Lost Beauty

This book is dedicated to my sister;
Tracy McMahan

Tracy, we have been through a lot together
When I've been strong you have followed me
When I've felt weak you have pulled me along
Thanks Sis!

Lost Beauty
by
Vicky J. Siegrist

Lost Beauty
By
Vicky J. Siegrist
www.vickysiegrist.com

Cover design
By
S. Parker
www.Sarahspencil.com

ISBN: 978-0-9820977-7-9

All rights reserved. No part of this book may be produced or transmitted in any form or by any means, electronic or mechanical, including photocopying, recording, or by any information storage and retrieval system, without permission in writing from the copyright owner.

Lost Beauty

Chapter 1.	Magnus	Page 1
Chapter 2.	Noteese	Page 15
Chapter 3.	Fanton.	Page 27
Chapter 4.	The Ship	Page 40
Chapter 5.	Henasee	Page 52
Chapter 6.	Lost Beauty	Page 64
Chapter 7.	Daniel	Page 78
Chapter 8.	Kingston	Page 92
Chapter 9.	Beauty or Scars	Page 105
Chapter 10.	Revenge	Page 121
Chapter 11.	A New Life	Page 134
Chapter 12.	Father Comes Home	Page 143
Chapter 13.	Going Home	Page 160
Chapter 14.	The Pretend Wedding	Page 171
Chapter 15.	Lies and Deceit	Page 185
Chapter 16.	Children	Page 199
Chapter 17.	Lost Friendship	Page 213
Chapter 18.	Tess	Page 229
Chapter 19.	No Beauty Needed	Page 243
Chapter 20.	Beautiful and Precious	Page 258
Chapter 21.	Fantons Beauty	Page 274
Chapter 22.	Young Love	Page 286
Chapter 23.	The Spell	Page 299
Chapter 24.	Believing	Page 305
Chapter 25.	Temper Tantrum	Page 309
Chapter 26.	Canta Carra	Page 315
Chapter 27.	Spells are Made to be Broken	Page 335

Chapter 1
Magnus

In a world of witches and potions, Magnus dreamed of only one thing. Magnus wanted to sail across the silver-red water to find the land called Noteese. Noteese is said to have riches of gold, diamonds, and silver. Magnus first learned of Noteese listening at her bedroom door many years ago to the heated arguments of her father and his friends. "One trip, "she had recognized the voice of one of her father's friends. "One trip is all we would have to make to be rich beyond our dreams and even our children's, children's dreams. "You know the dangers?" She had heard her father argue back. No talk was ever spoken again after that night about Noteese. Magnus had heard stories from some of the servant's years later about a ship headed to Noteese and a terrible accident. She was told many of her father's friends had been killed. She had approached her father one day on the subject of Noteese, and he had become very angry. "I never want you to speak that name again Magnus, do you understand? People think it will change their lives for the better, and all it does is bring them to their deaths." Magnus had watched as her father stomped out of the house, slamming the door behind him. Still holding onto her dream, she went to the only person she knew who would answer her questions. "It's very understandable," her uncle told her, smoking his cane pipe. "Your father had five of his close friends die trying to find Noteese. The weather became bad, and their ship was never heard from again. Your father blames himself for not trying harder to talk them out of going to Noteese."
"I heard him try to tell them it was dangerous, Uncle."
"Yes, many had tried to talk them out of it, but they could only see the riches they would be getting and not the dangers. "
"Has anyone ever come back from Noteese, Uncle?"
"Three men have returned, and they all came back very wealthy men. Each had his own ship and traveled for over a year-round trip. Nathan Banner is one of them, and I've heard he is planning to leave again in the spring. He swore for over two years that he would never make the trip again. However, his brother and his partner swindled most of his money away. He says he'll have to sail to

Noteese or he'll go under soon."
"Where does Banner live, Uncle?"
"What concern is it to you, Magnus? He would not take a girl on his travels. Even if he did, your father would have you beheaded if you ever tried to go."
Magnus nodded certain on both accounts. Her 19th birthday was coming up in four months, and her father had started looking for a suitable mate for her. She loved her father, but sometimes she wished she could be free of all his rules. Free to live her life as she wanted to and not be ordered about by an over-stern father and a protective mother. Since Magnus was their only child after two other babies died in childbirth, her mother was so protective that she sometimes smothered Magnus. Her father often treated her like she was his property, something he had grown and would one day exchange for a plow or maybe a herd of cattle.
"Magnus? Are you in there?" her uncle asked for the second time.
"I'm sorry." She shook her head to clear her thoughts. "I was just thinking about how great it would be to sail to Noteese and—"
"No! You don't." Her uncle blew smoke out his nose like a chimney. "You get those thoughts right out of your pretty little head. If your father ever found out I was telling you stories of Noteese, he would skin me alive. Now, off with you right now." Her uncle pointed to the other side of the dock. "I'll talk no more on the subject."
Magnus stood up, knowing her uncle was done talking about Noteese. He could be as stubborn as her father at times. "Ok, Uncle," she laughed. "I'll not talk of that place again."
Magnus smiled to herself on her walk home. "I need to get Nathan Banner to agree to take me on his ship," she said to a small tree she passed. "I could?" She tried to think of an answer. "Why would he want me?" she asked a stray dog. "Why would he let me? I have to figure this out, "she yelled out in frustration, bringing a few eyes on her from the other side of the sidewalk. "Ok, Magnus," she berated herself. "Stop acting like a nut. People are watching you. I have to find out a way to be on that ship," she cried out again, not caring this time if passersby thought she was odd or not.
"Magnalynn!" her mother called as Magnus entered the front door.
"I hate when she calls me that name," Magnus said under her breath

to their butler Jeffreys after he shut the door behind her.

"You had better get a move on, miss. Your mother has been looking for you for hours."

"What have I done now?" Magnus turned to ask him.

"I'm not quite sure, miss."

"There you are, Magnus," her mother said coming from the kitchen, with her hands firmly on her hips. "You were supposed to be back hours ago. Your father and I were starting to worry."

"I was fine, Mother. I went to see Uncle Bernard, and I guess I lost track of the time."

"Magnus," her mother's nose flares red, "your father and I have told you we don't like you hanging out by the docks. You could get robbed or something worse."

"I was fine, Mother. I was with Uncle Bernard the whole time."

Her mother's face didn't change. "You know I don't want you spending time with him."

"He's nice, Mother, and Father said it was all right."

"Why your father ever agreed to letting you be friends with Bernard is a mystery to me," her mother scoffed. Hearing the clock chime five, her mother jumped. "It's getting late, Magnus. Go get cleaned up for dinner. Your father has company he's bringing home tonight."

Magnus hated dinner guests. It usually meant she'd be stuck at the dinner table half the night. "Is it someone we know?" she whined.

"No, it's someone your father is doing business with. His name is Banner or something like that." Magnus stopped walking and turned to her mother. "Nathan Banner?'

"Yes, that's his name. Do you know him, Magnus?"

"No, I've just heard the name somewhere. I better get cleaned up." Magnus smiled at her mother and ran up the stairs before her mother started asking more questions.

Magnus and her maid Sally took great care in preparing Magnus for dinner. Sally combed Magnus's long blonde hair until it sparkled in the candlelight and curled tiny wisps of ringlets around her face. Looking through her closet, Magnus picked out one of her favorite gowns. It was a floor-length gown made of navy blue silk, with a v-shaped neckline made of the finest pearl-color lace. Her dressmaker found the blue silk material in Spain and had brought it back, saying it would make her eyes seem even bluer than they already were. After holding up the material, Magnus agreed wholeheartedly on the color complementing her appearance. One thing Magnus had always been confident of was her beauty and how it affected the people around her. She had been told since childhood how beautiful she was, and even complete strangers stopped her on the street to smile at her or nod their heads as if she were the finest of royalty. Finally, she winked at Sally in the mirror.

"My reflection is going to come in handy. I'm going to use my beauty to get on Nathan Banner's ship.'

"Please," Sally whispered, and looked around as if there were spies throughout the room. "Please, Magnus, your dream of Noteese will only cause you pain."

"Sally," Magnus whispered back. "I'll be fine. I promise." She still has no idea how she would persuade Nathan Banner or her parents to let her go to Noteese. With her head held high, she walked down the grand staircase to dinner.

Dinner was not going her way, she noticed, looking from her father to Mr. Banner. Mr. Banner, as she was introduced to him, had not been enchanted with her beauty one bit. With dinner almost over, her father and Mr. Banner were so engrossed in the business of what Mr. Banner would be storing on his ship. They hardly noticed Magnus and her mother were still sitting at the table. An hour went by before her father looked up shyly and smiled at her mother.

"I'm sorry, my dear. Why don't you and Magnus have your dessert in the sitting room? We've still got a lot more to go over." He nodded at Banner. Her father pulled out her mother's chair, and she stood to leave.

"Come, Magnus." Her mother smiled as Mr. Banner stood behind Magnus's chair to assist her in standing.

"I don't mind listening to them, Mother."

"Magnus," her mother said in a tone that allowed no argument.

"I'm coming, Mother." Magnus stood and looked into Mr. Banner's eyes.

As he acknowledged her beauty with a tilt of his head and a glance, Magnus smiled, trying to make the moment last longer.

"Thank you." Magnus curtsied, but she noticed it fell on deaf ears as her father and Mr. Banner were already back in conversation.

"You think it will take you that long this time?" she heard her father ask.

"We ran out of supplies two weeks before we landed at Noteese the last trip. If not for a few loyal men, I'm afraid I might have been fish bait," Banner laughed.

"Let's go over the list again," her father said, straight-faced.

"I knew I could count on you, Darman," she heard Mr. Banner say.

"You have a good name in the business." "Thank you" was the last thing Magnus heard before her mother grabbed her by the arm and pulled her from the room.

"I'll get dessert," Magnus's mother told her. "And you stay out of there. That has nothing to do with you," her mother finished, pointing at the two men at the table.

"Aren't you curious, Mother? That man has been to Noteese and back."

"No, Magnus, I'm not curious. Your father and I have a good life with his trade business and ships. I've never needed or wanted more."

"I want more, Mother."

"Oh, Magnus." Her mother hugged her. "You're too young to know what you want. My mother told me the same thing when I didn't want to marry and then I was introduced to your father. You have nothing to worry about, darling. Your father and I will pick a nice young man with a good future ahead of him for you. You'll see, you'll be very happy, Magnus."

"Mother!" Magnus cried out. "I don't want to marry."

"Oh hush, Magnus," her mother said, and turned to walk to the kitchen for their dessert.

"Why won't anyone listen to me?" Magnus cried into an empty room.

"Why are you so gloomy, Mag?" Henasee, Magnus's best friend, asked the next day on the way to the street market.

"I . . ." Magnus started and then stopped and then started again. "Have you ever wanted to leave? You know just get on a ship and sail away?"

Henasee stopped walking. "You're talking about Noteese again, aren't you?"

"Maybe." Magnus continued walking, and Henasee raced to catch up. "Maybe I am."

"Magnus, you know better. If your parents hear you talking about Noteese, they'll marry you to the first guy who comes along."

Magnus stopped again. "I'm not talking to my parents, Henasee. I'm talking to you."

"I know, and it makes me nervous, Mag. If your parents marry you quickly, I think my father will take that as a sign and marry me off, too."

Magnus squeezed her friend's hand. "Don't you wish we could live our own lives, Hen?"

Henasee looked around before she spoke. She leaned over and whispered into Magnus's ear. "The last time we talked about this, someone overheard us, and I got a whipping when I got home. My father says it is ungodly to think about disobeying your parents. So please, Magnus, stop talking about ships and freedom. I will marry and raise a family here, just like my mother did and her mother before her."

"Will you be happy, Henasee?"

A tear slid down Henasee's face, and Magnus wiped it away with her hand. "Ok, Hen, I will not talk of it again." Magnus smiled and pulled on Henasee's hand to get her walking. "Not again today." Magnus laughed.

Magnus came to a stop in front of an old rundown building. A sign in the window of the shop read "Dreams or Dares by Fanton."

"Why are you stopping here, Magnus?" Henasee asked, pulling on her friend's arm. "My mother says she's a witch of some sorts."

"I'm just going to look around, Hen."

"I'm not going in there," Henasee said to Magnus, walking past the window.

"I'll meet you in 20 minutes at the mill," Magnus yelled at a fast-moving Henasee. Magnus opened the door slowly and jumped when a small bell jingled. Looking around the dirty rundown space, she felt silly for coming in. Hearing a noise from the next room, she called out, "Is anyone here?"

"I'll be with you in a minute," a gruff voice yelled from behind a black curtain. The voice sounded so angry it scared Magnus half out of her wits. Shaking from head to toe, Magnus turned to grab the door handle to leave.

"You leave before you ask your question?" the gruff voice asked from behind her.

Magnus took a shallow breath and turned slowly around. Not prepared for what she saw in front of her, she let out a startled cry and took a step back.

"No need to be afraid, my dear. My burns are not contagious," the old witch snarled.

Magnus stared at the witch. Her face was covered in dark red and purple scars. Her hair lay long and limp far past her shoulders. The colors Magnus was unsure of. Some of the long strands looked to be black, brown, and white while the strands around her face were gray with a burnt look to them. Magnus looked again at the witch's face and backed away. Her eyes, Magnus noticed, were pitch-black and appeared to be the shape of a snake's eyes. "Yes," she thought. "Uncle Bernard has such a painting on board his ship. It's a painting of a large green and gold snake. Its eyes are the same shape."

"Are you satisfied?" the witch whispered, catching Magnus by surprise. With a hint of sarcasm in her voice, she laughed. "I am Fanton, the beauty everyone speaks of behind my back."

"I didn't mean to . . . "Magnus tried to say something but couldn't think of anything to say.

"You didn't mean to what? Be afraid? Or stare?"

Magnus opened her mouth, but nothing came out.

"I understand my beauty is gone." Fanton laughed at Magnus's discomfort and walked across the room. "It has been two, years gone now."

"How? I mean. I know what you mean."

"Come." The witch pointed with a scarred hand at a chair for Magnus to sit in across from her. "It was a long time ago. I was 16 and a beauty like you," she said, pointing at Magnus's face. "My life was ahead of me. I met a young man named Hallmen. He was very handsome and very rich."

Magnus looked at Fanton's face and noticed she spoke as if she were in a dream.

"My mother and father forbade me to see him. But our love was too strong to keep us apart. After months of sneaking around, Hallmen asked me to run away with him to be married. At least," she paused, "I thought we were to wed. He had other plans. I found out later he

was already married. We were to spend the night together in town, and the next morning we were to be married. But . . ." Fanton paused and took a deep breath. "It seems his wife had gotten word he was staying in town with me. When she set our room on fire, she thought both of us would die. She later took her own life, I heard after I recovered. When she found out her husband was dead and I had been burned past recognition, I was told she laughed at my punishment and put a gun to her own head, killing herself."
Magnus looked away.
"No, my beauty." The witch grabbed her chin. "You look long and hard at my scars. This is what deceit and lies can bring you. A life of solitude and loneliness. I lied to my family every day. Because I thought he loved only me. My lies and his lies changed my life forever. No man has ever been able to look past my scars. Sure, many men have wanted me, but not for my beauty." Fanton laughed, making Magnus feel uncomfortable. She tried to pull her face back, and the witch laughed and released Magnus's chin.
"So now, my pretty," Fanton hissed, "you ask me your question."
"I want to go to Noteese," Magnus said, raising her head to look into Fanton's snake-like eyes.
"Even after my story of deceit and lies, you still wish to do this?"
"I must go," Magnus cried out. "I must leave before my father marries me off."
"I once thought that would be the end of my life, too, Magnus. Now look at me." The witch pointed at the scars on her hands.
Magnus sat back. "How do you know my name?"
"You are a very pretty girl, and everyone knows the name of a pretty girl." Fanton laughed. "It's the ones who aren't so pretty that are forgotten."
"I must go," Magnus told her.
"It will not be easy," Fanton hissed. "There will be times you'll wish you had never met my face. But if this is what your heart truly desires, I will help grant it."
Magnus let out the breath she had been holding. "This is what I truly want." Magnus smiled shyly. Fanton stood up so quickly, Magnus almost screamed again. Walking away from Magnus, Fanton turned and looked past her at the door.
"Come back tomorrow at this time. Bring some clothes for

traveling. Boys' clothes. They will never let you on the ship as a girl."

Magnus smiled. She had never thought of that before. Sneaking on the ship as a boy.

"Remember, you will not be returning home so bring what you need." Fanton turned her head. "I will get five gold coins." Magnus was surprised by the cost but didn't say anything in case the witch changed her mind. "You are not to tell anyone or the deal is off." Fanton shook her head and walked behind the curtain. "I'll tell no one," Magnus said to the curtain. "I'll see you tomorrow." Magnus started to say something else, but instead she reached for the door and ran to the mill to meet up with Henasee.

Later, packing wasn't as easy a task as Magnus thought it would be. Her mother had always kept her dressed in the finest gowns. Nothing in her closet came close to looking like boys' clothing. Throwing herself on bed, she thought about telling Henasee. Henasee's little brother's clothes would fit her nicely. No, she told herself. I can't tell her before it's time to leave Henasee might get scared and tell her parents. Looking out her window, Magnus smiled. "Yes," she yelled into her empty room. Ben will have clothes. She laughed out loud and threw her shawl over her shoulders.

Sneaking down the back steps of her house, she listened for the slightest sound. When she didn't hear anything, she opened a side door, looked both ways, and ran across the grass to the barn. Making sure no one saw her, she quietly opened the barn door and sneaked in. Looking around, she saw a dim light coming from the back room where Ben and his father, the head groundskeeper, sleep. Panicking when she heard voices coming, she stepped behind one of her father's buggies and crouched down. She sucked in a breath just as Ben and one of the other workers walked by and left the barn. "That was close," she whispered quietly, patting her chest trying to get her heart to slow down.

On shaky legs, she hurried to Ben's room and went straight to an old dresser that stood in the corner. Beside the dresser was an old pair of work boots she picked up. Opening the top drawer of the dresser, she smiled when she found two pairs of pants and three shirts nicely folded. Magnus scooped them up and placed them and the boots in a potato sack lying on the floor. Opening the next drawer, she found socks and a dark green sweater she placed in the potato sack on top of the pants and shirts. With her bag full, she placed the note she had written hours before. "I'm sorry," the note read. "I did not mean to become a thief, but I have no choice at this time. I am leaving more than enough money to replace the things I've taken. Please tell no one of my sins. Thank you, a friend."

Magnus rushed up the back staircase of her house and hid the potato sack filled with boy's clothing in the back of her closet. Sitting on her bed, she went over her plan in her head. "I will come back rich, and Mother and Father will forgive me." Hugging her pillow to her chest, she worried about how her mother would react on finding her gone.

A knock on her door startled her, and she turned to tell Sally to come in. Instead of Sally, Magnus watched as her mother breezed into her room. A moment of weakness almost made Magnus break down in tears and tell her mother the whole story.

But before the moment was over, her mother reached her hand out and patted a hair in place on Magnus's head. "I must talk to Sally about your hair, Magnus. It's always falling out of curl. She needs to hold the iron on it longer." Magnus reached up and placed the straight strand of hair behind her ear.

Without looking her way, her mother "tsks" about Magnus's room. "Really, darling, your father has paid good money for your gowns, and this is no way to treat them." Magnus looked at the pile of gowns she had thrown out of the closet looking for boy's clothing. "I was going through them, Mother. I," she hesitated, "I was looking through them. I know you and Father want me to meet someone special, and I was making sure my wardrobe was . . . "Magnus couldn't think up another lie.

To her relief, her mother wasn't listening anyway. "We are having dinner guests tonight, Magnus. Your father wants you to dress for the occasion. Your father has invited one of his business acquaintances, his wife, and son to dinner.

"So, Father has decided to start looking for my husband," Magnus cried, jumping off the bed and scaring her mother. "Magnus," her mother scoffed, holding her chest. "Don't move around so. Young ladies do not jump around like crickets."

"I thought he would wait until after my birthday."
"You knew the day would come, dear. Your father says he seem like a very nice young man." Magnus saw her mother stiffen for a battle. Magnus opened her mouth to begin her ranting and raving then stopped and smiled sweetly. Knowing it was only one night and after tomorrow her mother or father would no longer be running her life, her smile grew. "Ok, mother," she said, kissing her mother's cheek. "I'll hurry and dress for dinner. I'll be down in a little bit, to meet Father's guests." Magnus's mother blinked and looked at her daughter as if she is talking to a stranger. Not knowing what else to say or do, her mother smiled slightly and turned and left the room.
Hurrying down the grand staircase, Magnus's mother went in search of her husband. Not waiting to knock or be called into the room, she sailed into her husband's den. "Darling," her husband said, standing up from his desk and coming to her side. "What is it? You look flushed."
"It's Magnus," her mother stammered.
"Has something happened to her?" he asks, alarmed.
"I told her about our dinner guests." Her mother sighed, sitting on the sofa. Magnus's father paced. "She will come down to dinner," he yelled, "and she will act the role of a lady. It's time for that girl to be married, Francine, and she's not going to ruin it. The Westons are a fine family and will be a welcome addition to our family. I will not hear of Magnus acting out again.
"No, Darman," his wife said, a little shaken. "She was more than pleased to meet the Westons. She is getting ready as we speak." Darman sat down beside his wife.
"She is pleasant about meeting them?"
"Yes, dear. She said she'd be down in a bit." Darman took his wife's hand in his.
"What do you think she's up to, Francine? I just hope she doesn't embarrass us again."
His wife shivered. "There's not a family in town Magnus hasn't offended or scared off. It's taken me a long time to find a family that hasn't heard of Magnus and her views on marrying."
"I know, darling, and this young man sounds just right for Magnus."

"Well, Francine," her husband squeezed her hand. "Maybe Magnus is finally ready to marry." They look at each other and then turned to stare into the fireplace deep in their own thoughts.

Dinner was going exactly how Magnus thought it would. Her father's taste in young men was still horrible. Charles Weston I was a greasy-haired man who kept smiling at her and then at his son Charles Weston II, who besides his greasy hair being brown instead of gray, looked the spitting image of a younger version of his father. Mrs. Weston, Magnus noticed, never lifted her head up and tried hard not to answer too many questions. Sitting at her left, Charles II, whom Magnus nicknamed Junior in her head, tried too hard to keep Magnus in conversation throughout the meal. Magnus decided to be polite because this would be her last dinner with her parents until after she returned from Noteese.

Answering Junior's questions to be polite, it surprised Magnus when he reached his hand under the table and squeezed her leg. She looked around the table to see if anyone noticed she had jumped. Seeing no one was bothered, Magnus gave Charles Junior a look that meant I hate you. Laughing and asking her about her hobbies, Charles squeezed her leg again but a little higher. Not wanting to make a scene, Magnus scooted to the far side of her chair away from him. The look in his eye, she noticed, was amusement, and he leaned even closer to her.

"Look," Charles senior laughed, pointing at them. "I think our children like each other." Magnus looked up to see her parents beaming from ear to ear. When she looked back at Charles Junior, he had a large smile across his face. "Maybe we'll be partners after all," Charles Senior stated to her father, who nodded and smiled her way.

Magnus knew if she wasn't leaving in the morning she would hit Charles Junior in the face with her plate and tell her parents what a creep he really was. But not wanting to stir up her parents on her last night at home; she smiled at everyone around the table and tried her hardest to keep away from Charles Junior's reach. With dinner and polite drinks in the sitting room over, Magnus was happy to tell the Weston family good night.

Not wanting the night to end, Magnus sat by her mother on the couch in the sitting room until her mother announced she was going to bed.

"I'll walk with you, Mother," Magnus told her, giving her father a kiss good night on the cheek.

"Thank you, Magnus." He smiled at her.

"You, too, Father, thank you for everything." Magnus noticed her father looked a bit shocked and smiled at him again.

Magnus held her mother's arm as they headed up the staircase to bed. "Are you all right, Magnus?" her mother asked, concerned. "I'm fine, Mother. It's just that I'm in love. I know." Her mother laughed and hugged her. "You're smitten with Charles Weston." Magnus almost laughed out loud. "Your father and I couldn't be happier, darling. Mr. Weston and your father will make great partners, and one day Charles II will own it all. You're going to have a very exciting life, Magnus." Magnus was about to tell her mother what a skin crawl Charles Junior was. But looking into her eyes, she didn't have the heart to spend these last few moments in her company disappointing her. "You are smitten with him, aren't you, dear?" There was so much hope in her mother's voice. Magnus didn't' have the heart to deny it. "Yes, Mother, I am smitten with Junior, I mean Charles."

"Oh, that's what we prayed for," her mother cried, giving her a hug. "You have made your father and me very happy, Magnus. We can have a summer wedding. I know he'll propose after he talks to your father. He's already asked for an appointment with him. This is just the best news." Her mother continued hugging her. "I love you, darling." Her mother hugs her again at her bedroom door.

"I love you, too, Mother." Magnus tried to hide them, but the tears came running down her cheek. "Oh, darling," her mother hugged her again. "This is everything your father and I have ever wanted for you."

" I know, Mother." Magnus cried harder.

"You stop your crying, dear. Everything will be all right." For the first time in years, Magnus's mother helped Magnus dress for bed and tucked her in, kissing her goodnight.

Magnus got out of bed and dressed in one of her boy's outfits before the crack of dawn. She placed a note on her bedside table that read: Mother, I'll be riding this morning with Henasee and possibly be staying over for dinner, love Magnus. She looked around her bedroom one last time. Picking up the potato sack of clothing and tucking the five gold coins she had snuck out of her father's den into her pants pocket, she turned and quietly crept out of her house.

Chapter 2
Noteese

Meeting up with Henasee was a true part of her morning. Henasee did not return Magnus's smile as Magnus rode closer to her.

"What are you up to, Mag?"

"I'm not up to anything." Magnus smiled trying to throw Henasee's suspicions off.

"Right, Mag." Henasee lifted her eyes to the sky. "First you want me to meet you at this unsightly hour," Henasee moaned, pointing at the still dark sky. "Now you show up dressed like a boy. What are you up to, Magnus? Talk quickly, or I'm going home and getting back into my bed."

Magnus looked away for a minute and then turned back to look at her friend. Dropping down from her horse, she walked over to Henasee, who did the same.

"Ok, tell me, Mag." Magnus took Henasee's arm and led her to a fallen tree branch and pulled her down to sit with her. "Ok, Magnus, we're sitting. Now tell me before I drive myself crazy worrying about what you've got planned in that head of yours."

"Ok." Magnus paused.

"Tell me already," Henasee screamed.

"I'm going to Noteese." Henasee stared so long at her without blinking, Magnus started to get worried and shook her arm. "Hen, stop that."

"What do you want me to do?" Henasee asked slowly. "Jump up and down knowing my best friend is going off to get herself killed?"

"Oh, Henasee." Magnus touched her cheek. "I'm not going to get killed. I'm going to come back rich beyond our wildest dreams. I going to be so rich my parents will not have to find me a husband to marry."

"Don't do this, Magnus," Henasee said, starting to cry.

"Henasee, I'll come back and when I do, we'll be free to travel and see the world. We will live our lives without our parents trying to trap us in loveless marriages. This is for the best."

"Magnus, please." Henasee squeezed her arm. "You know how dangerous that trip is. You've repeated those stories so much I have nightmares about them."

"It will work out, Hen, trust me."

"No." Henasee stood. "Is this your plan, Magnus? To dress and act like a boy? You won't pull it off. You still look like a pretty girl wearing boy's clothing. Have you thought how your mother will feel when you don't come home tonight?"

Magnus backed away. "Yes," she screamed back. "I have thought about how much my parents will be hurt. But this is something I have to do. I can't marry Charles Weston II. He's a pig, Henasee." Magnus felt herself losing control but couldn't stop herself. "Please, Henasee, I wasn't going to tell you, but I couldn't just leave without saying good-bye. My parents had Charles and his family to dinner last night. He grabbed my leg under the table."

Henasee's face went white. "Did you tell your mother?"

"She and Father love him and are all ready making plans for the wedding. He is disgusting, Hen. And even if they don't make me marry him, there will be more just like him lined up at my door."

Henasee sat back down. "I don't know, Mag. You're liable to get killed."

"It's better than living with Weston Junior and his family for the rest of my life."

Henasee smiled through her tears. "I'll keep your secret," she told her.

"Oh thank you, Hen." Magnus hugged her. "I'll come back, you'll see. I'll come back, and all our dreams will come true."

"You better come back," Henasee cried in return.

Pulling themselves together, they mounted their horses. "How do you plan on getting on board?"

"You're probably not going to like the answer." Magnus shrugged her shoulders and turned her horse toward town.

"Tell me anyway, Magnus."

"Fanton," Magnus said, looking away from Henasee.

"You're putting your life in the hands of a witch!" Henasee yelled back.

"It was my only choice," Magnus said, matter of fact.

"I hope you know what you're doing."

"I'll be fine." Magnus smiled at her friend. Knowing Henasee was scared for her, she repeated, "I promise."

Magnus and Henasee tied their horses on the outskirts of town and walked to Fanton's shop. "This place makes my skin crawl." Henasee shivered, rubbing her arms.
"You can't come in anyway. I promised not to tell anyone." Henasee looked at the shop window. "That's fine with me. That's one place I never want to enter."
"You go down by the docks, Hen, and when she tells me where I have to go, I'll come down and say good-bye to you."
"Ok," Henasee said, looking at Magnus and then at the shop door again. Magnus watched as Henasee turned and ran down the sidewalk toward the docks.
Magnus opened the door to the witch's shop slowly. Expecting the witch to be waiting, she was surprised when the room was empty. Placing her sack of clothing next to the chair she had sat in the day before, she looked around the shop. She spotted three pictures on one wall and walked over to view them closer. The first picture she looked at was most disturbing; she looked at it a little jumpy. The artist was so graphic about every detail the picture looked almost too real. Magnus looked at the witch tied to a large stake in the picture. Looking closer, she could almost feel the heat coming from the fire burning at the witch's feet. "This can't be real," she said, reaching out to touch the fire in the picture.
"Don't touch that!" Fanton yelled from behind her. Magnus jumped and turned around. Fanton's face had even more scars on it than yesterday. And for the first time Magnus was afraid for her safety. "I didn't mean any harm," she started to say.
But Fanton cut off her sentence. "It is not yours to touch," Fanton snapped at her. Magnus started to apologize again, but Fanton pushed past her. "Did you bring the money?" Fanton asked taking a small tin box off a shelf and placing it on the table in front of Magnus.
"I brought what you asked," Magnus told her, trying to get a little of her composure back. "Yesterday," Magnus thought, "watching Fanton scoop up the money and place it in her shirt, I felt sorry for her. But today she is different."
"Sit," the witch ordered. "I said sit," she told Magnus again when she doesn't move. Magnus sat down where the witch ordered. "You still want to change your destiny?" Fanton snarled in Magnus's face.

Magnus nods without saying a word. "No matter what the cost?" Fanton shook a bony finger at Magnus. Magnus nodded again. "So be it!" the witch screamed, sending spit in Magnus face. Magnus was so scared she couldn't lift her hand to remove it. "Say it," Fanton yelled at her again. "Say you want to change your destiny."

"Yes," Magnus screamed, wondering when her voice had gotten so loud. "Yes, I want to change my destiny."

"Then let it be done," the witch screamed in unison. "Let it be done. No one will ever know you again as the person who sits before me today." Fanton opened the tin box and took out a small green box. Magnus started to relax watching Fanton speak over the box. "This is her show." Magnus smiled to herself. "Let her play it out. She's probably already got my fare paid for on the ship." Fanton finished speaking and looked up at Magnus.

"You laugh?" The witch scoffed at her. "You remember this moment, Magnus, for you will play it over and over in your head. You will one day curse the name Fanton. You will not remember this was of your doing and nothing I could have done would have prevented it. You chose to change your destiny. I am only a tool to help you." Magnus looked around the room, wishing Fanton would hurry up. She wanted to get down to the docks to say good-bye to Henasee. Plus, she was starting to get a headache from Fanton screaming at her all the time. Fanton placed the green box close to Magnus, and Magnus smiled thinly, hoping Fanton's show was almost through. Opening the box slowly, Fanton lifted the lid and blew into the box. A green powder covered Magnus's face, and she wiped with her hands trying to get it off. Magnus tried to take deep breaths but found herself wheezing instead.

"What have you done to me?" she cried between bouts of coughing. Looking around the room, she felt herself spinning like a top. "What's happening?" she cried out again.

"This is what you asked for." Fanton laughed. "This is your destiny." Fanton's laughter started ringing in Magnus's ears so loudly she thought she may be sick. "Stop it, Fanton," Magnus heard herself cry. "Stop it right now!" Magnus could no longer see because the room was filled with so much green smoke. She began to panic when her breathing slowed down so much she could feel every breath she took coming and going from her chest. "Please,"

Magnus whispered.

Magnus could hear Fanton's laughter echo in the background. "Did you think changing your destiny and the destiny of the people you love would be easy?" Fanton choked on her laughter. "You are a fool." The witch laughed and pointed at Magnus's face. "Your beauty would have given you a good life. You have a family that loves and adores you. Yet it is not enough for you. You must be free to do as you please. Your lies and deceit will rule your life from this day forward. As for your beauty," Fanton said with tears of laughter in her eyes, "your beauty is now mine."

Magnus can't understand what the witch was saying. Magnus moved her head from side to side, trying to make it stop hurting. A cry escaped Magnus's mouth. "This can't be happening" she thought she said, but no words escaped her mouth. Magnus blinked and tries to lift her head up off the table. "No," she was finally able to whisper. "No!" Fanton laughed. "It is too late to change back now. It's way too late." Magnus heard Fanton laugh again. Magnus's head lay sideways on the table. She tried to lift it but could not. Magnus tried to focus on Fanton. Looking into Fanton's face, Magnus's eyes widened in fear as Fanton's scars started to disappear. One by one, her scars got lighter and then disappeared, showing off soft white skin. "What?" Magnus tried to ask. Fanton lifted up her hand and caressed it with her other hand, which was now beautifully manicured. Magnus was so confused as to what was happening she could only stare at the witch's transformation. Magnus watched as Fanton's long scraggly hair became jet-black and shinny. Blinking, she watched as Fanton's cat-like eyes became a dark green with silver specks. "She is beautiful." Magnus tried to understand. "Why did she hide her beauty? What kind of game is she playing?" Fanton rubbed her cheek and looked at Magnus. "I will cherish my beauty forever." She laughed at Magnus. 'Or should I say I will cherish your beauty." Fanton's laughter echoed in the room.

"Please," Magnus was finally able to say, but Fanton didn't answer her. She slipped behind a curtain.

When she returned, Magnus couldn't believe her eyes. The woman before her was maybe a year or two older than she and she was breath-taking. From her fancy dress to her feathered hat. Long, glossy, black hair poked out from under her hat, and silky white skin covered her face. "This can't be her?" Magnus tried to make sense of what had just happened. "No, this must be an act of some kind. This can't be Fanton. Help me? "Magnus whispered, lifting a hand toward the breathtaking lady.

"I have done all I can for you," Fanton's voice screeched from the lady. Magnus was so shocked she dropped her hand. She had thought she had been dreaming or was under the effects of a drug Fanton had slipped her. How could this beautiful woman standing in front of her be Fanton? "You will need these," Fanton told her, throwing a piece of paper and a small purse on the table next to her. "The ship leaves in three days. Give this to the dock man they call Kentar. He will know what to do." Magnus wanted to ask more questions, but her eyes were so heavy she couldn't keep them open. Fanton watched on the dock as the ship was being loaded.

"Are you sure you don't want to board, darling?"

"I'm fine, dear," she said, squeezing Nathan Banner's arm. "I like the bustle of everyone working together."

"I can't believe my good fortune," Banner gushed at his new bride. "You, my dear," he said, cupping his hand around her waist, "you are everything a man could ever dream of." Fanton giggled lightly, holding her fan in front of her face to hide the look of disgust in her eyes.

"It is my good fortune to have found you, darling," she returned to him. Fanton had laughed at her good fortune two nights earlier when a waitress had pointed out Nathan Banner sitting at a nearby table. Fanton had known he would fall fast for her. Men were drawn to beauty, and she was just that, a beautiful woman. On first sight, she had wondered why he couldn't have been a nicer-looking man. With graying hair and a protruding stomach, she had to make herself sound interested in him. She laughed behind her fan at the memory of Nathan first seeing her. He slurred his words as if he were drunk. She had left her table and boldly walked over to his and sat down unannounced.

"May . . . I . . . help ... you . . . miss?" he stumbled out of his mouth.

"My name," she stated, "is Fanton Brew. I would like to secure fare on your ship headed to Noteese."

Banner stared at her as if she were mad. "I am sorry, Madame, but my ship is not taking passengers."

Fanton started to panic but caught herself. "I would cause no trouble, sir." She smiled sweetly.

Nathan's thin smile erased. "It is not you, my dear lady. A woman would not be safe among a group of, um, sailors. It would be very dangerous for you to travel alone."

"I had hoped to come along with my husband." She smiled to herself to see disappointment at her statement come across Banner's face. "I'm afraid even with a husband, my fair lady," he said sadly, "I could not say yes. It would still be too dangerous."

Fanton continued as if he hadn't interrupted. "I meant even if I did have a husband."

Banner's whole demeanor had perked up after she had announced there was no husband in her life. "Forgive my manners," he had laughed, waving over one of the serving ladies. "We will have a bottle of your best brandy," he told her and waved her away. It had only taken Nathan Banner six hours to propose marriage to her. She had giggled her happiness at his question.

Married only a few hours now, Nathan was ready to board his ship with his new bride. Fanton wanted to pull out of Nathan's grip. But she dared not take a chance he would change his mind about taking her with him. She dared not show her true feelings about him until they were at Noteese. She has heard many horror stories of women on board a ship full of lonely men. She had no plans on regaining her beauty to go through something like that. No, she was going to be the dutiful wife all the way to Noteese. Then she smiled behind her fan. Then she would kill him. With thoughts of his death lifting her spirits, she let Nathan Banner escort her onto his ship. Her smile deepened as she passed Kentar, and he nodded his head.

"What a beautiful day," Fanton laughed, looking around the ship.

"Yes." Nathan laughed, too. "This day is most glorious."

"What happened? Magnus asked, holding her head. The pain in her body was so severe she couldn't open her eyes. "Where am I?" she moaned, trying to sit up.

A hand held her shoulder down. "Don't try to sit up. You have been very sick. I can't believe you are still with us," the kind voice continued.

"Where am I?" Magnus asked, trying to focus on the voice and her surroundings.

"You are safe. Now try to rest."

"Why can't I see?" Magnus screamed.

"You must rest now," the voice became very stern. "You'll have plenty of time for questions later."

Magnus fell into a fitful sleep as the doctor put cream on her face, arms, and legs. "I can't believe she's survived this long," he said turning to his wife.

"What do you think happened to her, Horus?" his wife, asked, shaking her head.

"It looks as if someone has thrown kerosene on her and lit it on fire," he said sadly.

"Why would anyone do such a horrible thing? She's no more than a child."

"I have no answers, my dear. The man who brought her last night said to fix her burns and get her ready to travel. He said he'd be back in two days."

"Two days, Horus!" his wife bellowed. "This poor child won't be ready to travel in two days. It may be months or even years before this girl can travel."

"Listen, Margie." The doctor took her arm and walked her across the room. "There's nothing more I can do for her. She probably won't live out the week."

"But, Horus, to let him take her? She's in so much pain."

"I know, Margie, but he's willing to pay good for her keep, and you know," he whispered, "we can use the money. He must care for her to bring her here."

"It just don't seem right," his wife sighed, wiping her hands on her white apron.

"I'm not happy about sending her off either, Margie. But even if she survives, what kind of life is she going to have burnt up like that? It would be better if the good Lord just takes her."

"Horus Cane!" his wife yelled. "Who are you to decide life or death? I'll hear no more talk of people passing on."

"I'm sorry, dear. But you've seen her body. Over half of it is burned beyond repair."

"I know," Margie cried out, tears streaming down her face. "May God be with the poor little thing."

Magnus woke to a soft voice humming, a song she had heard her mother once sing at their piano. "Mother?" she asked, her eyes still heavily closed.

"I see you're awake." The pleasant voice sounded closer.

Magnus tried again to open her eyes but failed. "Where am I?" Magnus asked the voice.

"You're safe, my dear," came her reply. "Here, take a sip, dear. It has been hours since you have drunk anything." Magnus lifted her head slightly and sipped from the cup offered her. "Now that's better." A hand patted her lightly on the shoulder.

"Who are you?" Magnus asked the soft voice.

"I'm sorry. I should have introduced myself before. My name is Margie. My husband is the doctor in this town."

"What town is this?" Magnus asked slowly.

"We are in Port."

"Port?"

"Yes, Port Dodge."

"How did I get here?"

"I'm not sure, honey," Margie told her. "You should save all your questions for my husband. He'll be back shortly."

"Please." Magnus reached out her hand.

Margie was careful not to hurt the bandages and took her hand softly. "You must rest, my dear. You have been through a horrible ordeal."

"I don't understand," Magnus cried. "What happened to me?"

"You don't remember what happened, dear?"

"No," Magnus replied. "I hurt so bad," she moaned.

Margie jumped at the sound of the bell on the front door." I have to get the door, dear. I'll be right back." Magnus tried to call her back, but her pain was so great she fell back into a dark sleep.

"That feels good," Magnus whispered as a cool cloth was placed on her forehead.

"You were burning up from fever," Margie's voice told her. Margie smiled down sadly at the bandages on the poor girl's eyes. Wiping away a tear, she changed the bandages on her arms and legs before removing the ones on her face and eyes.

Magnus could feel her eyes become lighter and tried to open them. When her eyes did not obey, she cried out, "What is happening to me?"

Margie reached for her hand before Magnus could touch her face. "You have been hurt badly, my child. In time you will be better. For now, you must rest and let your body heal."

"How bad is it?" Magnus asked Margie.

"I am not a doctor, my dear. You must wait for Horus to come home. He will be able to answer your questions."

"Please." Magnus reached out a hand.

Margie took her hand and sat on the side of the bed.

"What has happened to me?"

Margie wiped at her own tears. "You have been burned, my dear."

"Burnt?" Magnus tried to understand.

"Yes, you are burned over half of your body. Horus has been putting cream on you and giving you medicine for the pain."

"How long have I been here?"

"Over two days, now," Margie told her.

"Does anyone know why I was burned? Was there some kind of house fire?"

"No," Margie tried to soothe her. "The man who brought you here only told us you had been burned."

Magnus started to cry. "Why can't I remember? I must know something."

"What is your name?" Margie asked her.

Magnus started to cry harder. "I don't know. I can't remember."

"You must not get upset." Margie got the rest of the bandages and sat down again by Magnus. "You have been through a great deal. Horus once told me sometimes the brain needs to rest after you've been hurt. So instead of getting all fussed up, let's get some broth in you and maybe a little bit of tea. We'll wait for Horus and see what he says." Margie was relieved when Magnus settled down and returned to resting. "I'll be right back with your broth and tea." Hurrying out of the room, Margie said a quick prayer for the frail little thing in bed.

Magnus took two sips of broth and one small sip of tea before falling back into darkness.

Margie opened the door after the first knock.

"I've come for the girl," the man standing in her doorway told her.

In her 58 years of life, Margie had never before seen anything as handsome as the man standing at her front door. She was not usually tongue tied, but the very size of the man left her breathless. His body filled her six-foot doorway. "I've come for the girl," he repeated, breaking the spell on her tongue.

"Yes, come in," she invited. "My husband will be back in a few minutes. He has gone to get her more medicine to take with her. Sit," she pointed at the kitchen table." I was just about to put a pot of coffee on." Margie watched as Kentar sat on the bench at her table. With his long blond hair and bronze skin, he was breath taking. Kentar looked at Margie and turned back to the table.

"I didn't mean to stare. It's just that we don't get a lot of . . . men like you around here." Margie busied herself with the coffee and was relieved when Horus opened the front door.

"You're here," Horus said, flushed. "Give me about 15 minutes to get her ready."

Kentar nodded and sat back down. Margie carried the two coffee cups over to the table and sat on a chair across from the handsome stranger.

"I am used to people looking at me," Kentar stated, and took the coffee cup from her. "I am not from here, and let's say people are curious."

"Curious?" Margie laughed, back to her old self. "I'm bettin' they're downright stunned. God did place a heap of good looks on you." Margie laughed again, offering him a sugar bowl. "Here, mister," Maggie offered a piece of bread with thick butter on it. "You look like you haven't eaten lately."

Kentar took the bread and bit into it deeply. "Kentar," he said after his last bite of bread. "My name is Kentar."

Margie offered her hand. "I'm Margie. Horus and I have been doctoring people for almost 40 years in this town."

"I met your husband years ago," Kentar said and returned to his coffee.

Margie was surprised but didn't pry.

Horus came out, sweat running down his face.

"Are you sure you must take her?" Margie asked as Kentar stood. Kentar reached into his pocket and pulled out three gold coins and placed them on the table. "We sail today," he spoke to Horus. "Is she ready?"

"Yes." Horus turned and walked into Magnus's room.

Kentar reached down carefully and picked the poor girl up. Margie was sure he would take good care of her. Magnus's arm fell to her side, and Kentar turned to the doctor.

"She was in a lot of pain," Horus choked out. "I gave her this." He handed Kentar a small brown bottle. "Give it to her for the pain as often as you can. When it runs out," he turned and handed him two more bottles, "use these." Margie smiled at Horus. She knew he had already spent the money the stranger had given him getting those medicines to send with the girl. "Make sure you keep her burns clean and dry. If they become festered, you'll lose her." Kentar nodded and carried Magnus out of the room.

"Wait," Margie said to Kentar, and they all turned as she rushed out of the room. Horus watched the doorway, ready for this big man with this girl to leave his house. Margie returned carrying a white knitted shawl. "It's getting chilly out. She'll need this," she said, lovingly tucking it over Magnus's sleeping form. "You take good care of her."

Kentar looked from Margie to Horus without saying anything and turned and left their house.

"Oh, Horus," Margie cried. "Do you think she'll be all right?"

"I'm not sure, dear. He seemed like a good man. He was so gentle picking her up as not to hurt her. We can only hope, dear"Margie squawked in surprise, scaring Horus. "What is it, Margie?"

"Look, Horus. Look here!" She pointed at the table. Horus looked at the table and squawked just like his wife. "There must be twenty gold coins in that pouch," Margie laughed. Horus picked the pouch up and dumped it on the table, and he and Margie danced around the room. Margie laughed and cried. "Anyone who would pay money like that will take good care of the girl. Margie, my dear," Horus laughed. "Let's go to town."

Kentar walked to the side of the doctor's house and lifted Magnus up into a carriage. Opening a brown leather chest, he placed her inside on a soft comforter. He packed clothing around her and checked to make sure there were enough air holes. When he was satisfied, he closed the lid and placed a lock on it. After climbing up on the carriage seat, he drove

Chapter 3
Fanton

Nathan placed Fanton on her feet after he carried her through the door of their compartment. "This is where we'll be living, darling." Nathan waved his arms around proudly. Fanton laughed and looked around the room. "I had some things brought over this morning for your comfort, dear." Fanton couldn't believe how rich the room looked. A big wooden table with eight chairs lined one side of the room. On the other wall, a huge fireplace stood with windows on both sides. A sitting area with two full red couches and three chairs made of the finest crushed velvet sat in the middle of the room.
A large mirror hung over one of the couches, and Fanton stopped to admire herself. She smiled at her reflection proudly. Her gold gown brought out the speckles in her green eyes, and her pearly white skin looked flawless in the mirror. Fanton didn't notice she'd been staring at herself until Nathan put his arms around her waist and pulled her to him. "You are a very beautiful woman," he whispered in her ear. Fanton loved hearing of her beauty and let Nathan turn her in his arms and kiss her for the first time. Never in his wildest dreams would someone as beautiful as Fanton want him and yet here she was his new wife. As fast as she came into his arms, she pulled away from him. Nathan was not bothered. He had seen her play shy before, and he rather enjoyed the cat-and-mouse games she played. "Let me show you where we will be sleeping." He offered his arm.
When Nathan opened a heavy wooden door, Fanton's mouth fell open. The cabin was almost the size of the living quarters. In the center of the room, a grand king-size bed was placed with brown silk blankets and pillows of every shade. Fanton rushed to a pink vanity with a soft chair and a large mirror in front of it. "This is for you, darling." Fanton sat in the chair and smiled at Nathan from the mirror. "This is not it, darling."
Holding out his hand, he led her to a large closet. "I knew you would not have time to buy clothing for the trip. So I had some things sent from a shop in town." Fanton opened the door and could not help crying out with laughter. Rows of gowns in silk and cashmere lay in

rows and rows on hangers. Sitting in boxes were shoes of every sort and everything she would need to go with her gowns. Fanton rummaged through the rows, going from gown to gown. Never had she seen so many beautiful things in one place. Never had anything like this been meant for her. Filled with tenderness, she reached out her hand to Nathan.

Nathan swept her up and carried her to their bed. Without thinking, Fanton became his wife in body and soul. Afterwards, Nathan held her in his arms, cooing love words to her. Fanton looked around the room and smiled at all the new things she would have after she killed her husband.

"I have another surprise for you," Nathan said, jumping from their bed and rushing to a wooden dresser. Opening it, he lifted out a small gold box and carried it back to her side of the bed. "We married so fast I didn't have time to get you one." Nathan opened the box, and Fanton's eyes lit up with excitement.

"It is beautiful," she said, taking the blue diamond ring from the box. Fanton placed it on her finger and rushed naked to the mirror. She held the ring up to see its reflection and smiles at it in the mirror. Nathan watches as his wife poses naked with the ring in the mirror. Never in his life had he wanted something as much as he wanted this woman, and he planned to keep her, no matter what the cost.

Kentar waved to some of the ship's men to help him carry a trunk on board. Helping them place it on the ground, he watched as the two men carried the trunk with Magnus to put it on board. One of the men tripped, and Kentar ran ahead and took the handle from him.

"Move out of my way!" he said as he pushed the man aside. "Get back on board. Maybe you'll be of some use there." Kentar glared at the ship and then at the other man.

"Do you think you can carry your end without dropping it?" he yelled at the one man left.

"Yes, sir," the man yelled back. "I won't drop my end."

"Shut up and get moving then," Kentar yelled back.

They walked the trunk across the deck and down two flights of stairs. Kentar ordered the man to set it down gently as he opened a lock on one of the cabin doors.

"Come on." He ordered the man to pick the trunk up and helped him carry it into the cabin. "We'll put it there." Kentar pointed at a rug on the floor.

Placing the trunk down gently, the man stood up, hoping to see what all the fuss was about in the trunk. "Get out," Kentar yelled at him, "and shut the door behind you."

Kentar unlocked the trunk and placed his hand on Magnus's forehead. Magnus moaned quietly but fell back into a deep sleep. Kentar reached his arms around her and wasn't surprised when she moaned again. He picked her up and placed her on the small bed in the corner. He gently pulled the covers up around her and sat in a chair at the side of her bed.

Reaching for a glass, he poured a small amount of water from a pitcher. Lifting Magnus's head up, he spoke firmly. "You must drink." Not getting a response, he shook her with his arm still behind her shoulder. "You must drink," he said again firmly. Her pain was so great she cried out. Kentar started to move her again and she cried out in pain. He noticed her lips part, and he placed the glass to her lips. A few drops fall into her mouth, and Magnus closed her mouth and fell back into unconsciousness.

Fanton put a light blue robe on and tied the belt around her small waist. Stopping to look at the mirror over her vanity, she smiled at her reflection. This is my destiny. She laughed at her beauty. Nathan cleared his throat. "What is your destiny, darling?"

"Why you are," she said, rushing to his side. Nathan smiled and took her into his arms.

"That's what I like to hear, darling." Fanton hugged him back, while counting the different ways in her head she might kill him. "I adore you, my darling," he whispered in her ear.

"As I you," she whispered back.

"Let me show you how much I adore you," he said taking her arm and pulling her toward the sleeping cabin.

"Darling," she pulled back. "Let us have some champagne to celebrate first."

"I don't need champagne to celebrate," he laughs and pulled her to him, kissing her passionately. "You are most beautiful, Fanton."

Loving the sound of her beauty, Fanton stepped out of his arms and turned to watch his eyes as she untied her silk robe. Nathan's eyes watered with wanting. Fanton opened her gown, slowly letting it slip down her shoulders and catch on the curves of her hips.

Knowing he wanted her, she pulled her head back and laughed. Longing overtook him, and Nathan scooped her into his arms and carried her to their bed. Nathan could not believe the feel of her skin beneath his hands. The finest of silks did not compare to its softness. He had been with many women, but none came close to the beauty of Fanton. Fanton moved in his arms. The sheer pleasure of Nathan wanting her was lighting her fuel. "Your skin is that of fine silk," Nathan swooned. Fanton laughed and pulled away so he could feast upon her beauty. "I am enchanted by your loveliness, my dear." Nathan noticed Fanton loved her beauty to be not only noticed but also talked about. "I have never tasted skin," he said, kissing her shoulder, "as soft as yours." Fanton lay her head back as if on a rush to the skies. "Your hands are that of a china doll," Nathan said kissing each finger. "I could live here in this room forever," he growled, pulling her closer. "Just to feast on your beauty is more than one man ever deserves." Fanton was so caught up in hearing about her beauty she let Nathan take her, and she found herself giving as much as she got from him.

Wrapped together in the middle of the bed, neither heard a door close from the other room.

"That, my darling, was fantastic." Nathan smiled and climbed off the bed, dressing quickly. "I must see to some things, but don't dress, darling. I want you right there when I return."

Fanton was out of the bed and pulling dresses out of her closet as soon as she heard the door close. Pulling on a light lavender gown, she brushed her hair and pulled it up in a twist, and then put on slippers to match. She checked herself in the mirror before leaving the cabin.

Kentar lit the candle sitting on the bed table. He hated waiting and was relieved when a knock came on the door. Opening the door halfway, he took the tray of food from Scan. "Here's your dinner, sir," Scan told him. Kentar took the tray and, without saying a word, shut the door in the man's face. "You're welcome," Scan said to the closed door. "No trouble at all, sir," he mumbled under his breath, going back up the steps.

Fanton let out the breath she had been keeping and came out from under the steps. She heard Scan talking and ducked behind them. She knew there would be no reason or excuse she could give Nathan for being in the men's quarters, being the captain's wife and the only woman on board. Not the only woman. She laughed to herself. The only desirable woman on board. It could be dangerous down here. Kentar knew by the slight knock it was Fanton. Opening the door, he looked into her face. "You are once again the most beautiful." Fanton's lips curved up, and her tongue slipped out to lick her top lip. Without thinking, Kentar grabbed Fanton's waist with one hand and pulled her to his hard chest. "I have missed you, Kentar." Kentar gave no reply. He tilted her head back and engulfed her in a kiss that made her cling to the muscles on his chest. Kentar rubbed his hands up and down her body, and she lay against him, gasping in his arms. "Please do not stop," she begged as he pushed her away from him. Kentar pulled her into the room, not realizing in their moment of passion they had been in the hallway.

She tried to return to his arms, but he pushed her away. "How long do you have this time, Fanton?" Fanton looked at the scar that was returning on her hand.

"Months, maybe less."

"You must go before you're seen. Do not come here again."

"The girl." Fanton pointed. "She must stay alive, or the spell will be broken and we will both die."

"Why have you done this again, Fanton? I told you I want no part of stealing these girls' beauty. Not for a few months' pleasure."

"Kentar," Fanton cried, reaching for his hand. "I have not let you see my scars in fear you would no longer love me."

Kentar became angry. "You have never let me near you when your scars return. How do you know how my love would act or feel? You do not know my heart."

"I know how men are, Kentar. They long for beauty and beautiful women."

"Like your husband," he screamed at her.

Fanton took a step back. "I was there, Fanton. I saw you in his arms. I saw you return his lovemaking."

"No," she cried out. "I was only—"

"Only what, Fanton? Practicing your beauty?"

Fanton's eyes filled and tears ran down her face. "I didn't mean to," Fanton cried, covering her face.

Kentar pulled her hands down and pulled her to him, letting her tears run down the opening in his shirt. "I would never have left you with or without your beauty. Ours was a great love, and you walked away from it as if it meant nothing. A note after two years is all I get asking to pick up this girl and bring her to the ship."

"I did this for us, Kentar."

"Can't you see our love can't live on after this? You need to go back to your husband's bed before he finds you missing." Kentar stepped away from her.

Fanton reached for him, and he pointed to the door. "Go before you get us both killed, Fanton." Fanton looked at him one last time and rushed from the room.

Magnus lay quietly on the bed, listening to Fanton and the man who brought her here called Kentar talk. Magnus had awakened to hear words of love and taking away young girls' beauty. Magnus noticed her pain was letting up and had even been able to move her arms and legs more freely. This man was Fanton's helper, and when she got better, she wanted them both to pay for what they had done to her. Magnus lay quietly, thinking about all the things Horus had told her before she left with Kentar. "I have treated three other girls in years past. When I couldn't figure out Fanton's spells, I went to the smartest person I know."

"Who?" Magnus had whispered. "Granny Marbella. She is a witch. She lives up in the hills. The spell you have hurts at first when the scars appear, but they heal fast. To outsiders, the scars may look new and raw, but in fact, they are many, many years old." Magnus was just happy some of the pain was stopping. "In a couple of days, the pain will be gone. Will the scars be gone too?" Magnus had asked him.

"The spell Fanton uses takes the beauty from young girls and gives it to her. In return, the girls get her scars." Magnus continued. "In return, I get her scars. You have treated other girls? Have any of them recovered?"

"They have gone on to live long lives, but no, their beauty has never returned."

"Can Marbella help me?"

"She did not know what spell Fanton used."

Magnus laughed in a low voice. "I know the spell. She spoke in French. My mother made me learn French. She said it would sound worldly one day when we went shopping for a husband."

"Your parents, they don't believe in love?"

"Only if they've picked it out for me," she grumbled.

"I'm sorry," Horus said, gently patting her hand. "Maybe they'll pick a good one for you."

Magnus let out a sigh. "It doesn't really matter anymore. No one will want me." Horus sighed, too.

"You must find the potion she used on you and reverse it. Say the words aloud, and you will have your beauty back. I must get you ready. He has come for you."

"Who?" she asked.

"He calls himself Kentar; he has brought two girls here before. He works with Fanton, I am sure." Horus finished dressing her eyes. "I have filled these bottles with ginger water. Maybe if they think you are very ill you'll have a better chance of finding the potion for your beauty."

"Thank you very much, Horus. Thank Margie, too."

"Margie must know none of this. I'm afraid she would chase that witch down with a stick and beat her."

Magnus tried a laugh. "I'm sure she would."

"You lay still. I'll get him. And Magnus—"Horus became very serious. "Wait until you get to Noteese to reverse the spell. Do not get your beauty back on that ship. It would be very dangerous."

"I promise," she told him.

Magnus lifted the eye patch up and looked around the empty room. Kentar had left hours ago and had not yet returned. Looking at the tray of stew and bread, she slowly crept from the bed and sat in the chair to eat.

Fanton stopped with a look of horror on her face in the middle of her cabin.

"So you have decided to come back," Nathan yelled, coming at her.

"Nathan, I was just—"

"Don't lie to me, witch!" he screamed, grabbing her arms roughly.

"Nathan, what do you mean?" Fanton cried out in alarm. She knew with her potions packed in her bag she was at his mercy.

"I'm a wealthy man, Fanton. I ask questions, and I get answers. I knew who you were before you got to my table. I must admit, I planned on just bedding you that night. But your offer of keeping

my bed warm all the way to Noteese held my interest. Why would I deny myself your company," he laughed, "and especially in my bed?" Nathan started dragging her toward the bedroom cabin.
"Please, not like this, Nathan."
"You chose the rules, my darling, not I," he said as he threw her down on the bed. As he took off his robe, she could see pure hatred in his eyes. "Remember, darling, if the captain's not happy, no one is." Inches from her face, he snarled. "If you ever meet him again, I will throw you and Kentar overboard."
Fanton was too angry to cry. Nathan used her as if she were a street beggar. When he was done, he stood over her naked body. "This is where you will be every night from now on. If you leave the cabin without my permission, Kentar will be shot."
"How did you know?" she asked.
"I saw you exchange looks on the docks. You married a very jealous man, darling." Not looking back, he walked out and slammed the door.
Magnus hurried and placed the lid over the tray when she heard footsteps. Kentar carried another tray into the room and set it on the table by her bed. "You must eat," he said into the silent room.
Magnus moved her head slowly.
"Where am I?"
"You are on a ship to Noteese."
"Why?" she asked again.
"That is what you traded your beauty for, isn't it?"
Magnus wanted to slap his face but lay quietly instead.
"You must drink more, or you will die," he threatened.
The pain, agony, and sorrow of what she had been through made Magnus snap. She pulled the bandages off her eyes and sat up so fast Kentar almost fell from his chair. "What do you care if I live or die?" she screamed in his face.
Kentar looked at her as if she were a ghost. He reacted angrily, grabbing her by the throat. "You have been acting all this time?" He squeezed her throat a little tighter, and when she started to gasp, he released her and pushed her down on the bed. Magnus clutched her throat, gasping for air. "I should have noticed," he spit at her. "Your burns are no longer new. They are aged as if they were still on Fan . . ."

"Were you going to say, Fanton?" Magnus choked out. "I know about you and her." Kentar reached out to take Magnus by the throat again. Magnus dropped her hand. "Go ahead, and squeeze the very life out of me."

Kentar dropped his hand.

"I see." Magnus looked at him with disgust. "You know the spell she used on me. You may kill me, but as long as I have her skin, you will be killing Fanton, too. Go ahead, kill me. I have no desire to live like this." Magnus's eyes watered as she lifted her hand out to him. Kentar swore and walked out of the cabin, slamming the door behind him.

Magnus wasted no time jumping out of bed and searching the room. Finding her potato sack of clothing, she hurried to dress in a pair of Ben's pants and a flannel shirt with a white shirt under it. Fishing through the bag, she pulled out an old pair of work boots she'd found in Ben's room. Sitting on the chair Kentar had sat on; she chastised herself for giving herself away so soon. She promised herself she would be more careful around Kentar. It would not do for him to know the spell Fanton had used could be reversed. She shook her head, knowing Kentar was a very dangerous man. After watching him with Fanton, Magnus had no doubt he would kill when it came to Fanton.

"Good," Kentar said, looking at Magnus. "It's best no one on board knows you're a girl. It could be very dangerous. Even for someone who looks like you," he finished. "Even ugly girls start looking good to men on board a ship after weeks." Magnus gave him a dirty look and turned to look out the window.

"You would be smart to remember your life depends on you keeping that secret."

Magnus could feel his eyes burning into the side of her head and answered, "I'll be careful."

"Good," Kentar shot back. "See that you do."

Magnus wanted to stand up and hit him, but instead she followed him out of the room. Taking two steps to his one and sometimes running to keep up, she stayed right behind him. Feeling her leg muscles stretch after weeks in bed, she was happy to at least be out of the cabin.

Magnus rushed to keep up, and Kentar led her to the galley. "This is Mack." Kentar pointed at a heavyset old man. Mack looked up from his boiling pot of what appeared to be pork and potatoes and shook his head at Kentar with a half smile.

When Mack looked past Kentar, his smile faded away. "That sure is an ugly boy, Kentar. Where'd you get him off the bottom of the sea?" Mack laughed at his own joke.

Kentar's face cracked into a smile. "Yah," he replied. "He was at the very bottom under a rock." Both men laugh in unison.

Magnus turned her head as a tear ran down her cheek.

"He sure is ugly," Mack continued.

"Do you think you can find him some work, Mack?"

"Don't know, Kentar. If any of the men see him touching food, they might not eat," Mack laughed, holding his side.

Kentar looked at Magnus's discomfort and joined Mack in his laughter.

It took a while, but Mack finally calmed down. "What's your name, boy?" Magnus looked over at Kentar. "Don't tell me he's a mute?"

"He's no mute." Kentar glared at her. "He's just being stubborn, that's all."

Mack touched a long chain hanging on the wall behind him. "I can fix stubborn real quick," he told Kentar, rubbing the chain lovingly. "Real quick."

Magnus took a step back, and Kentar grabbed her shoulder and pulled her forward. "His name is Mathew. Everyone calls him Scar."

Mack laughed again, looking at Magnus.

"Let me know if he causes you any trouble," Kentar told Mack and turned and left the room.

"You know how to start a fire, boy?" Mack asked Magnus. Magnus jumped as Mack grabbed for the chain on the wall. "You answer when you're spoken to, boy. I'll have none of that head shaking. Magnus started nodding and caught herself. "Yes, sir."

"I can't hear you!" Mack yelled back.

"Yes, sir!" Magnus yelled back at him. "Yes, sir!"

"Now you do what you're told, and we'll get along just fine."

"Yes, sir!" Magnus yelled again.

"You put some wood in that there stove." Mack pointed to a huge steel stove sitting in the corner. "That's where we cook most of our meals. We got over 30 men on board, and they get mean when their food is late. So get movin.'"

Mack turned and started peeling a large bowl of potatoes. Magnus busied herself filling the old wood-burning stove from a pile of wood behind the door. Magnus wiped a tear that strayed down her cheek and picked up another piece of wood for the stove.

"Someday," she thought of her Uncle Bernard, "I'm going to thank him for all the different things he taught me throughout the years. Like hunting, fishing, and building this fire." A smile lit up her face, thinking how devastated her mother would be seeing her dressed like a boy building a fire. Looking at the flames take fire, she whispered, "Please, God, don't let my mother worry too much why I'm gone." Magnus looked up to see Mack glaring back at her.

"I don't want no nut working for me. You stop talkin' to yourself. Or I'll give you the whooping of your life," he finished by looking at the chain on the wall.

Magnus started to look away but thought better of the idea. "Yes, sir!" she yelled from across the room. "That's better," Mack mumbled, and returned to cutting his potatoes.

"She's got to be here somewhere, darling."
"Where can she be, Darman?" Magnus's mother continued to cry. "It's been two days, and there's been no word of her."
"I have men looking for her night and day. You know how she can be, Francine. She probably is worried about marrying Charles, and she's gone somewhere to think it over."
"Yes." Francine peeked from behind her hanky. "Yes, that's what she's done, Darman. She ran away to think things over. She'll be back before we know it," she ended on another sob.

A knock on the door brought them both to their feet. "Hurry, it might be something about the girls." Henasee's father was led into the sitting room by Jeffreys, looking the worse for wear. "No word on Henasee?" Darman asked him.

"No, nothing yet. Her mother is beside herself with worry. Henasee has never run off before".

"We're afraid it might be Magnus's doing."

"Yes." Henasee's father shakes his head. "We have come up with the same conclusion. I don't know what I'm going to do first." Henasee's father scratched his head. "Hug her, whip her, or marry her off to the first fellow that comes along." Darman choked out an agreement. "That's why we figure Magnus took off. She had just met an interesting young man. We think she ran off because she got scared."

Ben stood at the doorway waiting to be noticed.
"What is it, Ben?" Darman asked.
"I found this note in my clothes drawers, sir."
"Let me have that." Darman snatched the note out of Ben's hand. "Why didn't you bring this in earlier?"
Francine hurried to Darman's side. "Is it something about Magnus?"
"It's Magnus's handwriting, that's for sure," Darman told her, handing her the note. "It is from Magnus," Francine cried, returning to the couch to sit before she fell. "What does it say?" Henasee's father asked, almost losing control. "It says she's taking some of Ben's clothing and she's leaving money for them. And that she's sorry for becoming a thief. What does all that mean?" Henasee's father yelled at Darman.
"I don't know," he replied. "When did you find the note?" Henasee's father screamed at Ben.
Ben backed away from the large man in front of him.
"They've been missing for days. Why wouldn't you have come forward sooner?"
"Unless..." Henasee's father grabbed Ben's shirt collar and picked him up two inches, staring in his eyes with rage. "Unless you are part of their disappearance!" Henasee's father screamed in his face. "Where's my daughter? You little... I'll kill you," Henasee's father screamed again at a terrified Ben. "I'll kill you if you don't tell me where she is."
Ben's eyes bulged, and his breathing started to get raspy.
"Stop him, Darman," Francine cried. "He's hurting the boy. Ben would never do anything to Magnus or Henasee."
Pulling on his friend's sleeve, Darman told him in a calm he didn't feel, "Let the boy go, John. Let him go."
John pulled once more on Ben's collar and released him.
Ben fell to the floor, gasping for air.

When Ben could breathe without choking he looked at Magnus's father. "I haven't been home since the day they came up missing, Sir. I've rode with every posse that's left the estate."
That's why I just found the letter. I was going to change into some fresh clothes, and I found the letter in the drawer." John's shoulder went down, and they could hear him sobbing quietly.
"I'm sorry, Darman, I didn't mean to hurt the boy. It's just been so much on Penny and me to have Henasee missing like this." John looked at Ben sadly. "I'm sorry, Ben. You've been nothing but kind to my girl. Saddling her horse and riding home with her after dark. I should be ashamed I'd think you had anything to do with her missing, Ben."
"Please," Francine walked up to Ben, "please forgive all of us. We're so worried about the girls being out there on their own. None of us are thinking right anymore."
Ben shook his head at Francine, and left the room.
"I can't believe I attacked the boy." John shook his head and took the brandy Darman handed him.
"We're all on edge, John. I almost grabbed him myself."
"Where do you think they are, Darman?"
"I'm not sure, John. But Francine and I aren't giving up hope that Magnus will come home soon."

Chapter 4
The Ship

Fanton dressed in an olive lace gown. Brushing her hair until it shone, she couldn't believe what she has gotten herself into. Looking at the rows of gowns and accessories in her dressing closet, she realized Nathan had taken great care to have a lady's needs met on board his ship. She thought she had snared a rich man, but it was he who had snared her. If not her, she was now sure it would have been someone else. Nathan always intended to bring along a lady friend to travel with. She wished she could go to Kentar. He would know what to do about Nathan. But she could not chance Nathan having Kentar hurt or worse killed. Nathan was the captain of the ship, and his men would kill for him or be killed. No, she was going to have to figure out Nathan on her own. One thing she was quite sure of, she smiled at her reflection, was the way she would l kill him. "I will drive a knife deep into his chest," she imagined and laughed out loud. Oh. Her smile deepened picturing blood rushing from his chest.

"I see you're in high spirits," Nathan said from the cabin door.
"Who wouldn't be happy after a night like ours, darling?"
Nathan knew Fanton was only playing. However, he didn't care. He planned all along to use her and throw her over board before getting to Noteese. Therefore, he smiled back at her performance and poured a drink.

"I know this one guy," the young voice continued, "that never did get his sea legs. The poor guy didn't keep anything in his stomach the whole trip."
Henasee lifted her hair out of her face and concentrated on where the voice was coming from.
"I see you're feeling better?" A young man with shoulder-length brown hair and hazel eyes stood looking down at her.
In return, Henasee turned her head and lost what was left in her stomach in a bucket next to the bed she was lying in.
"I might have made that statement prematurely," the young voice continued.

"You sure have," Henasee interrupted in between getting sick and gasping for air. "Yes, anything." The young man bent down by her bed to listen to her request.

"Please be quiet for a minute?" Henasee finished her statement with another set of her stomach churning.

The young man bounced to his feet. "I am very sorry," he said sitting back in his seat. "I should have thought more of your circumstances. I apologize, miss, you must be very uncomfortable, and here I am adding to your misfortune. I can only hope you can find it in your heart to forgive me."

Henasee's usually sweet demeanor had finally reached its breaking point. Placing her hands on either side of her body, she took a breath and pulled herself up into a sitting position. Focusing her eyes, she looked directly into the young man's eyes. As she opened her mouth, a wave of nausea came over her again.

"I am sorry," he started again.

Henasee fell back on the bed, too tired to think. The young man appeared at her side again.

'You've been so ill. I guess when I saw your eyes open I thought maybe you were getting better. These last couple of weeks, I wasn't sure if or even when you would be waking up. But here you are."

Henasee leaned over the bed to be sick again, and the young man held her hair out of the way.

"I know I shouldn't have snuck you on board the ship. But I couldn't just leave you in the alley. Your burns, even though they look bad, seem to be old burns."

Henasee leaned over the bed and continued to be sick. After 20 minutes, she lay back down on the bed. Henasee looked into the young man's face.

"Burns?" she asked. "I don't understand." Feeling the young man's discomfort, Henasee tried to sit up.

"No," he pushed her down gently. "You'll only make yourself sick again."

Henasee reached her hand out to touch his arm and recoiled. "It wasn't a dream," she cried out in horror. "I really am a monster," she cried, looking at the scars on her hand.

"You are no monster," the young man told her, taking her hand in his. Henasee continued to cry. "You must calm down, Miss. It will only make you sick again." Feeling her eyes swim and her stomach knot up Henasee tried to calm herself.

"Please calm yourself. I know who did this to you, and it can be reversed."

Henasee looked at the young man. "My face? I feel them on my face.'

"You need to rest. We'll talk later when you're feeling better."

Henasee closed her eyes and says a prayer. "Please, God give me the strength to get through this nightmare."

"It will be over soon," the young man whispered, patting her hand.

"Your name? she asked. "What is your name?"

"I am Rivers."

"And you?" he asked Henasee.

"Henasee."

"What a beautiful name."

"Thank you," she whispered shyly. "It was my grandmother's name. My mother named me after her because she said I look so much like her. My mother?" Henasee sat up quickly. "Where's my mother?"

Starting to panic that someone might hear her, Rivers sat on the bed next to her. "I will tell you everything I know if you calm down and be quiet. This is no place for anyone to hear a woman screaming."

"You said you brought me onto a ship."

"Yes. I found you in the alley next to Fanton's shop."

"Fanton?" Henasee cried out in alarm. "Magnus? Did you see Magnus?"

Rivers shook his head. "Listen, you must be quiet. If someone hears you, we'll both be in danger."

Henasee looked at the serious look on Rivers face and quieted down.

"No, I only found you. I tried to carry you into Fanton's shop, but it was locked tight."

"Magnus," Henasee cried quietly.

"Who is she?" he asked, concerned.

'She's my best friend. I was supposed to meet her by the docks. She had gone to see Fanton. Fanton was going to help her get on the ship. I tried to talk her out of going in, but once Magnus has a thought, it's hard to get her to change it. It was starting to get dark, and I was getting worried. I went back to the shop. Magnus was sitting at a table with her head down." Henasee took a breath waiting for her nausea to pass and then continued. "I tried to open the door, but it was locked. I could see a woman inside walking around. She was most beautiful. She yelled at me to go away. I told her I wasn't leaving without Magnus. When she laughed, I told her I would return with help. She opened the door and stepped aside for me to reach Magnus. I hadn't noticed the room was filled with green smoke until I tried to take a breath. I don't remember much after that. I think I fell and hit my head."

"You do have a rather nice-sized knot on your head," Rivers said. "I found you a little bit after dark lying in the alley. I didn't have time to figure out what to do with you so I brought you on board, and you're hiding in my cabin."

"Your cabin?"

"Yes." Rivers nodded.

"Where?"

"On a ship headed for Noteese."

"Noteese?" Henasee screamed.

"Stop that," Rivers warned again. "Maybe you don't mind being thrown over, but I'm not a ready to be fish food."

"Noteese?" she whispered loudly. "I can't go to Noteese. My parents will go crazy. My father's already warned me about finding me a good husband and marrying me off. He'll have my head." Henasee continued waving her hands in the air. "This is crazy."

"Fanton is on board the ship."

Henasee sat up and lay right back down. "She's on the ship?"

"Yes, and if we play our cards right, the spell can be reversed."

"Spell?"

"Yes, what she used to take your beauty."

"I don't understand."

"Fanton has done this before. Taken a girl's beauty for an exchange of something the girl wants."

"I've never even met her."

"Yes, but your friend Magnus has. She must have been exchanging your friend's beauty with something. And you walked in on the middle of the spell."

"Making me a part of it," she finished. "Magnus!" Henasee scolded.

"She wanted to go to Noteese. But I can't see her giving her beauty in exchange."

"That's where Fanton keeps things a little vague. She doesn't exactly put things down on paper. Most of the girls are so determined to get what they want they don't ask about the cost."

"Going to Noteese was Magnus's only dream in the world," Henasee sighed. "I'm sure if Fanton told her she could get her on the ship, Magnus would have jumped at the chance."

"You were just in the wrong place at the wrong time," he told her.

"You said there were other girls?"

"Yes. Rita was just a girl. She went to Fanton to have her help her find a rich husband. Rita's family live comfortably, but Rita had always wanted more. Fanton promised Rita riches beyond her wildest dreams in exchange for her beauty. Rita didn't hesitate. I found Rita hours later covered in scars lying beside five gold coins. With her own beauty restored, Fanton met a wealthy man and left town."

"What happened to Rita?"

"Her parents were killed on the way to find her. She inherited everything her parents owned. In her town, it made her a very wealthy woman. She lived by herself, afraid to go into town because of all the ridicule over her scars. Rita came to me one day and asked for my help in finding Fanton. I searched and searched. But I could not find her or anyone who knew of her whereabouts. Weeks turned into months and no sign of Fanton. Rita was beside herself with unhappiness. The man she had hoped to lure with her riches was engaged to someone else. She found wealth had left her lonely and unhappy."

"Did Rita get her beauty back?" Henasee asked concerned.

"Her beauty returned," Rivers continued, "but at a very great cost."

"I will pay anything," Henasee said, clutching Rivers arm. "Anything."

"I knew of another witch. Her name is Ahaira. I told Rita she should be our last resort. But Rita wouldn't listen. She was tired of searching for Fanton so she decided she would meet with Ahaira. Ahaira lived in a bad part of town. I didn't want Rita down there on her own so I went with her. I tried many times to talk Rita out of going, but her mind was set, and there was no changing it. She said she would rather die than live her life as a freak."

Henasee nodded in understanding.

"The docks where Ahaira lived were dirty, and filthy people of all sorts lived down there. Even with her burns and scars, men approached us to ask her for favors. Holding her tightly to my side, we went from shop to shop asking if anyone knew where Ahaira was. At the last shop, a man pointed to a side door in the ally.' She's there,' he told us. 'You would be wise to walk away now.' It had been many years since I had seen Ahaira. I had heard many stories about her and none were good. I tried to persuade Rita one last time. But her mind was set."

"What happened?" Henasee asked her eyes as wide as saucers.

"Ahaira was waiting for us. She had us sit down on chairs across the table from her. Sit, my children, she said. Every hair on the back of my neck was standing up. She was as beautiful and as scary as I had remembered. Ahaira looked past me and said, 'I heard you have grown up well, Rivers?' I was too afraid to move. You are very brave for a young man. Not many grown men would have walked through that door."

Rita was shaking. I could feel her leg bumping mine under the table. But she looked right into Ahaira's eyes without flinching. "He came with me," she told Ahaira. "I am the one who came for help."

"You found greed not to be your friend," Ahaira laughed.

"I didn't know this would happen," Rita told Ahaira.

"What did you think would happen?"

"I didn't know," Rita cried out.

" Then you should have asked," Ahaira told her flatly. Rita started to cry, and Ahaira clapped her hands to quiet her.

"Is Ahaira the one who helped Rita get her beauty back?" Henasee butted in.

"The story will only take longer if you butt in," Rivers scolded Henasee.

"Then please," she placed her arm over her eyes. "Please do continue."

"Ahaira opened a small glass case and pulled out a small blue bottle, placing it on the table. 'This will give you back your beauty,' Ahaira starts to tell Rita. But Rita did not let her finish. She grabbed the bottle off the table and swallowed the whole contents down. I tried to get it away from her, but it was too late. Rita turned to me with a

blank stare on her face. 'Rita you didn't ask the cost,' I told her."
I looked at Ahaira, who was laughing hysterically. "What is the cost?" I asked her. "You have learned nothing from your first experience with greed. You sold your beauty for greed, and you don't even know the price you just paid to get it back. You are a very selfish girl," Ahaira spat at Rita.
"Please, please," Rita started to cry. "Please tell me the cost." Ahaira waved her hands in the air.
"It has been done," she screamed.
I turned to Rita, and she slipped to the floor. Right in front of my eyes, the scars started to disappear from Rita's hands and then her face. Rita was healing, and her beauty was returning with every passing minute. She was even more striking than before Fanton had taken her beauty.
"What was the cost?" Henasee pleaded with Rivers.
"The cost came," Rivers said sadly, "when she opened her eyes. Her once shiny blue eyes were clouded over. I looked up at Ahaira, a question on my lips, when Ahaira's deep gray eyes came to life with a deep blue color. I had been so nervous I hadn't noticed Ahaira was blind."
"She took her eyesight?" Henasee cried out.
"No," Rivers corrected her. "Ahaira took nothing. Rita had sold it for her beauty. Rita had recovered her beauty, but it was something she would never see again. What happened to her? Her house burnt down a few days later, and she lost everything. She became so bitter with the loss of her eyesight no man would have her. I heard her grandfather eventually took her in, and that's where she remains to this day."
Henasee hit Rivers as hard as she could in the arm.
"Ow," he snapped. "What did you do that for?"
"I hit you for telling me that stupid story, you idiot. Did you think that was going to keep me warm and cozy in my dreams tonight?"
"I was just trying to help".
"Help! Now I can have my eyesight gone or keep these scars for the rest of my life." Henasee raised her arm up to hit him again, and he jumped off the bed.
"Stop that," he yelled. "I'm not into hitting little girls, but I'll make an exception if you hit me again."

"I'm not a little girl." She covered her eyes and started to cry. "I'm almost 19 years old."

"I guess it's hard to tell your age," Rivers said from across the room. "You have a lot going on right now. "

"You mean with these scars all over me."

"Well, I mean." He stopped. "Do you think you might be able to keep some broth down?"

"No," she moaned. "It's too soon."

"I need to get up top. So no one comes looking for me. I'm going to lock the door. Don't open for anyone but me. Remember, you're safe as long as you're in here." Henasee said nothing, and Rivers turned and left.

With the stove giving off a lot of heat, Magnus turned back to Mack. "The fire is hot," she yelled to him. Mack looked up surprised. "I didn't figure you'd be much help." Magnus started to smile.

"Don't get cocky on me, boy. Get to peeling those carrots. No more sir," Mack yelled back. "It's Mack."

"Yes, sir, I mean yes, Mack," she corrected herself.

Mack watched as Scar carried the carrots to the sink and started peeling them. "Strange boy," he thought, "but it looks like he's a good worker."

Preparing the food, serving it, and cleaning up the kitchen afterwards had Magnus's body screaming out in pain. "You need to take this tray up to the captain's wife." Magnus started to nod. "Yes, Mack," she yelled.

Knocking on the door, she waited to hear "come in" before entering. Opening the door, she saw Nathan Banner sitting at a large desk going over paperwork or something. Placing the tray on the table, she let out a small scream.

"What is it, lad?" Nathan Banner rose from his chair.

"A mouse ran across the floor, sir," Magnus recovered enough to say, after seeing Fanton standing by a tall mirror.

"You need to get tougher than that if you're on board my ship, boy. The men will eat you alive hearing you say something like that. You don't look like you need any more comments coming your way," Banner said, pointing at her face. Magnus wondered what he would think if he knew he had just had dinner with her family a couple of

nights ago.
Fanton had not moved from the moment Magnus entered the room. If Magnus told Nathan of the spell, he'd be liable to throw them both overboard.
"Don't pick on the lad, darling," Fanton cooed. "He's a little squeamish. That's all. I'm sure with you as his captain he will become a fine sailor." With his ego praised, Nathan went back to his desk.
"You," Magnus whispered to Fanton. "How did you get on board?"
Fanton looked from Nathan to Magnus and whispered back, 'I am married to the captain."
"Look what you've done to me," Magnus whispered back.
"No, you did this to yourself," Fanton corrected. "I warned you."
"You didn't warn me about this."
"Is there something wrong, dear?" Nathan asked.
"No, darling, I am telling the lad what to bring for breakfast."
Nathan smiled and returned to his papers.
"I want my beauty back, Fanton."
"It is no longer yours. You sold it."
"Is the boy about done?" Nathan looked up again.
"Yes, darling, he's leaving now."
"I'll see you in the morning," Fanton told Magnus.
"Really, darling, wouldn't you rather have a more comely boy bring our meals?"
Fanton's lips turned up in a smirk. "No, darling, this one will do."
Magnus bowed her head and left the room, shutting the door quietly behind her. In the hall, she hit the wall with her fist. "I will get you back, Fanton," were her last words before she rubbed her throbbing hand.

Fanton opened the door and, forgetting herself, almost walked into Kentar's arms. Stepping back enough to still smell his scent, she looked into his eyes.
"I've come to talk to the captain," he said, looking past her.
"What is it?" Nathan yelled from his table.
"A ship is approaching, captain."
"Who is it?"
"Pirates maybe," Kentar told him. "They're not flying a flag.

They're approaching fast."

"How close?" Nathan snapped.

"We can see their sails".

"Lock the door," Nathan said, turning to Fanton. "Let no one in. You should be safe here."

Nathan grabbed his revolver and sword, and Kentar followed him out. Fanton shut and locked the door behind them, wishing she could have kissed Kentar before he left and knowing that it was impossible. "Soon, my darling," she whispered at the closed door. "Soon we will be together."

Seeing Nathan and Kentar leave the cabin, Magnus started to follow. Kentar turned but didn't stop walking. "Go to Fanton. You stay with her until this is over."

"What is over?" Magnus asked him, but he was already rushing up the stairs to the deck. Magnus walked back to the captain's cabin and knocked on the door. "Let me in, Fanton," she yelled. "It's me. Kentar sent me." Hearing "Kentar," Fanton threw open the door. "He told me to stay with you."

"What are you going to do? Scream and cry if we're attacked."

"Oh, shut up." Magnus pushed past her. "It's strange," Magnus though, "but as a beautiful woman, Fanton doesn't look like she could hurt a rabbit."

"I'm not the one who needs to worry," Magnus laughed at Fanton.

"What do you mean?"

"If we are attacked by pirates, I doubt they'll take me to play with." Magnus laughed at Fanton. "It feels good to have you look as scared as I was," Magnus laughed again. Magnus watched as the color drained from Fanton's face. "Oh, no, Fanton, you must not be afraid. Why you're the one who traded my ride to Noteese for my beauty. You must be pleased that in a few short minutes many men will want to, let's say, share your beauty with you." Magnus knew she was being cruel, but she couldn't help it. They both might die at any minute, and she thought Fanton should share some of her pain as well as her beauty.

"You sold your beauty. I warned you. I even tried to talk you out of it. This is not my doing, Magnus, this was yours."

Magnus started to say something back but stopped. "You're right, Fanton, I would have given anything to come to Noteese. If I had the

choice again, I might think differently. But I'm not sure."
Fanton waited for Magnus to start screaming again.
"Listen." Magnus heard footsteps coming closer. "We must hide," she told Fanton.
"There's no place to hide," Fanton screamed back. "They'll rape me. You must hide me."
"Magnus tried to shake Fanton off her, but Fanton wouldn't let go. Voices and screaming started to get louder, and Fanton screamed in terror.
"Stop it." Magnus shook her. "They'll hear you."
"What difference does that make? They're coming this way. Hide me," she screamed over and over. "You are the one who wanted to change your destiny," she screamed in Magnus's face. "I tried to talk you out of it. I told you, you would blame me one day."
"You never told me the price," Magnus yelled back.
"You never asked!" Fanton screamed over the men now hitting on the solid wooden door. "You were so worried about changing your destiny you never asked."
Magnus started to say something and stopped. "You're right, Fanton, I wanted so badly to be free I never asked."
Fanton stopped screaming. "Then you will hide me?"
"Yes," Magnus told her. "I will hide you." Magnus rushed around the room. "There's no place to hide you, Fanton. I don't know what to do."
Fanton rushed to a cabinet and pulled open a purse. Magnus thought at least she had a gun. Fanton pulled out the green box she had placed between them at the table. Magnus backed away from her.
"You've got to be kidding," Magnus told Fanton. "You would give me my beauty back now with men outside who will rape and kill me."
Fanton wasn't listening to Magnus. She was listening to the men trying to break through the door. With shaking hands, Fanton pulled the lid off and blew the green powder into Magnus's face. Magnus grabbed for the bottle, and the remainder of it landed on Fanton. Fanton cried out in pain and fell to the floor. Magnus made it to the couch and dove behind it on the floor.
Wood broke free from the door, and men rushed in. "What have we got here?" one of them yelled. "This can't be her?"

"Take her!" another voice yells. "Let's get out of here before someone spots us. The boys have been keeping them pretty busy up top." Magnus heard Fanton cry out in pain and lay quietly behind the couch.

Chapter 5
Henasee

Rivers unlocked the cabin door to Henasee's cabin and steps inside. "You must remain quiet and lock the door after I leave. Don't open it for anyone but me. There are pirates on board".
"You're going to leave me here alone with pirates on board?" Henasee cried out.
"I must help my friends."
"But what if you don't come back?" Henasee asked Rivers.
Rivers hesitated before closing the door. "Then, my fair lady, I will meet you in the place my father calls heaven." Smiling one last time at her, Rivers shut the door. He left after he heard Henasee turn the lock in the door.
Too nervous to sit, Henasee paced back and forth in the small cabin, listening to screams of pain and horror.
Magnus could hear people shuffling around her, but she couldn't see them because of the green smoke Fanton had released in her face. Trying to lift her head up, she heard a cry she knew to be Fanton's. "Release me at once," she heard Fanton scream. "I am the captain's wife, and he will have your heads for this treatment."
Magnus heard men laughing. "He must have been real hard up to have married the likes of you," a gruff voice laughed. "You are the ugliest thing I've seen in a while. Isn't she, boys?" Magnus could hear the unified agreement.
Magnus crawled on her stomach away from the voices. She felt a soft wall in front of her and figured it was the other couch she'd seen earlier. Dragging her legs, she pulled herself as close as she could to the couch, and to her surprise, with her small frame she slipped underneath it and rested her head on the hard floor. Magnus lay under the couch, trying to slow down her breathing.
"Where's the gold?" the gruff voice yelled above the place where Magnus hid.
"I know of no gold," Fanton yelled back. "You are the captain's wife, and you know of no gold?" Magnus heard a slap and a cry come out of Fanton. The sounds of drawers being ripped open and

furniture being broken were all around Magnus as she prayed. "Please God,' she whispered, "please don't let them find me." Magnus kept her eyes closed from the burning of the powder and kept praying as the sounds of the room being destroyed continued. "We better get out of here, Gage," Magnus heard one of the men yell. "I hear people coming." Magnus's relief was taken away quickly as the couch was thrown off her body. "What have we got here?" The same gruff voice she'd just heard with Fanton laughed. "We found ourselves . . ." Magnus waited for him to say a beauty and she knew what her fate would be, but instead the gruff voice laughed out loud. "We've got ourselves anther ugly one, boys." Magnus went limp as the gruff man pulled her to her feet.
"What do we do with them, Gage?" a voice called from the room. "You want me to kill them?"
"No, bring them, maybe the captain will pay to get them back." He laughs, looking at Magnus. "Or maybe we can throw them overboard for the sharks."
Magnus didn't put up a fight. She was too tired to think. It was a relief not to have her beauty back at this time, but she knew it also meant she was always going to be without it. The potion didn't work. If she lived through this ordeal, she was always going to be horribly scarred. At that moment in her life, Magnus didn't care if she lived or died as she was dragged out of the captain's cabin, escorted by six or seven rough-looking men.
"Henasee, it's me," Rivers said, knocking on the locked door. "Let me in." When no one answered, Rivers knocked louder. Starting to panic, Rivers beat on the door with his fist.
"They took that ugly boy you had hiding in there," a voice said over Rivers back.
"What do you mean they took him?" Rivers said, drawing his sword to the man's face.
"I watched from under the stairs. A bunch of them pirates, they had the captain's wife. At least I thought it was the captain's wife. She was dressed real pretty like, but when she got close, she was burnt all over."
Rivers drew his sword tighter to the man's neck. "What about the gir . . . the boy they took?"
"The boy you had hiding in that room? One of the men pushed the

captain's wife, and the boy opened the door. There was some commotion, and they took the boy, too. They were ranting and raving about having three ugly ones to sell back to the captain."

"There will be no selling anyone back to the captain," Rivers stated, heading for the stairs.

"I don't know," the other man said, running up the stairs behind Rivers. "The captain seems pretty smitten with his new bride."

"The captain is dead," Rivers told him without turning or stopping. "I saw his body up top. We lost half the crew, but we still have enough men to sail," Rivers finished before the man behind him can ask.

Kentar reached the captain's quarters at the same time Rivers did.

"She's gone," he told Kentar. "They took her."

"What about Henasee?" Kentar asked him.

"They've got her and Magnus."

"This is a mess," Kentar said, rubbing his head. "If they kill either of those girls, Fanton will die, too."

"I know," Rivers returned with a glare. "I told Henasee to stay put, but she opened the door."

"You should have stayed with her," Kentar yelled at Rivers.

"You didn't do so great yourself, Kentar. Those pirates have Fanton and who knows what they'll do to her."

'Wait," Rivers said, with his hand in the air. "The man who watched them take Henasee said the captain's wife was covered in scars. That means that Fanton used the reverse spell on Magnus."

Kentar glared again at Rivers.

"Well, at least Fanton doesn't have her beauty."

"Oh, shut up, Rivers. Go find out how many are alive and let's set sail before something worse happens to your sister. She's aboard Ahaira's ship now. She doesn't have long to stay alive. Ahaira will kill her this time."

"Magnus started to get her eyesight back but didn't look up when another person was thrown into the line of people who were taking her and Fanton off the ship. She looked up when she heard a familiar voice cries out.

"Get your hands off me, you big oaf," Henasee screamed.

"This one is a feisty one," a bearded man with a deep gash in his chin yelled. "Can I keep this one?" he asked as if he'd found a new pet.

"Just bring her, Boots, we don't have much more time. We need to get back to our ship."

Hurrying up the line by pushing and dragging Fanton and Henasee, Magnus looked over at Henasee and couldn't believe it was her. If not for her voice, Magnus would have never recognized her. Getting carried aboard the ship had been one of the most humiliating things Magnus had ever endured. The man had half carried and half dragged her. He didn't care where he put his hands on her and how hard he grabbed her. Already her arms were starting to bruise. Magnus stopped to look at her arm again. "Oh no," she cried in her head. "The scars are starting to disappear." As much as she wanted to have her beauty back, Magnus knew this was not the place or time. Afraid her face might be changing back to her beauty also, Magnus reached up with her free arm and pulled down her hat to cover most of her face.

The man dragging her laughed out loud. "I would hide my face, too. You sure are an ugly thing. I'm surprised the cap'n figured you to be a girl. You don't have to worry about me," the man continued to laugh. "I like my girls to be easy on the eyes. I guess there's a couple of the men on board that won't care how yah look," he laughed.

"Shut up," the man Magnus figured was the leader yelled back to the man holding her. "Take them to my cabin," he pointed to a heavyset man, "and wait for me." Magnus followed behind Fanton, and Henasee.

Once inside, Fanton let out a scream. "This is Ahaira's ship," she said to the heavy man standing in front of the door.

"You will have time to ask questions later," he yelled back at Fanton. "Now sit down and be quiet, or I'll tie you somewhere." Fanton seemed to believe what he was saying, Magnus noticed, as Fanton turned and walked to a sofa and sat down quietly. Magnus moved slowly toward Henasee and took her hand. Henasee started to pull away.

"No, Hen," pulling off her stocking cap, "it's me, Magnus."

"Magnus?" Henasee cried out. "Sh, come sit over here," Magnus pulled on her arm.

"No," Henasee screamed and pulled away from her. "You did this to me."

"I said, sit down and be quiet," the man ordered from the door.
"You had to go see the witch," Henasee screamed again.
The man at the door looked around the room angry.
"I asked you not to go," Henasee continued," but no. Magnus always gets her own way, no matter who it hurts. You're not even ugly," Henasee cried out. "I came back to save you from that witch and look what happened to you and me, Magnus. You haven't changed at all. You are as beautiful as the day I came to save you."
Magnus looked over at the guard, but he, she noticed, is was white as chalk. "I did have my beauty taken away, Henasee, it's just now returned."
"What is going on with you?" he screamed at Magnus.
"Oh, yah Magnus, sure," Henasee continued ranting. "Sure, you know exactly what I've been going through because you've been like this, too. Sure, Magnus, tell me some more. Tell me the witch only took your beauty for a short time."
Magnus grabbed Henasee's arm. "Fanton gave it back to me when she heard the pirates coming."
Henasee stopped fighting. "What do you mean she gave it back?"
"The spell can be reversed," Magnus told her.
"What do you mean reversed?"
"Yes, if you know the words and . . ." Magnus stopped and turned to Fanton, who looked quite ill. "I didn't repeat the words, Fanton. What happens if I didn't repeat the words, Fanton? Magnus said, shaking Fanton's shoulders. "What happens if I didn't repeat the spell?"
Fanton looked past Magnus with a blank stare. "The spell will be weak."
"What does that mean, Fanton? Tell me," Magnus screamed. "Tell me!"
"It means your beauty will come and go," Fanton said weakly.
Magnus looked at her arm, and already the scars were reappearing. "No, please, please, God," she cried out, and threw herself in a chair. Henasee took a seat on the opposite side of Fanton, put her head in her hands, and cried quietly.
Magnus lifted her head up as the door swung open. A man with a patch on his eye came in with a beautiful lady with long black hair.
"Fanton," the lady laughed. "I see you are still up to no good." She

looked from Henasee to Magnus.

"Ahaira?" Fanton gasped.

Henasee looked up, scared to be meeting the witch who had blinded Rita.

"Which one is she?" Ahaira asked the man with the patch.

"That one there, I think," he pointed at Magnus.

"Come with me." Ahaira pointed at Magnus. Magnus paused until the man with the patch started coming her way. She stood and followed Ahaira out the door. Henasee was so mad still she never looked up to see Magnus look back at her.

Kentar and Rivers returned to the deck at the same time. "We're getting ready to set sail. They've got a two-hour start," Rivers told him. "We've lost half the men and Banner. I've been trying to figure out why Ahaira would take such a risk."

"Yah, me, too," Kentar told him. "It almost seems like they knew the girls were on board. They led us to believe it was a pirate ship. But it was Ahaira's vessel. What would Ahaira want with the girls?"

"I don't know." Rivers shook his head. "I hope we're not too late to get Fanton out of there before Ahaira takes her revenge."

Magnus followed Ahaira into a cabin. "Sit over there." Ahaira pointed to a green chair by a blazing fireplace. Magnus sat down and put her hands in her lap. "Warm them by the fire, Magnus," Ahaira told her. Magnus looked at the woman Fanton called Ahaira. "What do you want with us?"

"I am not sure I understand what you mean," she replied.

"Henasee and me, what are you going to do to us?" Magnus finished, out of breath. "We meant no harm. All I wanted to do is go to Noteese. I didn't mean to drag Henasee into it."

"You must have known there would be dangers in your plan."

Magnus started to cry. "I didn't know we would lose our beauty and Henasee would hate me. I don't even know what my mother and father are going through," Magnus gasped between sobs. "I didn't mean for any of this to happen." Magnus closed her eyes and covered her face with her hands. "I am so sorry," she cried.

"Well, it's good to know you're sorry for your actions, young lady." Magnus lifted her head.

"Uncle Bernard?"

"It's me." He smiled from the doorway. Magnus stood and ran into his open arms. "Oh, child," Bernard said with a sigh. "We'd thought we had lost you forever. There was no letter of good-bye. Your poor parents are beside themselves."

Magnus clung to her uncle, weeping openly. "I didn't think any of this out, Uncle. I wanted to go to Noteese, and I could think of nothing else."

"Here, here, child." Bernard patted her back. "Stop this carrying on and come sit by the fire. All that matters is you are safe with me." Bernard led Magnus to the chair she had been sitting in and sat her down. "Now tell me what happened."

Magnus thought she'd only been talking for a few minutes until she noticed it was dark out of one of the small windows.

"Well." Her uncle shook his head. "You sure have had an adventure to talk about in years to come."

"My, mother and father? How were they?"

"Your mother was doing a lot better than your father. I think he blames himself for pushing that snot-nosed brat on you. He had heard from Sally what the boy had done at the table to you." Sally. Magnus smiled through her tears. "Your father was quite upset you would run off instead of coming to him. He had thought at first it was only nerves. Then maybe first love. But when Sally came forward to tell him what that monster had done, your father was sure you left instead of marrying the young twit."

"I had made plans before I met Charles, Uncle."

"I was afraid of that." Her uncle stood and paced. "Your father will never forgive me for filling your head with all those stories of Noteese."

"It's not your fault, Uncle. I was bound and determined to sail to Noteese, and nothing you or anyone could have said would have made a difference."

Magnus stood and walked to the window. "So now we go home?" Magnus asked.

"No, we sail to Noteese."

"We're still going to Noteese?"

"Yes, Magnus, we are still going to Noteese." Magnus looked around the room and for the first time noticed Ahaira was not with them. Turning back to the window, she noticed the scars had returned on her hands. Magnus turned to ask her uncle a question and noticed the color drain from his face. "It is horrible, I know," she said, lowering her face.

"It was just a shock, my dear. I was not prepared for such a drastic change in you."

Magnus looked up and smiled sadly. "I know. The first time I saw my reflection, I screamed out in terror. I thought a monster was standing behind me."

"Oh, my dear." Her uncle approached her. "We'll get your beauty back. You said Fanton did this to you, and they brought her with you."

"Yes, her and Henasee."

"Henasee's beauty is gone, too?

"Yes, she went back to help me and ran into Fanton. She is very angry at me."

"Well, Magnus, this is one of your bigger . . ."

"Mistakes?" she answered for him.

"I would call this one more of an explosion."

Magnus nodded. "Uncle? Where is Henasee?"

"I'll send for her shortly. I had no idea the other ugl . . . the other girl," he corrected, "would turn out to be Henasee."

"Maybe you'll be able to convince her I'm really sorry." Her uncle patted her hand. "I'll see what I can do. Right now, I think you could use some food and a good bath."

Kentar looked across the water. They anchored their ship miles away in an alcove so as not to be noticed. With the moon not full and the fog rolling in, he figured this was the time to rescue Fanton and the two girls. He knew he had to bring Magnus and Henasee back. If either girl was harmed or killed, the same thing would be bestowed on Fanton. He might be angry with Fanton, but he wanted no harm to come to her. He had carried a love for her for two years. Kentar looked over at Rivers. "I can do this. Stop watching me,"

"We've got to find them and get them off the ship with no funny business, Rivers."

"I know, I'll be on my best behavior," Rivers saluted. "Let's get going, Kentar, you're wasting time." Paddling the small boat through the water was easy for the two men. Both had been raised on the sea. No talk was needed. Pulling the rowboat up to the side of the ship, Kentar tied it to the anchor rope. Following close behind, he directed Rivers. "I know Ahaira's ship well. I worked on it for over a year before I met Fanton. You can get turned around easy in her stairwells." Rivers nodded.

Kentar climbed the anchor rope, and true to his word, Rivers was a few steps behind him. Landing on the deck, Kentar first looked around and placed his fingers to his lips as Rivers jumped down behind him. Kentar pulled his sword, and Rivers followed suit. "What the?" A tough-looking pirate turned and pulled his sword on Kentar. Kentar was too quick for the man and pierced him through the chest before the man could raise his blade. Rivers didn't miss a beat and jumped in front of another pirate who had drawn his sword in place of the man lying dead on the deck. "I can take care of this one, Kentar." After two hits, sword to sword, Rivers ran his blade through the pirate, dropping him to his death beside the pirate already on the deck. "I see you have improved" Kentar states.

"It was improve or die," Rivers returned.

"Good choice," Kentar nodded.

"I will see to Henasee," Magnus's uncle told her. "You need to eat and rest." Bernard pulled on a rope, the door opened, and a very nice-looking young man appeared. "Oh, it's you, Daniel." Magnus watched from the corner. She could see the young man was very good looking. His light blond hair was shoulder length, and his blue eyes twinkled in the fire light.

"I was getting some food for my niece." Daniel smiled and looked Magnus's way. Magnus turned her head and looked at the fire, too afraid of how he might react to seeing her without her beauty.

"Magnus, honey, this is Daniel."

"Hello, Daniel," she said without turning around.

"Honey, you're being rude. What an old fool I am. Magnus, I never thought of your feelings. Please forgive me."

"It's not your fault my beauty is gone, Uncle. It is all of my making."

"Still, Magnus, I should have considered your feelings about anyone seeing you."

"Until now, Uncle, I didn't know it would bother me."

Bernard looked at Magnus's back and then at Daniel. "My," he thought maybe the two of them could . . . "I have to see to Henasee.

Daniel, will you see to some food for my niece?" Daniel nodded and left the room. "Daniel will not try to look at you or pry into your business, Magnus. I would trust him with my own life. He is a good man and a good friend."

"Ok, Uncle." She turned, and he could see tears running down her cheeks.

"Don't cry, my sweet." Her uncle came to her and engulfed her in a big bear hug. "I will talk to Fanton myself. We will get you back to your old self."

Magnus sniffed. "I don't even remember who I was before I lost my beauty."

"Even with your beauty gone dear, I would know you anywhere. You are a most beautiful girl inside."

Magnus hugged her uncle. "You can always lift my spirits."

"You sit by the fire and let me see what I can do."

"Thank you, Uncle."

"You're welcome, my niece." He smiled and winked at her as he walked out the door. Daniel was back within 10 minutes carrying a huge tray of food. He placed the tray on a wooden table and pulled out a chair. Magnus lifted her head slightly, and Daniel pointed again. "You're not going away until I eat, are you?" Daniel shook his head no. "You sure are one of my uncle's dear friends. He doesn't take no for an answer either."

Magnus walked to the table looking at her feet. When she got within steps of the table, Daniel lifted up her chin with one hand. Magnus started to say no. But Daniel placed a finger on her lips. Pulling out her chair, he made a grand bow. Laughing for the first time in weeks, she sat down. Placing a plate and silverware in front of her, Daniel waved his arm to all the food on the tray. "Oh my, this could feed a whole town." Daniel smiled, and Magnus noticed he had dimples on each side of his cheek. Never had she been so attracted to a boy.

"Man," she thought to herself. "He's no boy." Daniel poured her tea out of a china pot and offered her a small china sugar bowl. "Thank you." She took it and flushed as their fingers accidentally rubbed together. Daniel bowed and left the room. Magnus ate until her stomach was so full she thought she might pop. Walking over to the fire, she put her hands out to warm them.

Fanton continued to stare at the floor as Henasee paced back and forth.

"Where do you think they took her?" she asked in front of Fanton. Fanton did not answer but continued to stare.

"I know Magnus can be overbearing at times, but she wouldn't hurt me on purpose. I shouldn't have let them take her. What kind of friend am I?"

Fanton lowered her head, and when she raised it, Henasee gasped. "Your scars, they are gone? How did you do that?" Fanton blinked but does not look Henasee's way. Henasee turned as the door handle moved.

Kentar slowly opened the door as Rivers dragged the guard into another cabin.

Fanton reached Kentar before he finished opening the door. "I knew you would come for me."

"No matter how I feel, Fanton, I would never let Ahaira hurt you." Rivers stepped from behind Kentar and Fanton. "You all right? he asked Fanton and then Henasee. Henasee rushed" into his arms without thinking. They've taken Magnus."

"We must go," Rivers told her.

"Not without Magnus."

"We don't have time. If they find us, we're all dead. Now come on, Henasee." Rivers took her hand, and they hurried out of the room and up the stairs.

"Listen," Kentar quieted them. Voices coming from the top of the stairs start to get louder.

"Get in here." Kentar opened a door, and Rivers and Henasee followed Kentar and Fanton into the room. Rivers listened as the voices stopped in front of the door and then after a few laughs start moving again. "Let's get out of her fast," Rivers said to Kentar. Henasee followed Rivers until they got to the deck. "We have to climb over the side," he told her when she stopped. "I won't let anything happen to you."

"I'm not going anywhere until you tell me what's going on." She pulled free from his hand.

"Come on, Rivers, people are coming."

"Henasee, we don't have time. If they find us here, they're going to kill us." Henasee took another step back. "Who is 'they,' Rivers? And why didn't you ask me who Magnus was?"

Rivers looked at Henasee. "We need to go."

"No," she said, turning to run.

Rivers grabbed her arm and spun her around. Henasee opened her mouth, about to scream, and Rivers punched her in the jaw. Henasee went limp, and Rivers picked her up and carried her over the side of the ship. Kentar lifted Fanton the rest of the way down the rope and started to untie it. Looking up, he could see Rivers was carrying Henasee, and he reached up to help lift her in the boat. "Let's get out of here," Rivers whispered as he laid Henasee on his coat.

Chapter 6
Lost Beauty

Magnus watched the fire burn until her eyes closed. Waking hours later, she wondered who put the blanket on her and removed her shoes. Cuddling deep into the overstuffed chair, she went back to sleep. Her dreams were happy, and she laughed at Henasee and her angry face. "You can't stay mad at me, Hen. You know you won't." Henasee smiled at her and opened her arms for Magnus to hug her. Magnus walked into her friend's arms. But as she reached her, Henasee's face changed. Her beauty was gone. Her smile was filled with an angry look, and she started to yell, "I hate you, Magnus. You did this to me. I will never forgive you!"

"No, Hen, please," Magnus screamed back. "I didn't mean for this to happen. Please, Hen, please don't hate me. I'm sorry," Magnus yelled. "I'm sorry."

Magnus cried her eyes dry and finally with one last shook opened them. "It's you," she smiles with tears still running down her face. Daniel smiled back at her. "I was dreaming of my friend," she told him. "I got her in this mess, and she's lost her beauty, too. I don't think she'll ever forgive me," Magnus continued. Daniel tilted his head. "Henasee won't forgive me unless I can get her beauty back for her. I really didn't mean to hurt anyone." Daniel shook his head, and Magnus smiled. "I just didn't want to marry Charles Junior." She shuddered. Daniel laughed and nodded. "Thank you for listening to me ramble on." Daniel lifted her hand to his lips and kissed it.

"Daniel!" Ahaira screamed from the doorway, making Magnus jump. "You mind your manners. You know that's Bernard's niece and not some trollop we've picked up off the streets." Magnus knew, even with the scars, her face was turning beet red. Daniel gave Ahaira a sour look. Magnus looked down and was somehow hurt her beauty has returned. She had thought Daniel liked her beyond her beauty. And the whole time he was talking to her, she had her beauty with her. "Oh," she said sadly, looking away from Daniel.

"Daniel, I'll need the tub filled. Could you get some men to fill it?"
Daniel nodded and bowed to Magnus before he left the room.
"I see your arms and hands are quite pretty, but your beauty on your face has not yet returned," Ahaira told Magnus. Magnus jumped up and looked into a small mirror on the wall.
"My beauty has not returned," she laughed.
Ahaira shook her head, thinking the girl a little deaf. "Fanton never could get things correct," Ahaira snarled.
"Fanton," Magnus turned to Ahaira, "reversed the spell when the pirates came on board."
Ahaira looked at Magnus. "She was throwing you to the wolves."
Magnus nodded. "I know why she did it. However, in her haste she didn't say the spell," Ahaira tsked.
"What does it mean? Fanton did not say the spell."
"It means the potion did not work correctly."
"What will happen to me?" Magnus turned back to the mirror.
"It means your beauty will come and go. As will Fanton's."
"Is there no way to stop it?"
"As long as Fanton lives, you will live. If she dies, you die. As long as you both live, you will share your beauty and her scars."
Magnus sat down on a chair before she fell down. "I knew I was in trouble, but I thought it was something that could be fixed."
"It is not smart to mess with destiny. Lies and deceit will overcome your life."
The door opened, and Magnus looked up to see Daniel and two other men carrying buckets of water. Walking past her, Daniel smiled once again, and Magnus felt better.

Ahaira smiled looking from Magnus to Daniel and thought, "Maybe", her smile deepened, "Daniel will find love after all."
Magnus was the first to look away. "She's not sure why she is drawn to Daniel, but she knows there is a strong connection with him."
Ahaira broke the silence. "I'm sure there is something you can be doing, Daniel." Daniel nodded at Ahaira and looked one more time at Magnus. "I will see to her needs, Daniel, you may go." Daniel smiled at Magnus and left the room.
Magnus wasted no time turning to Ahaira. "Thank you for coming for me."

"It is not my thanks to take," Ahaira said kindly. "Your uncle and I have been friends a long time. I would give up my life for him, as I'm sure he would do the same for me."

"Are you talking a painful death, Ahaira?" Bernard laughed from the doorway.

"Oh, darling." Ahaira came to his side. "I was only telling your niece of our friendship," she purred. Magnus was too shocked to speak.

"Don't look so dumbfounded, Magnus," her uncle laughed again. "Did you not think women found your uncle attractive?"

"No," Magnus spurted out. "I mean no, Uncle, I'm sure many women find you very attractive."

"Who?" Ahaira spit out at Magnus.

"I didn't mean anything by saying that," Magnus said to her uncle. Her uncle laughed aloud. "I'm afraid where Ahaira is concerned, no other women should be allowed to look at me." Magnus looked at Ahaira, who nodded.

Looking uncomfortable with the direction of the conversation, Bernard led Ahaira to a light blue chaise lounge and asked her to sit. Going to a side table, he poured himself and Ahaira bourbon and handed Ahaira her glass.

"Now, let's see." Bernard looked at Magnus. "I think we have more pressing things to talk about." Magnus tilted her head. "I'm referring to your beauty, my dear." Magnus's face turned deep red, making her scars even darker. "Yes," Bernard coughed, "let's figure out your beauty."

Magnus looked at Ahaira. "Is there a way to get my beauty back?"

"You are lucky; Fanton uses a very weak potion to take beauty for her own. I will need some of her blood and . . ." Ahaira noticed the blue tint to Magnus's face now. "It is not much. I need just a pinprick." Magnus relaxed and smiled at her uncle.

"Ahaira is very good with potions and such things," her uncle said fondly. "She'll have you back to normal before you can say thank you." Magnus felt happiness and relief surge through her body and took a sip from her water glass.

"What's that?" her uncle said, hearing the clamor in the hall. He opened the door, and a very thin man screamed, "They're gone, sir?"

"Who's gone?" her uncle screamed at the shaking man.

"The witch and the other girl are gone. I went to relieve Jape and found him unconscious on the floor. The door was open, and the witch and the girl were nowhere to be found."

"Henasee is missing?" Magnus asked the man as if she hadn't heard him the first time.

"Don't get upset, Magnus, we'll find her."

"We need to find them both." Ahaira stepped to the other side of Magnus. "You and Fanton are sharing the same potion in your bodies. It will not be long before the spell takes hold of you permanently."

"What does that mean?" Magnus looked at Ahaira, with tears running down her cheeks.

"It means when the spell has run its course whoever has the beauty at that time will own the beauty."

"And whoever has the scars," Magnus finished for Ahaira, "will own the scars?"

"I'm afraid so."

Magnus looked faint, and her uncle led her to the sofa.

"There is nothing more you can do tonight, Magnus. I think you need to rest."

"Henasee? Uncle, what about Henasee?"

"They must need her still to keep the spell alive," Ahaira informed Magnus. "They will not hurt her. To hurt your friend will only hurt Fanton."

"You mean Fanton and me, don't you?"

"Yes, if any of you should die before the spell is completed, you will all die."

"Ahaira!" Bernard hushed her with a squeeze on her arm. "Do not scare the girl."

"She is not a child, Bernard, she is a woman now. You must not treat her like a baby."

Bernard looked taken back. "I'm not treating her like a child," he claimed. "She just needs to rest, that's all."

"No, no," Ahaira laughed you don't treat her like a child. "Now go, Bernard. I will see to your niece."

Bernard bent down and kissed Magnus's scarred cheek.

"Everything will be fine, Magnus, I promise. You get some rest, and we'll talk again in the morning. You will be safe in here, and there will be a guard posted through the night right outside your door. If you get scared or even lonely, you send for me."

"Bernard!" Ahaira said, grabbing his arm and leading him to the door. "Go now." Bernard knew Ahaira was laughing the whole time and kissed her on the cheek before leaving the room to find Daniel. "He is quite the man," Ahaira said to the closed door.

"Now let's get you cleaned up," she said turning to Magnus.

"I haven't anything else," Magnus told her, rubbing her boys pants.

"I have plenty, my dear." Ahaira opened a door, and Magnus couldn't believe the amount of clothes there were. Robes, gowns, slippers, shoes of every fabric and even color poured from drawers and shelves. "All I need is your favorite color." Ahaira pointed and laughed with Magnus. Magnus laughed harder as Ahaira pulled out dress after dress and piled them on the floor next to Magnus.

Henasee rubbed her jaw and moans. Opening her eyes, she saw Rivers sitting in the same chair he had been in while she'd been seasick. Without thinking, Henasee jumped from her bed and threw her body on Rivers sleeping form. Henasee hit Rivers on any part of his body her hands could find.

"What the . . ." Rivers yelled into the darkness, trying to block her blows. "Stop it, Henasee, or I'll forget I'm a gentleman."

"Gentleman!" Henasee hit his arm and then his shoulder. "You are no gentleman." Rivers held Henasee's right arm to her side and after two more punches to the chest was able to hold her left arm down. "Now stop this right now, Henasee." Henasee nodded, but as soon as Rivers let her right arm free, she smacked him in the cheek. Surprised by the burning sensation on his cheek Rivers stood up and she dropped to the floor. Within seconds, Henasee was back on her feet and taking a left jab at Rivers' stomach. Grabbing her around the waist, Rivers pulled Henasee into his arms. Henasee was frustrated because she couldn't hurt him anymore or get free, and she broke into tears.

"Stop that, Henasee," Rivers pleaded. "I can't stand crying."

Henasee turned her head and continued crying. Picking her up under the legs, Rivers carried her to the chair he had been sleeping on and sat down with her on his lap and rocked her gently. "I'm sorry I had to hit you, Henasee, but you were going to give us all away. I can take care of myself, but my sister . . ."

Henasee came alive. She punched Rivers so hard in the jaw his head flew back. Jumping from the chair, she headed for the door. Rivers recovered quickly and reached out for Henasee before she got the door open. "Stop, Henasee," Rivers spoke into her hair. "Just let me explain."

Henasee went limp. She knew she was no match for Rivers strength. Half carrying and half dragging her, Rivers managed to get Henasee back to her bed. "Now sit still for a second, please," he asked when she started once again to struggle.

"Yes," Rivers said trying to look into Henasee's eyes. "Fanton is my sister. She is my half sister. We had the same father." Henasee tried to get up, but Rivers held her in place with his hands on her arms. "Fanton does not hunt down little girls to steal their beauty, Henasee. These girls come to her begging to change their lives no matter what the cost."

Henasee believed Rivers statement. She knew Magnus went to Fanton's shop. "You weren't supposed to be part of the spell, Henasee. You were at the shop by accident. The spell had already been cast when you walked into the shop. Fanton said she tried to catch you, but you looked frightened and ran out the door. Later I found you in the alley. Not knowing what to do with you, I brought you here. I was surprised myself to hear Fanton married Banner. I had to get her off that ship, Henasee. Ahaira and Fanton have hurt each other before. Ahaira knows Fanton is weak, and she would have destroyed her."

"Why didn't you leave me there? I would have been with Magnus. I see. Fanton needs me still. Doesn't she?" Henasee screamed at Rivers.

"You are connected to her as long as the spell is still alive," Rivers told her.

"What does that mean? Tell me Rivers what does it mean as long as the spell is alive?"

Kentar carried Fanton to the bed she shared with Nathan and lay her down gently. His hand went to her face to wipe the tears away from her cheeks. "I was so afraid you wouldn't find me," she cried into

Kentar's hand. Kentar took her hand, never once showing he noticed the scars, and brought it to his lips.
"I would have searched the world over to bring you back to me." Fanton closed her eyes as Kentar lowered his lips to hers. Without pausing, he lay down beside her on the bed, taking in her beauty. Forgetting about her scars, Fanton opened her arms to Kentar and whispered, "You are my true love, Kentar."
"As you have always been mine, my darling," he returned, pulling her on top of him to kiss her deeply.

Magnus was so busy looking at the night gowns Ahaira was tossing her way she didn't notice two men and Daniel carrying water in buckets into the next room. "I think I like the blue one," she laughed at Ahaira's face. "Did I make the wrong choice?" Magnus asked, perplexed by Ahaira's facial expression.
"No, my darling, you have made a very good choice. The color will match your blue eyes and your beautiful complexion, nicely."
Magnus reached her hand up to touch her cheek slowly and let out a small whimper. Touching her other cheek, she ran to a small mirror on the wall. With tears in her eyes, she caressed her cheek and then her chin. "You are quite beautiful," Ahaira told her.
Magnus continued looking at herself in the mirror. "I've always took my beauty for granted," Magnus said into the mirror. "I mean, if I wanted something being the pretty little girl got me it. People have always fawned over me. But until I traded my beauty like it was nothing, I never knew how much it meant to have it. Does that make sense?" she asked, turning for Ahaira's reaction.
"Many have wished to be someone else and later found out the cost of changing."
Magnus turned back to the mirror. "It probably won't stay this time either, will it?"
"No, I think not. You and Fanton have shared the spell twice now. Only fate will show who keeps the beauty and who keeps the scars."
Magnus looked at Ahaira. "If my beauty returns, I will never trade it for anything again."
Ahaira smiled sadly. "Never is a long time, my dear, especially when life changes every minute."
Kentar woke to empty arms and searched the bed in the dark.

"I am here, Kentar," Fanton cried. As he started to get up, she said in a distant voice, "No, do not come closer." Kentar started to head toward Fanton's voice. "No, Kentar, I will not have you see me this way."

"What is wrong?" he asked, concerned.

"My beauty it is gone."

"Fanton, I've told you this does not matter to me."

"No, Kentar, you must go."

"If I do not go this time, what then, Fanton?"

"I will throw myself into the sea the very first time I am alone, Kentar. You must believe me. I cannot bear the idea of you seeing me like this."

"Fanton let me help you through this."

"You can help me by leaving, Kentar, and not coming back until I call for you. Promise you won't come until I call."

"I will do as you ask," he said, dressing quickly. "I'll see you have whatever you need."

"Thank you," she said weakly.

"Good night," he whispered at the door.

Magnus stripped off the boy's clothes and stepped into the steel bathtub filled with steaming water and a rose fragrance. She sat down with a moan. "I've never loved something so much in my life," she laughed.

Ahaira took a sponge and washed Magnus's back softly. "This tub was a gift from your uncle many years ago. Besides my diamonds and clothes, I think this was my favorite gift."

"I can see why," Magnus laughed as Ahaira poured warm water over Magnus's short hair. "My mother would faint dead away if she could see my hair," Magnus giggled.

"It will grow back in time," Ahaira said as a matter of fact.

"True," Magnus answered her. "It's funny the things people take for granted, isn't it? Like my hair, I never cared one way or the other about it. Mostly, I hated having it combed and fussed over. Now with it almost gone," she said, feeling the length to her ear, "I wish I had it back."

"I wonder if you never had your beauty?" Ahaira asked, drying off Magnus's back, "would you want to be beautiful?"

Magnus turned to look at Ahaira. "I'm not sure. I've always had it."

"Does it make you a different person?" she asked Magnus.

"I don't feel differently. That is until people say something about it."

"I see," Ahaira said, placing the wet towel on the side of the tub. "When people talked of your beauty, it was ok, but now that it's gone, it's a bad thing?"

"Yes, I mean no. I guess it depends on who's talking about it."

"Then maybe it's not the beauty, maybe it's the people around you." Magnus didn't know how to answer. Kentar and Jake had made her feel ugly and unwanted. However, when she met Daniel, she was relieved he had liked her without her beauty. It meant a great deal to her that he liked her for herself. Herself, she wondered, she had never known before what herself might be.

"You, my dear, need some rest, now come with me." Magnus followed Ahaira into a giant bedroom and watched her pull back the blankets.

"This is my uncle's room?"

"Yes, it is," Ahaira answered.

"Where will he sleep if I have his room?" Magnus turned red from head to toe when Ahaira laughed aloud.

"You're right," Magnus laughed, still embarrassed. "I need to get some rest."

"Remember, if you need anything, Daniel will be right outside." Magnus looked at Ahaira. "He asked to stand guard over you," Ahaira said lightly, and lowered the light.

"I'll see you in the morning. Thank you very much."

"You're welcome dear, now good night," Ahaira said again and walked out the door, closing it quietly behind her. Magnus had a hard time falling asleep with the knowledge Daniel was on the other side of the door. Once she heard a noise as if he had leaned up against it, and it gave her goose bumps all over. "Go to sleep, Magnus," she told herself. Saying a quick prayer for her parents and Henasee, Magnus fell into a deep sleep for the first time in a week.

Henasee understood Rivers loyalty to Fanton. She had very strong feelings for her family as well. But her mother and father were not witches and did not take away his beauty and leave him with a body full of scars. Turning her head, she refused to listen to Rivers story of growing up with Fanton as a sister.

"I wish you would try to understand, Henasee. I didn't choose her to be my sister; she just is. Our father brought Fanton to live with us when I was 12 or 13 years old. She was only 15 years old, and her mother had thrown her out over some disagreement. We never did hear everything that had gone on between them. Fanton was angry and rebellious, but we became close after time.

Henasee turned her head farther to the window.

"Ok, be that way. I don't owe you any explanation," Rivers screamed at the back of her head. "If you won't talk, the least you can do is get some rest. We're shorthanded now, and everyone will be needed to get us to Noteese."

"Noteese?" Henasee turned her head and screamed. "We're headed to Noteese?"

"That's the plan," Rivers shot back. "We should be there in about six months if the weather holds out."

Henasee jumped up and stopped at Rivers side. "I thought we'd be going home."

"No," Rivers answers, "we are going to Noteese as planned."

Henasee gave Rivers an "I'd like to kill you" look and turned back around to stare out the window.

"I'll come for you in the morning. You would be wise to lock your door after me and not let anyone in now that the men left on board know you're a girl. It won't be safe to trust any of them." Henasee hugged herself without turning around.

"Good night then," Rivers said at the door before leaving.

Henasee was so mad at Magnus, Fanton, and Rivers she didn't dare open her mouth for fear of what would come out of it. Rivers let out a deep breath and opened the door and slammed it shut before heading up top to find Kentar.

Fanton dressed quickly in a beautiful gown of green forest with a matching hooded cape. Laughing, she looked in the mirror one last time and rushed from the room. Once on deck, she spotted Kentar and glided over to his side, taking his arm.

"I see you have returned to yourself," he said, squeezing her hand on his arm.

"I feel wonderful," Fanton laughed aloud.

Kentar waved one of the crew away and swept her into his arms and kissed her deeply.

Henasee couldn't believe her eyes. Fanton was not covered in scars with black and gray straw-like hair hanging down her back. "No," Henasee said to herself. "This can't be? How is her beauty back?" Henasee reached the rail to study herself as an arm grabbed her and jerked her around roughly.

"What are you doing here?" Rivers screamed in her shocked face. "I told you to stay in your room until I returned."

Henasee tried to pull out of his grasp. "Let go of me this instant."

"You are a spoiled little . . . brat," Rivers screamed back. "Why can't you do what you're told?"

"Let go of me," Henasee screamed again.

"I should," Rivers said, shaking Henasee's arm.

"You should what?" she screamed back.

Kentar marched to them and took Rivers's arm off Henasee's arm. "That is no way to treat a lady," he said to Rivers.

Rivers laughed. "This one is not a lady."

Henasee forgot herself and kicked Rivers as hard as she could in the shin.

He was so stunned and angry; he reached for Henasee's arm.

"Leave her alone, Rivers. She has been through enough these last few days."

Rivers looked from Henasee and then to Kentar. "You can take care of her if you're so worried about her, Kentar. Good riddance," Rivers laughed at Henasee. "Good riddance. I don't need this headache," he said swatting at the air and walking off.

"He's not all bad," Kentar laughed at Rivers's departing frame. "I think he likes you."

Henasee almost laughed aloud, but instead she looked at the scars on her hands. "No one will ever like me again," she whispered.

"Don't sell yourself short. Beauty is only the outside. I think Rivers saw past that a while ago. He's not usually this worried about anyone but himself. No, I think he sees the beauty that still forms around you."

Henasee smiled at Kentar. "I wish I felt my beauty."

"Maybe you just have to look deeper than you are."

"Fanton?" Henasee pointed. "She has her beauty back now?"

"For now," Kentar told Henasee. "It comes and goes now."
"She is very beautiful," Henasee stated.
"She does not see her beauty as I do. She only sees the reflection of her beauty. Someday I hope she sees what I see in her."
Henasee was surprised she understood what he meant. Kentar loved Fanton with or without her beauty, but Fanton did not believe in their love enough to believe him.
"There is much to be done," Kentar told Henasee. "Jage the cook was hurt badly, and the rest of the crew that's left is needed."
"What can I do?" she asked Kentar.
"Do you know how to cook?"
"I can cook," Henasee told him. "Magnus and I used to go down to the docks. Her Uncle Bernard taught us how to build fires and cook."
"We could use your help," he told her. "We have 20 healthy men and three down below who are wounded. I have given strict orders if any man touches you he will die."
Henasee looked into Kentar's eyes and saw this was the truth.
"No man will hurt you on this ship." Kentar pointed to a staircase. "Down below is the galley. You will find it well stocked. We would be most grateful for what you can make us."
Henasee smiled at Kentar. "I will do my best."
"I believe you will." He smiled back.
Henasee excelled in putting together a meal of stew made with dried meat and biscuits. Happy to have something to keep her busy, she placed three bowls of stew on a tray and headed down the hall to find the three wounded men. Jage was the first to look up from his bed. "God bless thee," he whispered. "I thought we were left here to die."
"There's no need for talk like that," Henasee corrected Jage.
Placing the tray on the table by Jage's bed, Henasee lifted his pillow a little so she could spoon his stew into his mouth.
"You are truly a beautiful saint," Jage told Henasee. Henasee laughed as she placed a spoonful of stew into Jage's mouth.
"Your wound," Henasee pointed at Jage's wrapped chest.
"Kentar, he sewed me up real good last night. He told me he was sending an angel to care for me, and I was to be nice."
Henasee smiled and placed another bite into Jage's mouth. "I see,"

she hushed Jage by spooning a bite of stew in his mouth. "You will be fine after you eat and get some rest." Jage nodded and opened his mouth for another bite of stew.
The next man Henasee fed was just as polite and thanked her as she put the empty bowl of stew back on the tray. "Bless you, ma'am," he yelled as Henasee closed the door. Henasee touched the last man's shoulder and was surprised when he didn't turn over. Having grown up around farm animals with births and deaths happening all the time she was not afraid. Closing her eyes, she said a prayer for the lost life she had found. Picking up her tray, she returned to the kitchen and then went to find Kentar.
"I will see everything is taken care of," Kentar told Henasee after she told him of the dead man.
"Everything is ready in the galley."
"I'll start sending them down. If you would get a tray ready for Fanton, I will deliver it myself."
Henasee agreed and wandered back to the galley to find four men sitting around the big wooden table in the middle of the room. One gruff-looking man started to say something, but thought better of it and closed his mouth as Kentar followed Henasee into the kitchen. Henasee fixed a tray with stew, biscuits, and some dry fruit she had found earlier for Fanton's tray. Pouring coffee into a small pot and placing silverware on the tray, she handed it to Kentar.
"This looks great," he told Henasee, making her grin from ear to ear. Walking to the door, Kentar turned to look at the men at the table. "Remember what I said." All four men nodded at the same time. Henasee turned her head not to laugh aloud. After the four men were fed and gone, Henasee set more places at the table. An old man with a long gray and black beard was the first to enter the room.
"Something smells real good in here, ma'am." Henasee smiled her thanks and pointed to a chair. Four more sets of men came and went before Henasee could sit down for a minute. "It's not an easy job, is it?" She heard from behind her.
"No," she said, smiling at Kentar.
"Are you hungry? You stay down," he insisted. "I can get my own food. Have you eaten yourself?" he asked Henasee.
"I . . . no, I guess I haven't."
"It won't help any of us if you get sick. You need to take better care

of yourself, Henasee."

Henasee laughed. "You sound like my parents." Kentar laughed with her and poured a bowl of stew for her, too.

Rivers watched from the door with a scowl on his face at Kentar and Henasee's easy banter. Kentar told a story about his father, and Henasee laughed aloud. As Rivers stepped into the room, both went silent as he walked over to the stove. Henasee took a bite of her stew while Kentar drank his coffee. "I'm not a leper," Rivers yelled into the silence. Kentar looked at a startled Henasee and winked. With his coffee finished, Kentar stood to leave.

"Thank you, Henasee, for the good food and the company."

"You are most welcome, Kentar," Henasee replied.

Rivers sat across the table from Henasee, and she stood to remove her empty bowl.

"You will not sit and talk to me as I eat?" Rivers asked Henasee.

"I have work to do," she told him.

"You didn't look as if you were working a minute ago."

"I was being polite," she snapped at Rivers.

"It seems your politeness has won out," Rivers continued. "Am I not worthy of your company?"

Henasee finished picking up her cup and spoon and turned away from Rivers. "You're still mad at me?"

Henasee turned and looked him in the eye. "You have no right to order me about as you do. I was worried for your safety. I am not a little girl, Rivers. My parents were looking for a husband for me. I was going to be a married woman by fall."

Rivers looks down at his bowl and asked, "Did they find you someone, Henasee?"

"My dad had a couple of young men in mind."

"Did you fancy either of them?"

"They were nice, but no, I didn't want to marry either one."

Rivers took a bite of his stew. "This is really good. Jage isn't really a cook so his meals didn't have much taste in them."

Henasee smiled. "That's what Kentar was saying." With Kentar's name mentioned, the mood in the room went cold once again, and Rivers stood to leave.

"Thank you for dinner."

"You're welcome," Henasee whispered to his back.

Chapter 7
Daniel

Magnus woke to find a beautiful olive gown on the end of her bed and hurried to dress. Finding her beauty gone was no surprise. She had awakened in the middle of the night to notice the returning scars on her hands from the light from the moon-filled window.
"I will make this a better day," she smiled into the mirror, beauty or no beauty. A knock on the door startled her, but she recovered. "Come in," she called. Daniel smiled carrying a tray of food and a pot of tea. Magnus had watched Daniel and Ahaira communicate and she had talked to Daniel as if he could talk back.
"Isn't it a lovely morning?" she asked Daniel. Magnus noticed the smile on his face got deeper as he nodded. "Daniel, may I ask you something?" she asked shyly. "How do you talk if you want to answer more than yes or no?"
 Daniel pulled a piece of paper with a pencil out of his pocket and wrote quickly. "Until now," he wrote, "yes and no questions were enough. You feel it, too? Don't you?" Daniel busied himself writing again. "I feel what is between you and I Magnus."
Magnus smile and reached for his hand but dropped it as the door was thrown open and her uncle came in. "I see your beauty is not with you, my dear. Ahaira said you had it last night. I was hoping you might get to keep it this time."
Magnus turned from Daniel and her uncle. "Really, Uncle, I'm fine."
"No, my darling, you will never be fine until your beauty is yours again for good."
"Uncle, I don't care about my beauty."
"Of course, you do, Magnus, you've just been through so much lately. There's no way you can go through life without your beauty." Magnus sat on the sofa, never looking up. "You are right, Uncle, it would be horrible to go through life like this." Magnus didn't notice as Daniel left the room and quietly closed the door.

Henasee loved her routine. She woke before dawn and baked, fried, and cooked breakfast for the crew. After everyone was fed, she took

breakfast to Jage and Tar and returned to the kitchen to eat with Kentar. Sharing her meals with Kentar and listening to his stories were her favorite times of the day.
With breakfast done and everything cleaned up, Henasee took a walk around the deck of the boat. "It's a nice day, ma'am," one crewmember said after another. Henasee enjoyed her walks because the sea was breathtaking at dawn.
"I thought I might find you here," Kentar said to Henasee.
"It's so lovely at this time of day," Henasee told him without turning around.
Kentar stepped up behind her and looked into the sky. "This is why I sail. The water and the sky own my heart."
"The water, the sky, and Fanton," Henasee corrected him.
Kentar laughed, and Henasee turned her head to ask why. "You have changed," he said, "looking over her face with shock."
Henasee looked down at her hands as tears ran down her face. "You are very beautiful, Henasee, inside and out." Kentar reached out and rubbed his thumb softly down her cheek. Henasee smiled into his eyes.

Neither noticed Fanton standing in the shadows cursing under her breath. "I will see you pay dearly, you tramp," Fanton said to herself as she walked away from the two lovers.
Henasee stepped back and Kentar let his hand drop.
"I'm sorry. I didn't mean to touch you. I was so surprised to see the change. I mean it is so drastic. I didn't mean."
"I know what you're trying to say," Henasee laughed. "Thank you, my feelings are still intact. I'm just not sure how I feel at this moment. Everyone here knows me as the girl with the scars."
"You're more than that, Henasee. "You're the girl who feeds us and looks after us. Most of the men call you Inspire."
"Inspire?" she asked. "It means the one with the heart."
Henasee's tears returned and once again ran down her cheeks.
"This isn't time for tears," Kentar smiled. "This is time for rejoicing."
Henasee looked uncertain.
"What's wrong, Henasee?"
"I think it was easier to hide behind my scars. Who was ever going

to look at me? There were no decisions to make about my future. I was never going to find anyone to love me looking like I did."
"I'm not so sure of that, Henasee. I know one young man who has been very moody these last months because you're still not talking to him."
Henasee half smiled and said, "Rivers?"
"Yes, Rivers," Kentar repeated. "I don't think he sees the scars when he looks at you."
Henasee sighed. "What do you think he'll see now?"
Kentar looked at her face and smiles. "He will see a very beautiful young lady," Kentar whispered.

Rivers mood hadn't changed in the months they had been on the ship. Henasee not only stopped talking to him she walked out of the room when he entered now, but most of the men stayed away from him, saying he was mean to the core. Not caring what they thought, Rivers did his work and stayed by himself the rest of the time. Hearing voices, he followed them to the front of the deck.
"Give it a chance," Rivers heard Kentar talking to someone.
"I've never thought about love before." Rivers heard a voice he knew to be Henasee's.
Henasee hurried off to find Rivers and tell him the reason she'd been avoiding him was that she had feelings for him. Now with her beauty back, she hoped he would return her feelings like Kentar said he would. Running from deck to deck, she finally saw Rivers standing at the side of the deck looking out in the ocean.
"I've been looking for you," she said quietly.
"That's funny," Rivers stated, not bothering to turn around. "For months, you've been avoiding me and now you hunt me down?"
"Well, yes, I have something I want to tell you."
"I have no need to hear anything you have to say, Henasee."
"Please, I'd like to explain."
"There's nothing to explain."
"If you would just listen for a minute," she tried to tell him.
Rivers turned to face her, his facial expression never changing.
"What is it you want, Henasee?"
"I wanted to tell you I'm sorry."
"Apology accepted," Rivers snapped and walked away.

Magnus was getting used to her time on board the ship. She spent time reading or talking to her uncle or Ahaira. She was used to her beauty coming and going daily, and it didn't change her days much. She hadn't seen much of Daniel since the day she'd asked him about the connection between them and he had agreed. When she asked Ahaira about it she said Daniel could be moody and he'd come around when he got over whatever was bothering him. Only two more days, her uncle had told her last night, and they would arrive at Noteese. Maybe then, Magnus hoped, she'd be able to ask Daniel why he had been avoiding her.

Henasee ran from the deck, down the stairs, and closed the door to her room before tears flooded her face. Never before had she been so humiliated. "I will hate you for the rest of my life," she said, calling out Rivers's name into her empty room. "You will never see how much you hurt me," she said, hitting her mattress repeatedly. "I curse the day I met you and your sister." Henasee continued crying out her hurt and anger in her empty cabin.
An hour later she screamed, "I have been through enough." She stood up and walked over to the only window in the room and looked up into the sky. "I will survive Rivers's rejection as I have survived losing my beauty and being taken from my family. I will not let Rivers or anyone rule my destiny." Looking at her reflection in the window Henasee smiled angrily and shook her head. "I have learned what life might be without my beauty and I would have survived. Now I will learn how to be beautiful again. Beautiful and wiser," she told her reflection. . "Much wiser, where Rivers is concerned, much wiser," she whispered as she wiped her tears and left the room.

"Noteese," Magnus heard one of the sailors call, "straight ahead." Magnus smiled as her Uncle Bernard puts his arm around her, drawing her close.
"I see today is not one of your good days, my dear."
Uncle. Magnus laughed sadly. "If not for people telling me my beauty was gone, I barely notice when it comes and goes now."
Uncle Bernard cleared his throat. "I thought you were hiding your

feelings, Magnus."

"No, Uncle, my beauty is not as important as I thought it was."

"I'm afraid I do not understand," Uncle Bernard said to Magnus.

"I'm not sure I do either, Uncle. I just know it's not the first thing I think of when I wake in the morning, and it's not the last thing I pray for when I go to sleep."

"You have been on board this ship for weeks, Magnus. Maybe it's easier because no one here dares say anything about your beauty for fear I'd throw them overboard."

Magnus laughed, hugging him deeply. "I kind of figured you put a scare in some of the men."

"How so?" Uncle Bernard laughed back.

"I've said good morning to a few men who, instead of answering, ran from the deck like chickens with their heads cut off."

Bernard's laughter could be heard across the ship, to Magnus's delight.

"Look, Magnus," Bernard pointed, "there stands the famous Noteese." Magnus couldn't believe the beauty of the island as she squinted against the water's glare.

"The ships Uncle?" Magnus asked, alarmed.

"No need to worry, Magnus. Those are not fighting vessels. They have come to make their fortune as we have. There is plenty to go around, and no one will worry about the other here."

"What about Henasee, Uncle?"

"Fanton is not too far behind us so don't worry. Ahaira says Henasee is no threat to them. She'll be fine."

"How will we get her back?"

"Let me worry about that, Magnus. You worry about how rich you're soon going to be."

Magnus smiled and hugged her uncle again.

"We will float tonight," Kentar told one of his men. Every man on board respected and feared Kentar as their new captain.

"Yes, sir, I'll spread the word."

Kentar opened the door to the cabin he shared with Fanton when she had her beauty. Lately he'd noticed a change in her, but no matter how much he asked, Fanton refused to talk about it.

"We will reach Noteese tomorrow," Kentar told Fanton, reaching for her arm.

Fanton pulled away angry. "I care nothing for Noteese," she yelled at him.

Kentar looked at Fanton. "Your beauty has returned, why are you so angry?"

"You know why I'm angry," she yelled at him.

"What is wrong?"

"You play games, Kentar. You play with my heart. All the time telling me my beauty means nothing, and the whole time you speak of another's beauty."

Kentar looked at Fanton as if she'd lost her mind. "I've spoke of no other beauty," he yelled back at Fanton. "I speak of only your beauty."

"You lie," she screamed and threw a white powder into his face. Words swam around him as Fanton spoke a chant filled with anger. Trying to hold himself up, Kentar held on to the back of the couch. Fanton finished her spell and laughed into the air as Kentar fell to the ground, gasping for air.

"You have killed our love?" he choked out before falling into a restless sleep.

"No, darling, you will not die. You will sleep and I will take care of her." Fanton hurried to retrieve the bag of clothes she had under the bed. "Good-bye, darling, she laughed as she quietly closes the door. Fanton approached the first crewman she saw. "Kentar wishes a boat to be dropped in the water." Afraid of making either Kentar or his witch mad, the man rushed to do Kentar's bidding.

Fanton hurried to the kitchen. Grabbing a cloth bag, she threw two loaves of bread and four apples in it.

"Fanton? Is that you?" Henasee asked from the doorway. "What are you doing?"

Fanton turned to stare at Henasee. "It is you," Fanton screamed. "You think your beauty can take anything?"

Henasee started to back out of the room. Fanton's anger was almost choking her. Worried for fear Fanton had gone mad, Henasee turned to run from the room.

"No, my beauty," Fanton said, grabbing Henasee's arm. "I will take you with me."

Henasee tried to pull away, but Fanton whispered in her ear, "If

anyone comes to your rescue, I will bring pain to their heart as you have brought pain to me."
Henasee tried to tell Fanton. "Please, I don't know what you're talking about. I have done nothing to you. It's you that has harmed me."
"You don't look as if you've been harmed," Fanton screamed again.
"Yes, I know my beauty has returned," Henasee told her trying to drag her feet.
"I care not of your beauty," Fanton screeched into the air. "It's your heart that has no beauty."
"I don't know what you're talking about."
"It's a heart that would take true love away without a care for the pain it might cause."
"Let me go," Henasee yelled, trying once again to free herself.
Fanton stopped, listening to the approaching footsteps. "You will be the cause of their deaths if you continue to fight me." Henasee watched as Fanton reached into her pocket and pulled out a small brown bottle.
"What is that?" she asked Fanton.
"It is your lover's death." Watching Henasee's face drain from all its colors but white Fanton laughed.
"How could you be so cruel?" Henasee cried at Fanton, thinking Fanton was going to kill Rivers, her own brother.
"It is you that has sent him astray. You will be the reason he loses his life, not I."
Henasee turned to look at the door, knowing the footsteps and now yelling sailors were getting closer. Not able to think of the feelings she would have at Fanton killing Rivers, she nodded. "Ok, I'll go with you."
Fanton squeezed Henasee's arm, bruising it before letting her go. Taking her to the side of the boat, she pointed for Henasee to go first. Henasee climbed down the rope and into the waiting boat. Fanton wasted no time in climbing down behind her. Once in the boat, she handed Henasee an oar, and they head toward Noteese.

Rivers was surprised to find the galley empty. He had recognized Fanton and Henasee's voices and had come running to find out what was going on. Finding the room empty turned his blood cold.

"Henasee!" he screamed as he gets to her cabin. When no answer came, he threw open the door. Taking the steps two at a time, he hurried to find Fanton. Seeing Kentar on the floor, Rivers rushed to the man's side. Judging from how still Kentar was lying, his friend was dead. Reaching for Kentar's arm, Rivers gave a sigh of relief. He and Kentar had been good friends for the year Kentar had been seeing Fanton. Not having many friends Rivers did not want to lose him.
"No, I am not dead, my friend," Kentar whispered into Rivers's face.
"What happened?"
"Fanton, she did this," Kentar said trying to sit up.
"Why?" Rivers asks, looking around.
"She has gone mad," Kentar told him. "Ranting and raving over my destroying our love by giving it to another." Kentar watched as Rivers's face turned from concern to anger. "Not you, too," he yelled hoarsely. "You and your sister are both crazy," he finished trying to sit up.
"I have seen you with her, Kentar. I have heard you talk of love and her beauty."
"What are you talking about? I love Fanton, no other."
"Don't treat me like a fool," Rivers yelled, as he stood up.
"You are the one acting like a fool, Rivers. I have done nothing to you or your sister."
"I heard you on the deck," Rivers yelled, walking away from Kentar.
"Heard me what?" Kentar screamed back finally starting to feel like himself again.
"Henasee," Rivers screamed. "I heard you tell Henasee she was beautiful. I heard you talk of love. You swore your love to my sister and betrayed her."
Kentar stopped trying to move and looked at Rivers. "You heard me talk to Henasee of her beauty but not of a love she and I share, you fool. Henasee was talking about the feelings she has for you."
Rivers stopped pacing and bent down next to Kentar. "I heard you tell her she was beautiful."
"I did, her beauty had only just returned. She herself was not aware of it. She turned, and I was not prepared for such a drastic change in

her. I reached out and touched her cheek and . . . Fanton must have seen me," Kentar finished. "She must have thought I wanted Henasee."

"Where is Fanton?" Kentar asked, worried.

"I can't find her," Rivers answered concerned. "I heard Fanton and Henasee arguing in the galley. By the time I got there, they were gone."

"Fanton believes Henasee and I are lovers." Kentar tried to sit again but was too weak. "You must find Henasee. Fanton is not in her right mind. Henasee is in danger. Leave me. I am too weak to move. Fanton did something to me."

Rivers looked Kentar up and down. "Fanton did this to you?"

"Yes, but it will soon wear off. Hurry, you must find Henasee before Fanton takes her anger out on her." Rivers ran from the room.

Magnus watched as the men from the ship put supplies in smaller boats. "We'll be staying on shore for a week or two," her uncle told her, "depending on how hard it is to find our treasures." Magnus was excited about finally being at Noteese. From where she stood, the water was a deep red. Looking over the side of the ship, she could see fish of all kinds swimming freely. "What a beautiful place," she told her uncle.

"Many would love to be standing in your shoes. We have had an easy time so far, Magnus, but Noteese can be very dangerous even with all its beauty. You must be very careful."

"I'll be careful," Magnus answered her uncle without much thought.

"No, Magnus." Her uncle turns her to face him. "I have heard stories of Noteese. Stories I have never told you. This land is beautiful, but as you now know, beauty is only the surface. Many bad things have happened to people on Noteese. So you must promise you will stay close and keep your eyes open."

Magnus felt from his hold on her arms her uncle was worried for her safety. "I promise, Uncle. I promise I'll be careful."

"Good," her uncle said, releasing her arms and hugging her.

Magnus packed the clothes Ahaira set out for her. Placing the last dress in her bag, Magnus walked over and opened her dresser drawer and took out her boys' clothes and carried them to the bag. "Never know," she laughed and closed the bag.

Rivers stopped in the doorway and saw Kentar had managed to pull himself up on one of the couches. "They're gone, Kentar. Both Fanton and Henasee are gone."
"If she took her with her, she's not going to hurt her, Rivers," Kentar moaned, stretching his left leg.
"How do you know that?"
"If she were going to kill her, you would have found her body. No, your sister wants me to come after Henasee. Fanton has had men use her, and now she thinks I have done the same."
"What will you do?"
"I will find Henasee, and I will turn away from your sister forever."
"You love Fanton," Rivers told Kentar.
"I loved Fanton. I no longer love the person she has become. I've tried for over a year to make her believe I could see the beauty within as I saw you do with Henasee."
Rivers nodded. "Yes, I loved Henasee before her beauty returned. I loved her spirit. She has a fighting attitude I have never met in anyone, and I came to respect her for never giving into pitying herself. With or without her beauty, Henasee is beautiful."
"Yes." Kentar looked at Rivers. "What you have found in Henasee is what I once thought I saw in Fanton."
"But you love her," Rivers interjected.
"No, my feelings have changed. I no longer can find the good in her. I no longer see her beauty within. Fanton has used her beauty to draw me away. I am no longer in love with her."
Rivers stepped in front of Kentar. "So, it is true you are in love with Henasee."
Kentar looked Rivers in the eyes. "I have feelings for her, but she doesn't have her heart set on me. She loves you."
Rivers took in a breath. "She has told you this?"
"Yes, and she tried to tell you."
Rivers put his head down. "She told me she had something to tell me, but I wouldn't listen."
"She thought with her beauty returned, you may care for her as deeply as she cared for you."

Rivers balled his hands. "I didn't even give her a chance to tell me. I yelled at her and walked away."

"She had treated you poorly for months."

"Yes, but I should have tried harder. Henasee has been through a lot. Being taken from her family and living with the scars Fanton had cursed her with. I should have been man enough to see she had been through grave pain. Instead of helping her through, I turned away from her. You're the one who has befriended her, Kentar, not I. I will forever be grateful."

Kentar stood slowly. "We must find her before Fanton goes completely mad." Rivers reached out to help Kentar.

"No, I'll be all right. Get supplies and a boat ready. We must leave for Noteese at once."

Henasee was surprised how easy the boat skimmed through the water with her and Fanton rowing. Months of hard work, cooking, and cleaning the galley had left her the strongest she'd ever been. Looking over at Fanton, Henasee noticed that Fanton looked tired and drained from rowing. With a plan to escape as soon as they landed the boat working in her head, Henasee slowed her pace.

The closer their boat got to shore, the brighter the Island of Noteese appeared. The water around them, Henasee noticed, was a deep red. The sand on the shore was so white the glare off the red water made it look like a light rose color. Trees and plants filled the far side of the sandy beach with so many different colors Henasee could not count them.

"This is amazing," Henasee said out loud.

"Take it all in," Fanton growled, "for this may be your earthly resting place."

Henasee stopped breathing for a second. Fanton really was planning on killing her and burying her here. "I have done nothing to you," she screamed at Fanton. "You have taken my beauty and left me to a life of hardship. I am an ocean away from my friends and family."

Fanton looked over at Henasee and laughed. "You talk of pain. You have taken the very heart from my chest and thrown it into the darkest sea. I will laugh as the last breath of air drains from your body."

"I have done nothing to you. It is you who has."

Fanton didn't wait for Henasee to say another word. The witch reached into her pocket and pulled out a handful of gray powder. Henasee watched Fanton with terror in her eyes. Never once forgetting the green powder at Fanton's shop that had taken her beauty, Henasee said a silent thank you for Uncle Bernard teaching her and Magnus how to swim. She stood and jumped over the side of the boat, diving deep into the water.

Fanton jumped up and screamed into the wake of Henasee's form, "I will hunt you down, and you will pay for the lies and deceit you have caused. There is no place to hide, do you hear me?" Fanton screamed louder, "I am going to kill you."

Rivers could see Henasee and Fanton's boat. Blinking his eyes against the sun, he watched as Henasee stood up and dove into the water.

"Hurry and get those things loaded," Rivers yelled at two men packing supplies on the small rowboat he and Kentar would be taking to Noteese. With the last box placed on the boat Rivers was relieved when Kentar appeared looking more like his old self.

"Is everything ready to go?" he asked Rivers.

"Yes," Rivers replies. "Fanton." Rivers pointed to her boat.

"Where is Henasee?"

"She jumped over the side."

"Let's get going," Kentar ordered. Knowing he was still too weak to be able to row to shore, Kentar ordered two of his men to climb into the boat. Turning before he climbed over the side to get into the boat, Kentar looked at one of the men left on the ship. "You will not listen to anyone but Rivers or me. If Fanton returns to the ship, do not let her come aboard."

The man paled instantly. "What should we do?"

"Kill her if need be," Kentar told him. "If she comes on board, she will have no trouble killing you."

Terrified, the man agreed to kill Fanton if she returned to the ship. He would rather kill Fanton than have Kentar come for him. "Yes, captain, I will kill her."

Rivers looked at the set expression on Kentar's face. "You are really going to have her killed?"

"She is out of control now. You would be best to stay clear of her, Rivers."

"She would not hurt me."

"She is no longer the sister you knew. I looked into her eyes before she poisoned me; there was no longer light in them. The sister you once knew is gone."
"Maybe we can get her back."
"No, she is not coming back. Her heart no longer exists. Even with her beauty coming and going, she can only see the scars. She will destroy everything she touches and never shed a tear."
"How can you talk about her like that?"
"I have seen her change. I have watched the evil grow and grow in her daily. The Fanton I once knew would never have tried to kill me. Yes, she has schemed and plotted to get what she wants. Her reasoning always being for love and happiness but now Fanton looks only to harm."
"Yes, but to kill her, Kentar?"
"She will stop at nothing to take Henasee's life. She will listen to no one. I myself cannot look her in the eyes and tell her I have no feelings for Henasee. She will never understand it was she herself that made my heart stop loving her and not Henasee. Henasee reminded me of what I thought Fanton once was. I once thought her to be young and kind and loving. I no longer see those things in Fanton. Fanton only sees what she wants to believe now, and Henasee is in danger."
Rivers picked up an oar and started rowing with the two other men.
"I hope you're wrong, Kentar."
"I'm not," Kentar stated, and looks across the water. "Fanton must be stopped at all cost."
***
Magnus laughed at her uncle's antics.
"Not there, man, put the cases over there."
Everyone was so excited about getting ashore they were tripping over each other to pack the three small rowing boats to go to Noteese.
"Daniel," her uncle yelled, "come here. You sit here by Magnus."
Magnus looked up from her seat.
"I want you to make sure if there's any trouble you guard her."
Daniel nodded and climbed down by Magnus.
"I've missed you," she smiles at Daniel.
Daniel looked at her and turned away. "I guess you've been busy?"

She continued. Daniel looked out over the water and nodded. "I hope I didn't say anything to offend you."
Daniel never turned his head and shook it no.
"Daniel." Magnus took his arm.
When he turned, Magnus caught her breath. He was handsome. Never had she seen a man who has eyes the color of green meadows like the hills back home. Magnus dropped her hand, afraid he might feel her shake.
Daniel could not take his eyes from hers. She was striking in every way. He missed spending time with her. But he had heard her tell her uncle her beauty was the most important thing to her. How could he compete with her beauty when he himself could not speak. When her beauty was gone, he felt her heart. He had watched daily her beauty come and go. He noticed the men on the ship had noticed, too. Night after night, walking along the deck he would hear the men talking of the beautiful Magnus. He knew he could never compete with the men who would be lining up at her door to offer her love and security. He was wealthy, that was for sure. Magnus didn't even now they were on one of his ships. Before they had been introduced, she had taken it for granted he was a serving boy. He figured because he couldn't talk she could see him only that way. He was going to tell her when he overheard her talking to her uncle about not wanting to live without her beauty.
"Daniel, please talk to me."
Daniel reached up and touched her cheek so fast Magnus wondered if she imagined it. Then he turned his head back to the water. Magnus, knowing Daniel was done, turned and watched the men finish packing the boat.

Chapter 8
Kingston

Henasee shook from head to toe as she stepped on Noteese soil. She stopped shaking when the warm sand under her feet started to warm her up. Knowing she must find a place to hide before Fanton got ashore, Henasee ran down the beach and up into a beautiful multicolored woods. Looking from tree to tree, Henasee couldn't believe the beauty of the place. Flowers laced every wall of the woods.

"It is lovely, isn't it?" came a voice from behind her.

Poised to run, Henasee looked behind her.

"I will not hurt you. The voice came again. I saw you jump from your boat. I thought you might need assistance. Many have come to Noteese but they have not swam."

Henasee felt herself staring but could not turn away. The man before her was more than breathtaking with his long, shiny black hair and dark eyes. Henasee could tell he was a wealthy man by the cut of his clothes. He was dressed in a dark navy blue overcoat, with matching pants and a white silk shirt. For the first time in months, Henasee looked at her hand and was thankful her beauty was intact. Relaxing her stance, Henasee looked the man in the eyes.

"My name is Kingston, Kingston Thighmas the third at your service." Henasee laughed as Kingston bowed deeply. "My ship and crew are on the other side of the island. I was scouting around when I happened to see two lovely ladies in a boat. I was waiting to help you ashore when to my horror you jumped overboard. I am most grateful you were not harmed, miss."

Henasee laughed at his exaggerated expressions. "I'm Henasee," she offered. "I was aboard the Mailler. It's a few miles out."

"Yes, I spotted it this morning. Are there more of you?"

"Yes, Fanton brought me here against my will."

"I see I was right. You are in danger."

"Yes," Henasee smiled again, forgetting herself in his eyes. "Yes, I am."

"Then I must save you." He smiled back at her, offering her his

hand. Henasee never blinked and offered her hand back. "I think we should find safety back at my ship." Henasee agreed as he kissed her hand and led her through the woods to the other side of the island.
"Over there," Kingston points "are my mother and two sisters." Henasee liked what she saw. It reminds her of her family.
Kingston's mother, a older lady with brown hair and a shade of gray around her face, was busy reading to her daughters. The girls, Henasee noticed, appeared to be in their early teens.
"No! Mother!" one of the girls yelled and stood up and ran down the beach.
Kingston laughed. "That would be Drella. She doesn't think much of book learning. She wants to be an artist of sorts and thinks reading and writing are a waste of her time."
"Drella," Kingston's mother yelled, "you come back here this instant."
Kingston laughed as Drella picked up speed, never looking back.
"She sure can run," Henasee laughed with him feeling safe with so many people around.
Kingston's mother's face turned beet red when she turned to see Kingston with a beautiful young girl laughing at Drella's parting figure.
"Oh, my goodness," his mother screeched, clutching her chest.
"That girl will be the death of me, I swear," Kingston's mother said as he approached with Henasee. "Kingston," his mother sniffed,. "you really do find the worst times to bring guests home."
Kingston laughed out loud. "Look around, Mother, we are on an island. I didn't just bring her home from a ball."
Kingston's mother's neck turned as red as her face. "You make a good point, darling," she said, looking Henasee over. "Where on earth did you find her?"
"This is Henasee, Mother. Henasee this is my mother, Lady Thighmas," he smiled bowing at his mother.
"Stop that, Kingston," his mother turned her attention back to Henasee.
Henasee placed her hands over her wet dress, embarrassed by the wet, see-through material and wondered how much Kingston had noticed. Henasee lowered her eyes and curtsied.
"She came out of the ocean, Mother." Kingston smiled at Henasee's

misfortune. "I merely offered her shelter."
"She needs a dry set of clothes and maybe a bite to eat," his mother replied.
"Two things I intended to take care of, Mother."
"You cannot dress the girl, Kingston," his mother snapped.
Kingston laughed at Henasee's pink cheeks. "You are very right, Mother. So if you would be so kind as to help, I would most appreciate you finding Henasee some dry clothing." Henasee was most grateful.
Kingston pointed but does not look at her wet clothing. "Henasee, you can go with my mother and sister. They will find you dry clothing."
Henasee wanted to reach out and smack the snicker off his face but instead smiled and nodded.
"I will see you in a while then." Kingston bowed and sneaked a peek, she noticed, and then walked away.
"Where are my manners?" Kingston's mother said, shooing Henasee toward a tent.

***

"Magnus, you stay close to Daniel, were her uncle's first words as their boats came ashore." Daniel, ever the gentleman, lifted her out of the boat and carried her to shore.
"Captain," one of the men shouted at Daniel. "Do you want us to stay together or split up?" Magnus watched as Daniel split his arms in the air and pointed.
"Captain?" she rolled over in her head. "No wonder he didn't want anything to do with me. He has his own ship and crew. I must have looked like a stupid little girl. Telling him of my feelings. He and his men must have got a good laugh from that." Turning away so he couldn't see the tears in her eyes, Magnus felt her heart had just exploded into a million pieces. "I will not be ruled by my heart again, "she promised herself.
She turned in time to see Daniel shake his head at Bernard, and grabbing her hand, they started down the sandy beach. It isn't hard to follow the two set of footprints in the sand. Daniel turned his head to see Bernard and Ahaira lead his men down another trail of footprints. He knew Bernard would protect his Aunt Ahaira with his life. Turning back, Daniel looked over at Magnus, who has stayed

quiet since they came ashore.

"I'm all right," she smiled sadly. "I've waited a long time to come to Noteese."

Daniel nodded, and they continue down the beach. Magnus could feel her beauty starts to return. Her arms, instead of sagging, became tight and felt tingly as she stretched them at her sides. Daniel looked over in amazement at her transformation. With her beauty back, Magnus felt healthier, and it was easy for her to keep up with Daniel and his men. Daniel stopped and with one hand pushed his men to continue forward.

With a look of concern in his eyes, Daniel reached for a piece of Magnus's hair and let it fall between his fingers. Magnus looked deep into his eyes, and the tears start to flow down her cheeks. He wanted to tell her he never knew the scars and her transformations could be painful. He had just watched as her face mirrored pain and then relief as her scars went away. Throwing his hand away, she turned and ran down the sandy beach. It didn't take Daniel even a minute to catch her.

Falling with her to the beach, he engulfed her in his arms. With his body wrapped around hers, he rolled her on her back and kissed her deeply. Magnus couldn't think for the feelings rushing through her body. Heat, electricity, and excitement exploded inside her. Kissing her with more force, Daniel became oblivious to his surroundings. He had missed her, and she was here with him now. Magnus leaned into Daniel like a drowning fish, gasping and pawing until she felt him pull away. Rolling off her, Daniel looked out into the water.

"No, please, Daniel, don't do this again. What have I done?"

Daniel was all ready standing and walking up the beach when Magnus recovered enough to stand. Looking down at her arm, she gasped. Her beauty had returned. She knows now why Daniel wanted her. Lowering her head with tears on her cheeks, she followed slowly behind him.

Daniel mentally shook himself. What had come over him? He was no mere child. Was his intension to take Magnus there on the beach? He had almost succumbed to her willingness and his longings. When he had looked over and saw her beauty returning, he had also noticed the pain she must go through when her beauty was not with her. He had noticed she was able to walk and breathe better. Never before had he thought about how she must feel to be beautiful one moment, and the next have her beauty and health gone. His emotions had gone out to her, and everything he had been thinking about her had exploded. But no, he would not take for granted her innocence. He would stay clear of any feelings he had for Magnus. She deserved better than him. She deserved a man who could talk to her, whisper words of love in her ear. No, he was not good enough for Magnus, and they both knew it.

"Welcome," Kingston smiled at Daniel, holding out his hand. "You said you'd be here." Daniel smiled and shook Kingston's hand. "You have already found a treasure, I see," Kingston smiled at Magnus.
Magnus noticed that Daniel did not look pleased with Kingston's flirtatious behavior. Daniel nodded and reached for Magnus's hand. Magnus stepped back and looked Kingston over with one sweep.
"I am Magnus," she smiles, holding out her hand like a proper young lady.
Kingston smiled at Magnus and brought her hand to his lips. "I am Kingston," he told her, bowing slightly. "May I offer you some refreshments?"
"I would love something to drink," Magnus flirted back. Looking over at Daniel, she was pleased to see him scowl. "Use me for my beauty and then throw me away. I will teach you a lesson in manners" she laughed in her head. "You will be sorry for your games, Daniel."
Daniel watched as his best friend Kingston walked Magnus to his camp. Walking out of the tent with Kingston's sister and mother behind her, Henasee stopped at the sight of a beautiful Magnus coming her way. Letting go of Kingston, Magnus ran to Henasee. Reaching out to hug her, Magnus stopped.
"I see you are fine and well," Henasee said rather sternly.
"Henasee, are you all right?" Magnus cried "I was so worried about you."
"You seem to be doing just fine," Henasee said dryly, looking from Magnus to Kingston.
"We have just arrived. We followed the tracks from the beach. I've only met Kingston." Magnus pointed for Kingston to agree.

"Yes," Kingston smiled from one to the other. "I just rescued her from an evil villain on the beach."

Henasee tried not to show her panic for Magnus, but it showed on her face.

Magnus shook her head, laughing. "He did not rescue me. I was looking for you with Daniel and his crew of men."

"Daniel?"

"Yes," Magnus nodded. "Daniel is the captain of the ship my uncle brought to find us. Listen, Henasee," Magnus approached her. "I'm sorry I've gotten you into this mess. I would never have hurt you for anything in the world. Not even a trip to Noteese for all the riches in the world."

Henasee started to look away but stopped when Magnus touched her arm. Henasee looked down to see traces of scars appearing on Magnus's arm. "You did lose your beauty? She points at Magnus's arm."

Magnus rubbed one of the scars. "I tried to tell you, Hen, but you wouldn't listen."

"I know. I was so mad at what I had been through I didn't want to believe you. I'm sorry, Magnus."

No, Henasee, it is I who am sorry. I never meant to pull you into my dream. I mean my nightmare," Magnus cried back.

Daniel shook his head as he walked into Kingston's camp. He would laugh if his heart wasn't breaking. Still, he was glad to see Magnus and her friend Henasee hugging and clinging to each other in the middle of the camp.

"I am so sorry."

"No, it is I who needs to apologize. You didn't make me go in there. I was worried about you so I came looking for you. I should have listened to my mother," Daniel heard Magnus cry out.

"No, you were right, Magnus. We would have been miserable if our parents had found us husbands."

Daniel felt as if someone had punched him in the stomach. Magnus married to another man was more then he could handle in his mind. Looking around, Daniel walked out of the camp. Kingston noticed the change in his friend and hurried to catch up with him.

"Wait a minute, my good man. You don't plan on leaving those two with me and escaping, do you?"

Daniel smiled at his friend and nodded.

"No, no, no, my friend. As beautiful as they are, I, too, am here to make a fortune, and I don't have time to watch over them. You know, we only have a few more weeks to return home or we will not make it back. Look, my friend." Kingston pointed at the sky. "The weather is already starting to change." Daniel nodded. "Then you will look after the women?" Kingston tilted his head at Daniel.

"No," Daniel shook his head.

"What do you mean no? They are not my responsibility."

Daniel laughed again and kept walking. "I will be back," he motioned to his friend, "tonight," he waved for the sun to come down.

Kingston relaxed a little and waved good-bye to Daniel. "I will see you tonight, my friend."

Magnus also watched as Daniel left the camp.

"So," Henasee interrupted Magnus's thoughts. "There seems to be something you're not telling me." She smiled, tilting her head at Daniel's retreating form.

"There's not much to say," Magnus sighed. "I'm in love with a man who loves only my beauty."

"No, Magnus, I saw how he was watching you. He seems to really care."

Magnus shook her head sadly. "No, I'm afraid he doesn't see the real me. He only sees what others see. And when my scars return, his love goes away."

Henasee understood what her friend felt. Rivers treated her the same way. "At least we're together," Henasee laughed, grabbing Magnus and hugging her again.

"We're together, and we're at Noteese," Magnus laughed with Henasee and looked around. "There is a fortune for the taking."

"Don't you two get any ideas! Kingston called from the edge of the camp. "Noteese may be beautiful, but it is still very dangerous."

Henasee and Magnus looked at each other and laughed. A couple of months ago, they might have been scared, but after what they had just lived through, not a lot intimidated them.

***

Rivers was the first to step out of the rowboat and head to shore.

"Wait," Kentar yelled after him. "We must stay together. Fanton is dangerous and for us to face her apart will only cause one of our deaths."

"You're wrong, Kentar," Rivers yelled back, still heading to shore. "Fanton would never harm me."

"I have seen her anger, Rivers. She is not the sister you knew."

Rivers stopped and waited for Kentar to catch up. "I will not let you kill her, Kentar."

"I wish there was another way. But you will see how she's changed when we find her," Kentar told him. "I only hope we're not too late to find Henasee before Fanton hurts her."

***

Fanton stood inside the woods beside a tree, watching Henasee hug her friend. Fanton's face held only loathing for the two girls. She recognized Magnus's friend from her shop and Ahaira's ship. She was also the tramp who has seduced Kentar away from her. "I will kill you," she said out loud. "I will kill you and your friend for what you have taken from me." Spitting on the ground, she disappeared back into the cave she had found only minutes before.

***

Rivers and Kentar followed footprints down the shore. Both were lost in their own thoughts. Looking for signs of Henasee, they were cautious when they followed the footprints to a campsite where a low light glowed.

"There," Kentar pointed to Henasee sitting by a fire laughing with Magnus.

"She's all right," Rivers whispered. Rivers pointed past the fire. "Look, Kentar, it's Kingston."

Kentar looked at Kingston. Daniel and Ahaira must be close.

"I don't see them," Rivers whispered again.

"Let's wait and see who happens along," Kentar whispered back. "Maybe we'll get lucky, and for now Henasee is safe."

Rivers sat down by a tree and leaned back. Kentar did the same, and they both watched the campsite quietly. "Look," Rivers pointed. "There's Ahaira." Kentar watches as Ahaira walked into the camp with an older man whom Magnus and Henasee ran to.

"I found her," Kentar and Rivers could hear Magnus scream from the camp. "Look, Uncle Bernard, I found Henasee."

"So you did, my dear." The older gentleman laughed, hugging both

girls. "So you did. How are you Henasee?" Bernard hugged them both again. "I know your parents are going to be very happy when you return home." Henasee stepped out of Bernard's arms.
"I'm afraid I will be grounded for the rest of my life."
"I think your parents will be grateful to have you safe at home," Bernard comforted her. "Your father stopped talking about marrying you off to the first young man that would take you before I left."
Henasee laughed and started to cry. "I didn't mean to hurt them. I was only trying to find Magnus."
"You are a very fine friend," Uncle Bernard told Henasee as he hugged Magnus again. "Magnus has told me how you came to find her and how your beauty was taken from you. You both have been through so much. I think your parents will go lightly when you return."
"Thank you," Henasee told Bernard and returned to his empty arm.
"This is no way to celebrate a happy reunion," Ahaira laughed. Henasee looked frightened as she looks over at Ahaira. "She's a witch, isn't she?"
"Yes, she is," Magnus smiles at her uncle. "But she has shown me nothing but kindness."
"If not for her, I would never have found you two," Bernard said, squeezing them to his sides. "I agree, Ahaira. This is a time for happiness and not sorrow. We will celebrate tonight, and tomorrow we will all be rich beyond our dreams."
Everyone in the camp hooted and hollered. Even Kingston's mother let out a little squeal.
"I will let you ladies freshen up, and I will return shortly." Bernard bowed to all and walked to Kingston's personal tent and disappeared inside.
The two men who had traveled with Magnus and Daniel started to collect wood for a fire. Other men from Kingston's camp started to gather food and place dishes on a long table.
"Come, ladies," Kingston's mother pointed. "We must dress for a party." Kingston's mother was excited, and her face was a bit flushed. Looking over, she smiled shyly at Henasee. "We have been here for months. I was starting to go stir crazy. A party is just what I need."

Henasee smiled back. "Do you travel with your son often?"
"No, this is my first trip. I was afraid if I didn't come Drella would somehow sneak on board."
Henasee and Magnus looked at each other, embarrassed.
"Yes, I can understand what your mothers must be going through. But they need not worry another night. You are in my charge now, and I will let no harm come to either one of you."
Magnus wasn't sure if she was happy or not with Kingston's mother's speech. She had been taking care of herself for months and was doing just fine. Looking over at Henasee, Magnus could see the same look on her friend's face. For now, Magnus would go along with her mothering, but tomorrow was going to be another thing all together. She had dreamed of Noteese, and no one, not even Kingston's mother, was going to hold her back now.

***

Daniel never saw what hit him. He just knew his head hurt when he tried to open his eyes. The light from the fire he was lying by is making his head hurt even more.
"So," Fanton laughed, "you are going to wake up. I thought I might have hit you too hard. You've been out for a long time."
Daniel opened his eyes and shut them again because of the pain running down his face. Looking beside him with one eye opened, he could see a large spot of blood. Trying to shake off the nausea, he looked past the fire and into Fanton's eyes.
"It was dark Daniel and I had no idea it was you or I wouldn't have hit you so hard."
Daniel glared at Fanton.
"You don't believe me? I am telling the truth. Daniel, I would never harm you."
Daniel turned his head, looking around the cave for a chance to escape.
"Please, Daniel. I know you are still angry, but I never meant to harm you." Daniel turned and looked at her again. "I know it must be hard to believe. When you left with Ahaira, I could not have you still called her our mother. I am your sister, and she had turned you away from me." Daniel shook his head no. "She did," Fanton screamed at him. "She made you believe lies against me. I didn't mean to cast the spell that took your voice, I was so angry with your

words. You told me I was no longer your sister, and I would never again be. I was so hurt." Daniel continued to stare at Fanton, hardly blinking." I tried to find you, Daniel, but you and Ahaira had disappeared like thieves in the night. I never meant for you to stay without your voice. You must believe me. I did not kill your father as Ahaira would have you believe."

Daniel watched as Fanton pulled a pouch from her hip pocket and approached him. He tried to back away sure she planned to kill him now. Fanton stopped and sat beside him, rubbing his cheek. "I am not going to hurt you, my brother. I was young and full of anger when you and I fought. I am no longer that foolish young girl. I no longer feel anger for your harsh words. I wish only to return what I have taken from you."

Fanton blew in her hand, and red powder covered Daniel's face. Coughing, he was surprised when sound came from his throat. "Yes, Daniel," Fanton cooed, "I have given you back what I stole from you." Before he could speak, Fanton turned and rushed from the cave. Sitting in her spot, Daniel saw she had left a knife. Turning on his back and working his hands together, he was able to cut the ropes from his wrist and ankles. Sitting by the fire, he spoke for the first time in almost a year. "Hello," his voice echoed in the cave. "Hello, hello, hello," he yelled again and again. Fanton stood outside the cave, tears running down her face and hands. "Yes, you are whole again. Maybe now you can forgive me." Fanton wiped her face and disappeared into the woods. Tomorrow she was going to kill Kentar and the two girls who had ruined her life. She would see them all pay, but for now she smiled at Daniel repeating hello from a distance in the cave.

***

"I don't know what happened to Drella," Kingston's mother yelled over the guitar music one of the sailors was playing. "She should have been back hours ago."

"You know how she gets, Mother," Kingston answered. "She's not going to come back until she's good and ready." Kingston's mother shook her head and looked out across the beach. Magnus wished Daniel was here with them and watched the shadows for him to appear. Watching as a shadow came down the beach, Magnus's heart started to race. But it was only the young girl they called Drella. As Drella got closer, Magnus could see she had made a mistake about the girl's age. Drella was the same age as Magnus and was small for her age. But as she got closer, there was no mistaking her age. She was very curvy, and with her blonde hair and deep blue eyes, she was very beautiful. Magnus knew why Drella was spoiled. Magnus was sure no one said no to anything this girl wanted. She was one of the most beautiful people Magnus had ever seen. Even with her shirt and skirt dirty from the sand, Drella was breathtaking. The sailor playing the guitar stopped and held his breath as Drella walked into the campfire light.

"There you are," Kingston scolded her. "Mother has been worried sick."

Drella looked from Kingston and then to her mother without a care on her face. "I took a walk and lost track of time," she told Kingston with a flip of her head.

Looking down at her hands, Magnus noticed her scars were returning, and reaching up to her face, she looked away from the fire.

Henasee reached for her arm. "Don't, Mag, we'll find Fanton, and you'll be your old self again."

"I don't know if I want to be my old self again," Magnus said, looking at Drella.

"She is something, isn't she?" Henasee whispered.

Drella looked from Henasee and then to Magnus. Her eyes stayed on Magnus's face as she watched scar after scar appear. "What have you got?" she asked, stepping backwards. Magnus felt her face. Kingston and his mother try hard not to stare, but the transformation was so different from the beautiful girl they had known all day.

"This," Kingston said, watching Magnus's reaction to them staring, "must be Fanton's work."

"Yes," Henasee spoke up first. "Fanton stole both of our beauty. I was lucky to get mine back, but Magnus's beauty still comes and goes with Fanton's."

Magnus sat down on a log and looked at her hands.

"How bad does it get?" Drella asked, still staring at Magnus.

Henasee gave Drella a dirty look, but Drella just shrugged her shoulders. "I'm not the only one who's going to ask her questions. When we return home, everyone will want to know why she turns ug. . ." Kingston stopped Drella before she could finish the word. "Enough from you, do you understand, Drella? Now go and get cleaned up." Drella did as Kingston told her and walked to her mother's tent and disappeared inside. Henasee sat down by Magnus. "She's right, Hen," Magnus cried. "People are going to say horrible things about me."

"Not everyone will say things, Magnus. Drella is a spoiled brat. She didn't care if she hurt your feelings or not. Besides, we're going to find Fanton and change you back."

"I hope so," Magnus sighed. "I thought I didn't care what people thought of me. But to tell the truth, I want my old self back again."

"It will happen, Magnus, I promise," Henasee said, smiling at her friend.

Magnus watched as Daniel walked up the beach and for the first time she was embarrassed about her appearance. Daniel is laughing and smiling from ear to ear. Waiting with everyone else to see why he was so happy, Magnus held her head down. Just as Daniel reached the campfire, Drella ran from the tent and into his arms. Magnus held herself, still not wanting to make a scene and cry out. Henasee reached over and took her hand in hers. Daniel picked up Drella and spun her around and around in the air. Drella laughed and reached out to hug him. Daniel pulled her close, and Drella surprised him with a passionate kiss on the mouth. Surprised, Daniel pushed her out of his arms.

Not being able to stand another second of Drella in Daniel's arms, Magnus stood up and ran down the beach. Pushing Drella off him one more time, Daniel ran after Magnus. He almost passed where she was sitting behind a pile of logs and rocks, when he heard her crying softly. Turning around, he walked back to a pile of rocks and looked over the top of them.

"Go away," Magnus cried out. "I don't want you to see me like this. I understand you can only care for me when I have my beauty," she sniffed. "Go back to Drella, she is most beautiful. I may never have my beauty for more than a few hours. I can't live like that, Daniel. You would want me one minute and not the next. Don't you know that breaks my heart every time you turn away from me?"

Chapter 9
Beauty or Scars

Daniel pulled her hands from her face." I want you all the time, Magnus with or without your scars. You are beautiful inside and out."

Magnus started to object when she caught her words. "Your voice? You have your voice."

"Fanton," he said. "She gave it back to me."

"What do you mean, back to you?"

"It's a long story. I would rather talk about you and me."

"You and me?" she asked him.

"I never cared whether you had your beauty or scars. I didn't think you would want to be with me because I was not a whole man."

"Daniel, you are more man than anyone I have ever met."

"My voice, Magnus, I felt not whole without my voice. I knew other men would fight for your attention, and I had no way to hold it being only part of a man."

"We have been very foolish, Daniel. Me for my thinking you only wanted me beauty and you for thinking a lack of a voice would make me not want you. I love you, Daniel, with or without your voice."

"I love you with or without your beauty, Magnus." Daniel opened his arms and Magnus came willingly into them. Their kiss started as a seal of their love and ended breathless.

"We had better go back now. Kingston's mother will think I've abducted you." Magnus stood to leave, and Daniel pulled her back into is arms. "Marry me, Magnus. Marry me tonight, this minute, so you will never doubt my love for you."

"What about Fanton?" Magnus delayed her excitement.

"She will not hurt us tonight. She would not have returned my voice if she were going to hurt me. Tonight is our night, Magnus."

Magnus reached her arms around his neck and pulled his head down to her lips. Kissing him until he pulled away, she smiled and said, "Yes, Daniel, I'll marry you today, tonight with or without my beauty. I am totally in love with you."

Daniel swept her up in his arms and twirled her around.
***

Everyone in camp was smiling when they return. "What are all the smiles about?" Magnus laughed.

"The breeze carried your voices," Henasee said, jumping up and hugging Magnus as Daniel set her on her feet. Kingston was right beside her giving hugs and shaking his friend's hand. "You are a very lucky man, my friend."

Daniel smiled and says, "Thank you, Kingston."

Kingston stared as if he'd seen a ghost. "I heard you talking, but to see it come out of your mouth is unreal. Fanton?"

"Yes," Daniel told him. "Fanton gave me back my voice."

Kingston reached out, hugged him, and laughed. "This will be the best wedding ever. Mother, help the bride get ready."

Kingston's mother jumped up laughing. "I will make her the prettiest bride ever."

Daniel turns to Magnus. "She already is." Magnus smiled and lets Kingston's mother lead her off to change. Magnus passed Drella, who seemed happy flirting with the guitar player.

Inside the tent, Kingston's mother went through trunk after trunk, looking for the right dress for Magnus to wear. "This is so exciting," she giggled, opening another trunk. With Kingston's mother's excitement, Henasee and Magnus soon joined in. All were laughing and talking all at once like little girls. "Mother?" Megan asked and pulled out a white silk gown. "How about this one?"

"That's perfect, darling," Kingston's mother cooed and reached for the gown.

"It's beautiful," Magnus told Kingston's mother. "Thank you so much."

" I love a good wedding," his mother sniffed. "Now let's get you into your wedding dress."

"Here," Megan handed Henasee a dark blue gown. "This should look great on you." Henasee smiled and took the gown. Magnus stepped behind a curtain and undressed and slipped the white gown over her head. As she stepped out, the three women stared at her as if she were a ghost.

"What's wrong?" Magnus cried out. "Is it that bad on me?"

"No, Magnus," Henasee approached her. "It's your beauty, Magnus,

it has returned." Megan walked to a table and brought back a hand mirror. With shaking hands, Magnus took the mirror and looked into it. When her beauty stared back at her, she started to cry.
"You will make a beautiful bride, my dear," Kingston's mother smiled, and Henasee and Megan nodded.
A wedding song echoed in the breeze as Magnus stepped out of the tent. With a look of surprise, she smiled into her uncle's eyes. "You didn't think you'd be getting married without me as an escort, did you?"
"Oh, Uncle Bernard," Magnus cried, hugging him. "I would be honored for you to escort me down the aisle. It is almost like father being here."
Bernard grunted "I'm not sure if your father would be walking you down the aisle or spanking your behind."
Magnus looked up with tears in her eyes. "Do you think they'll love him like I do?"
"I think in time they will see Daniel is a fine young man. He is a very wealthy lad. I'm sure your father will have no qualms about his family or their inheritance."
Magnus wanted to ask her uncle what he meant by wealthy, but the music had gotten louder, and Henasee was already walking down the aisle. "I think they're ready for us, Magnus." Magnus looked at her uncle and smiles.
Daniel has never before seen such a lovely sight as Magnus walking down the aisle. He knew at that moment he would give up his voice, his eyesight, and even his life to be with this woman, who would soon be his wife.
Bernard kissed Magnus on the cheek and gave her hand to Daniel. Magnus smiled with a glow of love surrounding , and Daniel smiled back returning her love with his eyes.
"Do you take this man," Kingston asked Magnus, "to be your husband?"
"I take him to be my husband," Magnus replied.
"Do you, Daniel, Kingston asked, "take Magnus—"
Daniel interrupted Kingston. "Yes, I take Magnus to be my wife."
"Then all I have to say," Kingston laughed, throwing his hands in the air, "is you are now husband and wife. You may . . ." Kingston laughed with everyone else as Daniel picked Magnus up and with

his mouth on hers swung her around and around. "Let's celebrate," Kingston yelled into the faces of his friends.

Magnus and Daniel danced through the night. Henasee danced with Kingston so much her legs hurt. Laughing and swaying to the music, Daniel whispered into Magnus's ear, "I will love you always, Magnus."

With tears on her cheeks, she returned his very words. "I will love you always, Daniel."

Nervous and excited, Magnus held Daniel's hand and followed him to a small tent on the edge of the camp.

"How did this happen? Daniel kissed Magnus on the lips. "Kingston is a very good friend."

Opening the flap and walking in, Magnus had to agree. An assortment of pillows lined the walls. In a corner, candles stood tall and glowing in small glass containers. Magnus smiled at Daniel as he pointed to a bed made of soft-looking blankets. "Has Kingston done this kind of thing for you before?"

Daniel pulled Magnus into his arms. "Never for my wife," he laughed kissing her deeply.

"Your wife?" Magnus laughed, pulling out of his arms. Daniel reached over and swept her off her feet.

"This," he swung her around, "is Kingston's world. But for tonight I accept his gracious offer. You are who I think of every morning, Magnus, and who I want to be with every night."

Daniel kissed her again, and this time the sparks between them ignited into flames of passion. Standing her on her feet, Daniel slowly unbuttoned the front of her dress. Magnus was nervous but tried her hardest not to let it show. Looking into her eyes, Daniel saw the fear. "No," he smiled, kissing her cheek. "I would never forgive myself if you felt fear from me, Magnus." Taking his hand off her dress, he touched her cheek, so softly Magnus could hardly feel it. With his left hand, he reached behind her dress and pulled her closer to him. "I won't pretend I haven't been with other women, Magnus. But God's honest truth. I have never wanted someone as much as I want you. I have thought of this moment for months. I . . ."

Magnus placed her finger on his lips. "I'm not afraid any more, Daniel. Not of you. I, too, have dreamed of lying in your arms. I, too..."

Daniel placed his lips on hers and slowly lowered her to the blankets. Kissing him felt so right and when they finally joined together, Magnus felt as if she had been waiting for him all her life. Lying in his arms was where she was meant to be.

"No worries," he whispered into her hair.

"Not a care in the world," she whispered back. Turning on his side to face her, Daniel traced the outline of her jaw. Magnus started to reach for his hand when in the candlelight she noticed the scars on her hand.

As she tried to move her head to the side, Daniel stopped her. "No, Magnus, you cannot hide every time your beauty goes away. If my voice was gone tomorrow, would you seek another to be your husband?"

"No, of course, I wouldn't."

"Then why do think so little of me? I love you, Magnus, with or without your beauty. You must trust in our love."

Magnus stopped trying to turn away and smiled up at Daniel. Once again, they made long, sweet love; this time healing the emotional pain the scars have given Magnus. When they were both satisfied and exhausted, they wrapped into each other's arms and fell asleep.

***

Rivers and Kentar sat on the edge of the woods, steaming in silence.

"If he touches her one more time, I'm going to shoot him," Rivers whispered to Kentar.

"No, my friend, I will slice open his neck with my knife."

"Not before I've shot him," Rivers whispered again. "She doesn't have to look like she's enjoying it so much. She's asking him to kiss her with every ounce of her body. Kingston is a user of women and a real cad." Rivers continued glaring at him.

"Be quiet, Rivers. She is well chaperoned. There are guards everywhere and Kingston's mother isn't going to let her wander off." As soon as the words were out of his mouth, Kentar regretted them as, hand in hand, Kingston and Henasee walked slowly down the beach away from the camp. "Where are you going?" Kentar asked as Rivers headed into the woods.

"I'm going to save Henasee's honor. Even if she doesn't want it saved," he said, disappearing into the woods. Kentar looked past

Rivers and spotted a small shadow run across the ground. Standing on his feet, he rushed after Fanton.

Kingston slowed his pace and pointed at the blue-colored moon.

"This place is amazing," Henasee told him, looking around. "Magnus used to tell me about Noteese, but I never dreamed it would be like this. Flowers the colors of gold and moons the colors of . . ." her voice ran off as Kingston turned her into his arms.

"Moons the color of your eyes," he said, lowering his lips to hers. Henasee was surprised and yet intrigued. Kingston was a very good kisser, and she was drawn to his handsome looks. Kissing him back, she was surprised when he pulled away.

"Have I done something wrong?"

"No," he said turning to face the water. "There are two kinds of women, Henasee. The ones I see," he choked out, "and the ones that are like you."

"Like me?" she asked with a little laugh.

"The kind of girl you marry."

Henasee laughed out loud. "It was only a kiss, Kingston. Surly you have kissed a girl and left her with her, let's say virtue intact."

Kingston smiled her way and turned back to the water. "My kisses have always brought them to their knees," he said, turning to face her. "There was no thought of tomorrow. Just fun and then on to . . ."

"On to your next adventure?" Henasee choked on another laugh. Henasee bent down and held her side, and Kingston ran to her.

"Are you all right, Henasee? Should I get help?" He was surprised and angered when he heard her gasping on a choked laugh. Kingston threw his hands in the air. "I was trying to be kind," he told her. Laughing out loud, now Henasee could catch her breath. Angry beyond words, Kingston turned and grumbled down the beach back to the campsite.

Watching in anger at Kingston's retreating form for leaving her out her alone, Rivers growled under his breath. Henasee watched and laughed as Kingston tripped over a log and had to stand back up.

"Don't worry about me," he yelled into the dark. "I'm fine."

Calming herself down, Henasee started to follow Kingston's footprints in the sand. Rivers waited for the right moment and when Henasee was in front of him, he jumped out and placed his hand around her mouth.

Holding her with the other hand, he said, "Don't scream, Henasee. It's me, Rivers."

Henasee turned around relieved that Rivers was all right and with her. With the words on her lips she started to tell him how happy she was to see him until she saw the same anger in his eyes as the day he told her to go away. "Let me go," she pulled away from him. "What do you want, Rivers? I am in no harm here."

"Fanton is still on the island."

"Then you should be looking for her and not sneaking around spying on me."

"Maybe someone should be watching you. You didn't have a problem throwing yourself in Kingston's arms, I noticed."

Henasee reached out and smacked Rivers across the face.

Reaching for her arm, he pulled her roughly to him. "You are trying my nerves, Henasee," he said as he pulled her face to his and kissed her deeply.

Henasee didn't know how long he kissed her, but she did know the minute he let her go. Almost losing her footing, she had to grab his arm for balance.

"I'll be back for you, Henasee. You stay close to Magnus and her uncle. They'll keep you safe. And, he says, turning back to face her, don't let Kingston put his lips on you again."

Henasee pulled herself together. "You can't tell me what to do, Rivers. I will decide who puts their lips on me." Watching him walk off, she reached her hand up to touch where he had just kissed her, and smiled into the night air. "I will decide, Rivers. I will decide."

***

Ahaira cuddled next to Bernard. "You are not afraid of what your brother will say about their wedding? "

"My brother's thoughts are made of making money and then making more money. He will love Daniel's bank account."

Ahaira laughed with Bernard. "More money than he has ever seen, I'm sure." She laughed again.

"He wanted Magnus to marry a rich man. Now he has it, my love," Bernard laughed, pulling her closer.

***

"What a beautiful morning," Kingston's mother said sitting at a wooden table.

Ahaira agreed. "I wish we had these beautiful things at home."
Kingston said, "In less than two weeks, we must be on our way."
Ahaira nodded. "Bernard knows, too. It is almost time to leave."
Kingston's mother leaned forward. "Has anyone seen any signs of Fanton?"

"No," Ahaira whispered back. "Bernard has his men searching, but nothing yet."

"She will show herself that's for sure," Kingston's mother said, patting her chest. "She is a bad one, that daughter of yours."

"I agree. Fanton has gotten meaner with age. Why she gave Daniel back his voice, I will never understand. I'm just thankful she did. He has had a hard life that one." Ahaira pointed at the small tent. "She seems like a nice girl."

Kingston's mother smiled. "I am very happy for Daniel. Magnus will make him a good wife. Talking about wives, has Bernard asked you yet?"

"No, but I think he will. He hasn't figured out he's in love with me yet. But as soon as he does. . ."

"It does take men longer to figure those things out" Kingston's mother laughed.

"Takes men longer to figure out what, ladies?" Ahaira turn to see Bernard walking up behind her chair.

"Nothing of importance, darling, just girl talk."

      He laughed and took a seat next to Ahaira.

"Oh," she laughed, "you have found us out. We were trying to figure out where you will start first. Will you collect gold or silver, my darling?"

"I'd feel a lot better if I knew where Fanton was. Until we find her everyone on the island is in danger. Kingston says we must collect our riches and leave or we may be trapped here for the winter."

"Yes, I am aware of the weather. I'm going to leave a couple men here to stand guard. You make sure the girls stay close to camp."

"Yes," Kingston's mother answered quickly. "We will not let them out of our sight."
***

Daniel kissed Magnus one last time before leaving the tent.
"Remember," he turned and smiled, "don't you or Henasee leave the camp. With Fanton out there, you are in danger."

"I promise," Magnus yawned. "We will stay close together until you return." Magnus sat up, holding the blanket to her chest. "And when you return," she smiled, dropping the blanket to show her perfect skin, "I will be right here waiting for you."
Daniel almost went back to her. Magnus smiled at the wanting in his eyes. "I will work as fast as one man can," he choked and left the tent.

"I don't see us having any trouble with Rivers," Kingston told Daniel and Bernard. "But Kentar has a mean streak in him when it comes to Fanton. Henasee has said Fanton brought her ashore without Kentar. In fact, Henasee and Kentar have become good friends."
"Ouch." Daniel shook his head. "That couldn't have set well with Fanton. She would kill any woman who even glanced at Kentar, let alone befriended him. Both girls have been warned to stay close to camp."
"Let's get going then," Kingston pointed in the direction of the cave. "I found a diamond mine just over that cliff. If we play our cards right, we should have enough on board our ship as to make us even wealthier men in less than 10 days. I know you don't need the money, Daniel, but my family is getting tight." Daniel laughed. He came on this trip to make sure his mother was safe from Fanton. After Fanton and their mother had fought, Fanton had promised to kill Ahaira. Knowing Fanton would kill her if she got the chance was the reason Daniel had came on this trip. His friend needing the funds Noteese had to make him wealthy was enough for Daniel to help Kingston. He also planned on finding Fanton and keeping Magnus and the people he loved safe. With the guards placed and knowing Kentar and Rivers were out there, Daniel felt a sense of ease.
"Let's get going then," Bernard announced. "Time is money."
Taking one more look around, Daniel followed them into the woods.

Kentar watched as the cave in front of him filled with smoke. "Good-bye, Fanton, he said sadly. "I will miss the woman I once loved."

Kentar placed more wood in the entrance of the cave and stood back to watch it burn.

"What are you doing?" Rivers yelled from behind him.

"I am putting your sister at peace," Kentar replied coldly.

Rivers pushed Kentar aside and rushed to the blazing fire. Trying to push past it but unable because of the smoke, he screamed her name. "Fanton, Fanton, Fanton. How could you do this?" Rivers turned to Kentar, rushing him and knocking him off his feet. "You have killed her. I will never forgive you for this," he said, straddling Kentar's chest.

Kentar knew he could knock Rivers off easily, but he owed him this moment of anger. He himself could not believe he had killed her. He only knew when he chased her in the cave if she ever came out, she would kill Henasee, and he could not let that happen. His love for Henasee was as deep as his love for Fanton had once been. No, he had made the right decision. Henasee was now safe.

"I didn't think you would be able to kill her," Kentar heard Rivers screaming.

Rivers finally stopped screaming and slid off Kentar. Standing up, he walked off into the woods without looking back. Kentar stood for hours watching the fire burn inside the cave entrance not thinking of anything or anyone. He was a man in a trance. Watching a love he once would have died for go away inch by inch with billow after billow of smoke. "I wish you well," he said, into the last bit of smoke hovering over his head. "I wish you well, Fanton."

Henasee recognized Rivers's form walking down the beach and ran to greet him. She stopped yards away from him when she saw the set of his jaw. "What is it?" she cried. "Rivers, what's happened to you?"

"You!" he screamed at her. "It's you. You have caused my family grief since the day I met you. You are evil, Henasee, and you make men love you, and you throw them away."

"What are you talking about, Rivers? Who did I throw away?"

"You play your games. One minute, you love this guy, and the next, you love this one."

"I don't know what you're talking about," she screamed back and turned to walk away. Rivers reached out and grabbed her arm. "You

let go, Rivers." She turned and hit him as hard as she could in the chest. Rivers grabbed her arms and took her to the ground. Fighting with all she had, Henasee connected with his right eye. "Get off me, she screamed into his face. Rivers continued to hold her arms and leaned in to kiss her.
"No, Rivers," she screamed again. "If you touch my lips like this, I will hate you forever." Rivers bent his head down, and at the last second before their lips touch, he stood and walked down the beach with his head bent. Henasee, shaken to the core, shook all the way back to camp. Magnus spotted her coming up the beach with her head down and ran to her side.
"What is it, Henasee?"
"Rivers," Henasee sobbed. "He was angry, and he . . ."
Magnus took Henasee into her arms. "Did he hurt you?"
"No, he scared me, that's all."
"It seems he did more than that," Magnus said, putting her finger through the hole on the shoulder of Henasee's dress.
"He was so angry at me," Henasee sobbed into Magnus's shoulder. "I tried to talk to him, but he wouldn't listen to me."
"Come on, Hen," Magnus coaxed. "Let's get you cleaned up."
Henasee let Magnus lead her back to camp.
Spotting the two girls Kingston's mother hurried out of her chair and rushed to them. "I'm not sure," Magnus told her, when she pointed at Henasee. "Rivers met her on the beach. I guess they argued, and that's all I've got out of her."
"Here, let me take her." Magnus gave Henasee's hand over to Kingston's mother and watched as she and her daughter lead Henasee into their tent. Magnus could hear Kingston's mother cooing and clucking over Henasee and smiled. Henasee was in good hands. Looking up and down the beach, Magnus felt cold even with the sun blazing down on her. Looking at her hands, she knew the scars were all over her now. "Another day," she smiles sadly. "But Daniel loves me," she said out loud, "and that's all that matters."
Watching from the woods, Fanton hissed, "Come this way, you she-devil. Just a couple of more steps closer and you will never touch my Kentar again. Yes, I know you love him. He even tried to kill me last night for you. But I am too smart. I climbed out a hole in the cave and watched as he placed wood after wood on my death

fire. Yes, I will laugh while I kill you, and I will make Kentar watch. Your days are limited, Magnus, they are limited." Watching Magnus turn and slip into a tent, Fanton swore and headed back to her new hiding place.

Magnus sat with Henasee until she fell asleep. Standing and stretching her legs, she noticed it was starting to get dark. Stepping out of the tent, she walked over to Kingston's mother and two sisters.

"How is she?" his mother asked.

"She's still resting."

"Poor thing," Kingston's mother shook her head. "I can't imagine what's gotten into Rivers. He's always been such a nice young man."

Magnus noticed that Drella snickered but doesn't comment on it.

"You know Rivers?"

"Oh, yes. They have been friends of my family for years. Ahaira and her children grew up next door to us."

"What do you mean, Ahaira and her children grew up next door to you?" Magnus asked, shocked.

"Yes, Fanton, Rivers, and Daniel."

"What do you mean?" Magnus said falling in the chair next to Kingston's mother.

"Ahaira and Fanton's mother. Didn't Daniel tell you Fanton is his . . ." Kingston's mother paused afraid she has said to much.

"Fanton is Daniel's what?" Magnus pushed forward.

"Fanton is Daniel's sister."

"Daniel's sister?" Magnus tried to calculate it in her brain, but it just didn't add up. "No, there's no way he could be Fanton's brother. Ahaira and he are mother and son? You must be mistaken. "

"No, they grew up next door to my mother and father's house. I had known them only a couple of years when I married Kingston's father, god rest his soul. But on many visits, my parents would tell me the trouble Ahaira and Fanton had made in the city. Many people were afraid of them and their black magic. But my mother always had a big heart, and she would make them cookies and candies to send over for the holidays."

"They are family?" Magnus asked dumfounded.

"Yes, my dear, they are all related. They used to be close, but Fanton

started using her powers to do no good. And Ahaira was just the opposite. People would come from miles around to have Ahaira fix a spell or potion Fanton had done to them."
"Daniel's voice?"
"Yes, it was Fanton. They had fought over some of her spells hurting people. He threatened to go to Ahaira. Fanton became angry and took his voice. I don't know the whole story," Kingston's mother said, looking around the camp. "I just know he has been without his voice and traveling with Ahaira for the last year or so."
Magnus sat staring at the water, trying to make sense of this new information. But try as she might, nothing would come to her.

"This is where I've been digging." Kingston pointed at a rock wall with a huge hole in it.
"My goodness, man," Bernard said, looking into the hole. "There are diamonds everywhere. I told you if we can work long hours for a few days, we'll never have to work again."
All three smiled at the diamonds glittering on the walls of the cave. Working in silence the three men filled bucket after bucket of rocks and stones. One filled the buckets and took them back to camp to work them out of the rocks. After each one had two buckets filled, they headed back to camp. Following the trail Kingston had made coming and going from the cave was easy. But the weight from the buckets made the trip back to camp very slow.
Kentar watched and followed their lead. Entering the cave the men had just left, he placed two more logs on the fire. Looking around the cave, he collected two buckets that he started to fill with rocks filled with diamonds. Working steady for hours, he walked outside and took in a breath of fresh air. Working out the kinks in his neck, he turned to walk back inside when darkness overcame him and he hit the ground hard.

Magnus was quiet during dinner. Daniel noticed, and when he tried to ask why, she told him they'd talk later.
Hurrying with his meal, he took her hand and headed toward their tent. Inside, she broke her silence.
"How long were you going to wait before you told me Fanton is your sister?"

"Kingston's mother," he said, pulling her down on their makeshift bed.

"Daniel, it doesn't matter who told me. I want you to answer my question. Were you going to tell me she's your sister?"

Daniel started kissing behind Magnus's ear.

"Stop it," she laughed, trying to push him away. "Daniel, I'm trying to talk to you."

"And I'm trying to," he whispered in her ear.

She giggled, and her face turned pink. "Not before we talk about your sister, I mean Fanton."

"That's a good way to ruin the mood, Magnus. Bring Fanton into our bedroom."

"I only want to know if it's true."

"Yes, it's true. I didn't pick her, I don't like her, and she took away my voice because I didn't like the things she was doing. I don't plan on her coming to dinner or being an aunt to our children. Our father was a very busy man and besides me I know of three other siblings; Fanton being my least favorite. Rivers and Killen I've only met a couple of times. They leave me alone and I return the favor."

"Children?" Magnus sighed. "You've thought about our children?"

"Of course, I've thought about our children silly. I had a lot of time to wish and dream on those lonely nights I stood watch."

"You thought about our children," Magnus sighed, again kissing his cheek.

"I thought about a little Magnus and a little Daniel running through the house, screaming for bottles, playing with balls, cuddling up with us by the fireplace to read books. Yes, Magnus, I've thought about our children."

Magnus almost knocked him off the bed getting to him so quick. "Now this is a lot more fun than bringing up my family." He laughed and kissed her back.

Henasee woke to darkness. Looking around, she could see Kingston's mother and his two sisters in their makeshift beds sleeping. Throwing off her blankets, Henasee sat up and found her way into the darkness to leave the tent. Looking around the camp, she could see the fire's embers had almost burnt out. Walking out into the darkness, she looked up and saw the full blue moon.

Walking across the campsite, she sat on a log facing the water. Listening to the water hit the shore, she thought about Rivers.
"I don't want to scare you," Kentar whispered.
"I'm not afraid of you," she said, turning to see his shadow on the beach. "I knew if Rivers was close you wouldn't be far behind."
Kentar walked the short distance and sat beside her on the log.
"You've seen Rivers?"
"Yes," she said, without looking at him.
"Did he tell you?"
"Tell me what?" she asked, without turning his way.
"I killed Fanton today."
Henasee turned to look him in his eyes. "You killed Fanton?"
"Yes," he answered. "She was going to kill you. I could not let that happen."
Henasee jumps to her feet. "You shouldn't have killed her."
Kentar stood and faced her. "I could not let her hurt you, Henasee. She was Rivers's sister. She was out of control. She wanted nothing more than to hurt you and Magnus. She thought you had turned me away from her."
Henasee looked into Kentar's face. "Did I turn you away from her, Kentar?"
Kentar took two steps and pulled her into his arms. "Yes, Henasee," he said, before kissing her. Henasee closed her eyes and felt the kiss go through her body. Putting his hand on her back, he pulled her closer for a deeper kiss. Not wanting the kiss to stop, she leaned into him. Minutes rushed by, and they finally pulled apart.
Breathless and dizzy from the kiss, she looked again into his eyes. "Why did you not say something?"
"You are in love with Rivers."
"No, Kentar. I thought I was in love with Rivers. But he is not who I thought he was."
Kentar took her in his arms and kissed her again. Hearing a rustling behind them, they pulled apart. "Stay with Magnus and your uncle," Kentar told her. "I must find Rivers and explain." Kissing her one last time, he turned away and walked down the beach and disappeared into the darkness.
Walking back to the camp, Henasee stopped and listened to a rustling in the woods ahead of her. Turning, she called out, "Daniel,

is that you?"

"No." Fanton stepped into the moonlight. "It's not Daniel."

Henasee turned to run, but Fanton threw the girl to the ground. Henasee tried to scream out, but Fanton stopped her by placing a dagger to her chest.

"If you scream," she hissed, "they will find your body."

Henasee stopped struggling and went limp. "Now stand up," Fanton ordered. Henasee did as she was told and stood up, shaking. Move. Fanton pointed toward the woods. Henasee looked around and, with a nudge from Fanton, walked into the woods.

Chapter 10
Revenge

"Where is she?" Magnus screamed when Kingston's mother came rushing from the tent.

"I don't know," his mother yelled back. "She must have gone out last night."

Kingston, Daniel, and Bernard searched the camp and the surrounding area.

"It looks like someone has taken her," Daniel said, returning to the camp. "There are prints on the sand."

"Daniel," Magnus cried, "you must find her."

"We will, darling, we will. Kingston and I are going to look for her right now. You stay in the camp with your uncle."

"Let me come, Daniel," she pleaded. "Henasee might need me."

"No, Magnus, you stay here. I promise we'll find her."

"Daniel, please."

"No, you stay here, where I know you'll be safe."

Seeing he wasn't going to change his mind, Magnus agreed to stay. "Please find her, Daniel."

"I will search every inch of this island. I promise."

Watching them walk out of the camp, Kingston's mother held Magnus as she cried.

"Where do you think Rivers took her?" Kingston asked Daniel as they walked out of the camp.

"I don't know," Daniel answered. "I just hope we're not too late. Fanton was pretty bold to come into the camp to take her."

"How do you know it wasn't Rivers?"

"Henasee fought with a woman in the sand," he told Kingston. "Fanton's prints were everywhere."

Kentar sat down by a tree for a minute. He was exhausted from looking for Rivers. With no signs of him, Kentar needed a minute to think. Henasee cared for him. How was he was going to tell Rivers he didn't know yet? He had killed Rivers's sister, and now he had taken the love Rivers thought he shared with Henasee. Hurting Rivers was the last thing Kentar had ever wanted to do. But his feelings for Henasee were strong, and he was not willing to give it away. Not even for his friend.

Looking around the woods, Kentar noticed black billows of smoke coming from somewhere on the island. Standing, he headed toward the smoke in the sky.

Daniel and Kingston both noticed the smoke in the sky at the same time. Picking up their pace, they headed toward the smoke.

Reaching the smoldering camp fire over an hour later, Daniel and Kingston looked around. Kentar rushed in behind them.

"Where is Henasee?" Daniel screamed at Kentar.

"She is at your camp," he screamed back.

"No." Kingston approached Kentar. "She was taken last night. There was a struggle on the beach."

Kentar looked around the camp. "Fanton is dead. I killed her myself."

"No," Rivers spoke from inside the woods. "Fanton is not dead. I tracked her footprints here. Remember, Kentar, if Fanton dies so do Henasee and Magnus."

"No," Kentar yelled back. "Henasee has been lifted from the spell. Her beauty has returned and has stayed."

Rivers walked up to the fire. "When you told me you had killed Fanton, I went to see Henasee. Yes, her beauty is still with her, but she would have been scarred or dead if you had killed Fanton. The spell has not been broken."

Kentar looked at the other three, and turned and ran back toward the campsite. "Fanton needs both of them to break the spell." Daniel's legs went weak, but he kept pace behind Kentar.

"Both?" Kingston yelled behind Daniel.

"She needs Magnus," Daniel yelled back.

Rivers looked around one more time and ran to catch up with Kingston, Daniel, and Kentar.

The campsite was filled with red smoke. Covering their faces, the men looked for Magnus, Bernard, Ahaira, and Kingston's mother and sisters. Finding his mother and sisters lying on the floor of their tent, Kingston went to them. Relieved to hear his mother cough, he reaches for Megan. Finding her breathing, he touched her face and shook her until she stirred.

"Where? Am I?" she choked out.

"You're all right, Megan. Where is Magnus?"
"Fanton came. Magnus was scared, Fanton pulled out a red powder, and we couldn't breathe. Mother is she ok? What about Drella?" Megan asked, almost near hysteria.
"They're fine," Kingston said, picking her up and setting her on her bed.
"I couldn't breathe, Kingston, and I heard Magnus scream and I tried to sit up, but I couldn't. Where did she take her?"
"It's all right," Kingston said, patting her hand. "We'll get her back."
"Oh, Kingston the things Fanton was saying to Magnus were horrible. She said she was going to kill her and Henasee, too."
Kingston covered Megan up with a blanket and left her long enough to place his mother and then Drella in their beds. He stood to open the flap on the tent when Megan cried out again.
"Don't leave us, Kingston, please."
Kingston walked to Megan's side and leaned down to kiss her.
"You're ok, Megan. I'll be right outside. I need to talk to Daniel, and I'll be right back."
"Tell Daniel Magnus fought to keep us alive, Kingston. Without her, Fanton would have killed us all."
Daniel searched the rest of the camp and met Kingston at the tent door. The guards are out cold - some kind of spell," he told Kingston. "It was Fanton," Kingston told Daniel. "She has Magnus. Megan says Magnus saved their lives."
Daniel was not surprised Magnus would give up her own safety to save others. "Does she know anything else?"
"She said Fanton told Magnus she was going to kill her." Daniel turned green. "It doesn't mean she already has, my friend. You will find her. I'm sorry I can't go."
"Your place is here with your family, Kingston. I understand. I will find my wife and bring her back."
"I know you will," Kingston told him touching Daniel's arm. "I know you will."
Rivers watched as Kentar looked up and down the beach and then turned and ran the opposite way. He knew Fanton planned the whole fire and even her own fake death. She was smart, and this time she'd gone too far. He was not going to let her touch one hair on

Henasee's head. He would not kill his sister, but he would keep her captive until the spell wore off. Even if that took Henasee off the island and left him here.

Finding her camp was as easy as Rivers thought it would be. Watching from behind a tree, he easily spotted Magnus and Henasee tied and gagged by a big boulder. Fanton sat by a roaring fire looking at her hand. Henasee looked up, and Rivers put his finger to his lips to hush any movement she might make to give him away.

"There is no need to stand in the dark, Rivers," Fanton said, looking at him. "I knew you would know how to find me."

Rivers cursed under his breath and walked into the light of the fire.

"I see you did not believe Kentar about my death?"

"Henasee and Magnus would have died, too," he answered. "At first, when Kentar told me you were dead, I believed him, but I remembered if you die, they also die."

"You know Kentar tried to kill me?"

"Yes," Rivers answered. "He could not let you kill Henasee or Magnus."

"I have already given them the potion that breaks their contact to me."

"Then why does Magnus still have the scars?" Rivers asked.

"She will take the scars to her death," Fanton laughed, "leaving me her beauty for the rest of my life."

"Henasee, why kill her?"

"You know she has taken Kentar from me. But do you know she returns his love, Rivers?"

Rivers looked at Henasee and back at Fanton. Swallowing his pain, he faced Fanton once again. "We cannot help who we love, Fanton."

"Kentar has always loved me. That is until these two came into my life. Beauty was not enough. They had to have my life and the love I shared with Kentar. They must die the death of a thousand women's pain. They have dishonored mine and Kentar's future. It was not I who came to them to beg and lie about my future. No, Rivers it was them who have destroyed my life with their greed and deceit."

"No, Fanton." Rivers stepped closer. "I will not let you hurt them."

Fanton stepped to the other side of the fire. "You will not stop me, Rivers."

"What will you do, Fanton? Kill me?"

"If I have to, I will. Please do not make me kill you. You have been a good brother to me and many times my only friend Rivers."
"Then stop this Fanton."
"I cannot."
Rivers started to step toward Fanton, but stopped when she pulled out her knife. "I said I didn't want to kill you, Rivers, but I will." Rivers stepped back as Fanton pointed the knife at his chest. Magnus and Henasee both cried into their cloth gags. "Kentar was right," Rivers screamed at her. "Your heart is black!"
"No," Rivers heard Henasee cry out. Looking over at her, he lost his footing, and Fanton stuck the blade of her knife deep into his chest. With screams of horror, both girls scrambled to stand. Pulling out her knife, Fanton stabbed Rivers again. Surprise crossed his eyes as he fell to the ground with both his eyes wide open staring at the sky. Unable to take it all in, Henasee fainted and fell the rest of the way to the ground. Magnus looked from Rivers to Fanton, who was wiping her knife off on a cloth hanging from her skirt.
"You made me do this," she screamed at Magnus. "You made me kill him. You are a selfish devil. You had everything, loving parents, and a nice home. But, no, that wasn't enough for a spoiled brat. You had to have more. You had to ruin my life. I will find pleasure in watching you and that harlot," Fanton said, pointing at Henasee's still body. "I will laugh as your last breath leaves your body. I will have your beauty, and you will have nothing."
Fanton started to walk up to Magnus when a hand grabbed Fanton's arm.
"You will not hurt her," Kentar screamed at Fanton. "You have done enough." He pointed at Rivers's dead body.
Fanton whirled around and plunged her knife at Kentar. Kentar turned her arm and drove Fanton's knife deep into her own chest. Looking at him in disbelief, she fell dead next to Rivers.
Daniel reached for Magnus and pulled her to her feet. Pulling her gag from her face, Daniel pulled her into his arms as she cried. "She was going to kill us. But Rivers stopped her and then you came and . . ."
"It's all right, darling; everything is going to be all right." Kentar removed the ropes from Henasee. Picking her up in his arms, he cradled her as if she were a fragile child. Henasee opened her eyes

and buried her head in his shoulder.
Rivers is dead.
"I know, Henasee," Kentar says, tightening his grip on her.
"She tried to kill us," Henasee said between sobs.
"She's dead now. She'll never hurt anyone again."
Henasee looked over at Fanton's blank stare. "How?"
"I stopped her from hurting Magnus." Henasee lifted her arms around Kentar's neck and wept openly.
Magnus put her arm around Daniel and let him lead her from the camp. Reaching the camp, Magnus saw her uncle sitting by the fire with a bandage on his head with a worried Ahaira leaning on his arm, with a bandage on her arm.
Bernard smiled and tried to stand, but Ahaira pushed him back down.
"You stay put Bernard," she told him. "You've got a nasty cut on your head."
Bernard stayed put and looked at Magnus. "Are you all right?"
"I'm all right, uncle," Magnus said, falling to her knees in front of him and taking his hand in hers. "What happened to you?"
"Fanton," Ahaira said, looking at Bernard. "She came out of nowhere by the rowboats. We were walking back, and she ambushed us with a log."
"It felt more like a rock," Bernard grunted.
Magnus asks. "Are you ok?"
"I'll be fine. What about you and Henasee are you alright?"
Magnus smiled up at Daniel. "We're fine, too."
"Fanton is dead," Daniel tells his mother. "She has been dead inside a long time, Daniel." Ahaira shook her head sadly. "Fanton let her powers take over her heart. Our powers are very strong and if you use them for evil they will eat away at the very heart of your soul. There was nothing left for Fanton in this world. She is in a place she can no longer kill and destroy everything around her."

The two ships were packed with gold, silver, and diamonds as they set sail. Magnus waved at Henasee from across the deck of Daniel's ship. Smiling to her friend, Henasee waved back from the other ship while holding onto Kentar's arm. She smiled knowing they would be leaving in two days. Kingston had told them he would be setting sail in less than two weeks. Daniel had laughed when Kingston told him he had one more money-making venture left before he left Noteese.

"Why didn't Magnus and I die?" Henasee asked Kentar.

"Fanton said it herself. She released you and Magnus from the spell in order to kill you and not die herself."

"Why did she have to kill Rivers?"

"Fanton never wanted any of her men to love another that's why she took Daniel's voice when he wanted to live with Ahaira. I think that night she saw in Rivers eyes that he loved you. She felt betrayed and killed him. I will never understand how she thought love had to be so selfish."

"Rivers might have loved me, but he loved her, too."

"In Fanton's world, if he loved you, there was no room in his heart to love her anymore."

Henasee reached up and kissed Kentar's cheek. "Poor Fanton," she sighed.

"Poor Fanton?"

"Yes," Henasee told him. "She had all the love she would have ever need in your heart and her selfishness drove it out."

Kentar touched her beautiful cheek before he pulled her against him and kissed her with a tenderness he has never felt before.

Magnus turned from the mirror and smiled sadly at Ahaira. "I thought my beauty would stay. Fanton said she took the spell off us."

"Spells are very strange," Ahaira smiled back. "Maybe one day your beauty will return for good. But don't let it hurt your life."

Magnus smiled at Daniel as he walked into the room and kissed her on the mouth. "I have learned a lot about myself and my worth."

"And what's that, my darling wife?"

Magnus smiled up at Daniel. "I have learned that I am more than my beauty. I have learned that you will love me no matter what changes my body makes in my lifetime." Daniel hugged her to his side.

"And," Magnus said in his ear, "I will love you always, Daniel."

Daniel lifted her face to his and smiled as her beauty returned on her face. Not wanting the moment to be ruined by telling her, her beauty has returned, he kissed her instead.

Fanton opened her eyes to darkness. Feeling the heat of the earth all around her, she started to claw at it. Her hatred for Magnus and Henasee fuel her strength, and soon she could see a tiny ray of moonlight come through to shine on her arm.

"Yes," she laughs. "I knew I would not die that easily."

Reaching down with a screech of laughter, she pulled the knife from her chest and used it to continue digging. Covered in mossy-colored dirt and blood, she finally pulled herself out of the grave Kentar had placed her in hours earlier.

"You, my darling, I will kill last," she said, thinking of Kentar. "I will enjoy watching your tramp die before your eyes. I will place her in a grave to be left all alone for eternity. And I will watch as your heart breaks into a million pieces as you have broken mine."

Fanton pulled a small cloth sack from her pocket and lifted her dress to examine her knife wound.

"Oh, my darling, you should have taken my heart out. Even you know a witch cannot live without a heart. Maybe you thought your betrayal would be enough to damage my heart so it would quit. You are wrong, Kentar," she says his name as she moaned from the pain of placing powder on her wound. "Once my heart was alive and filled with love for you and now my heart is alive and filled with vengeance. I will come for you and the betrayal of our love. You will know the same feelings I now know. Love is no stronger than beauty. When you have it, life is kind. When it's gone, you have nothing but pain and anger."

Fanton leaned back, waiting for the herbs to take effect. Looking up, she could see the clouds rolling under the stars. Closing her eyes, she fell into a deep sleep and dreamed of the love she and Kentar once had for each other. Waking to the morning light, she tried to sit up too fast and fell back in pain.

"I must get to the ship."

Lying down, she gave herself a minute to think. "I need the man who came aboard with Kentar. Yes, I need to find him." Gathering up every muscle in her body, Fanton sat up. When her head stopped spinning, she pulled herself up on a tree. Waiting until her legs were strong, she leaned on the tree. Taking a deep breath, she walked, catching herself from tree to tree. With half the day gone, she started

to worry she might not make it before nightfall. Concentrating, she moved on. Relief ran across her face as she saw the sailor they call Jage pacing in front of the rowboats.
Looking up, Jage watched in terror as Fanton half dragged and half limped toward him. Fanton snickered. She knew he would be afraid of her. In fact, she counted on his cowardly ways to her best advantage.
"Come here," she cried out.
When he didn't move, Fanton started to chant something at him. "I said come here," she cried out again. "Or you will live your final days here." She pointed at the beach to a lizard. Jage hurried to Fanton's side.
"Help me into a boat," she ordered. Jage hesitated. "I see," she snarled. "You have orders to keep me away."
"Yes," Jage said between shaking teeth. "But you're dead. I heard Kentar say he buried you up there." Jage pointed to the woods behind Fanton.
Fanton lifted her arm to show Jage. "He buried me, but I did not stay dead." Fanton watched as the color drains from Jage's face and neck. "Now you will do as I say, or I will turn you into a—"
"I'll do what you say," Jage answered in a rush. "I know you're a witch. The whole ship knows that."
"Then get me on one of those boats."
Jage took Fanton's arm and helped her to the first rowboat.
"How long before they set sail?"
Jage looked around trying to figure out away to escape.
"My powers are very strong," Fanton told him watching him look up and down the shore. "My powers brought me back to life. My powers," she continued, "will take your life if you betray me."
Jage stopped looking around and faced Fanton. "What do you want from me?"
"How long before they set sail?"
"Two days, Kentar said."
"Kingston, is he leaving with them?"
"No. He leaves within two weeks."
"Take me to Kingston's ship," she ordered.
"I can't do that," Jage answered her.
Fanton started her chanting, and Jage cried out, "Ok, I'll take you,

but there's nothing I can do after I get you there. Kentar will notice if I'm gone too long. If he sees the boat gone, he'll think I went for supplies off the ship. But he'll know something is up if I don't return."

Fanton snorted. "I have no reason to keep you, once I'm safe on the ship. I will need food for three or four days while I heal. And water. You get me those things, and I will let you go free."

Jage climbed in the rowboat and started to paddle. The night air was chilly, and Fanton reached for the blanket she knew was under the seat. Wrapping it around herself, she leaned back on the floor.

"You will be wise to let no one find out you helped me. Kentar would feed you to the fish. And if he doesn't kill you, I will kill you myself."

Jage tried to swallow, but his throat swelled up, and he choked instead. "I'll not be saying anything to nobody," he choked out. "Fanton lay back and closed her eyes."

Kentar and Daniel watched from a cliff as Jage and Fanton headed to Kingston's ship. "I always thought he was a trader," Kentar spat. "I doubt he had a choice. Fanton can be very persuasive when she wants her own way. What are we going to do?" Daniel asked.

"I'm not sure. I was afraid she might be able to heal herself. That's why I knew to watch for her. Fanton has a strong magic. It seems not even death can take her down."

"You didn't take her heart?" Daniel asked.

"I was not sure if it would kill Henasee or Magnus."

Daniel flinched. "Are you saying if Fanton dies Magnus may die?"

"The spell is still working or Magnus would have kept her beauty."

"And Henasee, is she still affected?"

"I'm not sure," Kentar answered. "That is the only reason I didn't take her heart."

Daniel watched as Jage lifted Fanton on board Kingston's ship. "What about Kingston and his family?"

"We can't tell him," Kentar answered. "It will only put Magnus and Henasee in danger again."

"But what about Fanton being on the ship with his sisters and mother" Daniel asked pointing toward the camp.

"Fanton should have no reason to hurt them. It is me she will want to harm now. She will hide on the ship and heal. She'll be waiting to return home."

"And then what do we do?" Daniel asked.

"Then we will have to find away to break the spell and cut her heart out," Kentar said flatly and headed back down the cliff. "I would not tell Magnus about this. The girls have been through enough for now. Let them have a nice trip home." Daniel had to agree. "To tell them now would only make them worry needlessly." Daniel spotted Magnus across the camp and picked up his pace.

"Where have you two been off to this time?" She laughed when he scooped her up and hugged her.

"Just a few things we had to finish up before going home."

"Home," Magnus gushed. "I never thought those words would sound so good. All these months away from my parents have made me miss them terribly."

"How do you think they'll act when you tell them you've brought home a husband?"

Magnus laughed softly as Daniel kissed her ear. "They will love you as I do."

"Hopefully not as you do," he laughed, taking her hand and leading her to their tent.

"Well, not as I do," she laughed back.

Kentar walked past the camp to sit by Henasee as she watched the waves roll out to shore. "You look deep in thought."

Henasee smiled and moved over, inviting him to sit on her blanket. "I thought I'd never see my home again. And now we're heading back."

"Are you sorry to go?"

"No," she smiled sadly. "This place is beautiful. But it's not like home. It is like a beautiful dream with all its riches and colors. But I would never want to live here."

"Where do you want to live, Henasee?"

Henasee turned shyly to face him. "With you Kentar I want to live with you."

Kentar placed a hand behind her neck and brought her mouth to his, kissing her softly at first and then more deeply. Minutes went by before he pulled away.

"Henasee your family is . . ."

"I know. They're different from your family Kentar," she finished for him.

"Yes, he laughed. "I'm not so sure your family will accept me."

Henasee looked out at the water again. "Then I will leave with you, Kentar. You and I will be rich. We will be able to travel the world if we like."

Kentar touched her cheek. "You said it yourself. You miss your home, and that is where you should be. Let's not waste our time figuring out our lives. Let's be happy for what we have now."

Kentar took Henasee's hand and pulled her to her feet as he stood. "For today we are together on a beautiful island. Our lives are whatever we make them."

Henasee laughed and ran to the water. Taking off her dress to reveal an under slip, she ran in, laughing. Kentar took off his sandals and ran in behind her. Diving deep into the water, it took him only seconds to catch up with her. Grabbing her around the waist, he pulled her backwards up against himself and kissed her neck.

"This could last forever," she whispered in his neck.

"Today is a part of forever," he said and turned her around into his arms. Henasee pressed her body against his so tightly she could feel the ripples of his chest against her stomach. Henasee kissed him.

"You are not a child, Henasee," Kentar said, pushing her away from his chest slightly. "You know what will happen if you continue to kiss me that way." Henasee leaned back into his arms and kissed him again. "Henasee, I'm not a young boy to play games with," he said pushing her out of his arms again.

Henasee pulled her slip over her head and returned to his arms. "I know you're not a young boy, Kentar."

She kissed him again. Kentar pulled her legs up around his waist, and together they floated in ecstasy. Kentar watched her face as she was filled with excitement and then passion. He knew Henasee would be a kind and loving partner, and she had just proved it by giving herself so openly. She held nothing back. She pressed forward when he pressed. They became dolphins playing, loving, and living together in their private water wonderland. Henasee clung to the last moments of their lovemaking. Kentar held her tightly but with a gentle touch, as if she were a light bird with feathers, a sparkling dust he's afraid might wipe off or leave

tarnished in some way. Henasee noticed his expression.
"This was not all you, Kentar. I wanted this to happen."
Kentar held her to him tightly. "We should not have done this until we—"
"I know," she answered, "until we know if we'll stay together. Today is our life together." She smiled, kissing his mouth again. Kentar looked into her eyes and returned her kiss for kiss.

Magnus had wonderful days on board the ship. She played chess with her uncle in the afternoons. At night, she strolled the deck with Daniel. Her favorite time was at night when she and Daniel proved their love for one another.
"I never knew life could be this good," she smiled at Daniel lying beside her.
"It is good," he smiled back.
"I didn't mean this." She pointed at the bed. "I mean being with you every day and being rich."
"I see," he laughed, tickling her under the blankets. "I am just a husband to please you. It is really the gold and diamonds that have your heart."
Magnus laughed, trying to back away from Daniel's tickling fingers. "No," she laughed, "you are worth your weight in gold."
"Oh," he tickled faster. "Now I am equal to your riches."
"I didn't mean that, she laughed, out of breath. "I meant . . ."
He stopped, seeing she had suddenly become serious.
"I mean I would give all my riches up for a moment with you, Daniel."
Seeing the tears form in her eyes, he was sorry he took the joke so far. "Magnus, sweet, don't do this." He brushed away a tear. "I was only joking with you. I, too, am glad we have the riches to take back home. We will want for nothing. Your parents will want for nothing.

Chapter 11
A New Life

We are going to have a great life together."
Magnus nodded and buried her head in his shoulder. "We're going to have a child, Daniel," she whispered.
Daniel didn't know what to say. "Are you sure? We only left Noteese two months ago."
Magnus looked him in the eyes. "Yes, I'm very sure, Daniel. We are going to have a baby."
"A baby!" he shouted, trying to get used to the idea. "We're going to have a baby?" he asked Magnus.
"We're going to have a baby," she repeated to him.
"We're going to have a baby," he shouted, finally believing what he was saying. "We're going to have a—"
"Baby," she laughed.
"A baby," he said pulling her closer. "We're going to have a baby."
Daniel didn't want to share the news with anyone for the night.
"We'll tell them tomorrow. Tonight it's just our family," he smiled, tenderly putting his hand on her stomach. Daniel and Magnus talked through the night about their plans for the future.

"What are your deep thoughts?" Kentar asked Henasee as she looked out over the dark sea.
"I was thinking about my family."
"You miss them terribly?"
"Yes, Magnus has always been the free spirit. I am more the 'do as you're told' type."
"Is that what you will do then?"
Henasee turned to face him.
"You have not touched me again since the day in the water. Why?"
"We can't play we're together, Henasee. People will get hurt. You and I will get hurt. You live a different life than I do. I can't see how the two can be joined. I have loved Fanton this last year. To start a new love with you is too hard to ask my heart to keep up with. You have a life with your family, and I have one at sea."

"You're not even willing to try?"
"It would only fail, in the long run. When we get you home, we must part," he said sadly and turned and walked away. Kentar slammed the door to his cabin. He hated hurting Henasee this way. But with Fanton on a ship right behind them, he had to leave Henasee with her family and lure Fanton away from her. Fanton wanted him, and he was going to let her have her way. He cared neither way how his life played out. He would try to make Fanton believe he loved her and try to get her to leave with him. Or she could have her revenge on him, and he would let her kill him without putting up a fight. Either way, Henasee would be safe to live out her life."

"Oh, my dear." Uncle Bernard hugged her again. "I am going to have a grand-nephew or niece. How delightful. I will have another wondering soul to get into trouble," he laughed, pointing to the ship. "Your father may not even bury my head after he has me beheaded." Magnus laughed and took Daniel's hand. "I will love every minute of your storytelling to my child, Uncle. You are the best uncle a girl has ever had. Without you, I would never have met Daniel and now," she put her hand on her stomach, "I have even more to be grateful for."
"Let's just hope your father sees it the same way."
Magnus smiled again and put away her worries.
"What is the fuss?" Ahaira asked, coming into stand by Bernard.
"Magnus is with child," Daniel smiled proudly. Magnus caught the look in Ahaira's eyes before Ahaira turned away. "If you two would be so kind I would like a minute alone with Ahaira," Magnus asked, smiling shyly.
"Is there something wrong, Magnus?" Daniel asks a little panicked.
"No, darling," she cooed. "It's just some women's talk. Some things I need to ask."
Daniel and Bernard looked at each other uncomfortably and started to walk to the door. Magnus laughed. "It's not that horrible."
"You take your time, dear." Uncle Bernard patted her shoulder. "Daniel and I will look for our lunch."
Magnus laughed again as the two hurried out the door and shut it quickly. "Women's talk," Magnus laughed. "My mom could always clear a room when she said women's talk."

Ahaira laughed, too. "Men are afraid of women's talk. Almost as if it were an evil spell they might get caught up in." Both ladies laughed and Ahaira took a seat on the couch. "Your news took me by surprise," she told Magnus.

"I saw your eyes." "What is it? Is there something wrong with my baby?"

Ahaira did not turn away but looked Magnus directly in the eye. "Your beauty still come and goes."

"Yes," Magnus replied. "I sometimes have it longer than others. But sometimes it doesn't come back as quickly as it used to."

"I see. I was afraid of that."

"Afraid of what?" Magnus asked. "The baby," Ahaira stated flatly. "The baby what?" Magnus cried. "Will my baby be ok? Please tell me."

Ahaira looked at Magnus's scars and shook her head. "Your baby will be born with the same curse her mother carries."

Magnus felt as if she'd been slapped. "My baby's beauty will come and go?"

"Yes, your baby will be the same as you. There is something I do not understand."

"What?" Magnus asked quietly.

"Did you see Kentar kill Fanton?"

"Yes, I saw him stab her."

"Did he cut her heart out?"

Magnus pulled away from Ahaira. "No, why would he do that?" she cried.

"If he didn't take her heart, she is not dead."

Magnus felt faint. "She must be dead."

"No, that is why your beauty has not returned to stay."

Magnus had never thought of that. She thought the spell had been messed up and that's why it still came and went. "Do you think she's on board this ship?"

"No," Ahaira looked around, "I would feel her presence if she were close."

"Henasee. We must get to Henasee."

"Kentar will keep her safe. I saw how he looked at her. He will die before he lets Fanton hurt your friend."

"Kentar?" Magnus asked her. "He knows she's not dead, doesn't

he?"
"He would know. He has lived with her off and on for the last year."

Daniel opened the door, and after looking at Magnus and Ahaira, he wished he could close it right back up with himself on the other side. "Daniel." Magnus was on her feet before he took another step. "Did you know Fanton is not dead?" Daniel tried to pass her with the tray holding their lunch but she wouldn't budge. "Daniel, I asked you? Did you know Fanton was not dead?"
Daniel looked at Magnus. "Yes."
Magnus didn't wait for an explanation. She ran crying from the room. Daniel set the tray down quickly and ran, trying to catch up. After opening the door to the cabin she shared with Daniel, Magnus slammed it shut and put the bolt lock on.
"Magnus." Daniel knocked on the hard wooden door. "Let me in."
"Go away, Daniel," Magnus screamed from the other side. "I have nothing to say to you."
"Let me explain."
"You've had plenty of chances to tell me Fanton is not dead. Why didn't you take the time then?" she screamed through the door.
"Magnus, let me in," he said, shaking the door.
"Go away."
Daniel tried for a few more minutes to get her to let him in. "I'll be back," he said, turning and leaving.
Magnus crumbled to her bed and cried herself to sleep.

Fanton sneaked through the halls of the ship, careful not to be seen. Getting food had been harder than she thought it would be. The ship's galley became pitch black after dark. She had gotten used to counting her steps from the doorway to get to the table. The first week she had bumped and bruised herself badly trying to maneuver in the dark. Now she had it down to a mere 30 steps in the dark. Finding a loaf of bread on the table, she turned to reach a counter. Feeling around, she took a handful of dried meat and dried fruit out of a basket. She was careful not to take too much as not to be found out. Happy with her findings, she counted the steps back to the doorway. Hurrying when she saw a light coming down the stairway, she rushed back to her cabin on the lower deck. Jage had told her no

one came to this end of the ship. It was said to be haunted.
Fanton laughed at her luck. She had supplies for another week, and besides water, she would need nothing. Her time was spent planning revenge on Kentar, Magnus, and Henasee. She loved thinking about the ways she would torture and kill them. "Except Kentar." she laughed out loud. "He will be mine once again." Blowing out her candle, Fanton sat quietly in the dark. A noise from outside her door seemed to be getting closer. With no lock on the door, there was nothing she could do but wait and listen. Fanton's heart beat faster as the voices got closer to her cabin door. Seeing light come under the door, Fanton held her breath. The knob started to turn, and Fanton reached in her pocket for her dagger.
The knob slowly turned, and Fanton leaned forward to attack. The door swung slowly open, and a lantern blinded Fanton's view.
"See, Megan," a girl's voice giggled, "I told you she wasn't a ghost." Megan stayed in the doorway, but Drella marches right up to Fanton with the lantern.
"You are Fanton, aren't you?" Drella asked without a stitch of fear. Fanton tried to focus her eyes, but the light was too bright. "Move the light," Fanton snapped.
Megan took a step backwards, but Drella didn't move. "I have you in a trap, witch. It is not the other way around."
"Let's go, Drella. We must tell Kingston she's on board. "
Fanton looked through the shadows, and her eyes started to adjust. She knew she could at any minute kill both girls, but there would be a search for them. For now, she decided to play captive to them. There would be plenty of time later to kill them both.
"Did you hear me, witch?" Drella said, lifting the lantern to Fanton's face.
"Yes," Fanton replied, releasing her hold on her knife. "You have caught me. I am now your very own servant. What is it I can do for you? Miss?"
Drella's face was covered in a smile. "I wish to have the love of my choosing."
"I can grant that," Fanton said flatly. "And what is it you trade for this love?"
"I will trade your life," Drella said boldly. "You know my brother would throw you overboard if he knew you were here. So if I get my

wish, I will not tell my brother of your whereabouts."
"It is so," Fanton said waving her arm in the air.
Drella laughed, and her smile broadened. She had loved Daniel for years, and now he would return her love. "Who then? Who is he?" Drella asked suspicious.
"It is Daniel," Fanton stated. "The love you want returned is from Daniel."
Drella was more than pleased, and Fanton made no effort to talk again. Fanton looked at the spoiled brat before her and started to laugh. But she covered it with a cough. She had watched as Daniel returned to the camp. She had seen for herself this girl throw herself at Daniel. Yes, she was sure it was Daniel's love the girl desired.
"You." Fanton turned to Megan. "What is it you wish for?"
Megan started to shake. "I have no wishes," she said, with her voice shaking. "I," she stammered, "I need nothing."
"Come now," Fanton said, feeling confident. "You must want something."
"No, I am very pleased with my life."
"There is nothing you have lost that would give you joy to have it back?" Fanton knew to push for an answer. The girl would slip and tell someone she was on board the ship without a promise for a granted wish.
"I," the girl thought for a moment. "I would wish for my father to return," she said shyly.
"Megan," Drella scolded. "Father has been gone for years. Not even she can bring him back."
Fanton watched as the hope drains from the young girl's face. "I have brought back many from death," Fanton said matter of fact. "I will grant you your wish if you promise to keep my presence here a secret."
Megan nodded, too scared to talk. Never in her wildest dreams did she think she would see her father again. Oh, how she wished she could tell Mother, Father would be coming soon.
But before she could pull up another thought, Fanton spoke again. "I will grant your wishes, but only if I'm not found out."
Drella looked over at Megan, who was nodding. Megan listened to her brother and Daniel talking about burying Fanton so if she could come back from the dead she was certain her father could, too.

"We will keep your secret," Drella said, turning to leave. "You should be more careful," she said, looking at Fanton's supplies spread out on the table. "Cook has been going crazy trying to figure out who the food thief is. I will bring you food and water every few days." Drella waited for Fanton to thank her, but nothing came. "I will see you in a few days then."

Fanton nodded, and Drella closed the door behind her. Fanton re-lit the candle on the table and broke off a piece of bread. "You are a fool, child. Blackmail is a game for adults, not children." She shook her head and placed a piece of bread in her mouth. "You will pay dearly for your wish," she promised as her eyes glowed with hatred. "Dearly," she repeated. She took small book from her pocket and opened it up. "A do ch lay ny coe la dar," she read from a page in the book. "Let him come in her dreams. Let him be with her in the night. Then stay with her through the light. A do ch la ny coe la dar," she said again and placed the book back into her pocket. With a smile of gratification, she took another bite of bread. Children shouldn't play with adults. She laughed.

Daniel was beside himself. Magnus would not allow him into their cabin. He thought a few hours would calm her down, but it had been three days now. She opened the door to her uncle and even Ahaira. But when he tried to enter, she slammed the door.

"Please, Magnus," he begged from the other side of the door. "Let me explain. I didn't mean to hurt you."

Magnus opened the door slowly and stepped aside.

"Are you ok?" he asked, concerned.

"I have eaten and I am fine."

"Magnus, I am so sorry. When Kentar and I saw Fanton, I couldn't believe she was still alive. Kentar had told me there was a chance she could still be alive."

"How?" Magnus asked.

"He didn't cut out her heart. He couldn't take the chance of it killing you or Henasee. We tried to leave as soon as we could. Then she would be trapped on the island, but she went aboard Kingston's ship."

"Kingston? Does he know she is aboard his ship?"

"No, we didn't tell him."

"Why, Daniel? Why? His family have been nothing but kind to us. They are in serious danger with Fanton aboard their ship."
"Kentar thinks she will wait until we dock to cause trouble. She is coming after him."
"You mean us, don't you?"
"She's coming after Henasee, Kentar, and me."
"And now our unborn child," Magnus finished on a gulp. "What are we going to do?" she cried, almost falling to the floor.
Daniel grabbed her around the waist and set her on the sofa. "I will not let her hurt you or our child, Magnus. You must trust me."
"This is my entire fault," Magnus wept into her hands.
"No, darling, you have done nothing wrong."
"Yes, Daniel," Magnus said through streaming tears. "It is I who lied and deceived the people I love for a chance to go to Noteese. And my punishment will be to lose everything I hold dear for my sins."
"Magnus, you didn't plan any of this."
"Fanton told me if I changed my destiny I would pay dearly. She must have known it meant giving up you and my child."
"Magnus, we aren't going to let her have our child."
"Did you know even if we can hide our child from Fanton it will be born with a beauty that comes and goes like mine?"
"Magnus, we will make our child feel loved and safe. He or she will have a good life. On my honor as your husband, she will never hurt you or our child."
Magnus faced her husband and looked deeply into his eyes.
"I am not a child, Magnus. I am your husband, and I will protect you and our child with everything in me."
Magnus stopped crying. "You're right, Daniel. She gave you back your voice. She would not hurt your child."
Daniel pulled her into his arms. And for the first time in days, Magnus felt safe for her child and herself.

Henasee took great care in brushing her hair and dressing in one of the gowns Kingston's mother insisted she take with her.
"You cannot meet your parents dressed in rags. Your mother would faint dead away."
Visualizing her mother fainting, Henasee did not put up a fight but

thanked Kingston's mother with a hug. Looking at the gold lace dress in the mirror, she was glad she had accepted. She understood all of Kentar's reasons for not being together, but if she had to live life without him, she wanted one more night of memories to cherish. Picking up the dinner tray she had prepared, she headed for his cabin. Kentar opened the door on the first knock. Looking at her, his heart almost exploded. He would carry this picture of her in his heart for the rest of his life.

"What are you doing, Henasee?"

"You must eat," she said, skirting around him with the tray. "And I must eat. So I thought we could eat together."

"You know this isn't a good idea," he said, watching her place the food on the table.

"I understand your reasons why we can't be together after we reach shore. But give me this one night, Kentar. I wish only to be held in your arms one last time. I will never ask you for another thing. After tonight, you will not even know I am aboard this ship. I will keep my distance as you asked."

Kentar took in a breath. "I would know you were on the ship, Henasee. I can feel you in the air. I can still taste your kisses on my mouth. When I think of you, my heart beats out your name. I would still know you were on board, Henasee."

"Then let us have tonight, Kentar. Let us have each other in the way we are meant to be together."

Kentar watched as a single tear formed in Henasee's eye and slowly glided down her cheek. With his heart breaking in a million pieces, he turned and walked out the door. Henasee waited for the door to close and crumbled to the floor crying. Listening to her cry almost made him go back in, but he knew he could never give her up if he held her in his arms one more time. Brushing a tear of his own off his cheek, he went up on deck.

***

Daniel was happy to spot Magnus across the deck laughing with her uncle. The idea of Fanton not hurting their child had put some of Magnus's worries to rest. Not for Daniel though. He knew Fanton could be the cruelest to those she held close. That included him and his unborn child. Fanton would stop at nothing to get revenge. He needed to come up with a plan and quickly.

Chapter 12
Father Comes Home

Megan covered her eyes with her hands. The pain of seeing him again was too much for her to look at. Waiting until her breathing came back to normal, she lowered her hand.
"Father," she cried, letting her tears fall freely on her light yellow traveling dress. "Is it you, Father?" She smiled as he turned to face her. "It is you," she cried, and ran to where he stood on the far side of the deck.
Her father bent down and scooped her up, giving her the biggest hug she had ever had.
"You really are here," she cried, hugging him back.
"Yes, my dearest daughter," he cried into her hair. "I really am here."
"But where have you been, Father? I've missed you so much."
"I've been with you the whole time, sweetheart. You just haven't looked hard enough."
"I'm sorry, Daddy. I should have looked harder."
"No, it's not your fault. I was hard to find."
"I don't understand, Daddy."
"I know, sweetie. It's hard to understand death. I hardly understand it myself."
"You're here, and that's all that matters."
"It sure is, sweetheart. And I'm never going to leave you again." Her father hugged her again and kissed her forehead. "Have you been a good little darling while Daddy's been gone?"
"Oh yes, Father, I've done my school, and I've helped Mother with. Oh, Daddy, Mother will be so happy you've returned." Megan smiled, but when her father's face turned to anger, she stepped back. "What is it, Daddy? Have I made you angry?"
"I must go now, Megan, but I'll be back at the same time tomorrow."
"No, Daddy," she cried, trying to take his hand.
But he pulled it away before she reached it. "You be a good little girl," he told her, his voice turning kind again.
"Please, Daddy, don't be mad at me."

"I'm not mad at you, Megan. Daddy could never be mad at his little girl. Now run along," he said, "patting her on the head, and I'll see you tomorrow."
"You promise, Daddy?"
"I promise."
Megan smiled through her tears and ran off to tell her mother that she has just talked to her father, and he was coming home soon.
"Mother!" Megan ran to her mother sunning on the top side deck. "I've got a surprise for you."
"Well, darling, you know I love surprises." Her mother smiled at her taking her extended hand. "Tell me, is it a special picture you made me? You know how I adore your artwork."
"No, Mother," Megan laughed, "it's much better than a picture."
"Is it a lovely story? I told Kingston just the other day how good your writing is. No one would ever guess you were only nine years old when they read your stories."
"NO, Mother!" Megan laughed, shaking her mother's hand. "It's Father."
Megan's mother's hand went limp. "Megan, you know I don't like to talk about your father."
"But, Mother, he's coming back."
"Megan, that's enough," her mother yelled, dropping her hand.
"No, Mother, really, Father is coming home."
"Megan!" her mother stood shaking from head to toe.
"Mother," Megan cried.
"This is a very cruel joke, Megan. I thought better of you."
Throwing off the hand Megan put on her arm, her mother stomped from the deck. Megan sat down and cried for a minute and then stopped.
"I will show you I am not cruel, Mother. When Father returns, you will see."

Magnus loved the sea air. Walking with her uncle was always interesting.
"I do believe you have more stories inside you than a hundred men, Uncle."
"I do have quite a lot of them," he laughed proudly.
"I can't believe we'll be home soon, Uncle. It seems like years have

gone by."

"We have been gone for almost a year now, Magnus."

"Magnus patted her stomach. "It won't be long before these little ones are ready to come out and see the world. I see you're not surprised when I said these little ones."

"Ahaira told me last night you were having twins. What did Daniel say to you having two babies?"

Magnus laughed at the memory. "I was lucky he was already sitting down. I think he might have fallen to the floor. Two babies at one time is quite remarkable. I can't believe how blessed I have become."

"Good things happen to good people, Magnus. You and Daniel deserve happiness."

"Thank you, Uncle. I have worried so much about Fanton's threats of hurting people with my lies. I've been afraid I'd wake up one morning and everything I've grown to love would be gone."

"No one is going to take Daniel or your children, Magnus. Daniel would not allow it."

Magnus squeezed her uncle's arm. That is what missing words??

Henasee stayed clear of Kentar. To look at him only causes her embarrassment and pain. She threw her gown in a heap on her cabin floor the day Kentar refused her advances. And that is where it still sat months later. She placed the boy's clothes Rivers had given her on and that's how she stayed - with her hair tucked into a cotton cap and her boy's clothing. She went back to helping Jage do the cooking and feeding of the men. That is, except for Kentar. When he walked in the room, she left in the other direction.

He hated hurting her, but there was nothing else he could do. She would be in danger to be with him. In no more than three weeks, he could hand her over to her parents, and she would be safe. Thinking about her marrying another man was something he couldn't bring himself to do. Instead, he worked with the men from morning to night and ate and slept. Thinking about her he knew was something he could not let his head or his heart do. If he did, he would never be able to let her go.

Fanton opened the bag of food Drella brought her that morning.

Having her and her sister bring her things had come in quite handy. She even had a brush and a small mirror on her bed side table. Her beauty coming and going still made her angry. But she used the anger in a most positive way. She used it to plan the torture and deaths of Magnus and Henasee. Looking at her reflection in the mirror, Fanton laughed at the scars on her face.

"Your deceit and lies will not destroy my life, Magnus. It is I, who will come out on top and destroy your world. You have taken Kentar, Daniel, and Rivers from me and you will pay with your very soul."

Fanton placed the mirror on the table and ate a dry piece of fruit.

"Father!" Megan ran to him as he opened his arms to her. "I knew you would be here."

"Hello, dearest," he smiled, giving her a big hug. "Where is your mother?" he asked, looking past her. "I was sure once you told her she'd come with you."

Megan looked in her father's eyes. "Mother got angry when I told her you were coming back, Father." Her father's shoulders sink toward the deck. "I have been gone a long time, sweetie. Maybe your mother doesn't want me to return?"

"No, Father, I think she was just surprised when I told her you were back."

"What did she say?" Megan looked away from her father. "Megan? You and I have never kept secrets from each other. Let's not start now."

Megan looked up at her father with fear in her eyes.

"What is it, darling?"

"Mother said I was cruel. She said I made the whole thing up, and it was a very mean joke."

Megan's father put his hand on her shoulder. "That was a very mean thing for your mother to say, Megan."

"I tried later to talk to her, but she would not listen."

"Well, that is a problem," her father said rubbing his gray hair. "I can't very well come back if your mother doesn't want me back."

"I want you, Father."

Oh sweetie. I want you, too.

"You're not going away again, are you?"

"I'm not sure. I need some time to think of a new plan. I just figured I'd be going home with you. But if your mother doesn't want me to come home. . ."
"Please, Father, I want you to."
"I need time to think, Megan. Give me some time."
"How much time?"
"Give me two days, and I'll meet you right here. I'll come up with some kind of plan."
Megan hugged her father, and he hugged her back. "It's probably best not to talk to Mommy about me anymore, Megan."
"Why, Father?"
"I'm afraid she may want me to go away for good."
"I won't let her, Daddy," Megan cried, throwing herself at him. "I won't let anyone take you away from me again."
"I'll think of something," he promised. "Now you run off before someone sees us and tells your mother."
Megan hugged her father one more time and ran off the deck, making sure no one saw her.
"What are you in such a hurry for?" her mother scolded her. "You almost ran right over me."
Megan stopped as if she'd seen a ghost. "I was going to work on my studies."
"That's what I like to hear. No more games," her mother said sternly. "Too much time has gotten you into mischief lately."
Megan looked at her mother with such hatred her mother flinched. "You know nothing of what I've been doing. You leave me alone."
Megan's mother almost fell backward when Megan reached up and pushed her mother out of the way. Trying not to faint, her mother held the wall and watched Megan walk down the staircase.

A tap on the door surprised Fanton. "You may enter." She was not surprised when Megan opened the door.
"I have seen him," she announced excitedly. "He is coming back for good, he promised."
Fanton shook her head sadly. "I am not so sure. Your mother has rejected him."
"I don't care what she wants. I want to be with him."
Then Fanton placed her hand on the bedside table. "Then there are

things you must do."

"I will do anything," Megan promised, "to have my father back for good."

"Even if it means you will lose your mother?"

Megan didn't even hesitate. "I will do anything it takes."

"Come closer, child," Fanton ordered. "I will need a prick of your blood."

Megan looked unsure but held her hand out to Fanton. Fanton took out her dagger and sliced it across Megan's hand. Surprised and scared, Megan fainted. Fanton reached into her pocket and pulled out a small vial, collecting some of Megan's blood. She put some of the same ointment on her hand as she had put on her gun wound. Minutes later, Megan started to come around.

"So you decide to wake up," Fanton laughed. "You are not such a tough little girl, are you?" Megan sat up, slowly examining her wrapped hand. "Did you think I would cut off your whole hand?"

"I don't know," Megan replied. "There was so much blood."

"Blood from the young," Fanton laughed, looking at the now-filled small bottle.

"What will you do with that?" Megan asked more to keep from fainting again then for the answer.

"I will show you when you need to know. Make sure you leave that bandage on for three days. Then your hand will be healed."

Megan looked at the bandage and then back to Fanton. "You will help me with my father like you promised, won't you?"

"I don't make promises lightly," Fanton snapped, scaring Megan all over again. "I had better go. You meet with your father like he told you."

Megan snapped her head around. "You know he came."

"I sent him," she answered. "Meet with your father. He will tell you what to do."

"I will," Megan promised and left the cabin.

"Please listen to me, Kingston," his mother said through tears and close to hysterics. "There is something wrong with Megan. She is different."

"Mother, stop worrying. Everyone gets crazy sooner or later at sea. We are almost home; everything will be fine."

"I'm worried for her mental health, Kingston. She's never been

aggressive before."
"If it will make you feel better, I will talk to her, Mother."
"Yes, yes you talk to her, Kingston. You two have always been close. I'll feel a lot better if you talk to her."
"I will go now, Mother."
"Thank you, dear. I will feel a lot better knowing you have seen her."

It took Kingston only a few minutes to find his sister. How lovely she is, he thought, walking up to her. She will one day be a true beauty as Drella is. "Except, he smiled, Megan has a heart of gold where Drella can be stubborn and quite the bother at times.
"There you are," Kingston smiled at his younger sister.
"Kingston," Megan turned with a smile.
"Mother is worried about you."
"Why would she be worried about me?" Megan asked with her sweetest voice.
"She said you seem to be angry at something."
"I'm tired of being on this ship all day." Megan smiled. "I'll be glad to be home. But no," she turned her head with a smirk, "I'm not angry. I have noticed," she says, turning back to face him, "Mother has been acting a little strangely."
"What do you mean?" Kingston asked, sitting in the chair next to her.
"She's been acting, I don't know? She seems a bit paranoid about me turning out like Drella. I've tried to tell her we are nothing alike, but you know how she is. Megan laughed. "Once she has something in her head, it's there to stay."
"If there was anything bothering you would tell me, right, Meg?"
"Of course, Kingston. You would be the first person I would tell."
"That's good. Ok, I guess I'll see you at dinner."
"Ok. Megan smiled and turned back to her school lessons."

"She seems fine, Mother. I just talked to her. She is lonely for home and her friends. I think we're all ready to be off this ship."
"Yes, maybe that's it," his mother said calmly. "I'll go find her and talk to her. We had a misunderstanding yesterday and I don't want to leave it like it ended."

"That sounds like a good idea, Mother."

Fanton knew Megan's knock and waited at the bedside table as the door swung slowly open.
"Miss Fanton?" Megan whispered in the doorway.
"Come in, child, before someone sees you."
Megan quickly stepped in the door and closed it.
"What brings you here?" Fanton asked with a thin smile on her lips.
"It's my father. He said to meet him today, and when I went to find him, he wasn't there. I'm afraid," Megan couldn't help but cry. "He might not come again."
"Sit down, child. Fanton pointed to the side of the bed. "I have talked to your father."
Megan sat down gently, afraid to disturb the blankets. "You've talked to him?" she asks.
"Yes, this very morning. He said even though he misses you and wants to come home, he's very hurt that your mother doesn't want to see him. He's not sure what to do."
"He must come back," Megan cried out, taking hold of Fanton's arm.
Fanton looked at her arm and then back to Megan. Devastated beyond her fear, Megan shook Fanton's arm up and down.
"Please, help me. I need my father. Please, I'll give you anything," she begged. "Just tell me what it is you need."
Fanton watched as Megan came and went from hysterics. "You must stop now," Fanton finally told Megan. "You must catch control. Your father needs you to be strong if he's to return."
"You said if?"
"Your mother is a very strong-willed person. If she continues to not want your father to return, he may very well stay gone."
"But how can I change her mind?"
"I'm afraid; Fanton said coyly, "there may be no way to change her mind."
"Then what must I do?"
"You must break her will," Fanton said matter of fact.
"Break her will?"
"Yes, you must take from her the very thing that keeps your father from returning."

"Her will," Megan nodded her head confidently. Megan started to rise and sat back down. "I don't know how to break her will."
"I will tell you," Fanton reassured her. "But you must do exactly as I say. If you don't, your father will be gone forever." Megan nodded.

Megan leaned up against the wall under the stairway leading to her mother's room.
"No, Kingston, I haven't talked to Megan," she heard her mother say as she and her brother walked past the stairwell. "She's off by herself somewhere." Megan listened as their voices got farther away. Coming out from behind the stairs, she looked around cautiously before entering her mother's cabin. Going straight to the wardrobe closet, Megan pulled out gown after gown. Taking a pair of scissors off her mother's vanity table, Megan cut up her mother's gowns. Working fast and listening for any sounds outside, Megan was pleased with herself and the pile of gowns that lay destroyed on the floor. Replacing the scissors on the vanity, she opened the door, looking both ways before she rushed from the cabin. Making her way to Drella's cabin, Megan stood for a full minute catching her breath before she knocked on Drella's door.
"What is it?"
"It's me, Megan."
"What do you want? I'm busy."
"It's Fanton," Megan whispers loudly from the hallway.
Drella opens the door in a huff. "What are you doing?" Drella asked, opening the door with a click and pulling Megan into her cabin. "Do you want to get her caught?"
"You didn't open the door," Megan retaliated.
"What is it about Fanton?"
"She wants to see you."
"When?"
"Now!"
"What for?" Drella whined. "There's nothing she can do for me until we get home. It is Daniel's love I want, and he's not aboard the ship."
Megan looked past Drella. "Maybe she needs to start the spell now so it will be strong when you see Daniel?"
Drella looked at Megan. "Is there something wrong with you?"

"No," Megan snapped at her. "Why would you ask a dumb question like that?"

"You're acting strange."

"I am not." Megan turned and glared at Drella. "I am no different than I've ever been." Megan turned to leave. "I told her I'd give you the message."

"When did you talk to Fanton, Megan? We haven't taken her food in four days."

"I talked to her this morning."

"Why would you go alone, Megan? We promised we wouldn't go without each other."

Megan looked back at Drella. "She is making my wish come true."

Drella started to laugh and caught herself. "What do you mean, Megan? Fanton can't make your wish come true. Daddy is dead."

"She came back from the dead," Megan said flatly. "She'll be able to bring back Father."

"Megan," Drella reached out for her hand and noticed the bandage. "What happened to your hand?"

Megan looked at the bandage and shrugged her shoulders.

"Did Fanton do this to you?" Megan turned to leave. "Answer me, Megan," Drella insisted. "Did Fanton do this?"

"Leave me alone," Megan said, shaking free of Drella's hold on her arm.

"You tell me or," Drella puffed her body out, "or I'll tell mother and Kingston about her."

Megan stopped fighting and calmed herself. Walking back into the cabin, she took a seat on Drella's bed and patted the seat next to her. "I'm sorry, Drella," Megan said sweetly. "No, Fanton didn't do this to me."

"What happened?" Drella asked all concerned.

"It was . . ." Megan paused. "It was Mother."

Drella jumped off the bed. "What are you talking about? Mother wouldn't hurt you."

"I found her ripping up her gowns. All the ones Father had gotten her. When I tried to stop her, she caught my hand with the scissors."

Drella looked at Megan's hand. "You're lying. Mother didn't do that to you; it was Fanton."

"No, Drella, Megan tried harder to convince her. "Mother was angry

when I told her I had talked to Father and he was . . ."
"What do you mean? You've talked to Father?"
"Yes, I've seen Father," Megan stated calmly. "He misses me very much. When I told Mother he was coming home, she got very angry. She doesn't miss him like I do. She doesn't want him to come home. Father was very hurt when I told him about Mother. But Fanton said she can fix it so Father can come back for good."
Drella sat back down beside her. "Megan, Father is dead. When you asked Fanton about bringing him back, I thought she would have Mother meet a new man and we'd have a stepfather. I never thought she would convince you Father is alive."
Megan stood up and headed for the door. "Father is coming back, Drella, you'll see."
"No!" Drella screamed at Megan's departing words. "Father isn't coming back, he's dead. And I'll not have Fanton telling you otherwise."
Megan turned around calmly. "Let's ask her together."
Drella grabbed her shawl, and they went in search of Fanton.

Fanton smiled at the knock on the door. Without waiting for an invitation, Drella pushed the door open. With no fear of the consequences, Drella marched up to Fanton with her hand raised. "Why would you be so cruel as to tell Megan our father will be returning?"
Fanton looked past Drella to Megan, whose shoulders sagged.
"I didn't mean to tell her," Megan cried out behind Drella.
"You must choose now," Fanton screamed at Megan. "Will it be your father or your sister that survives?"
Drella's mouth dropped open as she turned to look at Megan. In Megan's hand was a finely carved knife. "What are you doing with that knife, Megan?" Drella moved beside Fanton's bed, still looking at the knife Megan held. Megan started to walk closer to her.
"Megan, stop this!" Drella cried out. "You're scaring me!"
Megan continued to get closer.
"Stop this at once!" Drella ordered. "What have you done to her?" Drella screamed at Fanton.
"I am giving her wish to her, Fanton laughed. "She wants your father and only your father. She cares nothing about you." Fanton

laughed again. "Everyone went on with their lives. The same as before he went away. Everyone except," Fanton smiles at Megan, "except for your sister, that is. She wants him back, and I have granted her wish."

"This is crazy. Drella backed even closer to the bed. He's dead."

"He's not dead to her. Fanton pointed at Megan's face. She can see and talk to him any time she wants. That is, without you or your mother's interference."

Megan now stood in front of Drella.

"I won't let you do this to her," Drella said with a confidence she didn't have.

"It's too late to change her destiny," Fanton smiled at the knife. Drella watched in horror as Megan plunged the knife into her stomach. Drella looked at Megan and flinched as a smile came across Megan's face. Fanton watched as Drella fell to the bed. Megan would get her wish. She had a heart of gold to change for the return of her father. That heart. Fanton laughed at Megan cleaning off the knife with a piece of cloth. That heart no longer existed. Blood gurgled from Drella's mouth, and her eyes closed.

"We must hurry," Fanton said, pulling the sides of the blanket over Drella's body. "We must return her to her room before anyone looks for her."

Megan helped Fanton carry Drella's small body back to her room. Listening and ducking behind staircases and into empty rooms, they finally opened her cabin door. Placing her on the floor, Megan dropped the knife by Drella's body. Ripping a piece of Drella's dress off that had blood on it, Fanton handed it to Megan.

"You know what to do with this." Megan nodded, and they left the room.

Screams could be heard all over the ship.

"What is it?" Kingston rushed to his mother's side.

"Drella," his mother points to her daughter's body, "she's dead, Kingston." She's dead."

Kingston pushed past his mother and knelt down beside Drella. What happened to her? Looking at the knife, he looked back at his mother.

"I don't know!" his mother cried out. "I came to call her for dinner."

Kingston looked at Megan standing in the doorway, shaking her

head no. "Megan told me you and Drella were having a horrible fight."
Megan's mother turned to face Megan. "Why would you say a thing like that? I haven't seen Drella in hours."
Megan looked up at her mother, and her mother reached out and smacked her across the face. "You did this," her mother yelled at her. "It was you."
Kingston grabbed his mother's arm before she could hit Megan again.
"She was with me," he yelled. "She came to find me because she said you lost control, and she was afraid you might hurt Drella."
"Why would I hurt Drella?"
"Because you haven't been yourself lately," Kingston answered.
"I am perfectly fine," his mother snapped, trying to release her arm.
"I've seen your room mother and now this. He pointed at Drella.
"I didn't do this," she screamed louder. "It was her!" She pointed at a weeping Megan. "She did this, Kingston. "You must believe me. I would never," his mother cried, "hurt my children."
"Mother, you have already killed once."
Kingston's mother crumbled to the floor. "That was an accident, Kingston. The baby wouldn't stop crying, and I was so tired. I asked it to stop, and when it finally did, the baby was dead. The doctor said I was overtired, remember. Your father knew I didn't mean to quiet him forever. Didn't he, Kingston? Didn't your father know?"
"Yes, Mother. Kingston rocked her. "Father knew it was a horrible accident."
Kingston picked up his mother and carried her out of the room, with Megan following, walking past the torn gowns and the bloody piece of material. Kingston placed his mother on her bed.
"You rest, Mother," he said gently. "I'll be right back."
Leaving a man in the hallway to ensure his mother didn't leave the room, Kingston took Megan to her own room.
"I must take care of Drella. Will you be all right for a bit?"
Megan hugged Kingston and smiled sadly. "What are we going to do, Kingston?"
"I don't know," he answered honestly. "But we'll get through this, Meg, I promise."
Megan hugged him again and watched him walk away.

"You are a very good girl," her father said, holding out his arms to her. Megan ran into them.
Kingston wrapped Drella in one of her silk blankets and tied it with twine.
"I'm sorry," he cried as he finished tying the last string. Carrying her out of her cabin, he walked on deck. None of his men approached but stood and watched as he lifted the bundle over the side of the ship and dropped it into the red silver water. With his head bowed and eyes closed, he prayed for her journey to heaven. Returning to his mother's room, he was unsurprised to find her in a deep sleep. He remembered after she had killed his little brother that she had slept for months. She awoke only to eat a little and cry herself back to sleep. Why she turned on Drella, wasn't certain. They always bickered but never anything to worry about. Covering her up with a blanket, Kingston kissed her head.
Kingston's mother opened her eyes as soon as Kingston closed the door. Sitting up in bed, she looked around her room. Walking to the door, she quietly peered out. The guard on her door was sleeping in a chair leaned up against the wall. Opening her door enough to get out, she snuck over to Megan's room.
"It's all right, darling," Megan's mother heard a man's voice coming from Megan's room. "You did what you had to do. Now it'll be you and me forever." Megan's mother listened at the door. Drella would have told everyone about Fanton, and we couldn't risk that, now could we?"
"No, Father," Megan replied.
Megan's mother grabbed her chest and leaned against the wall. She knew his voice. She was married to him for almost 25 years. How can it be? She made her legs walk the distance to Megan's door and, with all her will, reached for the doorknob.
"You'll not hurt her, too, Mother." Kingston reached out and took her hand off the doorknob.
"It's your father, Kingston." He's in there."
Kingston could see the madness in her eyes now. "Mother, Father has been dead for a long time."
"No, Kingston, I heard him. He was just now talking to Megan. He's in there, Kingston."

"Did Father tell you to kill Drella, Mother?"
"Kingston," she gasped. "I did not kill Drella. It was Megan."
Megan opened her cabin door slowly. "Kingston, is that you?" she whispered.
"It's me, darling," her mother answered first.
"Please, Mother," Megan cried out. "Please don't hurt me. I'll do my studies without complaining. I promise to be better, Mother."
Kingston continued his hold on his mother."
"Let us in, darling. Kingston is here with me."
"Kingston?" Megan cries out again. "Are you there, Kingston?"
"I'm here, Megan."
"Megan opened the door the rest of the way. Her mother pushed past and rushed into her room.
"Where is he, Megan?"
"Where's who, Mother?"
"You know who I mean - your father." "Where's your father?"
Megan looked at Kingston and backed away from her mother.
"What are you talking about, Mother? Father is dead," Megan said, bursting into tears.
Kingston reached for his mother's arm before she could pin Megan into a corner. "Mother, leave her alone."
"No, Kingston. She was talking to him. I heard her with my own ears."
"Mother, listen to yourself. You're not making any sense."
Megan stepped closer to the door, and her mother lunged for her.
"No, you're not leaving until you tell me where he is."
Kingston reached for her, and just before he took her arm, something hit him hard on the head. He crumbled to the floor unconscious. Megan smiled at her father.
"Who are you smiling at?" her mother asked. Turning around, she looked into her husband's face. "Jeffrey?" she cried out.
"So you didn't want me to return?" he growled with hatred.
"I don't understand," she cried, clutching her throat.
"Maybe you'll understand this." He put a hand on her throat.
"Maybe it's time we traded places, Marian." You can come to this side, and I'll be with my little darling," he said, smiling at Megan.
Marian looked at Megan and then back at her dead husband. "What is this?" Marian thought. But she couldn't think clearly.

"Come," Jeffrey ordered. "You have a date with destiny. Taking her arm, he led her out of the room.
Megan ran to keep up with her father and mother.
"You didn't need me anymore, did you, Marian? That's why you didn't want me to come home?"
Marian cried real tears as he took her on deck. "I didn't know, Jeffrey."
"Megan was the only one who wanted me back."
"That's not true, Jeffrey. I wanted you. I've missed you so much."
"Stop your lies. I heard what you said to her. You called her cruel. You are the cruel one denying your own daughter of her father."
Standing by the deck, Jeffrey was almost glowing with a rich green aura.
"I didn't know it was you, Jeffrey, Marian pleaded. "Please don't do this she begged as he opened a gate that led straight to the water below.
"I will teach our daughter now," he laughed.
"You have taught her to kill her own sister."
"Drella was in the way," he laughed again. "Megan is my only concern. She will take care of Kingston and the house, and the treasure will be ours."
Marian watched as Megan looked up lovingly to her father. "I will not let you hurt another one of our children, Jeffrey. You must return to where you've come from. The man I loved would not have hurt his children." Jeffery's look never changed. "You are not my husband," Marian screamed. "You are a creation from hell. My Jeffrey would not have done this."
Megan became concerned. Her father was starting to disappear before her eyes. "No, you will not take him away from me," she yelled at her mother. "Throw her over, Father. Throw her over."
"You must help me, Megan. I am still not strong enough." Megan reached for her mother, and her mother stopped fighting. "I will not fight you, Megan," Marian smiled lovingly at her daughter holding out her arms. "I will not fight you, darling."
Megan walked into her mother's open arms. Holding her tightly, Marian walked toward the open gate. "You are not my Jeffrey," she tells him again. "And you will not destroy my children with your lies and deceit."

Kingston watched in horror as his mother jumped overboard with Megan in her grasp. "No!" he heard Megan scream as she was dragged over the side of the ship with her mother. Kingston rushed to the gate and looked for any signs of his mother and sister. Men came from everywhere on the ship to see what the commotion was. No one approached or spoke as they watched Kingston fall to his knees in grief.

Chapter 13
Going Home

"We will be home tomorrow," Kentar tells Henasee, scaring her out of her thoughts. "Are you not excited to see your parents?" he asked when she doesn't look at him.

"I will be happier at home than here," she said flatly, and stood and left the deck.

Kentar wanted to explain, but her hatred for him would keep her safe. His feelings would only be the death of her. Knowing how deeply Fanton can hate, he watched with a broken spirit as Henasee walked away.

"You are excited enough for the both of us," Daniel laughed at Magnus.

"Help me, Daniel. I can't get this over my stomach."

"Our children do not want to be contained," he laughed, helping her pull her dress over her huge stomach.

"It will be much easier if I look the part of a lady to my parents."

"You mean easier to introduce me?" he asked.

"Well, that, too." She laughed at his question. Having a daughter with beauty one minute and none the next may be a bit of a surprise for my mother. She raised me to be very prim and proper."

"I would say she did a very good job raising her daughter." Daniel kissed the back of her neck.

"Stop that." She shooed him away. "I mustn't look tussled."

"Tussled," he laughed. "That's a good name for it."

"Daniel," she pushed at his hands. "I need to look my best."

"Darling, I have never seen you look better. Your parents will love their grandchildren when they are born. They will be proud of their only daughter, and they will welcome me with open arms. What more can we ask for?"

Magnus went quiet. "You do think they'll be happy for us, don't you?"

"Yes, darling, I think they'll be happy for us."

"There they are!" Magnus waved at Henasee's ship. Although she

could see the ship in a distance daily, it was not the same as seeing Henasee or being able to talk to her. "I have missed her so much."
"I know you have, darling. Soon you'll be spending time with her and your mother. You will be setting and talking over all your adventures."
Adventures," Magnus sighed. "Now all I want for my family," she patted her stomach, "is to live a boring everyday existence as a normal family."

"Oh, darling," Daniel laughed, "we will never have a boring or normal life."
"That's not what I mean. I mean Fanton."
"Let's not ruin our day, darling, talking about her. Let's set our sights on our new life together."
Magnus smiled at Daniel. "Yes, our new life together."

Henasee saw Magnus on the deck standing next to Daniel. Oh how she wished she were arm in arm with Kentar, waiting to greet her parents with a love long-lasting. But that is not meant to be. As Henasee waved at her friend, tears ran down her cheeks.
People came from everywhere to watch the two ships that were said to have been to Noteese come into the harbor. Magnus and Daniel smiled and waved at the mob of people waiting on the docks. Magnus searched face after face, but the growing crowd made it too hard to spot her parents.
"We'll find them." Daniel squeezed her to his side. "They have no idea you're on board the ship."
Magnus's shoulders drooped. "I had almost forgotten. My parents must think the worst has happened to me by now."
"We will explain together, darling. You're not on your own, Magnus. You have me and them." He laughed, putting a hand protectively on her stomach. "You are no longer a little girl that can be scolded. You are my wife. And I will have no one treat you badly. Not even your parents."
Magnus looked over at Daniel. For the first time in months, she felt safe. He was no child; he was a man. He was her man and he would protect her and her children with everything he was. "Yes, Daniel," she smiled.

Walking off the boat to cheers and good wishes, Daniel held tightly to Magnus's hand. Uncle Bernard and Ahaira walked closely behind.

"Let's get you settled, and I will fetch your mother and father," Bernard said to Magnus. Daniel nodded. Daniel helped Magnus into a waiting wagon and climbed in behind.

"What about Henasee?" she asked, alarmed.

"It will be hours before they dock, darling. I will leave word where she can find you."

"Thank you," she answered.

Magnus couldn't believe how such a short walk from the wagon to the room could tire her out.

"Let's get you settled, darling," Daniel said, concerned for her.

"You rest," he says, pointing for the maid to pull back the blankets on the bed.

The young maid smiled and asked, "Is your baby due soon?"

Magnus smiled back. "No, they have two more months, give or take a week." She smiled at Daniel.

"Two?" the girl acts surprised.

"Yes." Magnus sat on the bed. "I'm having twins."

"I've never seen twins."

"I've never seen twins, either." Magnus laughed with Daniel. "But it looks like I soon will."

"My, twins. What a blessing." The girl gushed and finished getting Magnus ready for her nap.

Magnus smiled at Daniel. "Yes, what a blessing," she repeated.

Daniel kissed Magnus on the cheek. "Now get some rest, darling. It's going to be busy when your parents get here."

"Daniel?"

Daniel smiled. "Yes," he whispered in her ear. "Your beauty has returned."

"Oh," she sighed. "I want to tell my mother before she sees it for herself."

"She will think you're beautiful, no matter what, darling."

"Thank you." She smiled at Daniel and closed her eyes.

"Bernard!" Magnus's mother came across the parlor in a mad dash. "I heard you have returned. Is there any word of Magnus?" she asked, sobbing. "We have searched everywhere, and no one has any word on her or Henasee's whereabouts. You are our last hope." She cried, taking his hands.

"She is safe." Bernard caught her before she fell to her knees.

"Thank you, my lord," she cried out.

"Come sit," Bernard coaxed. "I will tell you about her."

"Bernard!" The door flew open, and Magnus's father was at his wife's side. "What has happened? You've no information on Magnus?"

"No," his wife cried openly. "She is safe. Our Magnus is safe."

Magnus's father sat his wife down on the sofa. "You have seen her, Bernard?"

"Yes, she is resting at the inn."

"Is something wrong?" her mother cried, trying to stand, only to have her husband push her gently back down on the sofa.

"She is just tired after the trip. I will take you to her shortly."

"What happened, Bernard?" her father asked. "Was she kidnapped?"

"No," Bernard answered. "You know Magnus. Once she gets something in her head, it's hard to stop her."

"You said she's all right?" her father asked again.

"Why didn't she come home?" her mother asked Bernard.

"There are some things she needs to tell you first."

"Bernard," her mother begged, "you're not lying to us?"

"She is all right." Bernard smiled at his brother and sister-in-law. "Magnus is better than she has ever been."

"Please, can we see her?" Magnus's mother pleaded.

Magnus felt better after her rest. Daniel, she can see by the dress lying across the sofa's back, was very busy while she slept.

"I wanted you to look your best for your mother."

"Thank you, Daniel."

Mandy, the young girl who helped her get ready for her rest, appeared behind Daniel. "If you would like, I can help your wife get ready for her visitors."

"Visitors?" Magnus looked to Daniel for answers.

"Your parents are here, darling. Do they know about you?"

"Yes, Bernard filled them in quite nicely on the ride over."

"Do they know about them?" She looked at her stomach.
"No, he thought you might want to tell them yourself."
Magnus smiled shyly. "I think they may guess on their own." Daniel laughed.

"No I will not wait until she's ready to see me," Magnus laughed, hearing her mother's voice.
"You may move aside, Bernard, or I will go through you. It's your choice. No one is going to stop me from seeing my daughter."
"Honey," Magnus smiled at her father's voice. "She will be out in a moment." "You will have your brother move this instant," Magnus's mother screamed through the door.
"Daniel," Magnus laughed, "will you invite my mother in please?" Daniel bowed and opened the door. "Magnus is ready for you."
Magnus's mother waited no longer. She pushed Bernard with all her might, barely moving him and slid through the doorway.
"Magnus," her mother cried from the doorway. "Is it really you?"
"Mother," Magnus replied, "I have missed you so much."
Magnus's mother was by Magnus's side in less than five steps.
"Mother," Magnus cried in her arms.
"Oh, darling. I thought we lost you forever."
"I'm sorry. I betrayed you and father."
"No, let's not talk of that now, you're home and you're safe. Daniel," her mother continued to cry. "He seems like a nice young man."
"You do like him, don't you?" Magnus cried in unison. "I love him so much, Mother."
"I'm sure we will love him the same, darling. Are you all right? Nothing bad happened to you?"
"It's a long story," Magnus cried, holding on to her mother.
Magnus's mother pulled back for a second and looked down at Magnus's stomach. "You are with child?"
Magnus let the tears continue to slide down her cheeks. "Yes, Mother." She pulled the blankets from her stomach. "I am with two children, Mother."
The men smiled at each other, listening to the two women yell out their happiness from the bedroom.
"I think this calls for a drink," Bernard announced and headed for

the brandy.
"I wholeheartedly agree, my brother."

"Count me in," Daniel followed behind Bernard. "This could be a very long night."
"I don't think you should plan on leaving anytime soon," Bernard laughed. "Magnus can use the cheering up."
Magnus's dad joined the two men at the bar. "Bernard has told me a little about this Fanton. He says she will be here in less than two weeks."
"Yes." Daniel becomes serious. "We must find a safe place for Magnus and the babies to be born."
Magnus's father stopped his drink in midair. "Babies?"
"I'm sorry, sir." Daniel looked at his drink. "I'm sure it would have been better to come from Magnus."
Magnus's father shed a tear and Daniel smiled at his future father-in-law. "That's how it hit me when Magnus told me about them."
Magnus's father reached out his hand, and Daniel took it and shook it, never looking away from his face. "I love her, sir."
"And I'm sure she loves you, too," he replied. "No one on earth could have gotten her to the altar if not for her undying love."
Daniel beamed from ear to ear.

Magnus was getting tired just from listening to her mother talk about the things she'd bought for her and the babies. When her husband took her aside when they returned home the night before and told her Magnus was in danger and must hide, she began to plan. "I will leave her safety up to you and Daniel. I am going to care for my daughter and our grandchildren." She laughed and then cried in her husband's arms.
"Your father said we will be leaving tomorrow, and there are still plenty of things you and the babies will need up at Chainridge. No harm will come to you at your father's childhood home. There are not many who have ever heard of it. Your father sent ahead to make sure it was aired and cleaned before we arrive."
Magnus smiled at her mother. "Thank you."
Her mother sat by her side. "It is I who am grateful, Magnus. You

tried to tell your father and me you weren't happy, but neither of us listened. That horrible boy we introduced you to. He made such a fuss after you came up missing. Then he went and married Kelley Maine's daughter. You remember little Joley."
Magnus cringed.
"I know, darling. Kelley told me in strictest confidence how horribly he treats poor Joley. I am so sorry we thought he would be a suitable husband for you."
"You didn't know," Magnus cried.
"I can't imagine how it might have been if you had married him instead of Daniel."
"Did someone say my name?"
Magnus smiled through her tears. "I was just telling my mother how lucky I am. How lucky we are."
He smiled at the two women. "Bernard will be here, darling. I'm going down to meet Kentar."
"Henasee?"
"Yes, darling, I will make sure she knows where you are. Your father is waiting with her parents at the dock." Magnus looked at him. "I'll make sure she's ok, darling."
"Thank you." She smiled.

Henasee picked up the gown she threw in the corner months ago and placed it on the bed. She slowly took off the boy's clothes she had been wearing and replaced them with the gown. Combing her fingers through her hair, she left her cabin for the last time. Waiting on deck was harder then she thought it would be. This was probably the last time she would ever see Kentar.
Even the men on board seemed sad the trip was ending.
"You take care of yourself, Henasee," one of the sailors told her, walking by with a heavy wooden box.
"Stay out of trouble if you can." Another one laughed, waving from one of the sails.
"It won't be the same around here," another sailor whistled sadly.
"You are a fine cook, lad." Jage patted her on the back. "We'll miss that apple stuff yah been making us."
Henasee smiled at them all. She would miss everyone on board. But especially she looked over at Kentar with a broken heart. Especially

him. Kentar turned to look at her and smiled.
Not returning his smile, Henasee walked to the other side of the ship. "It's time for you to go ashore, miss." Jage pointed to the ramp. "Will you be needing help getting off?"
Henasee almost laughed. For months, she had been treated like one of the men. Now because of a dress, she was a lady waiting to be led ashore. "What would you do if I said yes? she laughed at Jage.
Jage's ears turned red. "I'm not sure, he laughed uncomfortably.
"Then I won't." She smiled and kissed his cheek. "Thank you for everything, Jage."
"It is I who must thank you, miss."
"Not miss," she corrected. "I'm Henasee."
"Thank you, Henasee." He smiled back.
"You're welcome." She curtsied. Jage's ears were fully red by now.
Henasee took a step and stopped one last time to look around the ship. Turning back to the ramp, she started to run when she saw her mother with a handkerchief dabbing at her eyes.
"Mother! she cried out.
"Henasee!" her mother cried in return.
Both women fought to get past boxes and sailors to reach each other.
"Oh, Mother," Henasee cried in her arms.
"You're safe, darling. You're safe."
"So much has happened."
"I know, darling. Bernard has told us. How scared you must have been. Your father and I never stopped looking for you. I knew you'd come home to us. I just knew it."
"Henasee?" Henasee turned to see her father standing with his arms open.
Henasee couldn't believe this was the tough-spoken man she had always feared. His hair, instead of brown as she remembered it, was now almost completely gray. Instead of an angry growl on his lips, tears ran down his face. .
"Father," she cried, leaving her mother's arms to be engulfed in her father's arms. "Oh Father. I did not mean to leave and worry you and Mother."
"I know, Henasee. I know you were trying to protect Magnus. Bernard told us you were quite the hero."
"Henasee held on to her parents' arms as they left the ramp and got

into a wagon to head for home. Henasee paused at the wagon and looked up at the ship. Kentar smiled and waved one last time at her. "Come, dear," her mother took her hand. "It's time to go home." Henasee nodded at Kentar and got in the wagon.

"You have two of everything," Magnus laughed at her mother. "If you're going to have two babies, you need two of everything, darling."
Magnus loved being with her mother and she couldn't remember why she ever wanted to get away from her.
"I wish there was a way of telling if they are boys or girls," her mother laughed. "It would make preparing so much easier."
"Ahaira says they are both girls."
Magnus's mother looked up from the pile of baby clothes she was folding. "Do witches know such things?"
Magnus laughed so hard it hurt. The mother she used to know would have squealed at the idea of a witch guessing anything about her grandchildren.
"She seems to know a lot about a lot of things." Magnus laughed trying to stand up.
"I haven't pried, Magnus, but..."
"But what, Mother?"
"Your beauty - you said it comes and goes?"
"Yes, I'm surprised I've had it for these last few days. It comes and goes a lot more."
"Maybe it will stay?"
"That would be wonderful, Magnus smiled. "But as long as the curse is still alive, it will probably come and go."
"How bad does it get, honey?"
"It gets bad," Magnus said, looking in the mirror. "I never thought anyone would want me. Let alone love me without it. But Daniel treats me the same with or without it. Sometimes he waits to tell me it's gone or back."
Her mother smiled at her. "He does love you. It shows in his eyes."
"I am very lucky I found him."

"You're going to have a baby?" Henasee cried from the doorway.
"Oh, Hen," Magnus cried, turning to see her beautiful friend.

"No one told me you were going to have a baby."
"We're keeping it a secret," Magnus told her.
"Why on earth are you keeping it a secret? She's not dead, is she?"
Magnus shook her head.
"They killed her and buried her on Noteese."
"No, Hen." Magnus shook her head sadly. "Kentar and Daniel saw her getting on Kingston's ship. She used some kind of spell."
"Kentar knows she's alive?"
"Yes, he has since we left Noteese."
Henasee took a breath. "He changed after we set sail. He wouldn't even touch . . ." Henasee stopped and looked at Magnus's mother. He was so different.
Magnus shook her head. "He knew she would come for us."
Henasee let tears run down her face. "He was saving me."
Magnus took her friend in her arms.
Henasee pulled away. "What are you going to do? She pointed at the babies' safe in Magnus's stomach.
"We are going on a trip" her mother chimed in. "We are going on a very long and safe trip."
Henasee smiled at Magnus. "You're going to have a baby?"
"Two babies, her mother laughed. "Magnus is having twins."
"Twins?"
"I know," Magnus smiled. "It's like a dream."
"I'm glad it all worked out for you and Daniel, Mag."
"Thank you, Hen. It's been quite the adventure." Magnus sighed. "Now it's time to grow up and raise a family."
Henasee turned away so Magnus couldn't see her new tears.
"I'm sorry, Henasee." Magnus took her hand. "I wish things would have worked out for you, too."
Henasee smiled. "Enough about me. Let's talk about those little darlings you're carrying in there. My mother will love that. Magnus laughed. "She has come up with list after list of names for them."

"We leave in the morning," Daniel told Kentar. "You'll meet Kingston's ship?"
"I'll find her, Kentar told Daniel. "Fanton will not get off the ship without me noticing."
"Then what?" Daniel asked him.

"Then I promise my undying love and try to get her to leave with me."

"That's got to be a sacrifice for you." Daniel watched Kentar's face change.

"I'll be all right."

"I saw how you looked at Henasee. You're in love with her." Kentar looked out over the water. "If I want her safe, I must do this."

"I see." Daniel smiled. "You're going to be with Fanton to protect Henasee."

"There's no other way. Fanton would move heaven and earth looking for Henasee."

"You mean Henasee and Magnus," Daniel corrected him.

"You'll have to keep your wife safe."

"Nothing or no one will touch her," Daniel promised.

"I believe she is in good hands, Daniel. Bernard will take care of my business while I'm away. He's a good man. I would trust him myself if I needed to."

"Thank you, Kentar. You're probably saving Henasee's life."

"I only wish I could have told her," Kentar said, looking at a bird fly over them. "She thinks I'm cruel. I'm sure she hates me."

"She'll figure it out one day. You only have her best interest at stake. You are giving up your life for her safety. That is a strong price, Kentar."

Kentar shook Daniel's hand, and they parted ways.

"If you ever need me." Daniel turned to tell him, "tell Bernard. He's the only one who knows where we'll be."

"I will, Daniel," Kentar answered. "Good luck to you."

Chapter 14
The Pretend Wedding

Fanton held her knife at the sailor's throat. "I want you to drop the rowboat. If you move too quickly or try to alert anyone, I will see you dead. Now untie the rope."
"The man, knowing who she was, did as he was told. He lowered the rowboat slowly to the water."
"Now go!" She pointed over the side.
When the man hesitated, she cut his arm with her knife. Jumping from the pain, he glided over the side.
"Now row," she ordered. "If anyone sees us, you're dead."
The man let go of his arm, letting the blood run down his shirt and started to row. Once close to the shore, Fanton pointed to the beach. "Climb over and pull us ashore."
The man, weak from blood loss, climbed slowly over the side of the boat, grabbed the front of the boat, and started walking. Fanton stood without a word and swiped her knife across his throat. The man gurgled and fell dead in the water.
Fanton laughed at her good luck. She knew Kentar thought Kingston's ship was weeks behind them. But with his mother and sisters dead, Kingston pushed his men day and night to get home. Kingston set anchor, and his ship would be docking in the morning. Oh, how she wished she could see Kentar's face when he doesn't find her on the ship. She saw him and Daniel on the ledge the day she left Noteese. She knew Kentar well enough to know he was planning something for her return.
"You have lost, Kentar." She laughed into the night. "You have lost."
***
Henasee ran to the ship. "I know why you pushed me away," she whispered to Kentar's back.
"Then you know why you must leave," he answered without turning around. "She'll be here soon, Henasee, and she'll be coming after you and Magnus."
"I'm not afraid of her, Kentar. As long as you and I are together, we

can stand strong."

"She is a very dangerous woman. She will stop at nothing to get her revenge."

"There must be something we can do," Henasee said, touching his arm.

"I've known her a long time, Henasee. There is nothing we can do. If you won't stay away for yourself, stay away for me. If Fanton sees you with me, she will kill me on the spot."

Henasee took in a breath. "How thoughtless of me. I never once thought she would hurt you. I thought you were protecting me." Henasee turned to leave.

"Stop," he said, taking her arm and turning her around. "I only said that so you would go. You're in danger being with me."

"I want you, Kentar. I would rather have a moment in danger than to never have you touch me again."

Kentar looked at her face and then deeply into her eyes. "I feel the same. I have missed your touch, too."

Henasee moved slowly into his arms. Afraid he might pull away from her, she didn't look up. Lifting her face with his hand on her chin, he rubbed her lips with his thumb.

"I miss the touch of your lips," he said, as he rubbed them again. "I miss the touch of your hair," he said as his other hand glided across her hair. "You are so soft," he told her as he put his hand on her back and slowly moved it down to her waist.

Henasee willed him to kiss her with her eyes. Kentar looked at her with such caring and she closed her eyes for his kiss. When nothing happened, she opened her eyes. She could tell he wanted her, but he would not take the offer of her lips.

"We would have a beautiful night together, but it would change nothing, Henasee. Fanton will still be a danger tomorrow. We can't be seen together again. She must think you and I are a thing of the past."

Henasee touched his cheek and pulled out of his arms. "You are right, Kentar. I see what you mean now. We can never be. Fanton would destroy me and you for her revenge. Nothing good can come from anything between you and me. I will not look for you again," she told him and turned and walked away.

"It is for the best," he said to her retreating body. "You be safe,

Henasee."

"You, too, Kentar," she said never looking back.

***

"I'll be fine, Magnus. I'm not going to hide from Fanton the rest of my life. You have Daniel and the babies to protect. I will be fine. Fanton will not bother with me when she sees I am not with Kentar."

"I'm so sorry, Hen," Magnus cried, taking her hand.

"It wasn't meant to be," Henasee sighed, smiling sadly at Magnus. "I will survive."

"You will survive, Hen. You've grown so much this last year."

Henasee smiled at her beloved friend. "It has been a long year, hasn't it?"

"I'm so sorry I got you caught up in my web of lies and deceit, Hen."

"I'm over being mad at you," Henasee laughed. "I had an adventure of a lifetime, and now my adventure is over. It's time to figure out what I'm going to do with the rest of my life."

"What do your parents think?"

Henasee's smile grew bigger. "I am a very rich young lady, and they think I can decide for myself."

Magnus hugged her friend. "You'll find someone to love, Hen."

"Not right away," Henasee told Magnus. "My heart is still with Kentar."

"It's time to go darling," Daniel said from the doorway.

Magnus stood and hugged Henasee. "I will miss you."

"I will miss you, too, Magnus. My letters will come from Jeannie Pradue."

Henasee laughed. "Where did you get that name from?"

"I'm not sure. It just sounds so mysterious."

"That it does." Henasee laughed again.

Magnus settled in the carriage next to her mother. "Are you ready, dear?" her mother asked.

"I'm ready for a new adventure," Magnus smiled.

The days were long and the nights uncomfortable, but Magnus didn't complain. The trip to Chainridge was more than two weeks long. But the farther she got from Fanton, the safer Magnus would feel for her babies.

"Are you ok, darling?" her mother asked when Magnus moaned in her sleep.

"The babies have decided not to sleep tonight," Magnus moaned again.

"Here." Her mother sat up and began to rub Magnus's lower back. "That feels great."

"Your father rubbed my back many nights when I carried you. It relieves some of the pressure from the babies."

"Thank you," Magnus told her. "This always helped me. Not just for my back, mother, but for you and father coming with Daniel and me. I sure got everyone in a mess, didn't I?"

"Oh Magnus, you didn't mean for anyone to be in danger. You were making your destiny."

"Yes, but look at us. We're running for our lives."

"Magnus, I went through months of thinking I may never see you again. I had a lot of time to reflect on the things I did wrong. Following you to Chainridge to help raise my grandchildren is the only place I want to be now."

Magnus sniffed.

"Your father and I are very proud of you. You followed your dreams of Noteese. Now you're getting ready to start a family. You should concentrate on the joy you're going to bring people and less on our misfortunes."

Magnus laughed at her mother's way of saying an evil witch is out to get them. "I'll try." She smiled at her mother. "I will try."

Henasee watched from a distance as Kingston's ship docked in the harbor. Waiting with her father, she was surprised that, after half an hour, Kingston's mother and sisters hadn't run off the ship.

"I thought they'd be the first to leave the ship," she told her father. "I can't wait to see them. They were very kind to me at Noteese."

"It's a shame," a passerby said to his friend. "Yes, his whole family dead."

"Who's dead?" Henasee asked the stranger.

"Kingston's sisters and mother are dead. It seems the mother killed her daughters and then killed herself."

Henasee would have buckled to the ground if not for the support of her father. Shaking free from her father's hold, Henasee started to run. Pushing and shoving past people, she ran onto the ramp.

"Kingston?" she yelled at the first sailor she saw.

"He's over there," the man pointed.

Henasee lifted her skirt and rushed to him. Kingston saw her out of the corner of his eye and sent the sailor away he had been talking to. He had just seconds to open his arms before she was in them.

"Your mother is dead?" she cried.

"She jumped overboard taking Megan with her."

"And what of Drella? She's dead too?"

"My mother stabbed her in the chest."

"No, Kingston! Your mother didn't kill them!"

"I saw her take Megan over the side of the ship."

"It wasn't your mother."

Kingston pushed her back. "It was my mother, Henasee. I watched her jump overboard hanging onto Megan."

"Fanton is on board."

Kingston looked as if he'd seen a ghost. "Fanton? She's dead on Noteese."

"No," she hastily corrected him. "Kentar and Daniel saw her board your ship at Noteese. Some kind of spell brought her back from the dead."

Kingston's face changed from grief to anger. "Daniel and Kentar knew she was aboard my ship and said nothing?"

"They didn't think she would hurt anyone."

"She killed my family," Kingston screamed out, turning some of his men's heads. "If I would have known, I might have been able to save them. My mother tried to tell me something was wrong with Megan. I even thought she was acting strange. But I did nothing, and now they're all dead."

"I am so sorry, Kingston."

"It was not your fault, Henasee. You have been a victim like me. But Kentar and Daniel, I will never forgive. They helped kill my family, and I will never forgive them for that."

Kingston looked up and started to run. He hit Kentar so hard with his weight that they both flew into the water.

"No, Kingston, stop," Henasee screamed. "He must find Fanton."

Hearing her name again, Kingston swam to shore. "The witch is on board," he yelled to his crew. "Find her! I want her brought to me now."

His men scattered about the ship looking for Fanton. Kentar pulled himself on shore and stood.

"I will not fight you now, Kentar," Kingston yelled from the deck of his ship. "But be warned. The next time I see you, I plan to kill you on the spot."

Kentar nodded. He heard on shore about Kingston's mother and two sisters dying. He knew Fanton was to blame without anyone telling him. He would never forgive himself for not warning Kingston that Fanton was on board his ship.

"You can go to him now," Kingston snapped at Henasee. "I know you are with him."

"No," Henasee answered him. "Kentar and I are not a couple. If it's all right, I'd like to stay here with you." Kingston took her hand.

***

"Chainridge is beautiful, Mother."

"Yes, it is, darling."

"Why haven't we come here before?" Magnus asked her mother.

"Your father has never wanted to visit. He was unhappy as a child here, and when his mother passed away, he never came back."

Magnus watched out the window. Vines of reds and yellows had grown up one side of the house. "It is almost like a castle," Magnus told her mother.

"Yes, it is just as beautiful on the inside. Your children will love growing up here."

"Will it bother Father?"

"I don't think he's worried about it one minute. He's so proud of his pending grandchildren."

Magnus watched as maids and butlers scurried out the front door and formed a line. There were so many of them. She laughed as more people in uniforms paraded out the front door.

"Your father has always taken very good care of Chainridge. Most of the people working at Chainridge have been here all of their lives."

"It feels like a wonderful place to live," Magnus said as she looked over the manicured lawn. "It is most beautiful."

"Chainridge has its charm," her mother smiled.

***

Kentar wasted no time hunting for Fanton. Running from room to room, he looked under beds and in closets.

"You're sure no one seen anything?"

"No, sir," one of his men tells him. "She's not on board."

"One of the men has been missing since yesterday," one of Kingston's men told Kentar. "We noticed one of the boats was cut loose last night."

"We all thought Kane snuck out," one of the sailors piped in.

"We've been on board a long time. Not so strange for a man to sneak into town."

Kentar shook his head. Looking up, he saw Henasee consoling Kingston.

"She is not aboard," he walked over to tell them. "It looks like she went ashore last night."

Kingston looked as if he might strike Kentar, but he calmed down when Henasee placed her hand on his arm.

"Kentar will find her," she told Kingston. "That's what he does. He rescues unsuspecting people from Fanton."

"Kentar started to say something and thought better of it. Giving Kingston a minute to calm down, Kentar waited by the boat ramp.

"He wants something," Kingston says to Henasee. "He's going to ask you to watch out for me," she told him simply. "It is not safe for me now that Fanton is ashore. She wants me to suffer as I have made her suffer."

Kingston laughed. "You've made her suffer? She killed my family."

"I'm so sorry, Kingston."

"Fanton is a monster." Kingston held Henasee for a minute. Thank you for being here. I wasn't sure what I was going to do. I didn't want to go home alone. Our house was always so busy, with Megan and Drella running around. I'm afraid the silence will be deafening."

"I will help you through this, Kingston."

"Marry me, Henasee."

Henasee backed away from him as if she'd been slapped. "Why would you ask me to marry you?"

"Kentar will never be free of Fanton. You will never love another. I will not expect you to love me," Kingston continued. "By marrying me, Fanton will have no reason to harm you. She will see that you are not in love with Kentar."

Henasee watched as Kingston's face turns to pain. "I have a very selfish reason for asking you to marry me."

"What is that?" Henasee asked.

"I don't want to be alone," he said quietly. "I've always had them when I've come home, and the thought of having no one is too much to bear." Henasee watched as Kingston broke down in tears. "I'm sorry. I know I should be a man about this, but it hurts so much."

Henasee returned to Kingston's arms. "No one expects you not to feel the loss of your family, Kingston, no one. I will marry you."

"Kingston wiped at his tears. "I will make you very happy, Henasee, I promise."

"I'm sure you will, Kingston."

Kentar turned around and stared at the beach. He couldn't bear to watch Henasee in Kingston's arms.

"You needed to talk to me?" Kingston asked from behind Kentar.

"I need to ask you to watch out for Henasee. Fanton will try to harm her if she can."

"There is no need for you to worry about Henasee," Kingston stood tall. "As her husband, I will protect her from the witch."

Kentar looked from Kingston to Henasee.

Henasee nodded. "Yes, I've agreed to become Kingston's wife. I'm sure Fanton will be happy when she finds out my feelings are no longer tied up with you."

Kentar nodded in return and turned and left the ship. Turning, he looked at Henasee. "If you ever need my help, Daniel will know where to find me."

"I will be fine, Kentar," she replied and hugged Kingston's arm to her chest.

Kingston, Henasee noticed, is understandably a shadow of his old self.

"We must make plans," he laughed. "I want to be married and on our honeymoon by Saturday."

Henasee hugged him. "You must meet my parents."

"I will meet them this very day." He smiled at her, swinging her around the deck. "You have given my life back to me, Henasee. And I will make sure you are a very happy woman. We will build a home

and have a family."
"Henasee smiled and snuck a glance at Kentar's retreating figure. "You will be a good husband, Kingston. I'm sure of it," she whispered into his neck.
***
"How do I look?" Magnus asked her mother, patting at her crinkled gown.
"You look fine, dear," her mother said sheepishly. "I am sorry I screamed at your scar. I mean your lost beauty," her mother finished.
"Magnus smiled at the memory of two nights earlier. She had awoken from the twins moving around. Her mother, hearing her stir, woke and set up. She had taken one look at Magnus's face and screamed bloody murder. Daniel and her father stopped the carriage and wasted no time getting to her and her mother, only to find out her mother was screaming at Magnus's lost beauty.
"I am sorry about screaming at your lost beauty, my dear."
"Mother, I've told you not to worry about it anymore."
"Yes, I know, dear, but to scream at your own child is simply horrible."
"You didn't know it was me, Mother."
"You had warned me, Magnus. I should have been prepared."
"It's not something you can prepare for, Mother. I'm still not used to it myself."
"Well, your beauty is back now, dear."
Magnus laughed at her mother. "We wouldn't want to scare people at Chainridge, Mother." Her mother took in a breath. "I was teasing, Mother. Relax."
"Ladies, we are home." Her father bowed and opened the carriage door. "May I be the first to welcome you to Chainridge."
"It's most beautiful, Father."
"Chainridge has always had a charm about it." He smiled, taking his wife's hand.
"Thank you for bringing us here, Father."
"You are very welcome, my daughter."
Daniel moved in to help Magnus from the carriage. "You look beautiful today, my dear."
Magnus smiled into Daniel's eyes. "I feel beautiful today."

"Welcome!" an elderly man said as he rushed ahead of the growing line of servants. "Sir, it is good to see you."
"Lenard!" her father smiled extending his hand. "You have done well by the old place."
"Thank you, sir. It has been a privilege keeping Chainridge at its best."
"It seems you have well accomplished that."
"I am honored to do so, sir."
"This is my wife. This is my son-in-law Daniel and my daughter Magnus."
"It is my honor," Lenard said as he bowed to them all. "I have your rooms ready as you wished. If you'll follow me." Lenard pointed to the walkway. "I'll have your things brought in, shortly."
Daniel took Magnus's hand, and they followed her parents into Chainridge. Inside the house was beautiful with its stone walls and high ceilings.
"This is striking." Magnus looked from wall to wall. Her father pointed out pictures and told of their history. Magnus's mother laughed at their excitement.
"We should get her settled in. It has been a long trip."
Magnus's father smiled as he took Magnus's hands in his. "We will share many moments together at Chainridge. Your mother is right; you should rest."
Magnus hugged her father. "I will look forward to our time together, Father."
"This way, sir." Lenard climbed a huge winding staircase, drawing his hand forward for them to follow. "I've had your parents' room redone, sir. I thought you and your wife would enjoy the view."
Magnus looked at her father's reaction and smiled. A small tear formed at the side of his eye. Opening the door, Magnus could not believe the beauty of the room. Mahogany furniture matched the big poster bed. The fireplace was carved out of marble, and the windows had ceiling-to-floor white sheer curtains.
"This is lovely," her mother told her father, trying to take it all in.
"I hope you will be comfortable in here." Lenard bowed to her parents.
"This will be just fine," her father told him.
Magnus and Daniel followed Lenard down a long hallway. Opening

the door, Lenard stepped aside. "This is the east wing," Lenard said proudly. "Your father sent word of the children. This room has a lot of natural light. I thought this would be nice for you and your family."

Magnus looked around the light yellow room. The fireplace was set in a middle wall from the floor to the ceiling. A sitting area with light blue couches was arranged by the fireplace.

"I thought this would be comfortable." Lenard hurried to show them the couches. "I had these brought in from town."

Magnus rubbed the back of one of the couches. "They are beautiful, Lenard. Thank for your thoughtfulness."

Lenard's face filled with a smile. "Thank you, ma'am. Over here," he pointed to a door, "is a room for the children."

Magnus followed Lenard into the room. Its light lilac color was breathtaking.

"I've never seen a color this shade."

"It is lilac delight, Lenard laughed aloud proudly. "The decorator said it was all the latest thing."

"I can see why," Magnus gushed. "It is most becoming."

"We've had the babies' bassinets set up, but the rest of the decorating we thought you would like to do, ma'am."

Magnus was so touched, she hugged Lenard.

Not being used to acts of emotions, Lenard stood stiff-legged with a small grin on his face. "Mrs. Franchise, the decorator will be here at noon tomorrow. If that's suitable for you?"

"That is just fine," Magnus smiled back.

"I will leave you to rest. I'll send Corey into help you get ready. She is most reliable. I'm sure you will be very happy with her. We've also hired on two nannies. After talking with your father, we traced their backgrounds. Both come highly recommended."

"Thank you, Lenard. I'm sure they'll do nicely."

"If there's anything else you need, send word, and I will see to it." Lenard bowed and left Magnus and Daniel to look around their rooms.

"This is very nice," Daniel said, making one of the bassinets rock. "I can see you sitting in that rocker feeding one of our children." Daniel smiled at Magnus.

"I was thinking the same thing about you," she laughed back.

***

"Mother!" Henasee yelled from the top of the steps. "Will you please come here?"

"I'm coming," her mother laughed merrily. "I'm coming."

"I need your opinion on my dress. Should I wear the blue or the green?"

Her mother looked at both dresses. "I like the green one."

"Are you sure?" Henasee says, picking the dress up and placing it up against herself. "I want to look my best tonight."

"You will look beautiful, no matter what you wear. Your father and I are very excited to meet the young man who helped you at Noteese."

"Mother," Henasee whispers, "he is going to ask Father for my hand in marriage."

Henasee's mother almost fell to the floor. "My darling," she cried, "you have fallen in love?"

Henasee turned her head away from her mother's eyes. "I am very fond of Kingston, and I'm sure one day it will grow into love."

Her mother took her in her arms. "My baby is going to get married."

"Mother," Henasee pulled away a little. "We are going to get married on Saturday."

"Saturday? It's not possible, Henasee. There are too many arrangements that must be made."

"I know together we can pull it off, Mother. I've seen you organize lunches and dinners in a matter of days."

"Yes, but a whole wedding is much different."

"Then tomorrow we will start," Henasee said with conviction. "I am going to be married at the end of the week, and nothing will change it."

Henasee's mother shook her head and hugged her one more time.

Kingston arrived in a black formal tuxedo. Henasee's mother thought he was most good looking. With the introductions completed Henasee's mother smiled at Kingston.

"I will see what's taking Henasee so long. I know she wanted to look her best tonight."

Kingston smiled. "She is always most beautiful."

Both of Henasee's parents smiled in agreement.

"She has always been a lovely child," her father tells Kingston. Kingston followed Henasee's father into the sitting room, and her mother took the staircase to get Henasee.

Her mother took a moment to look at her beautiful daughter. The green gown made her light skin glow with freshness. When she turned to face her mother, they both teared up.

"You look lovely, my dear."

"Thank you, Mother."

Henasee took her mother's arm, and they took the steps together.

"I see you have found her," Henasee's father announced.

Kingston hurried to take Henasee's arm. "You look beautiful tonight," he told her in front of her parents.

Henasee's parents looked at each other and smiled. This young man was in love with their daughter, and it showed through his eyes.

"You look very handsome yourself," Henasee smiled back at Kingston. Henasee decided earlier that morning to be the best wife she could be to Kingston. He, like she, had been swept into Fanton's dealings. She was going to try to put the smile back on his face that she first saw him with.

Kingston relaxed and told story after story at dinner. "Would you like to take a walk?" he asked Henasee after they moved to the sitting room for dessert.

Henasee looked to her parents for an answer.

"A walk would be lovely tonight," her mother smiled. "I'll get your wrap."

Henasee smiled at her mother. Taking the wrap, Henasee and Kingston walked out into the gardens.

"Your parents are very nice."

"Yes, they are." She smiled shyly. "I'm not quite sure how to act around you, Kingston."

"I know, he laughed back. "I'm very attracted to you. He smiled, squeezing her hand.

"You are a very nice-looking man, she smiled back.

"Well, at least we have that in common."

"Have you changed your mind about us?" Henasee asked.

"No, I want us to marry, Henasee. You will be safe from Fanton, and I will have someone to come home to."

Henasee looked up in the sky. "Everything feels like a dream.

Noteese, Fanton..."
"You and I," he finished for her.
"If I am to marry, I'm glad it's not to some horrible person my parents picked out for me."
Kingston looked shocked.
"Did you think you were my only choice?" Henasee teased.
Kingston looked into her eyes.. "We will have fun together," he said taking her hand again and continuing their walk through the garden.

Chapter 15
Lies and Deceit

Fanton laughed at her reflection. She was more beautiful than ever with the blood she took from Megan. The spell Fanton used made her very youthful. No one would recognize her, she's sure, not even Kentar. Her hair was now a dark chestnut brown. But the biggest difference was her eyes. They were a very dark brown. Her skin looked as young as a teenager's. If not for her womanly figure, she could have been mistaken for a child. All together, she knew she was breathtaking. And from the looks of the men passing her on the walkway, she could have anyone or anything she wanted.

The first night off the ship was hard. But she secured a room in a bad part of town. Finding the ingredients to make her potion was even more difficult, but she finally found everything she needed. She slipped out of the inn late at night. She didn't want anyone to see the change in her. She was smart enough to take some of the rubies off the ship. So money was no problem.

Laughing to herself, Fanton headed to the nicest inn in town.

"I would like a room," she told the old man at the desk.

"I...," the man stumbled at her beauty. "I have a very nice room at the top of the hall. Do you have any bags?"

"No." Fanton looked behind her. "My things will be coming later."

Then the man said , sweat running down his neck, "I will show you to your room."

Fanton gave the man a full smile. "You have been most helpful."

The man smiled "Anything I can do for you, Madame."

Fanton took out a handful of coins and placed them on the counter. "I would be oh so grateful if you would see to a bath."

The man shook his head and came out from behind the counter. Picking up the coins Fanton laid down for him, he said, "I will see to it at once."

"And if you would keep my presence a secret, I will see to a handsome bonus for you."

Not waiting to answer, the man yelled for his wife.

"What are you yelling about?" A heavyset woman came from a back room.

"This," the man shushes his wife, "this is Ms… I'm sorry," the man says, turning to Fanton. "I didn't get your name."

Fanton pulled another handful of coins from her pocket. "I did not give it," she said placing the coins where she had placed the other coins on the counter.

His wife, seeing the money, hurried ahead.

"Stop pestering the woman, James," his wife snaps. "Show her to her room."

Fanton followed him down the hall. "This will do nicely," she told him, looking around the room.

"I'll send your bath right in."

"Thanks ever so much."

Fanton smiled, and the man scurried out of the room. Fanton was happy when the caretaker's wife came with the two men carrying the bathtub.

"I will need some errands done for me," Fanton told her. "Do you know of anyone I could use? I'm willing to pay nicely."

"I will run your errands, Miss," the caretaker's wife told Fanton. "James can run the inn. He's very good at it."

Fanton looked at the two men and back at the woman.

"I will fetch you some tea, Miss, and then get your list."

Fanton shook her head. She didn't want to discuss her needs in front of anyone who might spread the story she was here. Kentar, she knew , was very smart. He might figure out it was her. He knew she could change her image if need be. Using blood, she smiled to herself again, with the spell had never occurred to her before. The spell worked better than she could ever have dreamed.

The woman brought Fanton's tea, some towels, and an old cotton robe.

"I know this isn't what you're used to," the woman says, embarrassed. "But this is the best I have."

Fanton took the robe from the lady. "It will do nicely." Handing the lady a handful of money, Fanton put in her order for some clothes, shoes, and accessories to go with them. And she told the lady as she headed out the door, "Buy yourself a new robe, too."

The lady laughed and hurried from the room. "Thank you, miss. "Thank you."

Sitting down in the tub was the most relaxed she felt in weeks.
"Are you sure it's hot enough, darling?"
"Yes, Daniel. The water is fine."
"You have been through so much, with the ride here and carrying the babies. I just want you to relax and take it easy."
"Then you must learn to relax around me, Daniel."
"What do you mean?"
"You're a barrel of nerves, Daniel."
Daniel started to deny it and then sat by the tub. "I am a bit frazzled."
"Is it Fanton?" Magnus asked.
"No, no, no. It's the babies."
"The babies? Magnus asked surprised.
"Yes, being a father scares the demons out of me."
"Oh, Daniel," she laughed. "You are going to be a great father."
"How do you know? I never even knew who my father was."
"Because you're kind, Daniel, and you're generous. My parents already love and adore you. How couldn't our babies not adore you Daniel? They will love their father."
Daniel laughed, feeling better. "As they will love their mother," he said kissing her softly on the mouth.

Kingston entered the dining room in town. Looking around, he took a seat in the corner..
"Will you have a drink, sir?" his serving lady asked.
"Yes, I'll have a glass of white wine."
"A very plain drink for a man who looks like you," a voice said from behind.
Kingston turned to find the most beautiful woman he had ever encountered smiling at him.
"I beg your pardon?" he smiled back.
I said. I thought someone who looked like you would be drinking a more, let's say, manly drink."
Kingston laughed out loud. "I didn't know white wine was anything but manly."
The beautiful woman smiled back. "I am new in town." She tilted her head. "I've noticed you are dining alone. If I could be so bold, could I ask you to join me?"

Kingston hesitated.

"If you are waiting for your wife to join you I understand."

"No." He shook his head. "I'm not married yet. I mean I won't be married until tomorrow."

The beautiful lady smiled at him again. "Then for tonight you are still a single man."

"Kingston was so drawn to her that it was hard for him to take his eyes off her. "I guess there's no harm in sharing dinner together."

"Kingston stood and moved to her table.

"How about your wine? she laughed.

"I guess if I don't want my manhood questioned, I better order the best champagne in the place," Kingston laughed back.

"That was only a statement to get your attention," the lady purred.

"You have my attention, that's for sure. You said you are new in town?"

"Yes, she said politely. "I have some business to take care of."

"Kingston liked the way her hair hit the side of her neck. If he weren't marrying Henasee tomorrow, he'd have taken this one home with him.

"Dinner was lovely," the lady told him after their coffee arrived.

"The company was most delightful," Kingston replied. "I should be going," he told her and started to rise.

"If you would be so kind as to drop me at my inn," she requested.

Kingston looked around the room. Everyone else had already gone.

"It must be later than I thought," he said absentmindedly.

"Yes," the beautiful lady agreed. "That is why I asked for the escort."

"I would be honored," Kingston said with a nod of his head. Taking her arm, Kingston tried to ignore the beating of his heart. Beautiful women always made him feel empowered. This one was quite the exception. He wished for only one kiss from her. Then he would promise his faithfulness to Henasee. Yes, just one kiss was the only thought he had before helping her into his carriage and telling his driver to take them to his home.

She turned and smiled and licked her lips. "How do you know I want to come home with you?" she whispered in the carriage.

"You would have screamed your refusal when I said it," Kingston

told her, pulling her into his arms. "I wished for only one kiss," he said, releasing her. "But now I want more."
"What about your bride?" the beautiful woman asked before returning to his arms.
"She will never know," he answered. "She will never find out."
Stopping only long enough to get inside, Kingston carried the beautiful lady into his study. Sitting her on the sofa next to the fireplace, he slowly started to unbutton her dress. "You are most beautiful," he said as each button opened to show white creamy skin. She giggled and lowered her head back so he could kiss her neck.
"Your skin is the softest I have ever tasted," he whispered into her ear. "I have wanted to taste you all night."
Kingston rubbed her shoulders and then returned with his lips to travel down them.
"You are very good at what you know," she whispered breathlessly.
"It is easy when I have someone as beautiful as you. You have not yet told me your name," he said continuing his journey down the front of her gown with his lips.
"You will be married tomorrow. What difference does my name make?"
Kingston stopped for a second to see if there was anger in her words. When all he found was desire in her eyes, he pulled at the rest of the buttons on her dress and feasted his eyes on her bare breast. Hunger overtaking him, he pulled her to him. He was so engrossed in his desires he didn't hear the door to his study open.
"Kingston?" Henasee cried from the doorway.
"Oh my!" he cried back, trying to pull on his pants. "Henasee? What are you doing here?"
"I got word to come right away. I thought you were in danger."
"Why would anyone send word to you?"
"Henasee looked past him to the woman on the couch, who was half naked and not worried about covering herself up. "I see you are quite all right," Henasee snapped. "I'll leave you to your, your..."
Not knowing the right word to say, Henasee turned to leave.
"Please don't leave like this," he begged her.
"We were wrong to think we could marry, Kingston. You will always be a ladies' man, and I will always—"

"You will always love Kentar."
Henasee looked away.
"I didn't mean for this to happen," he told her.
"I know you didn't. I could not live as your wife while you were with other women, Kingston.
"I did not mean for this to happen, Henasee.
"I know you would not hurt me on purpose, Kingston but in the long run my heart would break being married to you."
Kingston followed Henasee to the door. He started to hug her, but she pulled away.
"It's for the best," she smiled sadly and walked out, closing the door behind her.
Shutting the door sadly, Kingston turned to find the beautiful lady gone and the outside door wide open. How can I blame her? he thought to himself. She must have been embarrassed. Taking his clothes, he headed upstairs to his room. Surprise and excitement came over him when he saw the beautiful lady lying naked across his bed.
"I thought you left."
"No," she laughed. "I only gave the illusion I left, just in case your bride decided to forgive you and stay."
"And what if I had brought her here?" He pointed to his bedroom.
"Then you would have missed this," she said sitting up and offering herself to him.
Kingston wasted no more time playing cat and mouse. He lifted her up into his arms and carried her to his pillows and let her down slowly. "Now this is where you should be," he laughed. Kingston made love to her over and over throughout the night. Never had he found such a knowing partner. If she would accept, he planned to ask her to stay for awhile.
"I will see to breakfast," he said after another lovemaking session.
"I am starved," she laughed, licking her lips.
"I will be right back."
Listening for him to leave, the lady reached for her purse and pulled a small gray bottle. Setting it behind a picture on the bedside table, she leaned back on the pillows. "It is a shame to kill you," she said, rubbing the top of her breast. You are a most enjoyable partner."
Kingston returned carrying a tray with a pot of coffee, some rolls,

and a jar of jam. "No one was up yet. I figured this will keep us for awhile."

The beautiful lady laughed. "You did well on your own."

Feeling his heart jump a beat, Kingston kissed her hand and set the tray between them on the bed.

"I would beg?" she asked shyly.

"You have only to ask, my beautiful lady."

"I take sugar in my coffee."

Kingston laughed out loud. "I will return in less than a minute."

She smiled and watched him leave. Reaching for the gray bottle, she turned the lid and poured the contents in Kingston's cup. Putting the bottle back in her purse, she waited patiently for him to return. Taking the sugar bowl from him, she kissed him tenderly on the mouth.

"What was that for?" He smiled at her.

"I have had a most unforgettable time."

"Kingston smiled and kissed her back. "That's what I want to talk to you about. He took a long drink of his coffee. "I would like to know if you might want to stay on a while?"

The beautiful lady smiled. "I wish I could, but I have other engagements to see to."

"But surely," Kingston said taking another drink of his coffee, "you could put the engagements off for a bit."

"I'm afraid it is not possible."

"But we've only just found each other," Kingston told her.

"I must be going," she told him. She stood up and started to retrieve her clothes.

"Can you come back this way? After you've finished your engagements?"

"It will be highly unlikely," she laughed, pulling her dress over her head.

"At least tell me your name," he asked.

"You already know my name." She laughed harder, tying her shoe.

"I do not know your name. You wouldn't tell me it."

"Aw, but you have a short memory. I am the one who killed your mother and sisters." She laughed out loud.

"Fanton?" Kingston cries out. "You can't be Fanton. You look nothing like her." Kingston tried to stand, but a wave of dizziness

fell over him. "What have you done?"
"I have sent you to be with your family," she laughed. "You should thank me. Now you will feel no more pain over their loss."
Kingston fell back on the bed choking and gasping for air.

"What do you mean he's dead?" Henasee asked her father.
"Last night. He was poisoned. The police are looking for the lady." Her father stopped. "I'm sorry, dear. It seems Kingston met a lady last night and took her home. They think the lady poisoned him."
Henasee sat on the sofa. "I went to see Kingston last night."
"You went over there? Why would you do that, darling?" her mother cried, coming to sit by her side.
"Mother I knew I shouldn't go, but the message sounded important. After everything Kingston has been through I knew he must need me to send for me so late at night."

"Jessy woke me right after midnight. She said a man came to the door with a message for me. It said that Kingston needed me to come right away. When I got there, he was with a woman. We decided marriage wasn't a good idea for the two of us. The lady was still there when I left. You say she killed him? Henasee asked, crying with her hands over her face.
"That's what the police are saying. They are looking everywhere for her."
"Do they know what she looks like? Maybe I should?"
"No, darling." Her mother put an arm around her. "I'm sure they have more than enough witnesses to find her. You would not be safe."
"This is crazy, Mother."
"Yes it is, darling."
"The lady who was with him," Henasee said taking her hands from her face. "She seemed proud to be caught. She didn't even try to hide herself from me."
Henasee's mother squeezed her shoulders.
"I just can't believe Kingston is dead," Henasee cried. "He didn't mean to hurt me when I found them together. Now he's dead? I don't understand."
"Who would do such a thing?" her mother asked her father.

"Fanton did this," Henasee answered with raw anger in her voice. "She must have hired the woman to kill him."
All heads turned as the butler came in the door.
"There is a man to see Miss Henasee at the door."
"Who is it, Niles?" her mother asked.
"He says his name is Kentar. He is waiting on the porch."
"Why didn't you let him in?" Henasee asked, moving like lightning.
"He is a most peculiar-looking man," Niles replied. We've never had anyone of his sort in the house before."
"Oh Niles. He's my friend." Henasee hurried to the door. "He didn't mean to leave you out here."
"I'm used to people not letting me in their houses, Henasee."
"Well you do look a bit frightening at times."
"Frightening?" he asked.
"You know, when you scowl like that."
"I don't scowl," Kentar replied.
"Henasee?" her father asked from behind. "Is everything ok out there?"
"Yes, Father. Everything is fine. It's a friend from Noteese."
"You have not had good luck with your friends from Noteese," her father answered.
"Father, please," she replied.
"Invite him in, Henasee. We do not visit with our guests on the front stoop."
Henasee looked back at her parents. Knowing they didn't plan to move until she invited Kentar inside, she asked, "Would you like to come in?"
Kentar nodded.
Henasee led him to the sitting room, with her parent's right behind her with their mouths wide open.
"I need a few minutes alone with him," she told her mother. "But we haven't even been introduced yet," her mother answered.
"I will introduce you in a while, Mother. Now please give me a few minutes."
Henasee's mother agreed and she and Henasee's father walked away.
"You are starting to stand up for yourself, I see."
"Nobody was going to do it if I didn't," she told Kentar.

"I came as soon as I heard about Kingston."
"They say the woman he picked up killed him."
"Yes, Kentar answered. "I think it was Fanton."
"No, I saw the lady. She didn't look anything like Fanton. She had brown hair and brown eyes. She couldn't have been any older than me."
"Fanton has many spells and potions to change herself with."
"Henasee sat down again. "I left her there with Kingston."
"Kentar crossed the room to be at her side. "You had no way of knowing that the lady was Fanton."
"She'll be coming for me soon."
"I know." Kentar placed his hand on hers. "That's why I have come. She knows the marriage was a fake. That's why she killed Kingston."
"They were . . ." Henasee tried to say it but couldn't.
"They were together," he finished.
"Yes," Henasee answered. "She was almost naked in front of me. Why?"
"She wanted to see if it bothered you. If it did, you were really in love with Kingston, and you and I were truly done."
"Kingston and I decided to call off the wedding in front of her. He said I would never stop loving you, and I said nothing."
"Kentar took a strand of hair off her face and tucked it behind her ear. "You said you would never stop loving me?" He rubbed her cheek.
Henasee looked at him and stood up. "I can't do this again, Kentar. One minute it's all right to love you, and the next it is not. I feel like my whole life is a jumping bean. It changes every few minutes. Is this the moment you take me in your arms and promise to be with me always? Or is this the moment you tell me we can never be together and you leave?"
"I was trying to save your life, Henasee."
"Because you're so much older and wiser," she yelled at him. "You are three years older than I am. You haven't lived the life as an adult much past me. I am not a little girl, Kentar, and I'm getting tired of you treating me like one."
"When you act like a child, I will treat you like a child."
"Henasee? her father yelled outside the door. "Is everything all right

in there?"
"Yes, Father. I'm sorry. We are just having a discussion."
"Well, if you need me," her father yelled through the door again, "I'm right outside, and so is Niles."
Henasee looked at Kentar and laughed.
"What are you laughing about?"
"I am picturing my father and Niles breaking down the door to save me. Niles is almost 70 years old."
Kentar laughed, too. "I might be in trouble."

"What do you think that young man wants?" Henasee's mother asked her father.
"I don't know. But I'm afraid this is the man she's been moping around about and not Kingston."
"Yes, I'm afraid you're right," her mother agreed, "She's not as upset as she should be about Kingston. Now they're laughing in there. What kind of a man is he?" her mother asked. "I've never seen anyone like him before, darling. He is so big and...
"Is the word 'handsome?' her husband baited her, and she smiled at him.
"Not as handsome as you are, my darling.
"That's much better," he said as he patted her hand. "Oh my goodness, Darling."
"What darling?"
"They will have beautiful children, won't they? her mother asked, worried.
"Let's not get ahead of ourselves, Francine."
"Yes, but Henasee said Fanton had something to do with Kingston's murder. She must think Fanton will be coming for her. What are we going to do?" her mother cried, almost hysterical. "What if that witch comes here and tries to hurt her?"
"Calm down, Francine. We're not going to let anyone hurt Henasee."
"But what if we can't protect her? You heard the stories of Kingston's family, and now he's dead."
"It won't do anyone any good if you start getting hysterical, Francine."
"What's the matter?" Henasee asked her father.

"It's your mother. She's afraid Fanton may be coming to harm you."
"Henasee looked at her father and then at Kentar. "That's what you think, too."
"That witch is coming here to harm you?" Henasee's father sat down beside his wife.
"What can we do?" her mother cried up at her.
"We're getting married."
"What?" Kentar asked at the same time her parents did.
"Yes, if Kentar and I marry, Fanton will follow us out of town. If not, she will come here to find me. I can't take the chance of you or Father getting hurt."
"You can't leave, Henasee. Your father and I aren't afraid of a witch."
Henasee smiled at her mother. "Kentar and I have fought Fanton and won before; we will win again."
Kentar, Henasee noticed, looked a little pale. "You have never married before?"
"No never," he answered.
"You look afraid," she told him.
"I'm not afraid of anything," Kentar answered.
"Good, then it's all set. You will take Kingston's place at the altar."
Kentar said nothing. His mind was too full for thought.
"Come, Mother. We must get ready for a wedding."
"What about the guests?"
"Only invite enough to get the word out after the ceremony. I want Fanton to hear of Kentar's and my wedding."

Henasee stepped back from the mirror and turned to her mother.
"You are the most beautiful thing I have ever seen, darling."
"I love him, Mother."
"Your father and I guessed he might be the one when we were listening in the hall."
"He loves me, too."
"We can see that, Henasee. It shows every time he looks at you."
"He only let me go so Fanton wouldn't come after me."
"We understand, darling. Once your father and I had your whole life planned out, and now we want only for you to be happy. If that means you are marrying Kentar, your father and I stand behind

you."

Henasee hugged her mother. "Thank you."

"You promise you'll be safe?"

"I promise, Mother. Fanton will not hurt what I have found with Kentar."

"I believe you," her mother said, hugging her again. "You have grown into a strong woman, Henasee, and we are very proud of you."

"Send my love to Magnus's mother. Tell her Kentar and I will take Fanton on a merry chance far from her and the babies."

Kentar returned in record time, dressed in a very stylish black suit and jacket. Henasee's father couldn't believe the difference in Kentar.

"You clean up nicely," he told Kentar.

"Henasee is worth the trouble," he told her father.

"We will trust you to keep her safe," he told Kentar.

"I will protect her with my life."

"I thought you might." Her father offered Kentar a drink. "The minister will be here in half an hour."

Kentar took his drink from Henasee's father with shaking hands.

"I was like that on my wedding day, too." He pointed at Kentar's shaking hands. "It's only one day out of the rest of your life."

Kentar looked at Henasee's father. "Was that day worth it to you?" he asked.

"I love my wife, and she gave me Henasee. Yes, it was well worth being nervous about it."

Kentar smiled and took a big gulp . "And," her father laughed, "my father-in-law to be gave me some very good brandy before the ceremony."

Kentar laughed back and took another big gulp of his drink.

Henasee walked slowly down the staircase with her head held high. Kentar looked at his bride, and his fears of their future dissipated. She was beautiful in her white flowing gown with a piece of lace draped over her face. Meeting her at the bottom of the steps, he took her hand.

"You are most beautiful," he told her.

Smiling into his eyes, she looked at him. "I love you, Kentar."
"I love you, too," Kentar answered, taking her arm and leading her into the drawing room.
They both were amazed at the sight in front of them. Lilacs of every color were everywhere in the room. Henasee smiled at her mother and father, who sat in chairs at the side of the flower-filled aisle. Looking to the side, she saw her mother's best friends. Turing her attention to Kentar, she smiled as he led her down the aisle.
Reaching the minister, they both turned and held hands.
"We are here," the minister began, "to join these two in marriage. We are in front of God and their families. If there is anyone who does not agree with this marriage, let them speak now."
A voice came from behind them. Henasee and Kentar turned to look. Standing in the doorway was the lady Henasee saw with Kingston the night before.
Kentar did not pause. He grabbed Henasee's arm and ran with her to the sitting room.
"We must leave," he told her.
"My parents?" She paused for only a minute.
"If we leave, she will follow."
"Henasee ran with Kentar to a side door, and he placed her in their wedding carriage.
"Trust me," he told her.
"I was going to make you my husband. I trust you."
Kentar lifted her up into the carriage and jumped to the driver's seat. The carriage rushed off down the dirt road.
"You are not welcome here, Henasee's father yelled at the woman who entered their home. Fanton turned without a word and left the house.
Henasee's mother cried out her name.
"No," her father told her. "He will protect our daughter. She will be safe with him."

Chapter 16
Children

Kentar didn't stop the carriage for hours. Knowing if he drives the horses too hard they would fall, he stopped the carriage by a creek. Opening the door, he expected to find a crying Henasee. But she was fine.

"That was close," she smiled coming out of the carriage.
"You seem to be handling this fine," Kentar told her.
"My family is safe now," she said climbing out of the carriage.
"I thought the marriage would do that."
"No," she said heading to the creek. "I figured Fanton would come to the wedding. I wanted her to leave my family alone."
"So!" Kentar followed her to the creek. "It was never your plan to marry me?"
"You left me time and time again, Kentar. What was I supposed to do? Trick you into being with me? I am better than that," she said, taking off her lace hairpiece. "If I told you we were going to trick Fanton, you would have said no."
Kentar looked at Henasee and back at the creek. "You are smarter than I thought."
"I am a lot more than you thought, she said, pulling the skirt from under her dress. "I needed to protect my family, and I did. Unlike you, Kentar, I protect what I love, not run away from it."
Kentar turned and brought the horses to the water. "I thought we would be married," he told her.
"Kingston asked me and believed he wanted to marry me. You walked away from me and never looked back at my feelings. No, Kentar, I'm glad I did not marry you. You are a runner, and I need someone who will not throw my love away so easily."
Kentar said nothing and handled the horses and helped her back into the carriage. Jumping back atop the carriage, he headed away from town.

"You're sure you want me to get your mother?"
"Yes, Daniel," Magnus groaned again. "Get my mother."
"I thought the babies had three more weeks before they would

come."

"Daniel," Magnus growled, "I need you to get her now."

Daniel looked at Magnus's face and got out of bed. "I'll get her now."

"Yes, Daniel, get her now!" Magnus told him. "Now!"

Magnus's mother came quickly to her room. "Is it time, honey?"

"Yes, Mother, it's time."

Her mother turned to Daniel. "Send up Sally and Mary. Tell Lenard to boil water and send for the doctor."

Daniel didn't take the time to dress but rushed from the room in his robe and slippers.

After telling Lenard the orders, Magnus's mother gave him, Daniel sat at the table.

"This is the hard part." Her father came from the hallway. "Waiting is as hard as having the baby I think."

"Yes," Sally laughed taking hot water from the stove. "Waiting is most painful."

Daniel and Magnus's father watched her leave the room.

"What did she mean?" Daniel asked Magnus's father.

"I'm not sure, but my wife's mother said the same thing when Magnus was born, and everything went just fine.

Happy to have each other, the two men sat at the table waiting for news of the babies being born.

"You're going to have to push, Magnus," her mother ordered.

"But the doctor isn't here."

"I will be here, Magnus. You must trust me."

Magnus looked at her mother and cried from the pain.

"Push," her mother ordered. "Push now."

Magnus looked past the pain and pushed down with all her might.

"I can see the head, darling," her mother told her. "Now push one more time."

Magnus bore down and pushed again.

"Yes, that's good, darling. Her mother took the baby and smiled at her daughter. "It's a girl, darling. You have a baby girl.

Magnus looked at the baby her mother handed to Sally. "Is she ok?"

"Darling, she's perfect. Now we must get your other baby out."

Magnus screamed from the pain. "I can't do it."

"You are strong, Magnus. You push," her mother screamed at her.

"Push now."
Magnus focused on her mother's voice, not the pain.
"It's almost out, darling. One more push."
Magnus grit her teeth and pushed with everything in her.
"That's my girl," her mother coaxed. "It's almost here. Yes, darling, only one more push."
"I can't, Mother."
"You can, darling. Push now."
Magnus screamed and pushed.
"She's out, darling. She's out."
Magnus cried and watched as her mother handed her baby to Mary.
"She's beautiful, darling."
"Oh, Mother, are they ok?"
"Yes, darling," her mother answered. "You did a fantastic job."
Magnus waited and tears ran down her face as her babies started to cry.
"They are beautiful, darling."
Magnus's mother waited to clean her daughter up. "Now you may see your daughters."
Magnus held out her arms as her mother placed her daughters in both of her arms. "They are beautiful," she cried.
"They are," her mother cried back.
"Daniel?" Magnus asked.
"Mary has gone to get him."
Daniel walked slowly into the room. Seeing Magnus hold their babies almost made his knees buckle.
"We have two daughters, Daniel."
"You look beautiful," he whispered, looking from Magnus to his two daughters. "They are as beautiful as their mother."
Magnus looked at Daniel and then at her two daughters.
"Daniel," she cried looking from one daughter to the other.
"She has her beauty," she cried, and then she looks at the other baby.
"Her beauty is not there." Magnus cried for her darling daughter with scars all over her face and body.
"It will be all right, darling," Daniel told her. "Her beauty will come like yours comes and goes. We will love our daughters as we love each other. Our family love will see us through anything."
"Are you sure? Magnus cried.

"Yes," he smiled down at his new family. "I am as sure as the love we share, Magnus."

Magnus's mother took one baby and handed it to Mary. Taking the other baby, she told her daughter to rest. "Everything will be fine, darling. Get some rest. We will clean your babies up and bring them back shortly."

Her mother and Mary carried the babies to the next room.

"They are not the same," Sally said, looking at the two babies on the table. "One is most beautiful, and the other one is quite ugly."

"You," Magnus's mother yelled at Sally. "You leave here now. I don't want you around these poor defenseless babies."

Sally looked at Magnus's mother and ran from the room. Mary looked at both babies but said nothing.

"She will leave tonight," Magnus's mother told her husband. "I want no talk like that around Magnus or Daniel.

"I will have Lenard escort her form Chainridge," her husband promised.

Lenard doesn't ask why but ordered a driver to take Sally from Chainridge.

"Magnus," Daniel told her as she continued to cry. These are our babies. We will raise them with love. They will be strong with or without their beauty.

Magnus stopped crying. "I've been a fool, Daniel. Of course, they are our daughters. We will raise them to be strong and independent of their beauty."

"Yes, Magnus." He smiled, taking her hand. "Our daughters will live happy lives. We will make sure of it."

"Can we see them again?" she asks him.

"Your mother is taking care of them. She'll bring them back shortly."

Magnus smiled as her mother and Mary returned her babies.

"Look," her mother smiled.

"They are both beautiful," Magnus cried out. "Magnus reached for her babies and smiling at them both her eyes filled with tears. Her daughters were identical. "They are very beautiful." She looked at Daniel.

Daniel looked at his mother-in-law. Both babies, he noticed, have no beauty.

"Your children are beautiful," she smiled at Daniel. "All babies are."

Daniel smiled at Magnus and sat with his new family. "They are both beautiful, darling," he said, touching his daughters' hands.

"You will mind your manners, Miss," Lenard told Sally. "Or you will find yourself walking back to town."

"I gave up good employment to come here and be thrown out on the streets."

"I have nothing to do with your staying or going, Miss. I was ordered to see you leave this house, and that's exactly what I plan on doing. Now if you would be so kind as to pack your things."

"I want to talk to the Madam."

"She is busy, and I don't think she'll be changing her mind."

"I will not leave," Sally screamed, "until I've had my say. I'm not the only one who will be saying the child has no beauty."

"Yes," Lenard whispered loud enough for her to hear. "But you were the first one to say it. That child will have enough problems in her life without the people closest to her hurting her feelings."

"She's just an infant, Sally laughed. "She didn't know what I was saying."

"That's true, but everyone in earshot knew what you meant. Now I'll ask you again. Please pack your things and be ready to leave within the hour."

"I will do no such thing," Sally yelled back.

"Then you leave me no choice."

Pulling on a pulley, Lenard watched Sally. Within minutes, two men dressed in black pants and matching jackets showed up. Sally knew them and watched as they approached. "You wouldn't dare touch me," she yelled at them.

"We would rather not," the older man said. "But if you don't cooperate, we will have to."

"I'm going." Sally stood and started for her room.

"No, this way," Lenard pointed at the front door. "I'll have someone bring your things out."

"You haven't heard the last of me," Sally's voice rang out through the hall as she pushed past the two men and went out to the waiting carriage.

Lenard gave the two men orders to drive her to town and waited with them until Sally's clothes were brought out.

"Here." Lenard put a small pouch of money on the seat by her. "This should help you until you get different employment."

Sally picked up the purse and shook it. "I deserve more," she snorted and sat back.

"I will see you pay," she fumed in the wagon. "No one throws me out like trash. You should have kept your family secrets to yourselves. She laughed into the dark carriage. "I will find that witch," she said to the empty carriage, "and I will tell her all about Magnus and her precious babies. She will pay for my information." Sally rested her head on the back of the carriage seat and played her plan over in her head.

"Magnus?" Daniel sat with her, looking at their daughters.

"You know, neither baby has her beauty, right?"

"Yes," Magnus looked at him and smiled. "I can see for myself, Daniel. But you look past my beauty coming and going. I can see past our daughters' beauty or not. Aren't they perfect?"

Daniel looked at the love in Magnus's eyes for their daughters and smiled. "They are beautiful, darling, just like their mother."

"How long before we will be able to go Chainridge?" Henasee asked Kentar at their next stop.

"It may be months before it's safe enough to try to see Magnus and Daniel. We must lead Fanton on a merry chase."

Henasee thought for a minute. "If we are leading her on a merry chase, I want to get some different clothes in the next town."

Kentar looked her up and down. "I think you look fine."

"I'm not traipsing around in this wedding dress."

"Why? it looks nice on you."

"It's hot and heavy," she snarled.

"I will stop as soon as I find a town."

"Thank you," she said, returning to the carriage.

Kentar shook his head at her departing stance. "You're welcome!" he yelled after her and climbed back onto the carriage. "Horses," he said, looking at the carriage. "We need horses."

Finding the next town was trickier than they thought. Hours later, Kentar pulled in front of an inn.

"We should be able to get our supplies here," he told Henasee.

"Here." Kentar offered her a purse filled with coins.

"Thank you," she said, snatching it out of his hand. "I will repay you as soon as I can."

"Some of it is yours." He smiled at her. "I traded some of the jewels in for it."

"Well then, thank you," she said, walking down the walkway toward a sign that's said "Merchant."

"I will get us a room for the night." He pointed to the open door in front of him.

Henasee didn't reply and walked into the merchant's shop. "I need some pants and shirts," she told the shopkeeper.

"Are they for your husband? he asked, looking at her wedding dress. Not caring to cause a fuss, Henasee smiled sweetly and told him, "Yes, my husband. He's not much bigger than I am. He'll need two pair of pants and some shirts. He also needs a pair of boots and a coat."

Excited about a big sale, the merchant gathered everything quickly. "Will there be anything else?"

"Yes," Henasee pointed, "I need a gun and some shells."

The merchant looked a little nervous but helped Henasee choose a gun and holster. "Are you sure your husband doesn't want to pick out his own gun?"

"I'm sure," Henasee said, looking the gun over and placing the shells in it. "This one will do nicely."

Kentar stood at the front of the inn when Henasee came out with her arms loaded. "Did you get everything you need?" he asked, not offering to help carry any of it.

"I did," she said curtly. "Did you get our rooms?"

"You mean room?"

"No," she looked at him. "I meant rooms."

"We have to look as if we've just been married. Now if you don't want people to get suspicious and talk, you'll go along with it." Henasee gave Kentar a dirty look.

"Now," he laughed, chucking her chin, "is that any way for my new bride to act?"

Henasee pulled away from his touch. "They will see a lot more if you don't keep your hands off me. I told you we're not married, and I'm not going to play the dutiful wife. Now keep your distance." Kentar laughed again and walked into the inn, with Henasee following behind with her heavy load.

"This is nice." Henasee looks around the room. "You will be comfortable on the sofa, I'm sure."
Kentar looked over at the sofa and then to the four-poster bed. "The bed is big enough for two."
"We are not sharing the bed," she snapped. "Now if you would order me a bath."
Kentar smiled, "A bath for two?"
"No," she snapped again. "I will be bathing alone."
"I see." He acted hurt.
"Oh stop it! You knew we would not be spending the night as husband and wife. We're together to make sure nothing happens to Magnus and the babies."
"This was going to be our wedding night," Kentar reminded her.
"I told you we were never going to be married. The minister wasn't even real."
"You got a fake minister?" Kentar yelled.
"Yes," she yelled back. "We were never going to marry."
"What was that 'I love you' on the staircase?"
"I was just setting the mood. In case Fanton was in earshot."
"Oh I see." Kentar grabbed his discarded jacket. "It was all a made-up plan. Did your parents know?"
"My mother helped me, yes. But, no, my father thought us to be madly in love."
"Well, at least he didn't make a fool out of me."
"You are the only one doing that Kentar."
Kentar was so mad that the veins on his neck stuck out. Grabbing her arm, he pulled her hard against his chest. Kissing her with frustration that turned into passion, he pulled away, leaving her breathless. "Sleep with the memory of that," he said, pushing her down on the bed, leaving the room, and slamming the door.
Henasee touched her swollen lips and lay back on the bed, smiling to herself. "You will learn to love me and not leave me," she

laughed. "I will teach you how, my love. I will teach you."
Kentar was out of the inn before he started to calm down. I shouldn't have let her get to me, he berated himself. Now she has the room and I have nothing, he thought, looking around the town. Maybe, he smiled at a sign, I can get a drink.
Kentar sat at the bar and ordered a whiskey.
"You new in town?" the bartender asked.
"Yep." Kentar took his drink and gulped it in one swallow.
"You that new married couple that just arrived?"
"Yep," Kentar answered, tapping his glass on the bar for another.
"It looks as if the honeymoon isn't going too well."
Kentar snarled at the bartender. "It's not what I had planned," he growled at the man.
"Young love," the old man laughed. "When it's good, it's really good, but when it's bad, it's terrible."
Kentar laughed at the man's joke. "Yah, when it's bad."
After four or five more drinks, Kentar went back to the inn. With the lights down low, it was harder to maneuver around, but he finally stumbled to his the door of his room. Falling against it hard, he heard other doors open and close.
"What are you doing?" Henasee asked, opening the door.
"I'm trying to go to bed," Kentar answered, slurring his words.
"You're drunk," Henasee whispered.
"I'm not drunk," Kentar yelled in reply.
"Get in here." She opened the door and pulled on his jacket.
Kentar fell into the room, almost knocking them both to the floor.
"You smell good," he said in her hair. "Like flowers."
"Kentar, stop it." She tried pushing him off of her.
"I miss holding you," he said, trying to pull her to him.
"Come," she pulled away. "Sit here." Henasee pointed to the bed.
"Kentar's eyes lit up. "Yes, that's exactly where I want us to be."
Kentar sat on the bed, and Henasee lifted his feet up on it, removing his shoes.
"Now you lay there, and I'll be right over."
Kentar smiled and lay back on the pillows, falling straight asleep.
"Thank goodness," Henasee laughed at a passed-out Kentar and pulled a blanket up over him. She reached over for a pillow and took her wedding gown with her to the sofa. Making her bed with the

dress, she climbed into it.

"Good night, darling," she laughed in the darkness. "I will see you in the morning."

"What is that sound?" Kentar screamed awake.

"I was just beating the dust out of my wedding dress," Henasee smiled, all innocent.

"Would you stop it? My head is killing me."

"I've had them send up some eggs and sausage for you. I thought you might be hungry."

"Not funny, Henasee," Kentar grabbed his head and sat up.

"I've already got us two nice horses and our things are packed, so as soon as you eat we can be on our way."

Kentar gave her a snarl that turned into a moan.

"You do look a little green this morning. Is there anything I can get you, darling?"

"Leave me alone," he yelled.

"All right. I'll take care of the bill and see you outside."

Kentar screamed as Henasee slammed the door on her way out. "I won't forget this," he said through gritted teeth. "You will get yours," he moaned, getting out of bed.

Kentar was impressed to find clothes sitting on a chair for him and dressed as quickly as his pounding head would let him. A knock on the door got his attention, and he sat back down on the bed.

"Yes!" he yelled.

The innkeeper's wife came merrily in. "Your wife said you had a bit of a hangover this morning. I brought you some hot coffee and two of these. Doc Hager gave me some to give my husband when he went out and came back with a headache. I saved them. I figured if he was stupid enough to drink so much he could own his own headache."

Kentar watched as the lady poured coffee out of a pot and into his coffee cup. "I was surprised to hear a big strapping fellow like you got drunk because he was so nervous on his wedding night. But a lot of strange things happen when you sell beds to strangers every night."

Kentar looked at the woman with his mouth open. "My wife said what?"

"She said you were embarrassed because you were, you know,

going to be with a woman for the first time, and you were scared. I would never have guessed it. The lady laughed, handing him his coffee and the two pills. Now take the pills, and you'll be good to go soon. It will get less stressful the more you do it, son. But drinking isn't going to help."

Kentar didn't know what to say so he took the pills and drank the coffee.

"Remember what I said, son. Practice makes perfect, and you'll get there."

Kentar watched as she left with a wave of her hand and a small laugh and closed the door.

"I see you're looking better," Henasee smiled on top of her new mare.

Kentar untied the reins to his stallion and climbed on. "I had some help from the inn owner's wife. It seems I have a nervous condition about . . ."

Henasee laughed. "She promised she wouldn't tell anyone."

"Well, she lied," he told her and turned his horse to leave town.

Henasee followed, laughing so hard tears ran down her face. "What did she say to you?"

"She said practice would make perfect," he yelled back.

Henasee stopped laughing and they rode in silence.

Following Kentar with Henasee was easier then Fanton thought it would be. They left a trail of people to find out their every move. Fanton sipped her tea. I see. She looked out the window. You are leading me on a wild goose chase. You are keeping me from Daniel and Magnus. Fanton took another sip of her tea.

"If I could have a word with you, Miss?" A young lady stood at Fanton's table.

"What do you need?" Fanton asked.

"I have some information on the babies."

"I need no information on babies," Fanton waves the girl away and returned to her tea.

"But Miss," the girl continued, "they are Magnus and Daniel's babies."

Fanton put her cup down hard enough to clink on the saucer, raising

eyebrows from other tables. "Sit," Fanton ordered the girl. "Tell me about the babies."
"They are twins, two girls born two weeks ago."
"How do you know about these babies?"
"I was there when they were born."
"Why are you not there now?" Sally put her head down.
"I said something about one of the babies, and I was dismissed."
"What was it you said?"
Sally hushed her voice. "One baby was very beautiful, and the other baby was . . ."
Fanton laughed out loud. "One baby was born beautiful, and the other was born without her beauty."
"Yes." Sally was happy not to repeat the ugly word again. It had brought her only hardship.
"What do you want for this information?"
"I want to be rich," Sally told Fanton.
Fanton clapped her hands together. "I can do that very easily. Come to my room tonight at 8. You will give me the information, and I will make you rich beyond your wildest dreams."
Sally stood, thanked Fanton, and rushed out of the dining room.

"Look at them," Magnus smiled at her mother. "Aren't they darling?"
"They are at that, my dear. Precious grabbed my hand today and wouldn't give it back."
"She does have her father's strength," Magnus whispered back.
"Beautiful looked around the room for more than an hour today."
"I'm afraid she has my curiosity." Magnus laughed quietly with her mother.
"I see they both have their beauty today," her mother told her.
"Yes, it comes and goes every three days. It still scares poor Mary, but Daniel and I are used to it."
"You are very good parents, Magnus. You will raise your children to see past their beauty coming and going."
"We will show them love comes in many different forms, and they will be loved always."
Magnus took her mother's hand, and they left Mary to watch over the babies."

"It feels so good not to be carrying all that weight." Magnus patted her stomach.
"You look great for just having two babies."
"I feel great," Magnus told her mother.
"Do you think there are more children in your future?"
Magnus turned white. "I'm not feeling that much better," she laughed nervously.
"I didn't mean today, darling. I meant in the years to come."
"I don't know," Magnus said truthfully.
Her mother patted her arm with a smile, and they went into the sitting room for tea.

Fanton had Sally sit across the table from her. "You said there are two babies?"
"Yes, Magnus gave birth to two girls."
"Both are healthy?"
"Yes, both babies were born healthy. But only one baby had her beauty. Yes, they were the same size and were born only minutes apart."
"Do you know their names?"
"My sister, Mary, still works with the babies. She came into town last week. She said their names are Beautiful and Precious."
Fanton slapped the table and laughed, scaring Sally.
"She says their beauty now comes and goes. She says it's scary at night when you're alone with them. One minute they're beautiful, and the next it is gone."
"How can babies be scary? Fanton snapped at Sally.
"I'm sorry. I didn't mean to say anything wrong."
Fanton changed her tone. "I mean, they are just harmless babies, aren't they?"
Sally smiled nervously. "Yes, they are harmless."
"You can tell me where they are?"
"Yes", Sally said, pulling out a piece of paper with directions on it to Chainridge.
"How did you find me?"
"I heard you were offering a reward for the whereabouts of a girl whose beauty comes and goes. I figured you meant Magnus."
"Yes, Magnus." Fanton rubbed her hands together. "I have looked

for her a long time."

"Do you know her?"

Fanton nods her head. "She is married to my brother."

Sally's eyes widen. "Then you are the babies' Aunt?"

"Yes," Fanton smiles at Sally, showing her perfect white teeth.

"You don't look any older than me."

Fanton laughed at Sally. "I am old on the inside."

"Is that enough information to make me rich?" Sally asked Fanton.

"You are going to be very happy in just a minute, my dear. I will see to it. Here." Fanton poured Sally a cup of tea. "Drink this. I will get your riches."

Sally took a sip of the tea and placed the cup back on the saucer. Looking around the room, she liked the feel of money and nice things. Smiling to herself, she took another sip of tea and fell off her chair.

"I'm sorry." Fanton stood above her with a grin on her face. "Did the tea not settle right?" Fanton stepped over Sally's dead body and left the room. Stopping outside, she put a note on the door that said, "Please let me sleep." Laughing, she left the inn.

Chapter 17
Lost Friendships

Henasee was tired and sore from riding from town to town. At least she was thankful that, after the first night, Kentar paid for separate rooms. So discomfort at night was not a problem. Their days were the same. They rode from town to town, asking if anyone had seen Fanton. No one had seen her so far. Henasee hoped that meant Fanton had given up looking for them. But Kentar was sure Fanton would never give up her revenge, not when he almost married Henasee in front of her.
"Let's head to Rover," Kentar pointed at a sign.
"What's in Rover?"
"The county fair," he answered, putting his horse into a gallop.
Henasee smiled and nudged her horse to follow behind Kentar.
"Look at all the people," she said to Kentar.
"I'll see if we can get some rooms," Kentar offered, getting down off his horse.
"I'm going to look around," she said over her shoulder.
"Not too far," he started to tell her, but she was already out of earshot.
"No room left in town," the innkeeper told Kentar. "I have a room over my place I can let you have for the night," an old man at the door told Kentar. "I saw you and your wife arrive a few minutes ago."
"Yes." Kentar smiled at the old man. "We came for the fair."
"A lot of folks do. It's a lot of fun for the folks around here. Most people never get off their farms so this is a good reason to bring the family and maybe win a contest or two."
The innkeeper laughed. "Old Hank, here, has won axe throwing four years running. With the looks of you," he said pointing at Kentar, "I'm guessing he's keeping his competition close to home."
Kentar laughed and shook the older man's hand. I thank you for the offer of the room. As for axe-throwing, I've never done it."
"You're kidding." The old man pumped Kentar's hand. "You'd be great at it. I'll go find my wife. I'll meet you here in 20 minutes," the

older man yelled after Kentar. "I need to get these supplies home before Becka has my hide."

Kentar laughed again and left to find Henasee. Minutes later, he found her standing at the window of the dressmaker.

"Do you miss all the finery?" he asked her.

"Sometimes I like dressing like a girl."

"You do make a very beautiful girl when you want to."

"Oh be quiet." She slapped at his hand and stormed off.

Kentar watched as Henasee turned around a corner, and he stepped into the dress shop.

Kentar waited for Henasee by the innkeeper's door. "I've been here more than 20 years," Hank told Kentar proudly. "I helped build the town. We didn't even have a store for three years after we settled. The men took turns going over to Far grove for supplies."

Kentar shook his head in awe. "I've always sailed the seas. I've never much been around farmers and such."

Hank laughed. "Well, how's it look-in to yah? Think you might like it out here?"

"Anywhere she is," Kentar watched as Henasee approached, is where I want to be."

Hank turned his head. "She's a mighty fine look-in girl. Just like my Becka." He smiled a lopsided grin. "She's a pretty little thing, too. I guess whether we're from the land or sea, we both got real lucky."

Kentar smiled at Hank and nodded. "We are that," he agreed.

Hank's place was only two miles from town, and Henasee laughed at his stories most of the way. Becka came out running out of the outhouse screaming my name. He laughed at the memory. "She thought some old cougar was shaking down the walls. I ran out there, and the old cat had kittens and she was moving into the outhouse. She's never lived it down. I can still get her riled up walking by and meowing when she's in there."

Henasee laughed out loud and Kentar smiled broadly.

"What a funny story, Hank." Henasee laughed some more.

"Me and Becka have been through our share. We had drought one year. Lost all our crops. We buried our boy." He pointed just over the hill. "Becka wanted him to wake up with the sun on his face every morning."

Henasee couldn't help the tears that flowed down her cheeks.

"No!" Hank reined in his horse. "Don't go crying. Becka will have my hide. We believe in the good Lord, and our Chad is in a better place. Now you stop that. We're almost there."
"Henasee smiled through her tears.
"This is it." Hank pointed around his yard.
Henasee liked what she saw. A creek ran down the side of the yard. The house had two stories and was made out of logs. A wraparound porch went across the front and down both sides. Across the yard was a horse corral and a big barn.
"This is lovely, Hank."
"Thanks," Hank puffed up with pride. "Becka and I have our hearts and sweat in this place."
"It shows," Kentar told him. "You have a real nice place here."
Becka was just how Henasee pictured her to be. She was a short, heavyset woman with a kind face. "Who we got here, Paw?"
"I found these two look-in for a room in town."
Becka placed her hand on her hip and laughed. "This is a bad time of year for that. Everybody and their brother is staying in town for the fair."
Henasee smiled.
"Where's my manners? You look like you've been drug all over the country," she told Henasee. "Let's get you inside." Henasee follows without hesitation.
"Hank, bring me in some water in from the well," Becka yelled from the doorway, never turning back.
"See why I love her," Hank laughed. "She knows how to get things done."
Kentar laughed at Hank's silly grin and helped him take the horses to the barn.
"You two been married long?" Becka asked Henasee.
"No, it's only been a couple of weeks."
"Oh, newlyweds. That's a fun part of the marriage."
Henasee turned away, not to get caught lying. "Yes, we've traveled around a lot."
"Trying to figure out where to set roots?"
"Yes," Henasee told her. "He's always loved the sea, and I was raised on a farm."
"A rich farm, I'm guessin.'"

"Why would you think that?" Henasee asked.

"You speak too fine to be from around here."

"I've never thought about that," Henasee told Becka. "The way someone looks, I've always understood them standing out. But never had I thought the way a person speaks can tell a lot about them."

"Plus," Becka continued, "you carry yourself nice."

"I carry myself nice?"

"Yes, like there's an air about you."

Henasee sat down at the table. "Is that a good thing?"

"Oh, yes dear. It's a very good thing. Women out here have to know how to take care of themselves; otherwise, the men would walk all over them."

Henasee understood and smiled. "Yes, Kentar can be a bit about himself sometimes."

"Same as my Hank. If I didn't keep him in place, he'd think he built this place all by his self."

Henasee laughed out loud. Kentar would sign his name on our farm, too, and then maybe remember I had helped.

"Men," Becka laughed. Can't live with 'um, and if you lose 'um, you want another one."

Henasee held her sides laughing when Hank and Kentar came into the cabin.

"I see you found out my Becka has a sense of humor."

Henasee laughed some more.

"I bet she's telling you how she keeps me in my place."

Henasee let out another roar, and Becka joined in. "Did I forget to tell you Hank knows I keep him in line?"

"Hank hugged a laughing Becka and filled the coffeepot with water from his bucket.

"Let me show you to your room, Becka told Henasee and Kentar when she calmed down.

The room she led them to was on the other end of the kitchen. "You can get the fire going so you'll have warm embers for tonight," she told Kentar. "Nothing worse than frozen floors to run across in the mornings, with the weather starting to get cold at night, we started using the fireplaces. Plus," she smiled at Henasee," it makes for a very romantic night." Becka laughed as Henasee's cheeks turned completely red.

Kentar loved Henasee's discomfort and kissed her cheek. "Yes, darling, it will be very romantic in here tonight."

Henasee backed away as if her embarrassment was at its end. "I can help with dinner, Becka."

"No, you get cleaned up and rest a spell. I've had stew on all day. It won't be nothing to throw it on the table."

"Are you sure?" Henasee tried to leave with her.

"No, you stay here with your husband," Becka insisted, pushing lightly on Henasee's arm. "I'll call when dinner's ready."

"The bed's nice." Kentar pushed on it and smiled up at Henasee. "Do you want to try it out, my devoted wife?"

Henasee hissed. "You stop that. It's bad enough having to lie to these nice people."

"You better get used to the idea of sharing my bed," Kentar stated.

"There's no sofa in here."

"There's a floor," Henasee hissed back.

"If you want to sleep on the floor and wake up stiff, it's all yours," Kentar laughed at her and stretched out on the bed.

"You are no gentleman," Henasee whispered.

"And you're not a very friendly wife," Kentar shot back and closed his eyes. "Now if you would be so kind as to be quiet, I'm going to take a little nap." With that said, he turned over on his side, ignoring her.

"Don't you turn your back on me," Henasee stomped to the side of the bed.

"Good." He reached out and grabbed her around the waist and pulled her down on the bed with him. "I was getting a little chilled." Pulling her closer, he closed his eyes once again.

"Let me go," she says, beating on his chest.

"You might want to lower your voice," he whispered in her ear. "You don't want our new friends thinking you're a little wild cat in the bedroom, do you?

Henasee hated this man next to her so much. She was sure that if she could reach her gun, she would have shot him dead.

"What are you thinking about?" Kentar asked, a little concerned.

"I was just having a pleasant daydream," she sighed back.

"Well, you looked a bit vicious with it."

"Good!" She smiled and drifted off to sleep.

Waking, Henasee looked around groggily. Kentar was nowhere to be found. But she could see he started a fire before he left. Stretching on the bed, she let the heat seep into her bones. Turning over, she sat up straight in bed and held up the same exact dress she had admired at the dress shop. Looking at the other boxes, she smiled. What a sweet thing to do. She rubbed the dress lovingly.

"Your husband said he bought you a dress. It looks real nice on you."
"Thank you," Henasee said, shyly rubbing it again. "I haven't been able to dress like a . . . "
"Like a lady," Becka finished for her.
"Yes, like a lady, in a long time."
"Well, it looks real good on you, honey."
"I think your husband will be right proud to show you off tonight."
"Show me off?"
"Yah," Becka laughed, "at the dance in town."
Henasee looked at Becka kind of funny.
"Haven't you ever been to a dance before?"
"No, my family never took me to one."
"You'll love it. It's a time to visit and get to know people. Real home people."
Henasee smiled at the thought of her parents meeting real home people.
"You'll do fine," Becka promised. Plus you'll get to dance with that handsome husband of yours. You'll be the envy of every woman there."
"You're not going and gettin' jealous on me again? Are yah, Becka?" Hank laughed from the doorway. "She's sure Pauline Langdon has the wants for me," he told Kentar with a nudge to his arm. Kentar laughed, too.
"That no-good roaster chaser has been trying to steal him away for 20 years."
"Yes's just friendly is all" Hank laughed again.
"There's nothing friendly about that cougar. Not unless you're another cougar." Becka looked at Hank for an answer.

"Nobody could get me out of here, Becka. You are more woman than any man deserves."
"That was a good answer, Hank." Becka laughed. "I think maybe I'll feed yah some dinner."
Hank patted Becka on the bottom.
"Don't go getting any ideas," she laughed. "We have guests."
Henasee looked over at Kentar, who was laughing under his breath. He smiled at her, and they all sat down to dinner.

"Thank you for the dress," she said later in their room.
"I wasn't sure of the size."
"It fits nicely," she smiled shyly.
"I thought that when I first seen you in it," Kentar smiled.
Henasee finished fixing her hair and turned to look at him.
"You are beautiful," he whispered, crossing the room. "Taking the side of her face in his hand, he bent his face and kissed her lips lightly. Nothing more was said between then as he took her arm and led her from the room.

"You have come with high recommendations," Francine told the nice-looking young lady, sitting on the sofa in the drawing room. "My uncle said you have twin girls."
"Yes, Francine smiled at her. "They are 4 months old. They are growing by leaps and bounds."
"Where will I be staying?" the young lady asked.
"We would like for you to stay in the home. We don't want to take a chance of the girls catching anything."
"I see." The young lady looked at her hands.
Francine tried to concentrate. The interview seemed to be running away from her. The young girl had somehow decided she would be running it. Francine cleared her throat. "Would you like some tea?"
"I would love some, thank you."
Francine didn't wait for anyone to come and headed out of the drawing room in search of a serving maid.
"What's the matter, darling?" her husband asked when he found her in the hallway.
"I think it's the stress of finding someone we trust with the babies."
"I thought you had an appointment this morning."

"Yes, I mean," his wife started again, "she's in the drawing room."
"Is there something wrong with her?"
"No," his wife answered quickly.
"Then what is the problem, dear?"
"I'm not sure," his wife tells him. "I'm not sure at all. I guess I'm worrying over nothing. The girl came with the highest credentials, Cameron Raleigh's niece.
"That is high," her husband whistled. "Nothing gets past old Raleigh."
"I'm just being silly." Francine excused herself and walked back into the sitting room. "Tea will be shortly."
"That's fine," the young girl smiled
"Would you like to see the girls?" Francine asked.
"I would love to see them." The young girl stood, excited. "I've never seen twins before. I was quite excited when my uncle told me about them."
"There is something I should tell you before I introduce you to them."
"Yes?" The young girl looked concerned.
"It's about the twins."
"Are they both healthy?"
"Yes, they are very healthy. It's about their beauty."
"Beauty? I don't understand." The girl looked perplexed.
"Their beauty comes and goes," Francine said in a rush.
"I've never heard of that before. Is it harmful to them?"
"No," Francine laughed nervously. "No, it just comes and goes every few days. It can be quite surprising if you're not used to it."
"I'm sure it will be fine, ma'am."
Francine put all her worries to rest and started to lead the young girl upstairs to meet the twins. "Do you go by your first name or your last?" Francine asked.
"Everyone has always called me Tess."
"That's a lovely name," Francine told her as they climbed the staircase. "They're right in this room here." Francine led her into the nursery.
Mary looked up from the rocking chair where she was rocking a very fussy Precious.
"She's got an air bubble or something, ma'am. I've tried everything,

and she's still fussy."
Tess walked over to Mary. "May I try?" she asked.
Mary handed Precious over. "I don't know what you can do, but here you are."
Precious stopped crying as soon as Tess put her up against her.
"I don't believe it," Mary said, looking at the almost sleeping baby.
Francine smiled at Tess and her granddaughter. "It looks like we need you if you want the job, Tess."
Tess smiled at Precious and then back at Francine. "How could I say no to this precious little thing?"
Francine laughed.
"What? Tess smiled again.
"The baby, her name is Precious."
Tess laughed and held the baby tighter.
"I'll get Magnus," Francine told Tess. "She'll want to meet you."
Tess walked over to the other bassinet. "My, you are two peas in a pod."
"Yes, they're beautiful today." Mary smiled at the sleeping baby in the bassinet. "She did tell you their beauty comes and goes."
"Yes, I was quite worried for their health, but she told me they were healthy little things."
"Yes, God has blessed them with their health." Mary smiled politely.
"She's in with the babies, honey."
Magnus smiled at the picture of Tess holding a very sound asleep Precious.
"Magnus darling," her mother pointed over at a very attractive young lady. "This is Tess Daloyal."
"It's very nice to meet you," Tess smiled up from looking at Precious.
"I'm thinking it's my good fortune to have you here. My mother has said you are great with Precious, and you come highly recommended."
"I had the good fortune to help my uncle with his two sons."
"You don't look old enough to have raised children."
"I was 16 when I went to work for him. His sons were 8 and 10. On their 12th birthdays, they went away to boarding school."
"Oh," Magnus shook a little. "I'm not sure I could do that."

"It is an honor to be chosen, and both boys wanted to make their father proud."
"Well, I'm happy then I only had girls. Magnus laughed, picking up Beautiful. "Are you hungry?" she asked the whimpering baby. Magnus laughed as Beautiful scrunched up her face and let out a loud mew. "I see you're starving," she tells her little daughter.
"I'll fetch the bottles, ma'am, Mary told her and went to the kitchen.
"You will work nights. Is that ok with you?"
"Yes," Tess smiles. "In fact, I do a lot of my best thinking at night."
Magnus smiled at the young lady and changed Beautiful's diaper before her bottle arrived. "They can be a handful at times. If you have any questions, my husband and I sleep right behind that door."
"I'm sure we'll be fine," Tess smiled at Magnus again.
"Mary will show you everything tonight, and then you'll have them on your own the next night."
"That sounds fine," Tess told Magnus.

Kentar lifted Henasee up into the back of the wagon. "You look wonderful in the moonlight," he told her.
"Thank you," she said flashing a genuine smile. it was something she hadn't felt in months.
"Let's forget about everything tonight," he whispered in her ear.
"Tonight we are young and in love. Tomorrow will be the same no matter how tonight goes."
Henasee put out her hand and he shook it.
"Tonight is ours," he laughed, kissing her cheek.
"Tonight is ours." She smiled and looked into his eyes.

The town was so lit up they could see it a mile away.
"I told you this is a big deal," Hank said proudly.
"I've never seen so many lights, Henasee told Kentar.
"They have everything from pie-eating contests to dancing. Don't forget the axe-throwing contest," Hank turned to tell them.
"Who can forget that, Hank? That's all you've been talkin' about for months." Becka laughed and it echoed throughout the fields.
Henasee tried to take everything in. "There's some kind of game or eating table set up down every walkway. Oh, my goodness," she laughed. "There are people everywhere."

"I told yah," Hank said as he climbed off the wagon, "It's a big at-do."
"What do we do first, wife?" Kentar asked Henasee.
"Let's walk around first," Henasee replied. "I want to see everything."
"Then it's everything I will show you."
"We'll meet back here around 11," Becka yelled after them.
"Hey," Hank yelled. "The axe-throwing contest is at the edge of town. It starts at 8, if you're interested?"
Kentar turned and laughed. "I told you, I've never thrown an axe."
"I bet you'd be a natural, Hank yelled back.
Kentar and Henasee waved at the older couple and disappeared into the crowd.
Here Kentar grabbed Henasee's hand and half-dragged her to a booth that had necklaces, bracelets, and rings for sale.
"What are you getting? she laughed, giddy with the excitement around her.
"You need a wedding ring," he smiled.
Henasee was so touched, tears came to her eyes.
"What can I get you?" a young man asked from behind a table.
"That ring right there, Kentar pointed at a silver band ring with different-colored stones all around it. Kentar took it from the young man and placed it on Henasee's finger.
"It's lovely," she smiled at him.
"Is it too loose?" Kentar asked.
"No," she smiled at the ring and then at Kentar. "It's perfect."
Kentar paid the man and they walked away hand in hand.
"You didn't have to do this." She looked at her hand and the ring.
"It's our night, remember? he replied. "What should we do now?"
"Let's find you a hat," she laughs.
"A hat?"
"Yes, a cowboy hat."
"No one will ever believe I'm a cowboy."
"We are in farm country, and everyone wears a cowboy hat."
Kentar looked around him. "I can see you're right about that. I haven't seen one man's head without a hat on it yet."
"We do want to fit in," Henasee coaxed.
"Yes, we do," Kentar laughed, looking for a booth that sold hats.

"There is a booth over there," Henasee pointed.

"I like this one," she said, picking up a dark tan hat. "Here try it."

Kentar placed the hat on his head and his eyes disappeared. "How do I look?"

"It's slightly big," Henasee laughed. "Try this one." She handed him a dark brown cowboy hat.

Kentar placed it on his head and tapped his fingers on the brim. "Pleased to make your acquaintance, miss," he said with a bow.

"That's the one," she said with a serious tone. "You look great in it."

"I will give a kiss for the young lady's kind words." Kentar bent so fast and kissed her lips that she wondered whether or not it happened.

Kentar laughed at her surprise. "I just wanted to thank you for the present."

"Oh," is all she said in reply.

"Now what do we do?"

She smiled at his hat. "You really do look good in that hat."

Henasee watched as woman after woman looked at Kentar. Feeling a bit jealous, she reached for his arm. Kentar knew not to laugh. She would have punched him and run off if she even thought he knew she was at the least bit jealous. Instead, he pulled her arm tightly through his and walked down the walkway looking at all the different items for sale.

"What about those?" Kentar pointed at baby blankets.

"Darling," she looked at him embarrassed. We don't have any little ones."

"Kentar flipped his eyes at her. "I meant your best friend's children."

"Magnus?"

"Yes, Magnus."

"Does this mean we're going to see her?" Henasee asked with hope in her voice.

"I think it's time those babies met their godmother, don't you?"

Henasee threw herself into Kentar's arms. "Thank you!" She kissed his cheek. "Thank you so much."

"Kentar pulled her closer and kissed her with such passion that it took her breath away. Pulling away, Henasee's cheeks turned red from people staring on the walkway.

"Don't be embarrassed," one lady passing by told her. "If my Emit looked like him, I'd kiss him anywhere and anytime."

Henasee and Kentar laughed. "I'm not sure whether they are boys or girls or one of each," she laughed. She was so caught up in the excitement of the fair, seeing Magnus, and being able to let her guard down about her feelings for Kentar that she felt like she was floating.

"Look at these." She pulled out two little patchwork quilts and showed them to Kentar. "I'll take these two, please," she turned and told the lady at the booth.

With the blankets safely wrapped and tied, Kentar and Henasee went in search of food and drink.

"Look over there," Henasee pointed to a pig being turned above an open fire. "Food."

Kentar smiled, pulling Henasee alongside. Sitting with their plates stacked with roasted pork, potatoes, and baked beans, they dug in.

"I didn't think I'd be able to eat anything after Becka's stew, but I'm starved."

Kentar motioned for her to look at his plate. Only minutes had passed and most of his meat and potatoes were gone.

"You were a bit hungry yourself?" she said lifting her eyebrows.

"On the ship, we ate fast and worked hard."

Henasee laughed. "I do remember, you're right about that. I sometimes didn't know if I'd pull back a nub when I placed food in front of some of the men."

"You're luckier than some were," Kentar laughed, taking another bite of his meat. "This is real good pork."

"You say it like you're an expert."

"My grandfather was a farmer. I went to live with him after my father was killed."

Henasee rested her hand on his arm. "I'm sorry."

"No, it's been a lot of years. I've always been thankful I had time with my Graps."

"Graps?"

"Yes, I called him Graps. I guess when I was younger I couldn't say m's very well. So I called him Graps. He said by the time I got old enough to teach me better he had gotten used to the name."

Henasee smiled at the thought of Kentar being a little boy. "I bet you were the cutest little boy."

"That's what all the girls used to tell me." He winked her way. "I couldn't go to town, and not have some women squeezing my cheeks or messing up my hair. Graps said it was a curse he wished God had given him."

"You poor thing," she laughed. "All the girls wanting to play with you."

"Yes." He put his fork down and turned to face her. "All the girls wanted to play with me. But there's only one girl I want to play with."

Henasee looked into his eyes and swallowed.

"Kiss him, girl," an old man's voice came from across the table.

"Yah," a woman's voice echoed in her head. "You don't want those other girls to kiss him first, do yah?"

Kentar laughed, looking around the table. The nicest-looking older couple had just sat down across from them.

"Thank you," he smiled at them. "I have been trying to get her to kiss me all day. But you know how shy a new bride can be?"

"You two just got married?" the lady asked Kentar.

"Yep!" he is proud to announce.

"This calls for a celebration," her husband yells out to the crowd. "These two just got hitched."

Everyone around them started to holler and clap. The music slowed down, and people left the makeshift dance floor.

"You should ask your missus to dance," the older lady coaxed.

"Yah, son," her husband smiled, "get your pretty wife to dance."

"Kentar turned to Henasee, who was bright red from all the attention.

"I guess it's up to you, honey. Are we going to dance or disappoint all these good folks?"

Henasee took Kentar's hand and let him pull her to her feet.

"We will dance now, darling," she whispered in his ear, "and I will kill you later in your sleep."

Kentar squeezed her waist tightly and twirled her on the dance floor.

"Then you've decided we will be sleeping in the same bed, I see."

"Before she could answer, he moved her tightly into his arms, and they moved along together as one on the dance floor. With everyone cheering and clapping, Henasee could hear nothing over the noise.

Being so close to Kentar, she could feel his lean, muscular body. His hands on her back felt like warm clothes after the fire had burnt to embers. His hand in hers felt as if it had been born with her, and it is where it was meant to be. As she looked into his eyes, every part of her wanted to lie down and be with him at that very moment.
Looking around, she felt faint at how she'd been thinking in front of all these people. Lie down right here and be with him! She shook her head to get rid of those thoughts.
"What are you thinking about?" Kentar asked.
"I was wondering if Magnus had boys, or girls, or one of each."
"Oh," Kentar answered, disappointed. "I think our song has ended."
"Yes," Henasee looked around, embarrassed once again. Why, she wondered, does he have to make me act so dumb?
"Miss?"
"Henasee turned to see a beautiful red-headed girl in a yellow sundress standing in front of them. "Do you mind if I ask him to dance?"
Henasee was so surprised she didn't answer the girl.
"I can speak for myself." Kentar gave the girl his most charming smile. "I would be honored to have this dance."
Henasee watched as Kentar and the redhead walked back to the dance floor.
"I wouldn't have given that one up without a fight," a girl whispered as Henasee walked back to her seat.
Henasee sat and watched Kentar dance with one woman after another. Watching was bad enough, but Kentar whisked them by her table so she could hear the women laugh and praise him.
"I'd be thinkin' about getting my man back, dearie."
Henasee looked at the lady they talked to earlier.
"He doesn't look to be having any better time than you are."
Henasee looked at Kentar, and for the first time, she saw the set of his jaw. She took it for granted he was having a good time. But no, he was being kind. Standing up, Henasee marched to the dance floor and tapped the lady in Kentar's arms on the shoulder.
"I've come to cut in and claim my husband," Henasee said without hesitation.
Kentar stopped dancing and let go of the lady's hand.
"I would be honored to dance with my wife." He bowed.

Henasee didn't even look at the woman who snorted and stomped off.

"Didn't you see my cries for help?" he asked quietly. "If I would have got any closer, we would have danced right across the top of the table in front of you."

Henasee laughed at the vision. "It took a kind lady to point out you weren't having any better time than I was."

"This is supposed to be our night, Henasee."

"I know," she sighed. "I'm sorry. I got scared and excited and scared."

Kentar laughed. "Let's start again."

"No." Henasee pulled out of his arms. "I like where we started." She showed him her ring. "I liked that part a lot."

Ok, let's finish what we started," Kentar smiled, picking her up off her feet and spinning to the music.

Henasee could hear sighs and moans as Kentar bent his lips to hers and kissed her with fire and passion. Sitting her down gently, he held her against him as she regained her footing.

"That was a very good . . . She can't think of a thing to say."

"Way to pick up where we left off?" he asked shakily.

"Yes, a very good way," she said, walking hand in hand off the dance floor with Kentar.

Chapter 18
Tess

"Tess," Magnus called from the hallway.
"I'm in here," a voice comes from the walk-in closet.
"What in the world are you doing in here?" Magnus asked, looking around the mounds of clothes on the floor.
"I'm trying to get some organization in here," Tess laughed.
"I tried when the girls were first born, but I lost."
Tess laughed. "I can see you lost."
"Shouldn't you be sleeping?" Magnus asked, concerned. "This will be your first night alone with the girls."
"I slept a couple of hours this afternoon, and I'll lie back down around 6."
Magnus smiled at Tess. "You sure are a Godsend. Mary said the girls adore you. She said they ate and went back to sleep in record time."
"I know how to tend to babies' needs," Tess smiled.
"Well, I guess I'll leave you to your organization."
"Thank you, ma'am," Tess yelled, getting back to work.

"I've never seen anything like her, Daniel. The babies have taken to her. My mother thinks she is the best thing in the world."
"And you, honey?" Daniel asked Magnus.
"I can't put my finger on it."
"Try," he asked again.
"She seems too good to be true. Like a . . ."
"Like a witch maybe?" he finished for her.
"Yes," Magnus said what she's been afraid to admit. "I was thinking if Fanton could take my beauty and replace her own with it, could it be possible for her to change her looks all together?"
"Yes, darling, I'm sure it's possible. Anything is possible when Fanton is involved. But," Daniel stood and paced. "Why the high recommendations from her uncle?"
"Daniel." Magnus stood and met him in the middle of the floor.
"We've never talked to Mr. Raleigh. When Tess arrived, she had her

references with her. What if she did something to the real Tess and upstairs right now Fanton is with our babies?"

"Slow down, Magnus. We must stay calm. Not everyone we come in contact with is going to be a witch in disguise." Daniel returned to pacing.

"It's not just me, is it?" Magnus pushes for an answer.

"No!" he turned and yelled. "Now give me a minute to think, Magnus. If it is her, we must be very careful. Fanton can do a lot of damage before we can get her to leave."

"She's going to be alone with the babies tonight, Daniel."

"No, she won't. I'll think of something."

"Daniel, it's our babies." Magnus started to cry.

"Stop, Magnus, we can't fall apart. I need you to help me figure this out."

"Ok." Magnus tried to calm down.

"We promised we would keep our children safe, and that is just what we're going to do."

"Whatever you want me to do, Daniel, I will."

"That's my girl. Go find your mother and bring her here. I'll find your father."

"Are you sure, Daniel?"

"The girl upstairs is Fanton. We're sure, Francine." Daniel sat by Magnus and took her hand. "We must work fast."

"What do we do?" her father asked.

Magnus had never been more proud or loved her parents than at this minute. Without thoughts of their own safety, they were going to protect her family.

"Magnus and I will need two hours to get everything ready. Francine," Daniel spoke directly to her, "have Mary help pack enough clothes for the girls to travel. Make sure Fanton, I mean Tess, has gone to lie down."

"I will," Francine nodded.

"You," Daniel turned to Magnus's father, "go to the barn and get a carriage ready to travel."

"You can consider it done." Her father saluted at Daniel. They all laughed, breaking some of the tension.

"I'll need Lenard to help," Daniel told them. "He seems to be a trustworthy man."

"He is," Magnus's father agreed.

"Ok, I guess this is good-bye."

Magnus and her mother clung to each other crying, while Daniel and her father shook hands and made each other promises to care for their loved ones.

"You be careful, dear."

"You be careful, too, mother. I love you," Magnus cried.

"I love you, too, Magnus."

"It's time to get started, ladies. I'm sorry, but if we don't get going, it might be too late."

"No, Daniel, I'm ready." Magnus turned from her mother and took Daniel's hand.

"I'm ready, too," her mother told her husband and reached for his hand.

Once out in the breezeway, they all headed in different directions. Magnus hurried upstairs to the babies' room. She was relieved to find Mary rocking Beautiful and Precious sleeping in her bassinet.

"What is wrong, Miss?" Mary asked, rising with Beautiful and placing her in her bassinet.

"We must get the babies ready to travel, Mary."

"Travel? Miss, they are still so young."

"Mary, you must be very quiet," Magnus warned. "The babies are in danger here."

"Danger!" Mary screamed. "Stop it right now, Mary. If you care at all for the girls, you must hold your tongue."

"I care about them, Miss. I'm even used to their beauty coming and going."

"I know, Mary, you hardly make notice of it anymore. Please, listen. We are leaving within the hour. You must get some clothes ready for the girls and pack your own things."

"Should I wake Tess to help?" Mary asked Magnus.

"No, Tess is not to be told," Magnus told her, taking her arm. "No one besides you is going. Now please go pack your things and bring them back here."

Mary nodded and rushed from the room. Magnus touched Precious's cheek and looked over at Beautiful.

"My little darlings," she told the two sleeping babies. "Your mother

loves you very much, and she will do anything to save you."
Precious stirred a bit but stayed asleep. "You sleep, my babies, for you are going on a great adventure. One like your mother and father went on. You will see new faces and new places. And you will be loved and cared for, my darlings, and you will be safe."
Mary hurried back carrying a pillowcase filled to overflowing. Magnus smiled. "That will do fine, Mary."
Mary smiled back, relieved. "I didn't know what else to do."
"Let's get the girls packed."
Twenty minutes later, Daniel stuck his head in the door. "Are you ready, Magnus?" he asked.
"As ready as I'll ever be."
Magnus picked up Precious all bundled up in blankets, and Daniel picked up Beautiful.
"You know what to do?" Daniel asked Francine.
"I know," Francine nodded and helped Mary with the babies' things.
"Let's get going."
Daniel took Magnus's hand, and they hurried down the staircase. Opening the door to the carriage, Daniel helped Magnus in and hands her Beautiful to put beside her on the seat. Hanging on to Precious, she reached out and touched Daniel's face.
"It's show time, are you ready?" Daniel asked Magnus.
"I'm ready."
"Magnus, please," her mother came screaming and crying from the front door. "Please, darling, I didn't mean to insinuate Precious is not a beautiful girl. I would never say my granddaughter had no beauty."
Magnus leaned her head out the carriage door and screamed, "You had no right to call her ug. I can't even repeat the word, Mother. You know I am very protective over the girls and their beauty coming and going."
"But to leave like this?" her mother's tears rain freely down her cheeks. "Please don't take my granddaughters from me."
"It is too late, Francine," Daniel yelled from on top of the carriage." You should have thought before you spoke."
Daniel raised the whip and snapped it in the air. The horses took off on a run, leaving Francine crying in the dust.
"Come in, darling." Her husband came to her side. "There is nothing

more that can be done."

"I didn't mean to say anything," Francine wailed.

"I know, darling, you know how Magnus is. She'll forgive you in a year or so."

Francine looked around the grand hallway and on seeing Tess running down the steps started crying again.

"I can't believe they are gone," Francine cried.

"Gone?" Tess yelled from the staircase.

Francine's skin stood up on her neck. She knew now Magnus was right. Tess Daloyal was in fact the witch they called Fanton.

"Yes," Francine spun around and falls to the ground like a rag doll. "Yes, they are gone. Daniel and Magnus have taken my granddaughters away. Magnus says she will never return as long as I am here."

Francine looked at her husband. "It's time for us to go home, darling."

Tess ran out the door and looked down the driveway.

"Tess," Francine called from inside the house. "You need not worry, dear. There are plenty of things for you to do, and you may stay on if you like. Our house is very nice, and we will be very kind to you."

Tess's face crinkled up, and her voice became gruff. "I'm not going anywhere with you," she hissed through her teeth. "I would like a ride to town if it's not too inconvenient?"

Francine looked at her husband and back at Tess.

"I will see to a carriage then," her husband told Tess. "Would half an hour be good?"

"Five minutes will be good," Tess snapped and headed up the stairs to her room.

Francine cried real tears as soon as Tess was out of sight.

"Stop, darling," her husband told her. "You were great. She's leaving right now."

"What about Magnus and Daniel? She's going after them."

"Yes," he calmed her. "But Daniel is a smart man, and they've got a good head start. By the time she gets to town, it will be too dark to follow them. She'll have to wait until tomorrow."

True to her word, Fanton came down the stairs with her suitcase in five minutes.

"Your carriage is waiting," Lenard told her and reached for her bag.
"Leave it alone," she growled and pulled her arm back.
"Very well," Lenard snapped back.
Fanton followed Lenard out the door and pushed past him when he tried to open the carriage door.
"Have a safe trip, ma'am," Lenard told her as the carriage pulled away.
Francine and her husband fell into each other's arms as soon as they heard the carriage leaving.

***

Henasee smiled at the older lady at the table, and the lady gave her a nod.
"What was that about?" Kentar asked, tightening his grip on her hand.
"Oh, just a wise woman, giving me some much-needed advice."
Kentar picked up the bundle of blankets, and they looked around for the axe-throwing contest.
"Over there." Kentar pointed at a row of men practicing throwing and retrieving axes.
"There's Hank." Henasee pointed.
Kentar stood beside a tree with his arms around her waist. "I can see just fine here," he whispered in her ear. "How about you?"
"I'm fine, too," she said cuddling into his arms.
An hour later, Hank held up his ribbon beaming from ear to ear.
"He's as good as he said he was. I can't believe he can throw like that." Henasee watched as Becka kissed Hank's cheek proudly.
"They have a good life, don't they?" she said dreamily.
"We have tonight, my love," he whispered in her hair. "Let's not think about anything but us."
Henasee turned daringly in his arms and kissed him without hesitation. Pulling away, she laughed at the expression on his face.
"What?" she asked.
"I don't know," he laughed, pulling her back into his arms. "But I like it."
Henasee laughed, too, and they walked off to congratulate Hank and Becka.

"I've never seen anything like that," Kentar smiled, offering his hand to Hank.

Hank smiled and shook Kentar's offered hand. "Thanks, I wasn't sure I had it all tied up. This year the competition was tough."

"You wiped the floor up with them," Becka laughed proudly.

"I did at that," Hank laughed and took Becka's hand as they walked back to the wagon. Holding Henasee tightly, Kentar watched the stars as they drove back to Hank and Becka's. Becka looked back and smiled at the young couple.

"Young love," Becka sighed.

Hank pinched her lightly on the fanny. "I'll show you some love," he laughed as she jumped. Becka laughed, too, and the rest of the trip was made in silence.

"I'll put the horses down," Kentar said, taking the reins from Hank.

"Thanks, I'm a bit tired," he said, winking at Becka.

"You go get your rest," Kentar laughed at the two lovebirds.

Hank didn't wait but turned and led Becka into the house.

"They are darling," Henasee laughed in their wake.

Kentar led the wagon in the barn with Henasee beside him. He unhooked the horses and gave them food and water in their stalls. Turning around, he was surprised not to find Henasee waiting for him. He looked around the barn one last time and started to leave.

"I thought this was going to be our night," Henasee called down from the loft.

Kentar looked up the ladder that led to the loft and caught his breath. Henasee stood naked at the top of the loft.

"I have never seen anything so beautiful in my life," he said, looking at her naked body. "If you were mine forever, I would never forget this one moment."

Henasee didn't turn away shyly but held her hands out for him to come to her. Kentar needed no words and hurried to climb the ladder and took her in his arms. Laying her down softly on her gown, he traced her face with his hand softly.

"I will cherish this night forever," he said before he lowered his head to kiss her.

Daniel pulled the reins in on the horses, and the carriage came to a stop. He opened the door, and Magnus shot out.

"I thought you'd never stop," she said, jumping out in boy's pants and a gray shirt.

"I had forgotten how good you look in boy's trousers," Daniel smiled at her.

"I thought it would be easier to travel on," Magnus smiled back. They both looked up at the sound of horses approaching.

"Just in time!" Daniel watched as two men rode up with extra horses tied to their carriages. Magnus smiled at the approaching men.

"You made good time," Daniel told one of the men as he jumps down off his horse.

"Lenard said no fooling around so we made double time."

"I appreciate your trouble," Daniel said, reaching in his pocket and pulling out a handful of bills. "This is for your trouble."

"Thanks," the man said, grabbing the money and shoving it in his pocket.

"Remember," Daniel warned him, "take your time going back. Stop at the next town, stay overnight and have some drinks on me."

"Yes, sir," the man laughed. "Oh," the man reached into his pocket and pulled out a piece of paper and handed it to Daniel. "Lenard sent this."

Daniel opened the letter and nodded at Magnus. Magnus turned and swiped at the tears on her cheeks.

"We should go," Daniel told Magnus.

Daniel took two duffel bags out of the carriage and tied them to the horses the men brought them. Magnus climbed on a brown mare and waited for Daniel to climb on his horse.

"Thanks again," Daniel waved, and he and Magnus cantered away.

"The babies?" Magnus asked when they are out of earshot of the two men.

"The note says Fanton left a soon as she found out we were gone. Your parents have the babies safe and sound, and they are taking them home, darling." Daniel reached for Magnus's hand as she cried.

"I was so afraid somehow Fanton would learn the babies weren't with us."

"I know, darling, but they're safe now."

"How long do you think we'll have to run, Daniel?"

"I wish I knew, darling. Fanton came for our children, and until they are safe, we must keep moving."

Magnus cried softly as they rode on.

Henasee tried to get Kentar to move faster, but he slowly took his time touching every inch of her.
"Kentar, please," she pleaded breathlessly.
"No, not yet," he whispered in her ear. "If I have but one night with you, it will not be rushed."
Henasee smiled and relaxed with his touch. "I would be in your arms forever if you asked," she moaned turning her head from side to side.
"If it were my choice, I would never let you go," he answered her. "Tonight is for us Henasee, tonight."
Henasee could not bear the agony anymore, and she coaxed him to take her. Needing her as if he were stranded in the desert digging for one ounce of water, Kentar pulled her on top of him.
"You are everything I have ever dreamed of," she cried out.
"And you are a beautiful dream," he returned, rubbing her hips.
"I love you, Kentar," she screamed out minutes later.
"As I you, my love. As I you."
Kentar woke to screams of terror coming from outside the barn. Henasee sat up to speak, and he covered her mouth.
"You stay here," he whispered into the darkness. "I'll see what's going on."
"Be careful," she whispered, grabbing for his arm.
Kentar placed his hand over hers. "You just stay put until I come back."
Henasee dressed quickly and hurried down the ladder of the loft. Making her way to a window, she wiped off the dust and looked out the window. Hank and Becka's house was engulfed in flames. She tries hard not to cry out, but a moan escaped her. Covering her mouth, she watched for any sign of movement. The flames from the house reached up to the sky, and the smoke was so thick Henasee had to squint to see through it.
"Come on, Kentar," she whispered. "Find them." Henasee cried out as an arm roughly pulled her backwards.
"You make a sound, and I'll snap your neck," a raspy voice whispered into her hair. "Now do as you're told, and I'll not kill your boyfriend."

Henasee went limp. She wasn't going to take a chance anyone would hurt Kentar.

"We're going to walk out the side door and get on my horse. Do you hear me?"

Henasee nodded, with the man's hand still on her mouth.

"If Kentar hears us, I'll put a bullet between his eyes."

Henasee nodded again. The man holding her, she noticed, knew Kentar's name. Fanton must have sent him to kill them both. The man slowly took his hand off her mouth and roughly grabbed her arm, digging his nails into it. Pain shot through Henasee's arm, but she didn't cry out.

"Come on," he whispered, dragging her behind him.

It was hard to see because of the smoke coming through the barn door, so Henasee let the mane drag her through the barn and outside. Covering her mouth with her other hand, she stifled a cough.

"Get up there," he ordered, grabbing her waist and pushing her on top of his horse.

Climbing up behind her, he reached for the reins. Kentar grabbed his arm and pulled the man down to the ground, bringing Henasee with him. Henasee tried to sit up, but the wind had left her lungs, and she lay gasping for air. Kentar hauled the man up to face him by the front of his shirt. Reaching inside his shirt, the man pulled out a knife. Kentar stepped back without fear in his eyes.

"I was hoping you'd do that," he growled, showing the man his front teeth. "Before I kill you, I want to know who sent you," Kentar spit at the man.

The man moved toward Kentar, waving the knife at him. Kentar, used to fighting, pinned the man to the ground in minutes. Putting the man's own knife to his throat, Kentar pushed the knife down to bring a drop of blood from a small cut.

"As I was saying, before I kill you, I want to know who sent you." The man tried to get up, but Kentar pushed him back down easily with the pressure of the knife. Kentar pushed on the knife, making a bigger slice in the man's neck.

"I'm asking one last time."

The man cried out, "It was a lady. She paid me to bring back the girl. She said she'd pay me good for her. I didn't ask why I."

Kentar stopped him with a kick to the ribs. "You thought killing an

innocent couple was worth making some money?"
Henasee came up behind him as Kentar pulled his foot back to kick the man again. "No Kentar," she said, taking his arm.
Kentar looked at the man and then at Henasee. "He killed Hank and Becka in their beds."
Henasee's face turned from hurt to anger. Walking up beside the man on the ground, she kicked him in the side with all her strength. "You will die for this," she screamed at him. "Let's put him in the house," she screamed at Kentar. "Burn him to death as he did them." The man's face turned ghost white. "No, please," he begged.
Kentar took Henasee's arm. "We would be no better than he is."
"I don't care anymore," Henasee screamed, close to hysterics. "When is this going to stop? She's killing everyone who shows us kindness. How can she be so callous as not to care who she hurts, and him!" Henasee walked to the man on the ground. "She paid him to kill two of the nicest people there ever was. Because she's jealous? Because she wants you back? This is crazy, Kentar," Henasee cried, out of control, turning to watch the roof fall into the burning house. "This is crazy," she cried again, crumbling to the ground.
The man watched as Kentar turned to grab her and jumped to his feet. Running without looking back, he jumped on his horse and kicked it in the sides with his boots.
 Kentar didn't even look up. We need to go, Henasee.
Henasee stayed on the ground, and he stooped down and picked her up.
"He shouldn't have hurt them, Kentar," she cried into his shoulder.
"I know, my love," he whispered, kissing her wet cheek. "No one should have hurt them. She's going to pay for this, Henasee. I promise." Kentar watched as the last wall fell from Hank and Becka's house. "I promise she'll pay."
Kentar saddled their horses as Henasee retrieved her shoes from the hay loft. The sun was starting to come up, and Henasee could see around the loft. Reaching down, she touched the spot she and Kentar had made love in just hours before. Lost in their world of passion and love, she never dreamed anything as horrible as this could happen. One minute, everything makes sense; the next, your life is turned upside down. "Kentar was right," she promised herself.

"Fanton is going to pay dearly for killing Becka and Hank". If it took a lifetime to pay her back, she would see to it herself.

With a few things packed from the barn to keep them warm at night, Kentar and Henasee rode off from Hank and Becka's property side by side.

"We need to make sure Magnus and Daniel are all right," Kentar told her when they stopped alongside a creek to give the horses water.

Henasee looked up from the creek. "We can see them?"

"I'm sure if Fanton found us she probably knows where they are."

"How far away are they?" she asked.

"Three days' ride," he answered.

"Three days?"

"I wanted to be close in case they needed help," he smiled at her.

Henasee smiled back. He could see the smile didn't reach her eyes. "I'd love to see the babies."

"Well, I think it's time the babies met you."

Henasee smiled and took Kentar's offered hand and let him pull her into his arms. Kissing her tenderly, he held her for a while, happy she was safe in his arms.

Magnus and Daniel stopped their horses on the edge of a cornfield.

"This looks like a good place to camp," Daniel said, helping Magnus off her horse.

Magnus looked around the field while Daniel gathered wood for a fire. Picking four ears of corn, Magnus sat down to pull the husks off.

"A woman who knows my heart," Daniel laughed, coming up behind her.

"Or," Magnus laughed back, "a woman who knows your stomach."

"Very funny," Daniel laughed with her.

"Do you think?" Magnus asked on a sigh.

"The babies are fine, darling. You can't worry yourself every minute of every day. It's not healthy for you or me. God has given us a beautiful family, Magnus. He won't let anything bad happen to our children."

"I know you're right, Daniel, I just miss them."

"Of course you miss them, darling," Daniel said, sitting down beside her.

"We both miss them, but you're their mother. One day they will know just how much you loved them."

"What do you mean?" she asked.

"You loved them enough to make sure they were kept safe no matter what the heartache to yourself."

Magnus hugged Daniel with all her strength. "How did I ever get so lucky?" she asked him.

"I am the one who is lucky, darling. It is I."

Daniel laid Magnus slowly on the ground and made love to her so gently it was as if it were their first time together. Afterwards, Magnus began to cry.

"I'm sorry you miss them so much, darling," Daniel said, pulling her into his arms again.

"I do miss them," Magnus sniffed, "but that's not why I'm crying."

"Then why?"

"Everything we have been through I would not go back and change my destiny back to my life without you."

"Wow," Daniel smiled, pulling her back to look into her eyes. "That's a big statement for you."

"I know," she laughed, hugging him again. "Even losing my beauty and being on the run hasn't changed my feelings of how lucky I am to have found you, Daniel."

"I feel the same, Magnus." Daniel's stomach growled, and Magnus laughed out loud. "Ok, you know my stomach," he laughed.

Filled to contentment on dried meats, fresh corn, and coffee from their supplies, Daniel cuddled next to Magnus on a makeshift bed of blankets. Looking up into the stars, Magnus closed her eyes and asked God to please keep her babies and her parents safe from Fanton.

"You say one for me, too," Daniel whispered in her ear, pulling her to him.

"I already did," she smiled." I can't believe how beautiful the sky becomes at night," she told him.

"I know," Daniel replied. "When we were sailing, it was the only thing to do on board the ship at night. If you weren't working, you were either eating or sleeping to work again. I used to look at the sky for hours on my night duty."

"I would never get tired of looking at the night sky," Magnus said quietly drifting off to sleep.
"I would never get tired of looking at you," Daniel said to her, kissing her cheek and falling asleep himself.

Chapter 19
No Beauty Needed

"You two get up slowly and raise your hands," a voice shouted, waking Magnus and Daniel up.

Magnus sat up, and Daniel reached for her arm.

"Slow down, darling, until I can see who we're dealing with. If I say run, you head into the cornfield."

Magnus looked into Daniel's eyes, and he knew she understands.

Standing slowly, Daniel stepped in front of Magnus.

"We meant no harm," Daniel yelled out.

Daniel saw the tip of a shotgun before a big man in a gray shirt and dark blue jeans walked slowly out of the cornfield. As soon as the man saw Magnus, he turned the scope of the gun to face the ground.

"I'm sorry, ma'am," the man said, nodding toward Magnus. "I've had problems with thieves, and I wasn't sure who those horses belonged to."

Magnus gave a nervous tilt of her head.

"We didn't mean to take advantage of your place," Daniel offered. "We've been traveling, and my wife got tired."

Magnus smiled and nodded her head.

"Like I said, I've had problems with thieves."

Daniel looked down at the empty corn cobs. "I'd like to pay you for those."

The man said nothing and waited for Daniel to put his hand in his pocket and pull out a wad of bills.

"I think I'll be taking all of that," the man nodded toward Daniel's hand. Daniel reached his hand out, and the man pointed to Magnus. "Give it to her. She can bring it to me."

Daniel paused a second, and the man lifted his gun up to point at Daniel's chest.

"No," Magnus cried out. "I'll bring it to you."

Magnus took the money from Daniel. Daniel pulled his hand back, and Magnus reached for it again.

"I can give the nice man his money, darling. He was kind enough to let us use his land for food and lodging."

Daniel smiled at Magnus and handed her the money. The man relaxed his gun and opened his hand to take the money from Magnus. Magnus reached out her hand and Daniel watched as her beauty started to go away. The man pulled his hand back as if it were burnt.

"What is that?" he screams watching as scars appeared on Magnus's arms.

"My wife has a disease. We've been traveling from place to place to see if there is a cure," Daniel said behind Magnus.

"It spreads so fast," Magnus said, turning over her hand to show scars on the back. "Please," Magnus smiled, reaching her hand out again. "Please take this for all you've done for us."

"I don't want it," the man screamed, backing up even more.

"No," Magnus said, following him farther into the woods. "I insist."

"Get away from me," the man yelled and tripped over a cornstalk, dropping his gun. "I don't want it."

"You must take it." Magnus pushed further. "You wanted it bad enough to threaten my husband's life. It must be very important to you to kill someone for."

"I wasn't going to kill him." The man starts to sweat. "I was just going to . . ."

"You were just going to rob us and let us think you would kill us." Magnus leered over him.

"Yes, I mean no. Please, ma'am, I have a family to care for."

"Is this a way for a father to act?" Magnus yelled at the man on the ground.

"No, ma'am, I shouldn't be acting the way I did."

"You're right," she yelled again. "You shouldn't. Now get up and go on now."

The man didn't wait for another word. He stood up and never looked back. Daniel laughed listening to the man stumble through the cornfield and pull himself back up to start running again. Magnus handed Daniel back his money, and they both started to laugh.

"I don't think he'll be robbing anyone anytime too soon."

"I don't think he'll stop running until his legs give out," Daniel laughed back. Daniel pulled Magnus to his chest. "I love you," he said, lifting her chin to kiss her.

"I was just lucky my beauty decided to go away at that very

moment."
"Listen to what you said, Magnus."
"What?" she asked him.
"You said you were lucky your beauty went away."
Magnus laughed and then started to cry.
"Losing your beauty just saved our lives, darling."
Magnus grabbed on to Daniel with all the love she felt. "This will be a story we will pass on to our daughters, darling. About the day their mother lost her beauty and saved their father's life," Magnus laughed into Daniel's shoulder.
"He was scared, wasn't he?" Daniel lifted his head up and laughed again, hearing the man in the cornfield still tripping over cornstalks.

"Chainridge is over the next hill," Kentar pointed. "We'll ride in as if we've always been here. In case someone is watching, they'll think we're out for a ride."
Henasee shook her head and smiled. "I can't believe I get to see Magnus and the babies."
Nothing was said as they rode up the road that would take them to Magnus and Daniel. Reaching the steps, Kentar lifted Henasee down from her horse. They walked up the stairs. Kentar banged on the door. Within a minute, the door flew open.
"May I help you?" a man dressed in black asked them. "You are Henasee." The man bowed at her.
"Yes," Henasee replied looking at him.
"Magnus described you and said you would be coming one day."
"Come, come in."
Henasee and Kentar followed the man into Chainridge.
"If you would be so kind as to follow me, Miss." The man led them into a sitting room and pointed to the couch. "Sit please."
Henasee sat down, and Kentar walked around the couch to stand behind her. Henasee watched as the man hurried and shut the door.
"We must not let others hear," the man said quietly. "Your friends are not here," he continued to whisper. "The witch Fanton came, and they—"
Henasee interrupted him. "Are they all right?" she asked. "Are the babies all right?" she asked with tears running down her face.
"Please, Miss, don't cry. They are all fine. The babies are with

Magnus's parents and Daniel and Magnus are…"

"Where are they?" Henasee started to get really upset.

"Henasee," Kentar placed his hand on her shoulder. "Let the man finish."

"The witch doesn't know where any of them are. Daniel came up with a plan," Lenard told them, rubbing his hands together nervously. "The witch thinks Daniel and Magnus ran off with the children because of a fight with Magnus's mother. But instead the babies were hidden in the west wing, and when the witch saw Daniel and Magnus take off, she left then herself. As soon as she was on her way, we packed up the babies and Magnus's parents and took them to safety."

"Magnus isn't with her children?" Henasee asked, still upset.

"No, Daniel knew they could not run with the baby girls being so small."

"Girls," Henasee cried out, standing to look into Lenard's face. "The babies are girls?"

Lenard relaxed and smiled for the first time. "They are beautiful little girls," he laughed. "They are very loved and cared for. She left you a letter, Miss."

Lenard walked to a desk on the other side of the room and pulled open a drawer. Reaching in, he took out an envelope. Bringing it back, he handed it to Henasee. Henasee opened the envelope and pulled out the letter.

"Dear Hen, If you're reading this, it means Fanton has found us, and we're probably on the run. I wish you could have been here with me when the girls were born. They are so beautiful, Hen, even when their beauty comes and goes. I named them Precious and Beautiful. Precious after you, my precious friend, and Beautiful after the thing I gave up to have my darling children. I am sorry for what I have gotten you into, and I hope someday we'll be able to sit and talk about everything. My parents are caring for the girls and will keep them safe as long as they can. But they can only do so much for so long. Fanton is very strong and very dangerous, as you know. I'm not sure how long my parents will be able to hide them. My father is preparing a ship to sail in less than 4 months from the date of this letter. I want you to join them and protect my daughters. I know you will do this for me, my friend. Kiss my babies for me. Thank you,

Love, Magnus"
Henasee handed the letter to Kentar.
"You look tired, Miss," Lenard observed. "You are most safe here. Let me show you to your room."
Henasee looked over at Kentar, who nodded.
"I am tired," she told Lenard.
"Come this way, Miss."
Henasee followed Lenard into the hall way and up a grand staircase.
"The babies?" Henasee asked, walking up the stairs behind Lenard. "What do they look like?"
Lenard stopped walking and turned to face Henasee. "They look just like their mother. Both of them are simply beautiful."
"You are very fond of them?" she smiled.
"This old place came alive with the birth of those two girls. When they left," Lenard sighed, "they took away the very happiness out of the place."
Henasee smiled at Lenard. "We shall pray for a very speedy return of the Chainridge girls then."
Henasee could see Lenard relax visibly. "Yes, Miss we will at that. I have a favor to ask, Miss."
"Yes," Henasee replied, "if I can it will be done."
"Daniel wanted me to stay behind in case you and your friend showed up. Now that you are safe here, I would ask you let me accompany you to the ship."
Henasee's smile grew wider. "Those two little darlings really did get under your skin."
"Truth be told, Miss, I miss them terribly."
Henasee walked into the room Lenard opened the door for her.

Henasee awoke into a room of darkness and started to cry out. Before she could make more than a single cry, Kentar was at her side.
"No, my lovely, you need not be afraid. I am at your side."
Henasee clung to Kentar. "I dreamt of the fire," she started to cry into Kentar's shoulder.
"I have not been able to let it go myself," Kentar whispered into Henasee's hair.
"They were good people, and they were very kind to us," Henasee

stated into the darkness. "She cannot get away with this, Kentar."
"I know, darling, we will think of something."
"I can't even think about what she would do if she got a hold of the babies," Henasee cried out, shaking from head to toe.
"We are not going to let her get a hold of the babies, Henasee. You must not make a problem that doesn't exist. We have lay low and then get to the ship without being seen. Then we will concentrate on keeping the baby's safe, not worrying about what if?"
Henasee pulled away from Kentar. "You are right," she told him. "I will not put such thoughts in my head. We will protect Magnus's little girls."
Kentar pulled Henasee onto his lap and kissed her neck. "We will share this night in a bed together," he said kissing her neck again. Henasee cuddled into him and sighed.
A knock on the door startled Henasee, which made Kentar laugh out loud. "You need not be so jumpy," he smiled and placed her gently on the bed. "I had Lenard get you a bath and bring our dinner up."
Henasee watched as Kentar lit a lamp. Her heart filled with so much love she wondered why it didn't burst out of her chest.
Lenard with two maids and two young boys carrying a bathing tub hurried into the room. Never looking up, each person did a different job and hurried out the door, only to appear again and again. When everything was to Lenard's standards, he ordered the two boys and maids to run along.
"This is very nice," Henasee smiled at Lenard.
"I hope everything is to your satisfaction, Miss?"
Henasee looked around the room. Candles were shining everywhere. A small table was set for two by a roaring fireplace. The bathing tub was placed on a rug beside the fireplace with steam rolling above it.
"I had the maid bring you some night clothing from Magnus's room," Lenard said, bowing. "If you are of no longer need of me, Miss? I will wish you a good night."
Lenard started to walk to the door.
"Wait." Henasee slid off the bed and headed to him. "There is one thing."
"Yes, Miss." Lenard looked around the room with a worried look on his face. Henasee reached out and kissed his cheek.

"That is for being so thoughtful." She smiled and looked around the room. Henasee kissed his other cheek. "That is for being such a loyal friend to Daniel and Magnus and their babies".

Lenard's face and neck turned completely red. Not wanting to open his mouth, afraid he may burst into unmanly tears, Lenard patted Henasee's hand and turned and left the room.

"I don't think his color will turn back to normal for weeks," Kentar laughed behind her.

Henasee turned and smiled. "He is a very kind man, and he loves those babies. He wants to come with us," she told Kentar.

"No, Hen, it's too dangerous. We have to be invisible until the ship sails. Another person will make it harder."

"I already gave him my word," she said, never taking her eyes way from his.

"Take it back," Kentar said flatly.

"I will not," she yelled at Kentar.

"Henasee, it will be too dangerous to have three of us traveling together."

"We will be extra careful," she snapped back.

Kentar shook his head and stepped out of the room, slamming the door.

"Go then!" she yelled at the closed door. "Go off and pout, Kentar, very mature, very mature."

Henasee looked at the closed door and shook her head. "Men!" she yelled. Walking over to the bathing tub, she undressed and climbed into it, slowly sitting down. Lying back she closed her eyes and enjoyed the hot water soaking around her.

"If I never live to . . ." she said into the empty room.

"If you never live to what?" Kentar asked, watching the water run across her body.

Henasee sat up so fast water shot out of the full tub. Kentar tried to dodge a stream of water she splashed at him but it soaked his shirt.

"I see you want to play," he laughed, taking off his shirt and pants and climbing in the other end of the bathing tub with her.

"I thought you were angry?" she asked him, lifting her leg over the side of the tub to give him more room.

"I was," he laughed. "But I am not a foolish man."

"What do you mean?"

"We have a night together safe from the world and all its anger. It took me two minutes to decide if I wanted to spend my night angry or here with you."

Henasee laughed and crawled to the other end of the tub with Kentar. "I think you made a very good choice, Kentar."

Kentar pulled her down on him. "I think I made a very good choice, too," he said, kissing her passionately.

With water everywhere, Kentar lifted Henasee out of the tub and carried her to the rug in front of the fireplace. Leaving her for only a minute, he returned with a soft light blue robe. Kentar placed it on her gently. Looking into his eyes, Henasee reached out her hand to him.

"We have all night, Henasee. I will not be rushed this time."

Henasee drew her hand back and stretched out on the rug, throwing off the robe. "I will not rush you, Kentar," she smiled, moving from side to side.

Kentar's neck muscles contracted. "You will drive me crazy with your wild ways Henasee." Kentar took the towel that was wrapped around his waist and let it drop to the floor.

"Now where were we?" he smiled, lifting up her head and kissing her lips ever so gently. She moaned. "I see it is not just the powers you hold over me. I must hold some myself."

Henasee pulled her head back and looked into Kentar's eyes. "You hold my heart in your hands, Kentar."

"As you do mine, Henasee," he said, kissing her again.

"I will never forget this night, Kentar."

"We will have many nights together, Henasee."

"You will not leave me?" Henasee asked him. "No matter the danger for yours or my life?"

"I will not leave you," he promised and stopped her questions with a deeper kiss.

Lost in her heart, Henasee kissed him back.

"How many more days, Daniel?" Magnus asked for the fourth time.

"We will meet the ship in three days, Magnus, and now for the fourth time, darling, stop worrying. Your father and I have everything planned out to the last minute. That way Fanton won't get word of us sailing until we're long gone."

"I know you two have a plan but what if?"
"Magnus," Daniel said sternly. "We agreed you would not obsess about this."
"Obsess?" Magnus screeched back at him. "I did not know being concerned was obsessed. Excuse me for worrying about everything I hold dear in the world." To hide her tears, Magnus turned her head away from Daniel. "My children are eight months old today," she whispered. "They probably don't even remember who I am."
"Stop, Magnus," Daniel asked, reaching out his hand.
"I can't help but worry, Daniel."
"I know, darling," he said, taking her hand. "Everything will be all right."
Magnus smiled at him with tears running down her cheeks.
"Promise me they will be all right, Daniel."
"Magnus, I promise the babies and your parents will be fine."

Kentar had all but forgotten his misgivings of not bringing Lenard. Lenard could ride as well as Kentar and was very handy on the trail.
"I will find some wood for a fire," Lenard told Kentar, heading to the woods along the place they were going to camp for the night.
"I know," Henasee smiled at Kentar. "He is a very handy man to have along."
"I must admit I have thought the same things these last couple of days. He finds firewood, makes the fire, and cooks better than three men."
"Maybe I was right?" she smiled again.
"Maybe," Kentar laughed and pulled her into his arms. "Just maybe," Kentar kissed her and held her to him.
Lenard walked farther and farther into the woods. Climbing up a steep hill, he looked around at the ground below. Spotting her, he waved for her to wait for him. Fanton sat on top of her horse smiling sweetly.
"Do you want us to kill him?" one of the two men with her asked her.
"No, I need him; he will die tomorrow when I have the girl."
"Ok," the man agreed.
"You have the money?" Lenard asked, his hand already stretched out.

"How are you going to get Kentar away from her?" Fanton asked him.

"I have brought these." Lenard pulled a piece of paper out of his pocket and unfolded it showing her two small pills. "The man I got it from says it will drop a bull where it stands."

"I don't want him dead," Fanton snapped. "I just want him down long enough to take the girl."

"He'll have a hell of a headache," Lenard laughed, "but he won't die."

"Good," Fanton laughed and handed Lenard an envelope. Lenard started to open it.

"You do not trust the money is there?" Fanton yelled at him.

Lenard took a step backwards and looked at both men. He hadn't noticed their guns before. Both had guns hanging from their sides and rifles sticking out of their saddles.

"I didn't mean anything," Lenard stuttered. "What time will you come for the girl?" he asked, still backing away from Fanton's gaze.

"Noon tomorrow," she told Lenard and turned her horse around. "Nothing better go wrong, or I will skin your hide off your bones, old man."

Lenard reached for his throat, scared to his very toes.

"Now go back before they wonder where you have been for so long."

Lenard hurried back to camp, picking up wood as he went.

"There you are," Henasee smiled, putting another log on the fire Kentar started. "I was starting to get worried about you."

"No need to worry, Miss. I'm still in one piece."

"How did it go?" Kentar asked Lenard, handing him a tin cup of coffee.

"She thinks I have turned on you, and she wants the girl. I mean she wants Henasee tomorrow by noon."

"Thank goodness you are a loyal friend," Henasee said, hugging Lenard.

Lenard hugged her back. "I would never give my worst enemy to that witch. She will get hers one day."

"Yes, I'm counting on it," Kentar told him.

"We need to get going," Lenard told them both. "She had two gunmen with her."

"How do you know they were gunmen?" Henasee asked him. "They are carrying enough guns to start a small war."

Henasee took Kentar's arm. "She plans to kill us this time, Kentar."

"No, darling," he said putting his hand around her waist. "She thinks Lenard has betrayed us. Thanks to Lenard's fast thinking, we are all still alive."

"I knew when she approached me in town she was up to no good," Lenard told them. "What kind of a monster would want to hurt priceless babies? She was angry when she thought Magnus had taken them away. She let her real self show by the way she left Chainridge. I would not have helped her kill a bug. When she approached me, she said I could be a very rich man if I got you out of the way long enough to get the girl."

Henasee cringed. "Why just me?"

"I walked away after I agreed to betray the two of you and snuck back down the alley. She was talking to a man about trading you for her Daniel and Magnus's children. She said, Kentar would get the babies for a trade for your life. When she had the babies, she planned on killing you both slowly."

Kentar gave Lenard a dirty look, and Lenard turned a shade of green. "I'm sorry, sir, I was so wrapped up in telling the story I forgot the Miss was in earshot."

"This is what you've been keeping from me?" Henasee said, pushing Kentar's arm off her.

"There was no need to go into details of our deaths, Henasee."

"I don't like it when you try to protect me, Kentar. If you haven't noticed, it always backfires on you."

"I am getting the picture." Kentar looked Lenard's way and gives him a glare.

Lenard felt it all the way to his toes. Lenard looked away from the two. "I will start the meal if no one objects."

Both Henasee and Kentar turned away from him.

"I told you what I thought was best for you to know, Henasee," Kentar said, reaching for her arm.

Henasee threw his hand off her arm. "I might have been naïve a year ago, Kentar, but I grew up fast. If we are to stay together, I will not have you keeping things from me."

Kentar started to say something, and she turned and walked off.

"Just keep your excuses, Kentar. From day one, you've treated me like I'm just a dumb girl, and I'm getting sick and tired of it. It's not just yours and my lives Fanton wants to end. It's Magnus's babies she's after. You should have told me," she finished and walked down to the river.

Kentar watched her climb over a small hill and disappear on the other side.

"I am truly sorry, sir," Lenard started to say.

"It wasn't your fault, Lenard. If not for you Fanton would have jumped us along the way. You have been a good friend. Henasee is right. I should have told her the whole story from the start."

Kentar looked at the empty space he had seen her a few minutes before.

I think that's all she wants to hear from you sir. Lenard smiles.

Kentar nodded and headed to the river walking with the knowledge that he could rely on Henasee as an adult and an equal made him smile. She was right. She hadn't been a young girl in a long time. She had grown from her experience into a beautiful young woman. She was smart, beautiful, and very wise for her age. He would never again leave her in the dark about anything. From now on, he was going to share everything with her. "Why not?" he laughed to himself. "She already owns my heart." Kentar's smile faded as he climbed over the small hill. He ran to the river. Beside the river, Kentar picked up a piece of Henasee's shirt. Looking around, he tried to find some sign of her.

"Henasee," he yelled into the open land. "Henasee?"

Lenard climbed over the small hill and hurried to Kentar's side.

"Fanton," Kentar screamed. "If you hurt her, I will choke the life out of you with my bare hands!"

Fanton looked over at Henasee sitting on top of a horse with one of her hired killers. Henasee looked back at Fanton.

"If you make a sound to alert him where we are he's a dead man." Henasee looked away from Fanton and said nothing.

"Now that's what I like, a smart girl," Fanton laughed again. "Let's get out of here," she told her men, and they rode off.

"Magnus, slow down." Daniel hurried behind her, trying to grab her arm.

"We are minutes away from seeing our girls, honey. I can't slow down."

"At least watch your footing. You're going to slip and get hurt."

"Then I'll crawl to my daughters, Daniel. Now let me go."

Magnus turned and rushed down another hallway.

"You're going to get us lost," Daniel yelled in her wake.

"Daniel, I lived on this boat for months. I know almost every inch of it."

"It wasn't filled to the rafters like it is now, Magnus."

"You told my mother to make sure we had everything we would need to raise the girls."

"I know, but I didn't tell her to fill up an entire ship."

"It's not that bad," Magnus laughed, almost tripping over another box.

"What could she have packed?" Daniel asked, climbing over a box and stepping on a bag of something that sounded like it shattered in a million pieces.

"Daniel." Magnus slowed down. "Be careful. You don't know what you're breaking."

Daniel rubbed his head as he tried to get his foot out of the bag. "I will, Magnus, I'll watch what I'm doing."

Magnus came to a closed door and stopped. "It's right there," she gushed.

"Well, aren't you going to go in?" Daniel asked her.

"I can't." Magnus stopped and turned to face him. "It's been months since we've seen them. What if they don't remember who I am? What if they cry, Daniel?"

"Oh, darling, they will remember you. Who could ever forget you after meeting you?"

"Oh, Daniel." Magnus fell into his arms crying. "I love you so much."

"I love you, too, darling." Daniel reached behind Magnus's head and drew her to him. He kissed her tenderly at first and then deepened the kiss.

"Oh, Daniel," she whispered in between kisses.

"Oh, my!" A screech came from the open doorway.

"Mother?" Magnus turned to say.

"Magnus, what on earth are you doing? I mean I can see what you're doing. I mean."

"Hello, Mother," Magnus smiled and gives her a hug. "I was just having last-minute jitters about seeing the girls again."

"I see." Her mother hugged her back.

"Are your jitters better now?" her mother asked, uncertain.

"Yes," Magnus nodded and smiled into her mother's face. "How have they been?"

"They are little angels, darling," her mother said proudly. "They can almost stand on their own."

Magnus sucked in a breath. "They can?"

"They are smarter than their age, Magnus. I swear Beautiful knows what people are talking about when she's around him."

Magnus looked at her mother as if she were touched.

"I know it sounds strange, dear, but they seem to know I'm not their mother. I'll be holding one of them, and they seem to be watching the door waiting for someone to come in."

"Maybe they do miss me, Mother."

"I think that's what it is," her mother cheered up. "They miss you."

Magnus slowly walked over to the bassinets. Peering over the side, she was surprised when Beautiful smiled at her. Not a smile for an eight-month-old infant but an older smile, a more knowing smile. Shaking off the uneasy feeling, Magnus reached for Beautiful.

Beautiful waited for Magnus to almost touch her, and she let out a scream that made even Daniel jump.

"What is that about?" Magnus asked, looking at her mother.

"I'm not sure, dear. We've had to let all but two nannies go. Beautiful won't allow them to touch her."

"Yes, but I'm her mother. I'm not just a nanny."

"Give her some time, darling. She needs time to get to know you again."

Magnus's eyes welled up with tears. "No, darling, it will be all right, you'll see. She was just frightened for a minute, that's all."

Magnus looked back at Beautiful, who seemed to be fast asleep. But when she turned her head to look at Daniel and back at Beautiful, she could swear she saw her daughter open and close her eyes real fast.

"I'll let her rest," Magnus said, a bit shaken. "How is Precious?"

"She has the perfect name. She is a precious little girl."
Magnus looked in Precious's bassinet and was thrilled to find Precious smiling like a tiny infant. Reaching in the bassinet, Magnus lifted Precious out ever so lightly.
"Hello, my darling."
Precious cooed and looks at her mother.
"You remember me, don't you, darling?"
Precious reached her hand up, and Magnus took it with her other hand. Precious smiled and squeezed her finger.
"She is a sweetheart," Magnus laughed. Magnus took Precious to a chair in the corner and sat down with her. Precious, Magnus noticed, never took her eyes from Magnus.
"I think I'm starting to see what you mean, Mother," Magnus said, watching Precious look at her. "Precious knows I'm her mother and is happy to see me. I think Beautiful is mad I've been gone."
"Darling, babies don't think for themselves like that. They're too young."
"Daniel, they're not ordinary babies."
Daniel approached Beautiful's bassinet and looked down at her. Beautiful's eyes opened up and stared at him.
"Ok, they are a bit creepy."

Chapter 20
Beautiful and Precious

"Daniel," Magnus scolded. "You can't call our babies creepy."
"Listen Magnus, Beautiful is looking at me as if she's thinking about saying something."
"I told you," Magnus's mother told them. "They've been getting, let's say, different with each passing day."
"They do seem a bit older than they are," Daniel said, watching Beautiful watch him. Daniel reached his arms in the bassinet, and Beautiful lifted her arms up to him. "She likes me," Daniel giggled.
"You are one of few, Daniel. She won't let very many touch her, Magnus. It's usually either Mary or me."
"Mary has been so kind to the girls," her mother smiled over at Daniel with Beautiful. "I don't know what I would have done all these months without her."
"I can't wait to see her," Magnus cooed at Precious.
"She should be along any minute. She usually sits with the girls at night so I can rest."
"Oh, Mother," Magnus cried, "thank you for watching over them."
"They are my grandchildren, of course I would look after them, darling. They are my precious little girls."
Daniel and Magnus both looked at their daughters as both babies turned and looked at their grandmother and laughed out loud.
A tap on the door made everyone jump. Magnus's mother stepped to the door and opened it.
"Mary," Magnus cried out.
"You are safe," Mary said, coming to Magnus's side and bending down to kiss her cheek. "I have worried about you."
"We are finally all together," Magnus smiled looking around the room. "Father, he is in good health?" she directed the question to her mother.
"He is younger than he has been in years, darling. He adores the girls and takes them for strolls on the deck. You would think they were his children."
"Have you heard from Henasee, Mother?"

"No, darling, nothing yet. But I'm sure we'll hear something soon. Your uncle sent word for them to meet us on the ship. I'm sure they'll be along soon."

"How wonderful to have the people I love most all safe for a change."

"I do agree with you there, my dear," her mother said, reaching her hands out to take Beautiful from Daniel. "I think it's time we get these two settled around for the night. Otherwise, they will not sleep at all."

Magnus smiled down at Precious. "She does look wide awake."

"They like the nighttime it seems better than the days," Mary smiled as she took Precious from Magnus. "It took many nights to switch them over."

Daniel kissed Beautiful's forehead and Beautiful smiled up at him. "Magnus," Daniel's speech seemed stressed. "Beautiful has markings on the inside of her hand."

Magnus stood and walked to Daniel. "What, darling?" Magnus asked him.

"It looks like two crosses joined in the middle. One of the crosses seems to be dripping blood from it."

Magnus looked at Beautiful's hand, but when she reached out to touch Beautiful, Beautiful let out a thunderous scream. "Oh, my," Magnus retracted her hand with a little cry. "She doesn't even want me to touch her."

"Don't fret, Magnus," her mother comforted her. "It has been a very big night for Beautiful. She will come around in a couple of days."

Magnus watched as Daniel turned Beautiful's hand around looking at the strange birthmark.

Mary stared in wonder. "Excuse me, sir, but I bathed her this morning, and there was no mark on her hand."

Magnus grabbed Daniel's arm and pulled him close. "It's from the blood of Fanton flowing in her veins, isn't it, Daniel? I mean, they are not ordinary babies."

"I'm sure that's what's going on, Magnus. All we can do is wait and see."

Magnus looked at Beautiful, wanting to take her from her mother and hold her close to her heart, but she knew she could not. Beautiful would not allow it. Magnus turned and held out her hands for Sally to hand her Precious.

"Look," Magnus showed Daniel. "She has markings on her hand, too."

"There is only one cross on her hand," Daniel told them. "Strange," he said, turning Precious's tiny hand around to look more closely at the mark. "Beautiful has two crosses with red spots coming from it, and Precious's markings seem to have a circle of light around her one cross."

"Oh, this is strange, Daniel."

"They are healthy little girls, Magnus. We will get through anything we have to, to protect our little girls."

"You're right Daniel," Magnus sniffed. "Our little darlings will grow up to be beautiful little ladies."

"Beautiful little nighttime ladies," Magnus's mother sniffed, "if they don't keep their bed schedule."

"Ok, Mother," Magnus laughed nervously. "We'll let them get their rest."

"This can all be figured out tomorrow, darling."

"I know, Mother," Magnus sighed, giving Precious back to Mary.

"They will be fine, Magnus," Mary reassured her.

"Thank you, Mary, for everything."

"No thank you's are needed, Miss. I love Beautiful and Precious. They are lovely children."

Magnus wiped a tear from her cheek. "They are both very beautiful, aren't they?"

"Yes, they are darling," Daniel said, placing his arm around her shoulders and leading her out of the room.

"You know we're not done talking about this, Daniel?"

"I didn't think we would be, darling, but for now let's find some dinner and a place for us to sleep for the night."

"Both of those things have been taken care of," a voice said from behind them. Magnus turned and happily stepped into her father's open arms.

"It's so good to see you, Father," she cried into his shoulder.

"You are safe at last, Magnus," her father said, hugging her tighter.

"We have prayed the good Lord would bring you back to us unharmed."

"I am unharmed, Father," she cried out in another burst of emotions.

"Daniel, my boy," her father smiled through his watery eyes, reaching out his hand to shake Daniel's. "Thank you so much for keeping her safe once again."

Magnus pulled away from her father. "I have done a very good job of keeping myself safe, Father." Magnus laughed when she saw her father had been baiting her. "Oh, Father." She stepped back into his arms. "I have missed you so."

"I have missed you, too, my daughter. We will have many talks and walks on our way to Noteese."

"Noteese?" Magnus asked, startled. "Why are we going to Noteese?"

"Ahaira said there is a rare plant there. It is known to have many uses. One is heard to break spells."

"You mean my beauty coming and going, Father? Daniel and I have come to a shared piece about that. I can live with or without it."

"No, Magnus, I am not talking about you, my dear."

"Then who, Father?"

"Your daughters, darling."

Magnus looked into her father's eyes. "Father, they will be raised with so much love, they will hardly notice when their beauty is gone. They will find men to marry as kind as their father. Beauty will not make or break their lives. They will have fine lives and be strong independent women."

"Magnus, dear," her father patted her hand. "It's not their beauty coming and going I'm concerned about. It's, it's . . ."

"Tell me, Father," she pleaded. "Please what is wrong with my babies?"

"Precious has shown no signs of anger yet, but Beautiful can be very . . ."

"Very what Father?"

"She can be mean, Magnus almost to the point of being cruel."

"Father, she's just a child. How can a child be cruel? They are only eight months old."

"I know, darling, but I have seen it with my own eyes. Beautiful clawed one nanny's face, and another she pulled hair out of her head by the roots. Leaving a bare bloody spot, where the hair had once been."

"But they are just babies, Father."

"They may be babies, Magnus, but the spell you were under has somehow changed them from being the same as other children. When Beautiful has her beauty, she is a very sweet child. When her beauty is gone, she is no longer the same sweet girl. You would be wise to be careful when you're with them."

"You want me to be afraid of my own children father? That's crazy," Magnus cried, starting to lose control. "What mother would be afraid of her children?"

"Magnus," Daniel came forward and took her arm and turned her to face him. "You have seen the girls. They are not normal babies. We will listen to your father and take them to Noteese. It's the only chance they have to have a normal life."

"Oh, Daniel," she cried.

"Magnus, we'll be fine, darling," he said with a confidence he didn't feel.

"This talk can wait until tomorrow, Magnus. Let's get you and Daniel fed and settled down for the night."

Magnus hugged her father again. "Thank you for being here, Father. I know this is not a trip you have ever wanted to take."

Magnus watched her father's face turn to sadness." I lost a lot of dear friends because of Noteese, but my granddaughters, I will travel to the ends of the Earth and back for them."

"I know you will, Father," she cried, holding him again. "I know you will."

Henasee tried her hardest not to lean back on the scary-looking hired killer. She knew that was what he was because Fanton laughed, telling her the story of finding the best hired killers in the area. Try as she might, they were riding so fast she had to lean back on the man riding with her.

"Settle in real cozy, darling. Slate here will make sure you don't fall off."

Henasee tried to sit up, but Slate pulled her back up against his chest. "Right here is where you feel best, darling."

Her head started to spin from the speed of the horse and the smell of stale alcohol coming from his mouth.

"Maybe you and I can have a private little party later," he said, putting an arm around her waist and pulling her even closer. : You know after everyone goes to bed."

Henasee gagged at the idea of this man touching her the way Kentar did. She didn't know what would happen to her, but she made herself a promise. She would die before this man ever had his way with her even if she had to take her own life. Having a plan even though it was not a good one made her relax a bit more. She caught her breath when she looked over and saw Fanton glaring at her. Henasee sat up straight and cringed at the pure hatred on Fanton's face. "I will not have to kill myself," Henasee knew in her mind. "Fanton has every intention of killing me and enjoying every minute of it."

"It will be a long and painful death for you, my pretty." Fanton said it so low Henasee wasn't sure she heard it. Looking away from Fanton and back left no doubt in Henasee's mind, Fanton had said those exact words out loud.

Hours into the trip, Fanton slowed her horse, and the two killers did the same.

"We mustn't get too far ahead of Kentar. We want him to catch us, remember?"

"Camp is only another hour, boss," one of the men told her.

"Yes, I know where camp is. I want Kentar to think we believe we've lost him and that is why we slow our pace. He'll see we've slowed down and try to sneak into camp."

"Then we kill him, boss?" the man beside Fanton asked.

"NO! you fool. I need him alive."

Fanton's face turned a deep shade of purple, and her beauty started to fade. Both men look shocked and scared. Henasee watched knowing how the change felt. The sympathy she may have felt for Fanton was short-lived when Fanton clawed at her arm.

"You and your friend will pay for all you have put me through." One thing Henasee could feel was Fanton's statement meant Slate would not be approaching her any time too soon. He had almost crawled off his saddle on hearing Fanton's speech.

"You mean she did that there to you, boss?" Slate asked, turning green.

"She and her friend did this to me."

Henasee started to say something, and then thought about it. "No", she thought to herself as she looked around at the two killers, "its best they are afraid of me. Let them think I can take beauty away from Fanton. I will seem more powerful, and it may come in handy."

Reaching the camp, Fanton got down from her horse and walked into a lighted log cabin. "Take her to the bunk house. If she escapes, I will see you both die."

Both men, Henasee noticed, look frightened at Fanton's words. Henasee knew firsthand Fanton would carry through with her threats. She and Kentar had been running for months, and Fanton had never stopped looking for them.

Henasee could hear Fanton yelling from inside the house. "Bring me the girl."

Henasee was surprised when a young girl about Henasee's age was brought screaming and crying from the barn. "No, please," the girl continued to cry out. "Please. I changed my mind. I just want to go home."

Henasee tried to run to help the girl, but stopped when Slate took his gun from its holster. "I will shoot you dead before you take two steps. Now get moving." He pointed his gun toward what Henasee knew was the bunkhouse. Once inside, Henasee covered her ears to stop the piercing screaming and crying from the young girl. Time stood still, and finally the girl's cries stopped.

Pointing for a young boy to drag the girl's body out, Fanton opened a gray bottle and sprinkled it in a small cup of the girl's blood. "I will change your destiny today," Kentar. Fanton laughed and drank the glass in one gulp.

Kentar slowed his horse to a gallop. He could see the camp from where he was.

"What are we going to do, sir?" Lenard asked out of breath from the ride.

"We aren't going to do anything, Lenard. I want you to go to the ship."

"Sir, I can help. I am a fine shot, and I—"

"No, Lenard I didn't mean that. I need you to warn Daniel and Magnus about Fanton being in the area. Do not tell them she has Henasee. I want them to leave as scheduled. Tell them if we're not there by tomorrow night to set sail."

"Sir? Are you sure?"

"Yes, Lenard. We must protect the babies. Henasee and I both agreed. We would never save ourselves and put those babies in danger."

"I hope Magnus and Daniel know what good friends they have," Lenard told him.

"They have a good friend in you, too, Lenard. You take care of them if we don't get there in time."

Lenard saluted Kentar. "I will protect them with my life, sir."

"I believe you will." Kentar saluted back.

Kentar left his horse in the woods and slowly walked to the side of the camp.

"She said you'd be coming," a voice said behind him. "If I don't see your hands, I'll pull the trigger."

Kentar lifted his hands above his sides.

"Now walk toward the cabin."

Kentar did as he was told, angry with himself for getting caught. The man nudged him in the back with the gun.

"Open the door."

Kentar opened the door and growled as Fanton rose from her chair to come to him." Where is she?" he screamed at Fanton.

"She is being well taken care of," Fanton laughed. Kentar reached out his hands and pulled Fanton closer. With one hand on her arm he put his other hand on her throat. "You will not kill me Kentar," she laughed. "You know the spell well. If I die Henasee will die also."

"If not for her, I would squeeze the very life from your body."

"You have forgotten our love so fast, Kentar."

"You killed our love, Fanton, with your murderous heart."

"I want one thing from you, Kentar."

"I have nothing left to give you, Fanton."

"We can be together again like before. We can go away from here away from Magnus, the babies, Daniel, and Henasee. We can start over."

"What about Henasee?" he asked releasing her arm.

"I will have her set free, Kentar. She can leave here tonight."

Kentar looked at Fanton and sighed. This is what he had known he would have to do all along. He just hoped Henasee would understand his decision. The thought of her hating him for the rest of her life brought him physical pain.

"I will leave with you," he told Fanton. Fanton rushed into Kentar's arms.

"I knew you could not forget our love darling. Love me now, Kentar," she begged. "Love me the way you used to love me." Kentar hesitated for a moment but in his heart he knew he must do as Fanton wants. He would make love to her and leave with her to save Henasee's life and future.

Henasee looked around the bunkhouse.

"Don't think about it," Slate told her, looking at an axe Henasee had spotted by the door.

Henasee gave him a little smile and sat back on a bunk bed. "I wasn't thinking about anything. I can see you're too strong for me to fight."

Slate stood up to show his height.

"I didn't notice you were so tall. My, you are a nice-sized man, aren't you?"

Slate started her way and stopped. "Wait a minute. That witch said you were the reason she lost her looks."

"I handed her the wrong potion bottle," Henasee giggled. "My friend and I used to be her assistants. We were ordered to clean and dust. How were we to know the bottle Fanton uses for her spells don't have names on them?" Henasee stretched out on the bunk and put one of her fingers in her mouth. "Of course, when Fanton got the wrong bottle, she fired us and she's been mad ever since. I've tried to tell her," Henasee yawned, showing her slim waist through her shirt. "I've tried to say I'm sorry, but she won't listen to me."

"She is a rough one," Slate agreed.

"Brent and I don't like her one bit. She scares the devil out of us."

"You don't look like you'd be scared of anything," Henasee flirted. "You being a big strong handsome man and all."

"No," he smiled. "I'm not much to look at."

"Who told you something like that?" Henasee said, patting the bed next to her.

"No one's ever come right out and said it," Slate said, nervously taking a step closer to her. "It's just women seem to run away when I look at 'um."

"It's probably because you're so big. Maybe they think they aren't woman enough to handle all that man."

Slate almost cooed with excitement. "I never have thought about it like that. You're right. They think I'm too much man."

"Well, let's see if they're right." Henasee patted the bed a bit more firmly.

"What about that witch? She might come in and—"

"Don't worry about Fanton. She's only mad at me. If she planned on killing me, she would have when she killed that young girl."

Slate thought a minute. "Yah, you're right. You'd already be dead."

"So let's stop talking about her and see just what kind of a man you are."

Slate wasted no time taking his holster, pants, and shirt off and throwing them one by one on the floor. Henasee stood as he reached for his flannel underwear.

"No," she said, taking his hand away and replacing it by his side.

"You close your eyes. This is the part I like to do," she said as she rubbed his chest and opened a button.

Slate took in a deep breath and closed his eyes. Henasee undid button after button so slowly. Sweat ran from Slates forehead."

"Hurry," he said, grabbing at her hand.

Henasee laughed and pulled away. "Now let's not get ahead of ourselves. We can do this slow and easy," she whispered in his ear.

"I'm ready now," he said his eyes flying open. "I don't need it slow and easy."

Henasee kissed his mouth and pulled away quickly. "You're right, I want you now." She ripped the front of his flannel shirt. "Take them off now," she screamed at him.

Slate was so excited he turned and removed his flannels. "There," he said with lust and a smile on his face. Turning to face her, his smile faded. Henasee pulled the trigger back on his gun.

Pointing it directly at his nose, she said, "I told you I wanted to go slow." Making him sit down, she started to wrap his hands with rope behind his back. Leaving one hand to hold the gun, it took longer, but she was finally satisfied when he couldn't budge.

"She'll kill me if you leave me here," he pleaded. "She would have killed you anyway, you fool."

Henasee slipped out of the camp and headed into the woods. Hearing a noise, she turned quickly and almost cried out loud.

Kentar's horse was tied to a tree. She knew he must be in the camp. Henasee walked to the end of the woods and looked out over the camp. "He must be in the cabin. Yes, Fanton must have him in there." Looking around and seeing no one, Henasee sneaked up to a window on the cabin and peered inside.

 Her heart shattered into a million pieces and ran to hide in every part of her body, turning her completely numb. Not being able to pull her eyes away from the entwined couple, she could think of nothing. Watching, she was oblivious to the commotion going on in the camp. "She can't have gotten far," seeped into Henasee's inner thoughts. "She can't have gotten far." Henasee broke her stare from the window and looked around the camp. Everyone, she noticed, had run into the woods toward Kentar's tied-up horse. Kentar, she hugged herself, her body hurting from every spot her heart had exploded. Looking one last time and wiping the tears from her face, Henasee turned and ran into the barn. After saddling the first horse she saw, she mounted it and rode out of the camp as fast as the horse would carry her.

Lenard reached the ship by morning. He was exhausted, but he couldn't wait to see the babies. They should be getting bigger by the day, he imagined.

"Lenard," Daniel yelled from on board the ship. "What are you doing here?"

Lenard hurried up the plank. "I've come to sail with you, sir."

"You were to wait for Henasee and Kentar at Chainridge."

"I did wait, sir, and they came. Kentar said not to wait for them; if they're not here tomorrow night to sail without them."

"Where are they?" Daniel asked him.

"Please, sir. I was told not to say anything."

 "Yes, but you do not work for Kentar. Is not Magnus's family where your loyalties remain?"

"Yes, sir, you are right," Lenard conceded. "We were traveling together, Henasee, Kentar and I. We thought we had a foolproof plan. Fanton had approached me, and I had agreed to change my loyalties for money."

"I don't believe that for one minute," Daniel said, shaking his head.

"Well, it was good that she believed me. I met with her and our deal was made. Only she had played me like a fiddle, sir. She waited until we took our eyes off Henasee, and she took her. Kentar and I followed her trail to her camp, but he wouldn't let me help. He ordered me here to make you sail by tomorrow night no matter if they came or not."

"We're not leaving without them," Daniel stated.

"He said he and Henasee had both made a pact. They would not save themselves and put the babies in any danger. You must know the babies have to come first, sir." Daniel stopped walking. "If Fanton gets a hold of them. . ."

Daniel turned to look at Lenard. "We will not talk of any of this in front of Magnus or her parents. We will tell them I sent for you as a surprise." Lenard nodded.

"Lenard," Magnus and her mother cried out at the same time. "You are here?" Magnus asked surprised.

"Yes, Miss," Lenard squeaked out. Lying was not his normal character, and it didn't come easy for him.

"Why aren't you at Chainridge waiting for Kentar and Henasee?" Magnus asked, coming closer to look in his eyes.

"I was, I mean. It was your husband, Miss, he sent for me as a surprise."

"Oh he did, did he?" Magnus looked unconvinced. "And just what did he say in this letter he sent to you, Lenard?"

"Please, Miss, it has been a long trip, and I am tired."

"You will be a lot more tired if we have to wait for you to tell us the truth, Lenard."

"But, Miss, I promised Dan . . ."

"So Daniel has you making up stories for him now?"

"Yes, I mean no!" Lenard screamed out flustered. "I didn't mean to lie, Miss. It's just he orders and you order. I am but one man with many employers."

"Right now you're standing in front of an angry employer so let's have it, Lenard." Magnus crossed her arms in front of her chest. "My husband is not here to protect you, so let's hear it."

Lenard tilted back on his heels. His hands started to shake, and his complexion was a slight color of gray.

"Lenard, are you all right?" Magnus got out of her mouth as Lenard fainted dead away and hit the floor.

"Oh, my goodness," Magnus's mother cried out. "You've scared the poor man half to death, Magnus."

"He's not dead, Mother," Magnus assured her kneeling down beside him. "He just got overexcited, that's all."

"Who wouldn't with you bullying him that way? You should be ashamed of yourself," her mother scolded.

Magnus pushed in beside her to look at Lenard. "He's not cut," Magnus said, looking at his head where he had hit the floor.

"He does have a lovely bump though," her mother said looking at a knot on Lenard's head as it grew.

"He will certainly have a headache when he wakes up," Magnus said, and her mother wholeheartedly agreed. "Yes, it is a very nasty bump."

"What's going on?" Daniel yelled from the end of the hallway. Rushing in, he looked to his wife and then at his mother-in-law.

"He fainted," Magnus said matter-of-factly.

"He fainted after you interrogated him with no mercy, darling," her mother said calmly.

"Mother!" Magnus snapped. "I did not interrogate him unmercifully."

"You were very unkind with your attacks, Magnus."

"He was lying to me, Mother. I was only trying to get at the truth." Magnus turned and looked at Daniel. "You didn't send for him, did you?"

Daniel evaded Magnus's look. "Right now, we need to get Lenard off the floor."

"You didn't answer me Daniel," she persisted. "It's a yes or no question. One you can answer while we're making Lenard comfortable."

"He has ridden all night, and now he's unconscious, Magnus. I think any talk besides getting him into a bed can wait for a few minutes."

"Daniel!" Magnus screamed, "tell me now!"

"No, I didn't send for him. Ok! Now will you help me get him up?"

"Where are Henasee and Kentar?"

"Come on, Magnus, let's get him moved, and then I'll tell you everything," Daniel promised. Daniel got two men from the deck to move Lenard into a single cabin and place him on the bed.

"I'll get some water and cloths," Magnus's mother said and scurried from the room.

"Thank you," Magnus told the two men as they left Lenard's room. "Now, Daniel, tell me now."

Daniel shook his head and looked out the small window. "Fanton has Henasee, and Kentar went to get her."

"You mean save her, don't you, Daniel? Kentar is smart, and if anyone can get her away from Fanton, it's Kentar. We must go after her," Magnus said grabbing at his shirt.

Daniel took her arms and held them gently. "They don't want us to come after them. Kentar told Lenard he and Henasee had made a pact. Neither would risk the chance Fanton would get a hold of our children."

"We can't let Fanton hurt her, Daniel."

"We must think of our girls, Magnus. Fanton must know we're getting ready to sail if she could find Kentar and Henasee so easy."

"Daniel, I will not leave her. You may go with me or stay here, but I'm not going to leave my friend. If anything else happens to her because of my choices, I will never be able to live with myself. Please, Daniel. Henasee is my best friend. If not for me, she would never have heard the name Fanton. She has been running for her life for months to keep my children safe. I cannot bear the idea of her giving up her life for me, too."

Daniel pulled her into his arms and kissed her hair. "You are right, darling. We will go after them."

Daniel made sure the ship was tied down tight and extra men were keeping guard. He had confidence in Edward Carter, the captain of the ship. Magnus's father had filled him in on Fanton, and Daniel was sure Carter could take care of any situation that came up while he is gone. Daniel knew the trip to Noteese would be longer this time. Magnus's had picked out supplies they would need to travel round for almost a year and then settle on Noteese for a couple of months.

Magnus was standing by the rail as Daniel approached her. "I see you are easily transformed into a boy."

Magnus smiled. "It will be easier to travel in pants."

"I didn't say I minded the look, darling. Your curves show through just fine from where I'm looking."

"We are trying to save my best friend, Daniel."

"I was just trying to lighten the mood, Magnus," Daniel said, pinching her bottom.

"Remind me later to be mad at you," Magnus said, turning her head at the sound of horses approaching. Magnus looked from the ten armed men on horses to her husband. "You did this."

"We can't have Fanton hurt your best friend, can we?"

Magnus threw herself into Daniel's arms. "Thank you, Daniel."

Daniel hugged her back and then pushed her away.

"We need to go," Daniel helped Magnus up top of her horse and climbed on his own. "Lenard said they are this way. We'll be riding hard, men. If your horse gets lame or you can't keep up, we're not stopping. Everyone understand?"

The men all nodded.

Magnus had to work to keep up with the men, but she didn't falter. Henasee needed her, and she was going to find her.

"Wait!" one of the front riders yelled. "There is something up ahead."

Knowing they were getting close to where Lenard told them the camp was after he woke up, Daniel reined in his horse, and everyone else followed suit. Daniel climbed off his horse and hurried to the body on the ground next to a very spooked horse. Slapping the frightened horse on the rump, he was relieved when it ran off. Bending down, he slowly turned the small body over.

"Magnus!" he yelled.

Magnus slid off her horse and ran to Daniel.

"Henasee!" Magnus cried out and fell to her knees. "Daniel, is she all right?"

"She's breathing," he said listening to her heartbeat. "I'm not sure if she's hit her head or what's going on with her. We need to get her back to the ship and send for the doctor." Daniel pointed to one of the men and he dismounted. "I need you to take her and my wife back to the ship."

"The reward?" the man started to argue.

"I'll take her back." A young man jumps from his horse and bent down to pick up Henasee.

"I'll see you are paid well, my friend," Daniel said, taking Henasee from him until he got back on his horse.

"I wasn't doing this for the money, sir. I wanted to sail with you."

"You get my wife and her friend back to the ship safely, and you have earned your place on board the ship."

The man tilted his hat and reached his arms out for a very still Henasee.

"Daniel," Magnus said, standing in front of him, "you be careful."

Daniel kissed her lips. "Nothing or no one could stop me from coming back to you or our girls, Magnus."

Daniel helped Magnus up on her horse and smiled at her.

"I love you."

"I love you, too, darling," he replied. "Now go and take care of your friend."

Chapter 21
Fantons Beauty

Kentar watched as Fantons beauty disappeared and he stood to dress.

Fanton sat up and watched him dress. "This is the face you begged to see, Kentar. This is the face you were going to love and make love to. 'Your beauty doesn't matter' you used to promise me when you pleaded for me to stay with you when my beauty disappeared. Now look at you. I disgust you. Do you feel you'll have to vomit at the sight of me, Kentar?"

"You are not the same person you were, Fanton. Our love would have been strong enough to survive your lost beauty."

"You lie, Kentar. You lied then, and you lie now. We had no love. The love we shared was all lies. Your lies, Kentar. They were your lies. I gave you my heart, and you pulled it from my chest. Now you will have what you have given me, a heart that will never be free to love again. I have given you back a life of lies."

"What do you mean?" Kentar asked, looking around. "Where is Henasee? What have you done with her?"

"I'm afraid your lovely mistress has escaped. She was here," Fanton pointed and laughed at the window. "She saw you with me."

Kentar pushed her aside when she tried to approach him.

"We were good together, Kentar. Last night proves that," she yelled in his face.

"I was only with you to save Henasee," he yelled back. "I would not have touched you with or without your beauty because you have no beauty inside."

"I can learn to be what you want me to be, Kentar."

"You will never be anything to me, Fanton. I love Henasee, and I plan on making her my life."

"You can have your life with her," Fanton screamed and picked up a bottle on the table. With her back to him she emptied out a small bottle into her hand. Smiling she turned and threw a black powder into his face. "She can have you now," she laughed, tears flooding her eyes.

"She will understand. Henasee knows you will do anything to keep

us apart."
"Yes, but will she believe what she seen with her own eyes?" Fanton laughed, pointing at the window again. "She saw you love me with every inch of your body. She watched as I satisfied you and you begged for more."
Kentar's head started to spin. "You had her watch?"
"No, but if I would have thought of it," she laughed. "She must have gotten away from Slate."
"If he touched her," Kentar threatened.
"I am sure she is long gone by now. She didn't look like she was going to stay around in case we had another show later."
If Fanton were a man, Kentar knew he would snap her neck at that very second. "I will find her and make her understand. If you come near me again, Fanton, I will kill you with my bare hands."
Fanton watched as Kentar left the cabin. Outside, Kentar was not surprised when no one tried to stop him. They all feared the witch inside, and if he could walk out on her, they were sure he had strong powers of his own.
"Where's my horse?" he yelled at the first man he saw.
"I'll get it, sir," the man told him and ran to retrieve Kentar's horse.

Kentar wasted no time. He jumped on his horse and rode out of Fanton's camp like the wind. He must find Henasee and tell her why she had seen him making love to Fanton.

An hour later, Daniel rode slowly into Fanton's camp. They looked around and could see most of the buildings in the camp look abandoned.
"You two look over there," Daniel pointed, "and the rest of you come with me."
Daniel walked up onto the cabin porch. Lifting his foot, he kicked the door in. Fanton sat looking at the fireplace.
"You have come to kill me, Daniel?" she said without emotion.
"I have come for Kentar and Henasee, Fanton! Where are they?"
"They are gone, Daniel. They both are gone."
"It is time you leave my family and friends alone, Fanton."
"I have lost everything, Daniel." Fanton turned, and he could see the tear stains on her cheeks.

"You have killed for your own needs and pleasures."

"Can't you see, Daniel?" Kentar drove me to this. "He said he would love me forever. He is the reason I had to kill, Daniel. I am not a bad person."

"You have not been a good person in a long time, Fanton. You are going where you will no longer be able to hurt anyone."

"You are going to kill me then," she smiled sadly.

"No, I'm not like you. I won't take the law into my own hands. Where you're going you won't have any potions or spells to cause people pain."

Fanton watched as the door slowly opened, and a sheriff and two deputies came in the door.

"That her right there?" the sheriff asked Daniel.

"Yes, that's her. Don't turn your back on her," Daniel warned him. "She'll slit your throat."

"Don't you worry about her getting the best of us, son. She's going where she can't do any more harm to anyone."

"Good-bye, Fanton," Daniel said sadly and turned to leave.

"Daniel?"

"Yes?" He turned to look at her.

"I can't be all bad. I had you love me once, didn't I?"

"Yes," he said, and turned and walked out the cabin door.

"There's another one over here," one of the deputies laughed.

"Come see this buck. He's all tied up and naked as a jaybird."

Daniel climbed on his horse, and he and his hired men rode out of the camp.

"Mother!" Magnus screamed coming up the gangplank. "Mother!"

"What is it, Magnus?" her mother came running after one of the men came to her cabin for her.

"Mother!" Magnus cried, pointing at Mathew carrying a still unconscious Henasee.

"Oh my goodness," her mother cried back. "Come this way," she ordered the young man carrying Henasee.

Magnus could see Henasee's one eye and part of her head was swollen.

"Where did you find her?"

"She was on the ground by a horse, Mother. She hasn't woken up yet," Magnus cried again.

"You," Magnus's mother pointed at one of the men on deck. "Find a doctor and bring him here."

"Yes, ma'am," he bowed as if he were speaking to royalty. "I will be back shortly."

"Well, don't dally," Magnus's mother snapped, and the man ran off the ship.

Magnus looked over at her mother. Even though the woman was as shaken and worried about Henasee as she was, she showed no outward sign of fear.

"Right in here." Her mother opened a door and hurried to the bed, pulling back the covers. "Put her right here." The man carrying Henasee placed her gently on the bed.

"I'll need some water and rags," she ordered the young man.

"I can get them, Mother," Magnus offered. "He's done a lot for us."

"No, I'm fine. I'll get them," he said and left the room.

"Let's get her out of these dirty clothes," Magnus's mother said, pulling Henasee's arm out of her shirt. "Look, Magnus, I think her arm is broken."

Magnus looked at the deep bruise on Henasee's arm.

"And here." Her mother touched a dark purple bruise on Henasee's ribs.

Henasee moaned, and they both jumped.

"You fight, Hen," Magnus whispered. "I'm here now. Nothing more can hurt you."

"Kentar," Henasee cried out.

"Daniel has gone for him. They should be back soon."

"No," Henasee started to move around the bed.

"Henasee," Magnus's mother held her shoulder. "You must not move. Your arm is broken, and you may have some broken ribs. You must stay still."

"Kentar will be here soon," Magnus repeated.

"No!" Henasee screamed. "I never want to see him again!"

Magnus sat back, surprised. "You don't want to see Kentar?"

"No, Magnus," she cried. "Please, Magnus, keep him away from me, far, far away from me. Promise you will," Henasee cried, trying to reach for Magnus's hand.

"I promise, Henasee. He will not get in this room. Is that's what you want?"

"Yes," she started to calm down before becoming unconscious again. "Yes, that's what I want."

Kentar reached the ship and tore from room to room looking for Henasee. As he reached for the door to Henasee's room, Magnus turned and saw him.

"Where is she?" he screamed.

"Quiet." Magnus shooed him into an open door of another cabin. "She must have got thrown from her horse. The doctor is in there with her right now."

"I want to see her," Kentar said, starting to leave the room.

"She doesn't want to see you, Kentar."

"I know. She saw Fanton and I . . ."

"I don't know what happened, and I'm sure you two will fix whatever it is. But for know you must respect her wishes and leave her alone. The doctor says we almost lost her. Now you can't just barge in there and explain. She needs time to heal and feel strong again. If you really care so deeply for her, Kentar, let her recover before you explain."

Kentar sat down in a chair with a thud.

Magnus noticed for the first time how ill he really was. "What has happened to you?"

Kentar looked up at Magnus, and the room began to spin again. Helping him, she laid him on the bed.

"I'll be right back. You stay there," Magnus ordered.

Kentar grabbed his head to stop the room from spinning. Magnus hurried back with the doctor. Checking his heart and pulse, the doctor shook his head.

"What has happened to him?"

"Poison, "Kentar said from the bed. "I was given poison."

"How long ago?"

"A couple of hours ago."

"If it were going to kill you, you'd already be dead," the doctor said matter of fact.

"Doctor!" Magnus scolded. "That is no way to talk to the sick."

"I'm sorry," the doctor cleared his throat. "I'm not usually in the company of young ladies when I'm caring for men. They are usually ranch hands."

"Well, I would think even ranch hands could use less threats and more treatment."

"I bet you do," Daniel laughed from the doorway.

"Daniel," Magnus cried going into his arms.

"Kentar, I see you made it back safe. I thought I'd find you hovered over Henasee?"

"Daniel," Magnus pinched his arm.

"Ouch!" he yelled. "Why'd you pinch me?"

Magnus pinched his arm again.

"Stop that, Magnus. That hurts."

"Well, be quiet for a minute and stop asking so many questions."

"I'll quit if you stop pinching me."

Magnus kissed his cheek and turned back to the doctor. "What can we do?"

"Put as much liquid in him as you can. The more he can get in him, the faster the poison will come out of him."

"What does he mean, poison?" Daniel asked, and backed away from Magnus in case she pinched him again.

"Fanton must have given Kentar poison. The doctor is checking him over."

"How's Henasee?" Daniel whispered, following her lead.

"She has a broken arm and some broken ribs. With rest, she should be fine."

"The ship needs to leave soon," Daniel told the doctor. "Will they both be ready to travel?"

"The girl will be sore for some time, but she can travel. As for him, it may be weeks or months before he is ready to travel. The poison is already making him weak."

"We don't have weeks to wait for him to recover," Daniel spit out.

"Daniel, please, be quiet."

"No, Magnus," Daniel grabbed her hand in case she thought to pinch him again. "Kentar knows we must leave on schedule."

"He's right," Kentar spoke from his bed. "You must leave as scheduled."

"Kentar," Magnus approached his bed. "I promised Henasee I would keep you away from her. You know she'll be sailing to

Noteese with us."

Kentar held his head. "Tell her it's not what she thought she seen, when she'll listen," Kentar moaned. "Fanton has a lot of tricks to make people believe what they see is real. I will wait for her to return."

"I'll tell her, Kentar," Magnus promised. "I will tell her."

Daniel came back with two men, and they helped carry Kentar off the ship.

"You take care of yourself, my friend," Daniel yelled after them.

"You take care of her," Kentar called back.

"I will, Kentar, I will," Daniel waved.

"We'll be sailing at the crack of dawn," Captain Carter came up to Daniel and told him. "A Mathew Doyle came on board last night," Carter continued. "He said you gave him permission to sail with us."

Daniel nodded, looking out over the sea.

"He seems to be a nice fellow, but we'll keep an eye on him for a while."

Daniel turned and smiled at Carter. "Is everything ready?" he asked Carter.

"Yes, sir, we're good to go. Everyone is on board now. We've gone through the supply list a dozen times. The ship's loaded and ready to sail."

"I'm glad to have you aboard, Carter," Daniel said, extending his hand.

"I thought I might find you out here," Magnus said, crossing the deck to stand by Daniel. "Everything has always made sense when I look up at the stars," he told her, putting his arm around her waist.

"Fanton is no longer a threat, but Kentar is being left behind," Daniel said, still gazing at the sky. "How can one person do so much destruction?" he asked, still looking up. "I mean," he continued, "without Fanton, you and I would never have met. The girls would not be asleep in their beds. So for that I feel grateful to her, but without her, people would not have died or suffered because of what she did. She calls it love and I call her love cruelty."

"Daniel," Magnus turned his face with her hand. "Fanton doesn't know what loving someone really means. She doesn't understand the give and take of love. She only knows how to take. Her love is one-sided. She has a love that only fulfills her needs. She doesn't care who she hurts or how she hurts them as long as she gets what she wants. Her love is a black love. It will never see the light of day."

Daniel smiled sadly at Magnus. "It still hurts to know my sister will be spending the rest of her life in prison."

"She will never be able to harm our children, Daniel."

"I will thank God every day for that, darling. I just hope some how she finds peace."

Fanton looked back from her horse to one of the deputies. She smiled at him, her beauty intact, and he shyly smiled back.

***

Even after months on board the ship, Beautiful would not let Magnus pick her up. "Do you think she'll ever realize I'm her mother?" Magnus asked Ahaira.

"She is a very smart little girl, Magnus. Give her time; she'll come around. She hasn't tried to hurt you, so I'd take that as a good sign."

Magnus laughed. "I'll take what I can get, right know. Mother said she scratched poor Nana again on the cheek."

"I saw what she did to Nana," Mary whispered. "It took some time getting the blood to stop pouring out of it. What would make her do something like that?" Mary asked Magnus.

"I don't know. Ahaira and Uncle Bernard seem to think the answer lies at Noteese."

"She is too beautiful to have a bad side," Mary said, reaching down and lifting Beautiful out of her bassinet.

"A bad side?" Magnus repeated.

"I didn't mean anything, Miss," Mary started to apologize.

"No, Mary," Magnus said, reaching for Mary's arm but stopping when Beautiful let out a scream. Pulling her arm back, Magnus let out a scream herself.

"What's all the commotion?" Daniel said, sticking his head in the door.

"I almost touched Beautiful," Magnus said with a tear sliding down her cheek.

"Still no progress, darling?"

"No, she still screams every time I come close."

"Give her time," Daniel said, kissing Magnus on the cheek. "She'll come around."

"That's the same thing Mary has been trying to tell me."

Daniel put his arms out and Beautiful smiled and cooed up at him. When he took her in his arms, she put her tiny arm on his shoulder.

"If I didn't know how old they are, I would swear they were acting like toddlers," Mary said, picking up Precious and handing her to Magnus.

"They are advanced, that's for sure," Daniel said, smiling at Magnus and Precious. "Are we ready for our walk, ladies?" Daniel asked.

"We are ready, Father," Magnus said brightly.

The room got quiet as Beautiful looked at Daniel and said, "Ready."

"Am I the only one who heard her?" he asked, his stomach in knots.

"No, sir," Mary choked out. "She said ready."

"Is it time for them to be talking?" Daniel asked Magnus.

"It is time for them to say words," she told Daniel.

"But Beautiful seems to understand what she's saying." Daniel held Beautiful away from him. "Are you ready, Beautiful?" he asked slowly.

"Walk, Father," Beautiful said clear as day.

"Yes, darling, Daddy will take you for a walk," Daniel laughed with his mouth hanging open. "Magnus, does Precious want to go for a w

Magnus looked down at Precious and back at Daniel. "She is sleeping, Daniel."

"Oh," he said, trying to think. "Well, I guess we'll walk," he said to Beautiful.

Beautiful gave him a big smile and looked over at the door.

"I don't know about you, darling," Daniel looked over at Magnus, "but I'm a bit spooked."

"Let's just take them for their walk, darling, and we'll talk later. There's no reason not to have a good morning with our beautiful little girls."

Magnus was surprised when Beautiful laughed out loud. "She's laughing at something I said," Magnus said, watching Beautiful laugh.

"What did you say?" Daniel asked.

"I said there is no reason we can't have a good morning," Magnus watched as Beautiful stopped laughing.

"You called them beautiful," Mary whispered.

"Try that, honey," Daniel coaxed.

"There's no reason not to have a good morning with our beautiful girls," Magnus repeated.

Daniel had to use both hands to hold Beautiful. "She laughed as if someone were tickling her. "She liked to be told she's beautiful," Daniel told Magnus.

"She is the most Beautiful little girl I've ever seen," Magnus cooed at her.

Beautiful laughed and reached for Magnus's hand. Magnus held out her hand, and Beautiful dug her nails in the palm of Magnus's hand. Magnus pulled her hand back and looked at the two tiny puncture wounds Beautiful had made with her nails.

"No, Beautiful," Daniel scolded. "You are not to hurt your mother."

Beautiful looked at Magnus and continued to laugh. Mary took Precious from Magnus, and Magnus ran crying from the room.

"I will be right back, Mary," Daniel said, placing Beautiful in her bassinet. Daniel found Magnus lying across their bed crying.

"Magnus, you must not take offence. It's the spell that makes her act this way. I'm sure of it. I remember my grandmother telling me stories of Fanton when she was small. She said she could be nice one minute and mean as Hades the next."

Magnus stopped crying and turns to Daniel. "We have one kind Precious daughter and one Beautiful daughter with a cruel streak in her, Daniel. What if there is no changing her? What if that cruel streak grows and grows. You've seen the cruelty Fanton has displayed. What if our daughter grows up to do the same?"

"Magnus, we don't know that yet. Ahaira says there is a plant on Noteese that may change the spell. Let's hope and pray she's right. If she is, our daughters will grow up with happy, normal lives."

"What if she's wrong Daniel? What if there is no cure? What then?" she asked, turning on the tears again.

Then Daniel picked her up and held her. "Then we will love them, Magnus. We will care for them, and we will love them." His voice shook as his tears fell into her hair.

Henasee dressed slowly with the help of Magnus's mother's maid. "I am getting up," she told the maid for the third time. "I've been in that bed long enough, and I am leaving this room today."

"I was told not to let you get out of bed," the maid continued.

"You may as well help me," Henasee snapped back, "or I will leave in my slip."

The older woman grabbed her chest. "You wouldn't dare," she cried out.

Henasee reached for the door knob.

"Ok," the woman yelled at her back. "I will help you get dressed."

"Thank you," Henasee said, out of breath. Truth be told, she could use a couple of more weeks in bed but lying in her room day after day has only made her miss Kentar more. At first when Magnus told her Kentar was not able to stay aboard the ship, she had felt happy and relieved. But with every passing day, she missed him more and more. Magnus had told her what Kentar had said about Fanton making people see what she wanted them to see. She was sure Kentar had been saving her life by being with Fanton.. Still, it hurt every time she pictured him making love to her. Knowing it was Fanton broke her heart.

"How long will you be out, Miss?" the maid asked.

"Not long," Henasee smiled. "I'm sorry. I just can't sit in here another day."

"I understand, Miss," the maid smiled sadly back, making Henasee wonder if everyone on board knew about what had happened. "No," she told herself, opening the door. "Magnus would never tell anyone what she had told her, not even Daniel."

Henasee climbed the stairs to the upper deck and stopped to steady herself.

"Are you sure you should be out and about by yourself?" a young man said, taking her arm and leading her to a chair on deck.

"I thought I was doing much better," Henasee said, feeling faint.

"You had a very hard fall," the young man continued.

"I don't mean to sound rude. But have we met?"

"We have met," the young man continued. "But you were out cold."

Henasee looked up and smiled. "You're the man that brought me to the ship, aren't you?"

"I can't believe you remember that," he smiled back.

"No," she laughed. "Magnus told me."

"Oh," he laughed again, "that makes more sense. You were sleeping pretty tight that night."

"I think my horse got spooked by something," she told the young man. "One minute I was riding like the wind, and the next I was flying through the air. Thank you," she told him. "Thank you for everything. Magnus says I only had a little more time and I would have . . ."

"No need to go there, ma'am," he said, gently placing his hand on her arm. "You're recovering nicely."

"Well, I thought I was until I climbed those stairs."

"Let me be of assistance again then."

"Without warning," he reached down and scooped her into his arms. Henasee was too startled to react and grabbed his neck with her good hand.

"Now," he told her, "I can carry you back down those steps and you can sit and sulk in your room, or I can take you for a walk around the deck? Which one does the lady prefer?"

Henasee moaned, and he stopped moving.

"I'm sorry. This was probably a bad idea. Are you in a lot of pain?" he asked concerned.

"Nothing a walk around the deck won't help cure," she smiled.

"Well then, we are off, fair lady."

"It might be easier if I knew your name?" she asked.

"I am Mathew Doyle at your service, ma'am."

"You may refer to me as Henasee and not ma'am," Henasee said looking around the deck. "It's funny how being in the sunlight can change the way you feel," she said, reaching her hand up toward the sky.

"I have heard the sun is good for your bones," Mathew told her.

"I can feel it warming my bones." She smiled and enjoyed their talk.

Chapter 22
Young Love

"What is it I heard? You took a walk on the deck this morning?" Magnus asked Henasee, coming into Henasee's room.
"Yes, I did." Henasee smiled at her friend.
"You look better for it, too." Magnus smiled back and sat on the side of Henasee's bed. "I also heard you met Mathew?"
Henasee laughed. "Don't going playing match maker, Mag. I still love Kentar."
Magnus looked down. "I'm sorry, I didn't mean."
"Oh stop, Magnus, you're my best friend. You can say anything you want to me.
I know you say it with love in your heart."
"It's just it has hurt me deeply to see you in so much pain over Kentar."
"That's what I was lying here thinking. It was nice to be with someone like Mathew. He's handsome, charming and he's not on the run from his ex-girlfriend."
"I can see your point." Magnus laughed.
"Mathew was sweet, and we didn't have to plan our next escape. We talked about the sun heating our bones. Do you know how long it's been to talk and not worry?"
Magnus smiled at Henasee. "I do know what you mean."
"I'm sure you do," Henasee smiled back." I'm not ready to care about anyone for awhile," Henasee told Magnus. "But it was nice to talk to Matthew."

"You should just walk up to her and start talking to her," Mathew told Carter.
"What if she's not ready to have another man interested in her?"
"I walk with her every day on the deck , and she looks more than ready to move on with her heart. Don't be a fool and let one of the other men get a head start on you."
Carter laughed. "I'll take your advice, Matthew, I promise."
"Approach her," Matthew told him. "She's a very charming girl.

Even if she doesn't like you, she will never show it."

"Thanks a lot, Matthew. With friends like you, who needs enemies?" Carter stomped off.

"Hey, I was only teasing," he yelled after a retreating Carter.

"Teasing about what?" Magnus asked Daniel.

"Carter likes Henasee."

"Oh, my." Magnus shrugged her shoulders. "I don't know how Henasee will take to two men fighting for her time."

"What's the news on Mathew?"

"She thinks he's charming and sweet," Magnus said, squeezing his arm.

"Carter does have a chance then. I bet my money on Carter."

"Why are you pushing for Carter?" she asked Daniel.

"He's a good man. Kentar ruined what he and Henasee could have had with Fanton out of the picture. I'd like to see her move on with her life."

"What's the matter with handsome and sweet, Matthew?" she asked.

"Nothing," Daniel laughed, if you don't mind brotherly and boring.

"Henasee said nothing about brotherly."

"She didn't have to." Daniel pulled Magnus tighter to his side. "When a girl really likes someone, she gets this far-off look in her eyes," he continued, "like she's looking into the sun."

Magnus laughed at his description. "Did I look as if I had looked into the sun when I met you for the first time?"

Daniel laughed and pulled her to his chest. "I don't know."

"Why?" Magnus pouted.

"Because I, my darling, was looking into the sun, the first time I saw you."

Magnus kissed him so hard he finished the kiss and scooped her up in his arms.

"What?" she laughed.

"If it's good enough for Henasee, it's good enough for my girl."

Magnus cuddled into his chest and watched as the sun went down off the side of the ship.

"Captain," Henasee smiled from her deck chair. "How are you this morning?" she asked politely.

"I am good," he stumbled out. "I am real good."
Henasee smiled wider as he tipped his hat and hurried off.
"You scared him off again didn't you?" Magnus laughed, taking the seat next to her.
"I only said good morning," Henasee laughed back.
"How can such an attractive man be so shy?" Magnus asked, looking over to where Carter was giving out orders. "The men would jump overboard if he asked them to, Daniel says. They are that loyal to him. What about you and Mathew?" Magnus asked her.
"We're friends. He kissed me one night under the stars. It was most romantic, but there were no sparks. Mathew and I are destined to remain friends."
Magnus laughed out loud again.
"What?" Henasee asked her.
"Daniel said it was a brother/sister affair, and I didn't believe him. How is your heart doing without Kentar in it?"
"I think about what we went through and I will always love him. Our love was fun and exciting. It meant living on the edge day and night. Never knowing what would happen the next day. But I cannot get the picture of him making love to Fanton out of my head. I know he was probably trying to save me but it was so real. He knew how to touch her and she knew how to touch him."
Magnus squeezed her friend's hand. "I am sorry you ever had to see that Hen."
"It will live in my mind forever, I'm afraid."
"Carter?" Magnus asked. Henasee smiled, watching Carter work on the other side of the ship. "What do you think of him?" Henasee continued to watch Carter work with ropes with two of his men and nodded her head yes.
"I understand that completely," Magnus laughed.
"Why's that?" Daniel puffed his chest out and approached them. Both girls laughed.
"Well, darling, for one thing, some people don't like people who eavesdrop on other people's conversations."
"Oh, no, no, no," Daniel pulled the pretend dagger out of his chest. "I was not eavesdropping. I was merely walking by."
Daniel, you have been listening for over 10 minutes back there.
Daniel smiled shyly at Henasee. "Well, I was trying to gather

information for Carter."

Henasee laughed out loud. "Carter needs information for what? May I ask?"

"He likes you," Daniel blurted out. "I mean he thinks you. I was sworn to secrecy," Daniel, Magnus noticed, was turning a bit red. "Carter is going to have my head."

"You aren't very good at keeping a secret, darling," Magnus laughed, watching Daniel start to sweat. Daniel looked from Magnus and then to Henasee, hoping he could find a way to escape. Henasee burst out laughing, and Magnus shook her head no, a notch.

"What did you do that for?" Daniel looked at Magnus.

"Do what?" Magnus asked him.

"You already told her about Carter, didn't you?"

Magnus turned her face to avoid Daniel's eyes.

"Oh, no you don't, my beautiful wife," Daniel said, turning her face back to face him. "Didn't you, Magnus? You told Henasee Carter likes her."

All three turned when they heard someone clear their throat. A very red-faced Carter stood looking at them all. "I'm sure you've all had a good laugh over me. Daniel," Carter said, glaring at Henasee. "Your mother-in-law is looking for you. She said it's something to do with the babies and come quickly."

Daniel started to say something to Carter but changed his mind. "We'll talk later," Magnus told Henasee, hurrying away to see to the babies.

"I'm sorry my attention toward you left such a foul taste in your mouth," Carter said to Henasee and turned and walks away.

Henasee didn't know whether to go after him and explain or hit him in the back of the head with her book. Brought up to act as a lady, she stood and went to her room to think about what had just happened.

"What is it, Mother? I heard you scream," Magnus said, rushing into the babies' cabin.

"It's their birthmarks, Magnus. Beautiful's has changed."

"Changed?" Daniel asked her.

"Yes, I was bathing Beautiful, and when I picked up her hand I . . ."

"You what, Mother?" Magnus asked concerned.

"Let me show you," her mother said, opening Beautiful's hand. Magnus looked but was careful not to get too close. Even after months on board the ship, Beautiful would not let Magnus come near her. "It's a snake of some kind," Magnus told Daniel, who was examining it himself. "Why would it change from the two crosses to a snake, Daniel?"

"I don't know, darling. Ahaira is as stumped as we are about the birthmarks. She says the potion Fanton used to take your beauty must have been a very strong spell. She says all we can do is wait and see what happens."

"I feel so helpless." Magnus started to cry.

"Honey, the girls are growing by leaps and bounds. They look happy and healthy. Everything else we'll have to put in God's hands."

"I know, Daniel." Magnus looked at him. It's not knowing what it all means. Magnus looked over at Mary who was holding Precious. "Has her birthmark changed, too?"

"No." Mary held up Precious's hand for Magnus to see. "She still has the one cross, no blood."

Time passed quickly on the boat as Henasee healed and the twins grew in leaps and bounds. "I can't believe the girls will be a year old tomorrow, Hen."

"It does seem to be going fast."

"Mother and I have planned a party for them."

"That sounds nice. I think everyone could use a nice celebration to break up their days."

"Did I hear celebration?" her Uncle Bernard laughed. Magnus hugged her Uncle. She loved having him on board and was grateful Ahaira joined him to help find a cure for the girls.

"Daniel." Magnus waved from the top deck. Daniel waved back and continued his strained conversation with Carter.

"Yes, sir, I'll look into how many supplies are left on board."

"Thank you, Carter," Daniel said and walked away.

"Has anything lightened up between you two?" Magnus asked, reaching Daniel.

"No, he prefers to keep our relationship all business. I have apologized until I'm blue in the face, and he just stares right through me."

"That's silly. It's been months now. He still won't acknowledge Henasee without growling at her."

"I'm tired of trying. He can stay in his own little world of unhappy."

"Daniel," Magnus scoffed at him. "That's not a very nice thing to say."

"I have tried to apologize to the man, Magnus, and he treats me like a leper. What else can I do?"

"I don't know, Daniel, but there must be something. We were all laughing about his crush on Henasee."

"No, Magnus, we were laughing because you can't keep a secret."

"Me!" she snapped. "I seem to remember the one that gave up the secret first was you, my darling."

"I'll my darling you," Daniel laughed, grabbing for her. Magnus ducked from him and ran down the deck, hiding behind a bunch of boxes. "You aren't getting away that easy," Daniel laughed, running after her. Daniel found her crouched behind a big sail. Quietly he sneaked up behind her and pulled her down on top of him as they landed in the sails. Screaming and laughing, Magnus kissed him as he pulled her closer.

"What in heaven's name!" Magnus's mother screamed. "Magnalynn, what has gotten into you? Even on this God-forsaken vessel, you are still supposed to act like a lady at all times. What if one of the men came along and saw you down there like anybody's trollop? I can't believe this is how you would act. Weren't you raised better than this?"

Magnus laughed quietly into Daniel's shoulder as her mother continued.

"What is all the commotion?" Magnus heard her father ask in the background.

"It's your daughter," Magnus's mother turned on her father. "She is down there," her mother pointed, "with Daniel acting like," her mother took a breath. "She's acting like a . . ."

"She's acting like a woman in love with her husband, darling?" Magnus could hear the steam going out of her mother. "Well, I know they're married, but there is a place and a time for everything and this is not the place."

Magnus peeked as her father whispered something in her mother's ear and her mother swatted at him.

"Come, darling." Her father took her mother by the hand. Magnus sucked in a breath when her mother giggled and walked off with her father. Magnus sat up, nodding.

"She is just a woman," Daniel said, pulling her back down, "who is in love with her husband."

Magnus laughed, returning Daniel's kiss.

"Look at her, Daniel," Magnus cried, watching Beautiful run across the deck. "She's been doing this all morning."

"She is sure-footed," he told Magnus. "Look at her make those turns. What about Precious?"

"She still prefers to walk not run," Magnus said, smiling over at her and Mary playing on a blanket.

"Your mother said Beautiful scratched her leg?" Daniel asked Magnus.

Magnus shook visibly. "Yes, Daniel, she did. Mother was holding Beautiful for a story. Precious was already sleeping. I glanced away, and when I looked back, Beautiful was laughing and looking at her fingers. She was laughing at the blood dripping from them, Daniel. Mother was so shocked she didn't scream until I asked her if she was all right. The thing is, Daniel, I had to run and get Mary before I could get Beautiful off mother. I sent for you when it happened, but Carter wasn't sure where you were."

"I was talking to Ahaira and your uncle. Beautiful got a hold of me last night." Daniel opened his shirt, and Magnus covered her mouth not to let out a scream. "It looks worse than it is," Daniel stopped her from crying out. "No, I don't want anyone to know. We'll just be more careful around her."

"Daniel, she only lets a couple of people care for her now, and now she's hurting them. What are we going to do?"

"Love her, Magnus, what more can we do? We only have a couple of weeks before we'll be at Noteese; maybe we'll find the answers there."

"So," Daniel asked Magnus's mother. "Beautiful's beauty was gone when she scratched you?"

"Yes, her beauty had been gone since that morning. Do you think there is a connection to her losing her beauty to her mean streak, Daniel?"

"I'm not sure, but Mary said she didn't have her beauty when she hurt Nana and the nanny. At least we'll know when we have to be extra careful around her."

Mary smiled at Beautiful while placing her in her bassinet for her nap. "You be a good little girl," Mary smiled. Beautiful smiled back at Mary and reached out to grab her arm. "No, Beautiful let go," Mary said nicely. "Beautiful, that's hurting." Mary started to panic. Daniel looked in Beautiful's bassinet. "Please," Mary cried out, "get her off me." Daniel tried to get Beautiful's hand off Mary's wrist. "Make her stop," Mary cried out.

Beautiful, Daniel noticed, was laughing and cooing. "Beautiful, let go," he screamed. "You're hurting her." Daniel tried to pry Beautiful's hand off without success. Daniel watched as Mary's hand turned red and then purple. "Beautiful!" he screamed. "Let go." Beautiful, Daniel noticed, was watching Mary's face. "Give me a blanket or a towel," he yelled to Magnus's mother, who was crying hysterically in the corner of the room. "Now!" he yelled at her.

Magnus's mother picked up a baby blanket and took it to Daniel. She avoided looking in the bassinet. The look of pain on Mary's face was enough for her nerves to handle at the moment. Daniel took the blanket and placed it over Beautiful's face. Beautiful released Mary, and Mary fell backwards. Daniel took her arm and led her to one of the rockers in the room. Picking up a towel, Daniel wrapped Mary's hand in it.

"Why would she do this, sir? She was acting as if she enjoyed causing me pain. I've never had problems with her before, sir."

"I know, Mary. It's the spell she has in her blood," Daniel told her. Looking over at the still bassinet, Mary moaned, "A spell of what, sir, cruelty?"

"Take her to see Ahaira," he addressed to his mother in law. Magnus's mother helped Mary to her feet.

Daniel walked over to Beautiful's bassinet and lifted the blanket up slowly. He was relieved to find her sleeping. "She looks like a beautiful normal baby girl," he thought rubbing the back of his neck to relieve some of the stress.

"Daniel!" Magnus came hurrying in the room.
Daniel put a finger to his lips. "She's sleeping." He pointed to Beautiful's bassinet.
"Mary? I just saw Mary and Mother. Beautiful hurt Mary?" Magnus whispered under her breath.
"Honey, not only did she hurt her, she acted like she was enjoying hurting her."
"That's crazy, Daniel," Magnus said, lifting her voice a little.
"Quiet, Magnus," Daniel whispered back. "Let's talk in the hall." He pointed to the door. Magnus followed Daniel out of the room.
"She couldn't have realized what she was doing, Daniel."
"I watched her face when she had a hold of Mary's arm. Beautiful was watching Mary's expression on her face. Magnus, when Mary cried out in pain, Beautiful laughed harder, and the strength she had was unreal. Try as I could, I couldn't get her hand off Mary's arm."
"I don't understand," Magnus said, grabbing onto Daniel's hand to stop herself from fainting dead away.
"Magnus, are you all right?" Daniel asked, putting his hand around her waist and leading her to another cabin. "Sit here," he told her, "and don't move."
Daniel headed two doors down to the cabin he shared with Magnus. He took the pitcher of water and a glass from the table and went back to Magnus.
"Here," he said, entering the room. "Drink this. It will calm your nerves."
Magnus took the offered glass and took three sips and set it down.
"Thank you," she said, placing the glass on a bedside table. "I don't know what's gotten into me," Magnus sighed.
"Or should you say who?" Daniel interrupted her. "When were you going to tell me you are with child, Magnus?"
Magnus didn't look up. "I was afraid to tell you, Daniel."
"Afraid?" Daniel's tone turned angry. "When have I ever made you afraid of telling me anything, Magnus?"
Magnus looked up with tears running down her face. "I was afraid when I said it out loud it would be real. Until now, I could pretend I wasn't carrying another child that could have the same problems Beautiful does."
Daniel's anger disappeared. "Magnus, have some faith. We are

heading to Noteese. A place your father swore never to set foot on. If he can do this, why can't you? We will find a cure for Beautiful and one for this child, too, if need be. Until then, we will be careful around Beautiful when her beauty is gone and show her love and attention the rest of the time."

Magnus put her hand on her stomach. "Daniel, we're going to have another baby."

"That's wonderful, darling," he said, pulling her close to him. "That's wonderful."

The men on the ship declined the invitation to the twins' one-year birthday party after they heard about Mary's encounter with Beautiful. The rest of the family set across the table with Beautiful and Precious laughing and clapping at each gift they were given.

The days on the ship were strained for Henasee. She stayed clear of Carter, who also went out of his way to stay clear of her. Daniel and his father-in-law took turns caring for Beautiful when her beauty was gone. Daniel noticed that when Beautiful's beauty is gone she was even more aggressive than she was before. The thing he and his father-in-law talked about without telling anyone was Beautiful's beauty was going away quicker and for longer periods of time.

"Are you sure you want to keep this information from Magnus?" his father-in-law asked him again.

'Magnus isn't having an easy time with the baby she's carrying. She's so afraid this baby will have the same issues that Beautiful does.'

'I can see why that could be a concern,' his father-in-law said, rubbing his arm.

"Did she get you?" Daniel asked.

His father-in-law lifted his sleeve.

"Is that a bite mark?" Daniel asked, examining the deep puncture wounds. "Her beauty is going away so fast I only turned my head for a second, and she had a hold of my arm. I tried covering her face, but she pulled the blanket off and bit down harder."

"You need to put something on that. It really looks bad."

"I'm keeping it clean and dry."

"If I haven't told you yet thank you for helping with her."

Daniel's father-in-law's eyes welled up. "They are my

granddaughters. I love them. I know she doesn't mean to hurt me. When she has her beauty, she is such a loving little thing; I almost forget what she's capable of."

"I know," Daniel agreed. "I can't believe she's the same child that can hurt me so fast and not care one bit about it. Carter says only a few more days, and we will land at Noteese."

"Ahaira says the plant is plentiful. We all need to say a couple of heavy prayers for that plant to work."

"I pray every day," Daniel agreed, "not only for Beautiful but for the child Magnus is carrying."

Both men stiffened as they heard Beautiful moving around in her bed. Looking around slowly, they smiled as Beautiful smiled at them with her beauty intact.

"That's my girl." Daniel walked to her and picks her up. "How's Daddy's little lady?" Daniel smiled, holding her at arm's length. Beautiful laughed and patted her hands.

"While everyone is doing well, maybe we should get some air," Daniel's father-in-law suggested.

"I think that's a wonderful idea, Grandfather," Daniel laughed putting Beautiful's shoes on. Daniel sat Beautiful on a chair and got Precious out of her bed and put her socks and shoes on.

"How's my little darling?" Daniel laughed ruffling her hair.

"Darling," Precious repeated.

"You are talking," Daniel laughed.

"Darling," Precious said again.

"Your mother will be so proud to hear you're talking, Precious."

"Mother!" Beautiful yelled from her chair. Daniel turned to look at her and lifted Precious up just as Beautiful threw a glass at him. Daniel moved with Precious to the other side of Precious's bassinet in time to dodge a plate and spoon. "Beautiful, that is enough. You stop this instant." Daniel watched as Beautiful's beauty was almost completely gone. "Watch yourself," Daniel yelled at his father-in-law. "We'll have to be more careful, with what's left in the room," Darman yelled back to Daniel.

Magnus opened the door, and both her father and Daniel yelled at the same time, "Get out!" Magnus looked from Daniel to her father and then over at Beautiful, who looked angry enough to kill.

"Magnus get out," Daniel yelled again. "Your father and I will fix

this." Magnus looked around the room again and slowly closed the door.
Not knowing what to do, Magnus went in search of Henasee.
"What's wrong?" Henasee jumped out of her deck chair and reached for a trembling Magnus.
"It's Beautiful. She's acting out again. I think my father and Daniel are keeping things from me."
"They are only trying to keep you calm because of the baby."
"I know, but it's better to know than to worry. Henasee, what are we going to do if the plant doesn't take away Beautiful's spell? She is so angry and cruel when her beauty is gone. I know this sounds mean, but I'm afraid of her. Isn't that a horrible thing to say about your own child?" Magnus asked, starting to cry.
"Magnus," Henasee led her to a chair by her bed. "You have every reason to be afraid of Beautiful. She's not a normal child. I've seen what she can do when her beauty is gone and she's angry. We have to hang on to the hope of that plant working. We have no other choice."
"I'm so scared, Hen."
"I know, Magnus. We are all scared, but it will work out. I just know it will."
"Thank you for saying that, Henasee. You are a good friend."
Hours later, Magnus looked up as Daniel came carrying Precious and hanging on to Beautiful's hand.
"How's Father?" Magnus asked, looking behind Daniel.
"His hand is cut, but he'll be fine. He went to find your mother to fix him up."
"Daniel," Magnus cried out.
"Not now, darling," Daniel looked at Beautiful. "We are going to have a nice walk on deck before bedtime."
Magnus nodded and stood up.
"You carry Precious." Daniel smiled at Beautiful keeping everything light.
Magnus was careful not to touch Beautiful and took Precious from Daniel.
"Tell your mother something," Daniel smiled at Precious.
"Darling," Precious said proudly.
"You can talk?" Magnus cooed, delighted. "What a big girl you

are," Magnus continued.

"Walk!" Beautiful demanded. "Walk!"

Daniel looked down at Beautiful and smiled. "You're right, Beautiful, we came out to walk, and walk is what we're going to do."

Magnus followed a bit behind Daniel and Beautiful." So you've decided it's time to talk?" she asked Precious.

"Darling," Precious smiled at Magnus.

"Darling," Magnus smiled and laughed back. "What a lovely first word. Can you say Daddy?" Magnus coaxed.

Precious paused as if she were thinking. She opened her mouth and said, "Darling."

Magnus looked ahead to see Daniel pointing out stars to Beautiful. She seemed to be memorizing what he was saying, Magnus watched in awe. "Please, God," Magnus whispered, "please make her be ok. She is such a bright child," Magnus continued to pray. "When she has her beauty, she is kind and caring. Please let her have a normal childhood."

Precious put her hand in Magnus's hair and pulled hard. "Ouch," Magnus cried out, reaching for Precious's hand. "Precious, that hurts Mommy. You must let go," Magnus told her.

Daniel turned and came over to them, holding on to Beautiful's hand. Precious smiled and let go of Magnus's hair.

"That's a good girl," Magnus said, hugging her. "You must not pull hair, Precious," she said, hugging her again.

Daniel gave a sigh of relief. "I think we've had enough air for one night, ladies. It's off to bed."

Daniel took Precious from Magnus and took the girls back to their cabin.

Chapter 23
The Spell

"I saw the look on your face," Carter said from the shadows of the deck. "You thought Precious was going to hurt you like Beautiful would have."

Magnus turned to look at Carter. "Yes," she confessed, "I was afraid she was going to hurt me."

"The baby you're carrying, do you think it will be born with Beautiful's problems?"

"Ahaira told me the spell will probably be weaker this time, but she can't be sure."

"You and Daniel have been through a great deal together."

Magnus nodded. "Daniel didn't mean to hurt you."

"I am known for my pig-headedness," Carter laughed. "I will apologize the next time I see him."

"He'll like that. He's missed having you to talk to."

"I've watched him with Beautiful. He is a good father. No matter what she's putting him through he talks calmly to her. You would think he was scolding her for making pictures on a wall and not hurting people."

Magnus smiled sadly. "We're hoping Noteese has all the right answers."

"I do for you and Daniel, too," Carter told her.

"Have a good night," Magnus smiled and headed to tell the girls good night.

"You, too," Carter answered.

"That was a very nice thing to say," Henasee walked up to him.

"They are very good people," Carter replied. "Now if you'll excuse me, I better get back, too."

"Why will you forgive Daniel for spreading your secret and not forgive me for laughing at something you misunderstood?"

Carter looked at Henasee and looked out to the ocean. "I'm attracted to you," he said matter of fact. "I knew about you and Kentar. I think everyone on board knew of you and Kentar. I didn't want to rush you."

"You do not have to worry about that," Henasee giggled.

Carter laughed, too. "I did act like a fool," he announced, "and I'm afraid I didn't know how to take what I said back Henasee." Carter took a deep breath. "The women I've been with, they were only . . ." He paused.

"They were passing in the night?" Henasee finished for him.

"You're not that," he struggled to talk. "I mean I didn't want you to think I was looking for something until you are rejoined with Kentar."

"I see," Henasee looked into Carter's dark eyes. "I don't know what it will be like for me when I see Kentar again. I believed I was in love with him."

"You said you believed?" Carter asked her.

"I'm not sure. Kentar and I had an on-the-run-for-our-lives romance. I'm not sure how a relationship can build on something like that. I couldn't promise you anything right now, Carter. I know I'm tired of being lonely at night."

Carter took the three steps it takes to reach Henasee and drew her into his arms. He started by kissing her roughly, and when she stayed in his arms, his kiss lightened.

Henasee smiled as he released her. "I'm not going to run off," she whispered.

"No," he growled, "you're not going to run off." Carter picked her up and carried her to his cabin. Neither of them noticed the looks and smiles they received from some of the crew as Carter took her down the staircase. Carter opened the door to his cabin, still holding Henasee in his arms.

"This is beautiful," Henasee said, looking around his cabin. The light glow of the lantern gave the room a blue glow.

"You are beautiful," Carter said, not taking his eyes off her. "I have dreamed of this moment with you."

Henasee took in a breath and waited for his kiss. Carter kissed her mouth as he sat her gently on a soft wine-colored sofa. Henasee was surprised when he released her and stepped away into the shadows. She looked around the room. Everything in the room was beautiful. Pictures were aglow with flowers and sunrises. The side Carter was on is still too dark for her to see. "The pictures," she cleared her throat, are breathtaking. "Where did you get them?"

"I know the artist," Carter laughed. "Here," he said handing her a silk robe. "This is for you."

Henasee looked at the white see-through robe and back at Carter. "Trust me," he smiled. "I'll be right back." Henasee watched as Carter left the room. She stepped out of her dress and placed the robe on her body. Finding a mirror on the wall, she brushed her hair out with her fingers, and then she stood by the fireplace warming herself from the chill of the room.

"I knew your beauty would be breathtaking," Carter told her from the doorway. "No, don't," he told her when she tried to cover herself. "Come," he said and moved her to a thick white rug in front of the fireplaces. "Sit here," he asked her. Henasee smiled and sat down on the rug. Looking up, she was surprised when Carter didn't join her but yet again he walked away into the shadows.

"Carter?" she called out.

"I want to remember you like this always."

"I don't understand," Henasee called back to him.

Carter turned up the lantern and Henasee saw for the first time what he had in the shadows.

"These pictures," Henasee pointed to the walls. "You painted these, didn't you?" she asked him.

"They are mine," Carter confessed. "I have a love for this art."

"You are very talented."

"I am only a man that puts what he sees to a canvas."

Henasee laughed. "These are much more than that, Carter. They are inspirational."

"You are very kind to my whimsical hobby, dear lady."

Henasee laughed again. "Am I to be a part of your whimsical hobby?" She lifted an edge of the silk robe up.

"You are more of a dream come true." He smiled, walking over to her. "I would paint you if I may?" he asked kneeling beside her. Carter kissed her and released her so fast she almost fell backwards.

"I don't understand."

"I want to see into your soul, Henasee."

"I do not know how to show you my soul."

"I will paint you," he smiled.

Henasee nodded.

Carter laid her on the rug, turning her on her side. He placed one of her hands above her head and the other hand he laid across her waist, resting on the floor. He opened the front of her robe and let it fall open, not baring her breast.

"A woman's body is a beautiful thing." He ran a finger down the opening of the robe. "But it is also a very private thing that should only be shared with someone special." Henasee smiled up at him. Carter worked for hours on the painting. "That should be good for now," he smiled at Henasee.

Henasee sat up, closing her robe and stretched.

"No." Carter sat beside her. "Let me," he said, watching as he let the robe slide off her shoulders and onto the rug. Carter reached out and ran his finger down the same trail he had before, never once touching her breast. "You are very beautiful, Henasee. I want to show you how beautiful I think you are now."

Henasee licked her lips and closed her eyes.

"No," Carter told her, surprising her. "You will look at me because if you are willing to make love to me. You will see it is me, and every touch you feel will be from me."

Henasee opened her eyes. "I can see only you, Carter, and I will only feel you."

Carter pushed her gently back on the rug, and Henasee went freely with him. Hours later, Carter pulled her close and kissed the side of her head.

"That is how I feel about you, Henasee."

Henasee cuddled into him and took a deep breath.

:Are you all right?: he asked.

"It has never been like that before," she told him. "I mean Kentar was . . ." Henasee stopped embarrassed. "I didn't mean to talk about another man. When we just, I mean I didn't."

"Stop," Carter put a hand to her mouth. "I understand, Henasee. You were made to fit my body. You were in love with Kentar, and I'm guessing he was your first?"

Henasee smiled and nodded.

"Let's not try and figure what this is between us yet," he suggested. "Let's let it go and see where it grows. Now," he laughed, "I would love for you to wake up in my arms, or if you're worried about what people might say, I can sneak you back to your room."

Henasee looked out one of the small windows and laughed. "I think it might be too late for worrying about my virtue."
"I'm afraid you're right," he said, pulling her back into his arms and administering kisses to her again.

"Daniel are you sure we shouldn't separate the girls? What if Beautiful should hurt Precious?"
"We've tried, darling, and every time they're away from each other for more than a minute, they both scream and carry on. Once they are reunited, they stop their screaming. Your father, Nana, and I are very careful to ensure Precious doesn't get hurt in one of Beautiful's bad moments."
Bad moments. Magnus shook her head. "It doesn't sound as bad as when she loses her beauty and she tries to hurt or maim people."
"We will be at Noteese any day now, honey. Then all of this will be behind us. Our children and our lives will be happy and normal."
"Normal," Magnus laughed. "I have fought having a normal life since I was a child, and now it's the only thing I pray for. I want a normal life with normal children."
"It will happen, darling. You wait and see," Daniel said, pulling her to him. "I must get back to relieve your father for breakfast," Daniel said, hugging Magnus and walking away.
Magnus watched him leave and smiled when she headed down the hallway as Henasee tried to sneak out of Carter's room. "Delivering breakfast to the captain?" Magnus laughed.
"Do you stand there every morning hoping to catch me, or is this just my lucky day?" Henasee laughed with Magnus.
"I can see your morning is going well."
"It was like a dream," Henasee gushed.
"I see," Magnus smiled and took Henasee's hand.
"Honestly, Mag, I can't remember when I've ever been this happy."
"I'm happy for you," Magnus told her, hugging her deeply.
"Thank you, Magnus. It's nice not to feel sad for a change."
"You deserve to be happy, Henasee."
"You do, too, Magnus."
"You're going to have a new baby and the girls will be cured," Henasee sobbed.
Carter walked out of his cabin to see Henasee and Magnus in

hysterical tears holding each other.
"Did something happen with Beautiful?" Carter asked, concerned.
Magnus and Henasee shook their heads no.
"What?" he yelled at them.
"I was telling her how special last night was," Henasee got out between sobs.
Carter turned red from his head and could feel the embarrassment tingling in his toes. "Ok," he smiled and looked at both of them. "I think I'll get to work, there's a lot to be done before we arrive at Noteese. I'll see you later?" He addressed the question to Henasee. Henasee nodded, and he smiled again and walked off.
"Isn't he beautiful?" Henasee said, watching him walk away.
"You do have good taste for picking very attractive men," Magnus agreed.
"My wife is already looking for replacements for me?" Daniel said behind them.
 "No," Magnus laughed. "I was just agreeing Carter is a very attractive man."
Henasee moved over so Daniel could slide up beside Magnus.
"I am the only attractive man in your life, my lovely wife."
Magnus giggled as Daniel patted her belly. "I am a one-man woman, Daniel." Daniel smiled and kissed her cheek.
"I am that one man," Daniel laughed, kissing her cheek again.
"Your father said he had a good night with the girls. He even got some sleep in. He sent me for coffee and more coffee."
Magnus's smile grew across her face. "Maybe everything will be all right after all."
"I told you not to worry, darling." Daniel patted her belly again. "And our family will be fine Magnus, just fine," he told her.

Chapter 24
Believing

"Noteese is just as beautiful as I remember it," Henasee told Carter.
"It is beautiful," Carter agreed, looking out over the vast colors of beaches and tropical flowers. "I've never seen so many colors," he told Henasee.
"Magnus and I sat one whole day and tried to count the different colors. We kept losing count. Look," Henasee pointed as the ship circles one side of Noteese. "Look as we get closer the water changes from red to blue."
"That is amazing," Carter said, looking to where the two colors meet.
"I know," Henasee smiled. "Kentar and I. . ."
"Don't stop," Carter encouraged her. "I know you were here with Kentar."
"No, it wasn't what I was going to say. Kentar and I talked of returning one day and swimming out to see how the two waters stayed separated."
"Maybe," Carter said, putting his arm around her, "maybe it's something you and I can find out together." Henasee settled into his arm and smiled up at him.

"Look, Daniel," Magnus laughed excitedly. "We are finally here." Daniel smiled at the sight of Noteese. "I never thought I'd be back here again," he said, holding onto Magnus's hand. "This is where our nightmares are put to rest." He smiled down at Magnus and lifted her up, swinging her around in the air.
Everyone on the ship is busy doing something. "Are we taking the girls ashore tonight?" Mary asked Magnus.
"No, Mary, we want everything set up before we move them. Are you afraid to stay alone with them?" Magnus asked her.
"No, I've spent time with your father and the girls. When Beautiful loses her beauty, I am very careful not to get too close to her She has not hurt me again. Your father told me to stay out of arm's length

with Beautiful when her beauty is gone. It's been working out nicely."

"Oh good," Magnus sighed. "If I haven't thanked you for everything you done for us," Magnus started to tell Mary.

Mary stopped her. "I love those little darlings, Magnus. Beautiful can't help she has a spell in her. Once we find that plant and give it to Beautiful, like Ahaira says, Beautiful will be just fine after that."

"You do believe it? Don't you Mary?"

"I believe everything is going to be fine now," Mary promised.

"Darling," Daniel addressed Magnus. "We are ready to go to shore. I've saved a spot for you. Your uncle and Ahaira are waiting. The sooner we find the plant Ahaira has described, the quicker Beautiful and Precious will stop losing their beauty. And . . ."

Magnus smiled. "The sooner our lives will become normal."

"What is normal?" Daniel laughed and took her hand leading her to the boat.

"You talked to my father?" Magnus asked Daniel. "He's with the girls right now. Mary will take her shift at 7:00, giving your father time to eat and relax for a couple of hours. Your father is taking night duty. If there are any problems, he will have one of the men wave a lantern. If no one notices, he will send someone to fetch us in a rowboat."

Magnus laughed. "You've thought of everything."

"Not this," Daniel turned her and kissed her deeply. "I haven't thought to tell you how beautiful you are today."

"Oh, Daniel," Magnus swatted at his chest. "You know my beauty is gone today."

"I can see past that, darling. I can see so much past that. You are a beautiful woman to me every day."

"Are you two coming or staying?" Uncle Bernard yelled.

"We're coming," Magnus laughed and let Daniel help her into the rowboat.

"I expect the girls are covered for the night," her uncle asked her. Magnus laughed, looking over at Daniel. "Daniel has thought of everything."

"Then it's off we go, Carter."

Carter nodded, and four men started to row. "We've got another boat coming soon with supplies," Carter pointed for Daniel and

Bernard to see.

"Tell us more about the plant, Ahaira," Daniel said, turning in her seat.

"It's a beautiful plant," she started. "I have seen only one in my lifetime. It was when I was a small child. My father had come across a enemy of my mother's. She had cast a spell on him. He was to never walk again. My mother used a leaf from a plant she called Canta carra, she said it meant the healing of pain. She ground the leaf up and made a tea out of it. After she gave it to my father, he slept for two days. When he awoke, he had use of his legs again."

Magnus reached over and squeezed Daniel's hand.

"I would not suggest for this baby," Ahaira pointed at Magnus's stomach.

Magnus looked at Ahaira. "I thought we could cure this baby, too."

"We do not yet know what this baby has. If we give the plant to take away a spell and there is no spell in this child, it could very well kill the child."

"Ahaira!" Bernard yelled. "There is no need to talk like that."

Ahaira glared at Bernard. "She is the one who asked. I only gave the answer."

"No more," he snapped again.

Ahaira turned around in her seat and refused to answer any more questions.

The rest of the trip was strained, and Magnus was happy to reach the island. She had been feeling sick, and now her legs were a little wobbly.

"Magnus," Daniel said, as he lifted her over the rowboat and carried her through the water, "everything will be all right. Ahaira is a bit dramatic at times. She didn't mean to scare you."

"She didn't say anything I haven't thought about, Daniel. We are going to be giving something to Beautiful that we don't know what it's going to do."

"We will believe God will help us through, Magnus. Beautiful can't grow up hurting people. One day she's liable to go too far."

Magnus looked at Daniel. "You've thought her anger is getting worse, too?"

"Darling, tonight we'll set up camp, and first thing in the morning Carter and I will hunt for the plant to cure Beautiful. Now you sit here and wait until I tell you to move."

Magnus smiled at Daniel. "I will, Daniel. I will sit right here until you tell me to move."

"I'm not playing, Magnus. You talked me into letting you come this far. Don't make me sorry I brought you."

"Ok, Daniel, I will stay put."

"Thank you." He bowed.

Chapter 25
Temper Tantrums

Mary brought two bowls of stew with bread and two small glasses of water.

"I see you're right on time," Magnus's father smiled helping her with the tray of food for the girls. "They are playing nicely together," he said, pointing at the girls in the corner. "Magnus and Francine sewed them new dolls, and they have been playing with them for hours."

Mary smiled and put the two bowls on the girls' small dinner table. Pulling out a chair, she said, "Precious are you hungry?"

Precious turned and smiled at Mary. "Hungry," she repeated.

"I'll be back at 11," he told Mary and waved good-bye to Precious. Precious climbed up in her chair and took the spoon Mary offered her.

"Good girl," Mary told her.

"Good girl," Precious repeated.

"Eat now."

"Eat now," Precious repeated.

Mary laughed and turned to look at Beautiful. "Are you ready to eat, too, Beautiful?" Mary asked her.

Beautiful didn't turn or acknowledge Mary had spoken.

"Beautiful?" Mary said again, taking a step closer. "Aren't you hungry, sweetie?" Mary turned to look at Precious when Precious drops her spoon and said, "Fall."

"Did your spoon fall, Precious?" Mary asked, bending to pick it up for her.

"Oh, my God!" Darman yelled when he opened the door to the girls' cabin. "Help me," he screamed into the hallway. "Someone help me."

One of the men on deck heard Darman and came running. "What's wrong, sir?"

"In here," Darman pointed at Mary hanging from one of the rafters by a scarf.

"What in heaven's creation?" the nervous man said, looking at Darman and then at the girls. "I've heard stories; did them little girls do this? I'm not going near them," the man said and started to back out of the door.
"Help me get her down," Darman screamed at him.
"Do something with them," the man pointed at Beautiful and Precious.
Darman could see the girls both had their beauty. "Girls," Darman said to them, "come here."
The man backed all the way down the hallway.
"Grandpa is going to play a game with you." Both girls clapped their hands and followed Darman into Magnus and Daniel's room. "I am going to count while you hide," Darman said out of breath. "One, two."
Beautiful and Precious giggled and looked for places to hide.
"Get her down," Darman yelled at the man still cowering at the end of the hallway. Minutes later, Darman and the man carried Mary's body from the room.
"Where do we put her?" the man asked Darman.
"In here," Darman pointed to an empty cabin. They placed Mary on the bed, and Darman covered her face with a sheet that was sitting on the end of the bed.
"We're not going to just leave her here, are we?"
"Give me a minute to think," Darman snapped at the man.
The man jumped as a door opened behind him. "Darman?" Francine called, seeing him in the doorway.
"Stay out, Francine."
"What is it, Darman? It's not the girls, is it?"
"Grandma," Francine heard Precious saying from Magnus's room.
"I'm coming, darling." Francine turned and opened Magnus's door.
"Francine," Darman yelled after her. "You be careful with them."

"Francine!" Darman yelled.
Francine opened the door and stepped inside. Darman pushed past the crewman and ran to Magnus's room.
"Francine!" he screamed as he opened the door. "Oh, my God!"
Darman knelt beside Francine. "Francine," he cried.
Francine looked up with tears running down her face. "She has a

knife, Darman."

"Beautiful stabbed you?"

Francine's eyes flutter. "No, Darman, it was Precious."

Francine closed her eyes for the last time, and Darman screamed so loud the room felt like it was alive with misery.

"Not her Lord, please." Beautiful and Precious came to stand by their grandfather.

"Go over there and sit down," he yelled at them. "I don't want you to move one inch." Both girls turned and ran to the bed, climbing on it with their beauty intact. Darman picked up Francine and carried her to their room.

"What am I going to do without you," he whispered to her as if he might wake her if he was too loud. "I have loved you most of my life." Darman looked down at the pool of blood that was gathering at his feet. "You didn't think they would hurt you, darling, and now you're gone."

Darman sat down on the bed with her. "Francine, please don't leave me. I will be lost without you."

"Sir," the man stepped in the doorway. "Should I motion for the captain?"

"NO!" Darman looked past the man. "I will take care of them. We will not be notifying anyone."

"But sir?" the captain said.

"I own this ship, and I give the orders."

"Yes sir."

"You may go," he said to the man. "Don't tell anyone of this." The man looked at Darman and then at Francine. "Or I will send those girls to find you."

The man looked up and cried out, "I won't tell a soul sir, not a soul." And then he ran off.

Darman sat with Francine on his lap for so long he lost track of the time. Looking around, he saw it is almost completely dark in his room. "I must go now, darling," he said as he gently placed Francine on their bed and fixed her dress. "I know how you hate to look wrinkled," he said, patting everything into place. "I need to take care of the girls, and I'll be right back." Darman kissed her forehead and left to find Beautiful and Precious.

"Now," Daniel returned to Magnus, "I will take you to dinner."
Magnus laughed. "I am hungry after watching everyone do all that work."
"Let's make a deal," Daniel laughed back. "The next time we come to Noteese and you're not with child, I will watch you build the camp."
Magnus laughed. "It's a deal, Daniel."
"I've been watching the ship. Nothing so far. Your father has everything under control, darling. Don't worry. By this time tomorrow, the girls will have their cure, and we will be a happy family."
"Do you think we can really believe it, Daniel?"
"We can believe it, Magnus. All the sad and crazy is long gone for us."

Darman emptied Francine's bottle of sleeping medicine into two small glasses. Hurrying to the galley, he got a teaspoon of dried milk and two coco beans. Putting everything in a pot, he poured water into the mixture and started the fire under the stove. Darman looked around and lit a lantern. He returned to Magnus and Daniel's room and gave a sigh of relief when he saw the two girls sleeping on the bed. Hurrying back to the galley, he found two sugar cookies the cook had been hiding and placed them on a plate on the tray with the glasses.
When the water was hot, Darman poured the concoction into the two glasses with the sleeping medicine in it. Darman walked back to the girls as if in a trance. "God, please forgive me for what I'm about to do."
Darman opened the door quietly and sat the tray on a bedside table. "Girls," he said in a shaky voice. "Grandpa has brought you a surprise."
Precious sat up and smiled. "Surprise?" she asked.
"Yes, my sweet, Grandpa has made a very special surprise for you. Drink up," he said, handing the drink to Precious.
Precious put the glass to her mouth, and Beautiful slapped it out of her hand.
"No!" she screamed at Darman.
Darman started to stand, but Beautiful grabbed his hair laying him

on the bed. Precious took the glass still on the table and started to pour it in Darman's mouth. Darman choked on the hot liquid.
"Bad grandpa!" Beautiful said.
"Bad Grandpa," Precious repeated.
"You are not normal children!" Darman screamed at them. "You must die."
"You must die," Precious repeated placing a pillow over Darman's head.
Darman tried to push the pillow off his face, but the strength of the girls was too much. Darman took a last breath and lay still.
Beautiful and Precious climbed off the bed and went out the door.
"Walk," Beautiful said to Precious.
"Walk," Precious repeated.
"What are you doing here?" the man who had helped Darman move Mary screamed.
"Walk," Beautiful said and Precious repeated.
"Where's your grandfather?" the man asked, sweating.
"Walk," Beautiful said again, and they both looked around and walked past him.
Beautiful watched as Precious walked behind a box and moved closer to the man standing by the rail of the boat. Beautiful approached him.
"I thought you went for a walk," the man screamed at Beautiful. Precious came up from behind the man and pushed him into the water. The man went over the side of the boat, hitting his head as he fell. Two men came running from different sides of the deck.
"What's going on?" they asked each other when they met n the middle of the deck.
"I thought I heard someone go over."
"It must be the storm that's coming in," one man pointed at the sky.
"Yah, you're right."
"Have you seen Ned?"
"Nope! I haven't seen him all night."
"No good," one man mumbled. "He knows we're shorthanded with most everyone on shore. I was hope in he'd pull his weight tonight."
"We are talkin' about the same Ned?"
"You're right. I don't know what I was thinking.' I got some things to get ready for shore tomorrow. I'll see you in a couple of hours,"

the man told him.

"Yep, see yah, Tom," Jake replied.

Jake lit his pipe and sat back in a deck chair. "This is the life," he smiled looking up to the stars. "No one around to say Jake do this, or Jake do that." Jake leaned back, and a rope came around his neck. He could feel tiny hands but couldn't see behind the chair and after fighting with all his strength, his hands finally fell to his sides.

"Sleep," Beautiful told Precious.

"Sleep," Precious repeated.

Beautiful and Precious went back to their rooms. Precious climbed in her bed and Beautiful climbed in hers, and they both pulled their blankets up over themselves and went to sleep.

"I thought better of you Jake," Ted screamed into the dark. "I know Ned's not a worker, but I thought I could count on you. What the? Jake?" Ted hurried to where Jake was lying. "What's going on?" he yelled, turning over Jakes body. "Oh, my God!" Ted screamed, dropping Jake back to the deck.

Running across the deck screaming, Ted couldn't find anyone. "Ned!" he screamed. Taking the steps two at a time, he went from room to room, opening door after door. Stopping at the bottom of the second tier, he saw a dark trail of blood. "What the?" He stopped and followed the blood with his eye. Opening the door slowly, he was relieved to see a lantern burning. He didn't have to touch her to know she was dead. Francine's body was already blue. "What's going on here?" he screamed out. "Is there anybody here?" Ted ran from the room and checked Magnus and Daniel's room. Finding Darman on the floor, Ted fell to his knees crying. "This is crazy," he said, taking the pillow off of Darman's face. Stumbling to get up, he ran from the room and headed up the staircase. He didn't see her until it was too late. Beautiful stepped onto the top step and pushed on his legs. Ted flew down the staircase, and his neck snapped as he hit the floor.

"Sleep," Beautiful turned and said to Precious.

"Sleep," Precious repeated.

Chapter 26
Canta Carra

"Why does everything you need always seem to be on the farthest corner of the world?" Carter laughed, pointing at another cliff they must find a way up.
"Ahaira said it would be closest to the sun," Daniel told him. "Something about the heat keeping it activated."
"Sounds a bit strange," Carter told him.
"I know," Daniel agreed, "but what Beautiful is going through is strange, too. She has the strength of 10 men and the cruelest personality when her beauty is gone. So maybe an activated plant is just what will cure her."
"I can't fight with that reasoning," Carter agreed and started up a slope on the mountain.
"You look like you've done this before," Daniel complimented Carter.
"I get around," Carter laughed.
"I heard you and Henasee visited last night."
"I think the whole ship heard about it before I came out of my cabin."
"Women are the voice of the world," Daniel laughed.
"I bet you wouldn't repeat that in front of Magnus," Carter laughed.
"I will deny I ever said it," Daniel laughed back.

"Magnus, you stay and take it easy, I'll have a few men go with me," her Uncle Bernard told her.
"I am tired," Magnus said, stretching on the chair Daniel had brought to shore for her. "I watched most of the night in case Father needed me."
"I'm sure your father and the girls did just fine." Bernard looked around to make sure the men were all working on the camp. "We're going to be here for a bit. We might as well have some comforts of home."
"Comforts?" Ahaira laughed. "You have brought almost everything in your house."

Bernard laughed. "I did bring a lot of comfort."
Magnus looked around at the men unpacking and setting up their areas to live in. "It's so good to be on solid ground," she smiled at her uncle. "Tell the girls their father will come for them tonight."
"I will, honey. You just sit and take it easy until Daniel gets back."

"Only a couple of more feet," Daniel said, looking back at Carter.
"And what?" Carter asked him. "We touch the sun?" Carter laughed, wiping sweat off his brow.
"I heard it said up is the hardest," Daniel enlightened him.
"Down is a long way," Carter said, peering over his shoulder.
Daniel reached for Carter's arm and helped pull him to the top of the cliff.
"Well, this is definitely the highest place on the island."
Daniel nodded. Looking around, Daniel laughed and clapped his hands. "How easy is this?" He reached down and started to pick a flower he knew to be Canta Carra. Ahaira had described it in full detail. Canta Carra was a bright orange flower with deep purple veins. The aroma would be of a very sweet orange.
"No!' Carter grabbed his hand. "She said we had to bring it still in the soil."
Daniel stopped and looked around. "How on earth are we going to do that?" Carter removed his shirt and placed it by the plant.
"Like this," he said, digging around the plant. "Then we'll wrap them in our shirts and carry them down tied on our backs." Daniel took off his shirt and placed it by another plant and started to dig with his hands.
"Look," Carter pointed. "Someone is taking one of the boats back to the ship."
"Bernard," Daniel told him, watching the boat glide across the water. "He said he would check on Darman if I wasn't back by noon. I'll be glad when this is all over," Daniel confessed.
"Your family has been through enough, that's for sure."
Daniel looked up at Carter. "I am sorry I didn't keep your confidence. Magnus has this way of goading me into saying things I wouldn't usually let slip out."
"Henasee and I are far from that now," Carter smiled.
"Good," Daniel smiled back. "She's a nice girl."

"That she is," Carter smiled to himself and placed the plant and soil inside his shirt.

Bernard knew approaching the ship that something wasn't right. He had left three men on board to make sure things went smoothly for Darman, but not one man was on the deck to greet them.
"Stay together," he told the four men he brought with him.
"Something isn't right." All the men agreed. The eerie quiet of the ship was making each one of them jumpy.
One of the men spotted Jake's body sprawled out on the floor.
"He's been strangled," one of the men screamed.
"Stop it," Bernard told the man. "We don't want to warn whoever did this."
"It's those little witches," one of the men screamed at Bernard.
"Yah, it's those little demons. They did this," another man screamed at Bernard.
"Stop this instant," Bernard yelled, losing his patience. "We'll find out what this is all about. Now cover him up." He pointed to a cloth tarp.
Two of the men took the tarp and placed it over Jake's body.
"Now let's stay calm."
One man nodded, but the others stared around the ship. Checking the deck and finding nothing else, they headed to the stairs.
"Oh, my God!" Bernard said, looking at Ned at the bottom of the steps, his head cocked to the side.
"They've killed Ned, too," one of the men screamed.
Bernard raised his hand to hit the man.
"You'll be fighting all of us," another man said grabbing Bernard's arm. "You know as well as we do those girls are the ones that did this. I say, we find them and kill them."
"Yah," the three other men agreed.
"What makes you think you can kill them?" Bernard asked the angry men.
Two of the men went ghost white while the other two looked at each other.
"I'm getting out of here," one of the men said and ran back to the rowboat.
"Light a lantern and wave it across the water. Daniel will come.

He'll know what to do."
Two of the men took off to light the lantern for Daniel. Bernard looked over at the one who was left. "I'm going down there. Are you coming?"
The man looked around and nodded. "I'm not staying here alone."
"Ok then. Stay close and keep an eye out for anything that doesn't seem right."
"None of this seems right," the man said looking past Bernard at Ned's dead body.
The first door Bernard opened, he cried out in pain.
"What?" the man said, bumping into Bernard's back.
"It's Francine. She's dead."
The man looked over Bernard's shoulder and saw Francine lying dead on the bed. Blood filled the white comforter. Shutting the door, Bernard wiped his brow. Another door down, Bernard opened it slowly. Bernard recognized Mary's legs and shoes sticking out from under the sheet. The man was so close to him, Bernard could feel the heat off his body.
"Who is that?" the man asked Bernard. Bernard pushed the man forward, and he slid past him to open Magnus and Daniel's cabin door. Lying on the floor was his beloved brother Darman.
"Oh, no," Bernard cried as he knelt down by Darman. Lifting his shoulders, Bernard pulled him to his chest and openly wept. The man at the door stepped in and shut the door.
"I don't think we should stay here," the man said, looking around. Bernard placed Darman back on the floor and wiped his face.
"I can't believe they're this strong."
"I think we should wait for their father," the man said looking around the room.
"I agree," Bernard told him, looking again at Darman.

"Look!" Daniel pointed at the reflection coming from the ship.
"Let's get going," he told Carter. "There's something wrong."
Daniel helped Carter with the rope that held his shirt on his back with the plant in it. "You don't want to tie it around your neck in case it gets hung up."
"Good idea," Carter agreed.

Magnus watched as the lantern glittered off the water. She watched with Henasee as two rowboats were put in the water and men jumped in them and started paddling.
"What do you thinks happened?" she asked, holding on to Henasee.
"It's probably nothing, Mag, just . . ."
"You can't even come up with a lie."
"All we can do is pray everything is fine, Mag."
"Daniel should be back soon," Magnus said, with tears running down her face. "He'll know what to do."

The two boats got to the ship at the same time.
"What's going on?" one man yelled up.
"They're dead," the man yelled down.
"Who's dead?"
"We found Jake and Ned's bodies so far. They're down below looking to see if there are any more dead bodies."
"What happened?" Another man from the boat yelled up.
"If you ask me, it's those girls. Everybody knows they're possessed."
"I'm coming down," the man holding the lantern told them. "I'm not staying aboard with them little witches. Let their father do something with them." All the men agreed.
"What are you doing down there?" Bernard yelled down to the men in the rowboats.
"We're not coming aboard," one man yelled, and they all agreed. Bernard watched as the men he came aboard with started to climb over the side and back into their rowboat.
"I'm getting out of here," one man told him. "I have my family I have to stay alive and go home, too. If something happens to me, they won't have anyone to care for them."
"We're in this together, men," Bernard addressed them by looking at each of their faces. "Daniel will fix this."
"Those babies killed all those people."
"You mean Jake and Ned?" one man asked him.
"No, there are three more dead down below. One has almost all her blood drained from her body."
Bernard started to panic looking at the faces of the men.
One man asked Bernard, "What are we going to do about those two

killers?"
"Let's wait for the captain and Daniel to get here."
"I'm not coming aboard," one man said, and the others agreed.
"Fine," Bernard agreed with them. "We'll wait it out like this. I will watch from up here, and you can stay in your boats."
The men looked around, and all agreed as long as they didn't have to board they were safe.

Carter knew Daniel was taking extra chances coming down the mountain. He understood if it were his family, he would get down any way he could to get to them, too.
"It's not going to do them any good if you fall," he told Daniel after he moved too fast and lost his footing.
Daniel took a breath and tried again. In less than an hour, they were at the bottom of the hill.
"Remind me never to go climbing with you again," Carter told him as they ran down the beach side by side. Magnus met Daniel halfway down the beach.
"You saw the lantern?" she asked him, breathless.
"Here, give this to Ahaira," Daniel said, untying the rope that held the plant in his shirt.
"I have one, too." Carter handed her his plant.
"Try to stay calm," he said to Magnus. "I'll be back as soon as I can. Tell Ahaira to have the plant ready when I return."
"I will," she promised him. Daniel kissed her face and marched down the beach for a rowboat with Carter.
"What do you think?" Carter asked him.
"I think it's going to be bad," Daniel said, pushing the rowboat into deeper water and climbing in. "I noticed the men were still in the boats and not on the ship."

Bernard tried not to cry as Daniel climbed up the rope and onto the ship. Looking at Bernard's face, Daniel's heart sank.
"They're all dead, Daniel."
Daniel almost fell.
"Francine, Darman, Mary, and at least two men we found dead."
"What about the girls?" Daniel asked him.
"Those girls of yours are the ones that killed them all," one man

yelled from a rowboat.
Daniel turned and gave the man a killer look, and the man sat back down.
"You men go back to shore." Daniel pointed to the two rowboats. "Tell my wife I'll be back shortly, and you have no more information. If any of you tell her different, I will hunt you down myself. Now go!" he yelled over the sea breeze.
The men wasted no time heading back to the island.
"Carter, you stay put and keep a look out for them. If you see them, don't go near them. You won't be able to tell them apart. If you get into any bad situation, jump overboard and take one of the boats to shore."
"She's killed five people," Bernard said seriously. "Don't be number six."
"Don't worry about me. I'll head over the side at the first outbreak of danger." Daniel shook his head and he and Bernard went in search of the girls.

Magnus watched as two boats headed to shore. "Here they come!" she yelled to Henasee, who we helping Ahaira ground up the plant. Henasee looked out to the water and then went back to helping Ahaira.
Magnus met the first boat and looked at the men's faces. "What happened?" she asked them.
"We don't know, Miss," one of the men talked for them all. "We never went aboard. Your husband said he'd be back shortly."
"You don't know anything?" she tried to ask again.
"We don't know nothing." The men helped drag the boat up on shore, and they all wandered off to their own makeshift areas.
When the second boat came in, Magnus tried another approach. "They said," she tilted her head toward two of the guys from the previous boat. "They said someone got hurt."
The man at the front of the boat stood up and clutched his fist. "He was told to leave that talk to Daniel. Daniel didn't want you to know about your parents being dead until he came to shore." Everything around Magnus started to spin and then everything went black.
"Magnus," she heard her name being called. "Come on, honey. It'll be all right. Try to open your eyes."

Magnus's eyes fluttered open. "Are my parents dead?" Magnus whispered to Henasee. "That's what the men are saying who came back from the ship." Magnus's eyes started to flutter again.
"No, Magnus, stay with me," Henasee told her. "I know this is hard, but when Daniel brings the girls ashore, they're going to need everyone who loves them. The men are afraid of them. You're going to have to be strong."
Magnus looked to the other side of the camp. A group of men were standing together talking and pointing.
"Ahaira thinks we should find another place to camp. Somewhere the girls will be safe."
"The cave!" Magnus told Henasee. "That's what I was thinking. Ahaira is going to help me move some supplies. You must guard the tea. She has it boiling on the fire."
Magnus sat up slowly. "I'll watch it," she promised.
"If Daniel gets back with the girls before we return, bring them to the cave. Otherwise, we'll be back in a couple of hours."
Magnus hugged Henasee. "You are the best friend ever."
"You just be careful." She pointed over at the men still swarming together. "There's nothing more dangerous than a bunch of scared people looking for a fight."
"I'll watch myself," Magnus promised. Magnus looked over at the men moments ago she had thought of as her friends. The looks on their faces showed they no longer felt that about her. Trying not to cry, she picked up a wooden spoon and stirred the tea a few times around. "Please, God, look after Daniel and my babies. I know it's not their fault. Fanton did this to them." Magnus bowed her head and started to cry. "No, Fanton didn't do this God. I am the one with all my lies and deceits. It is I who has brought this curse down on my children. If anyone should be punished it is me."
One of the men approached Magnus. "We are all in agreement," he yelled loudly enough for everyone to here. "We don't want you or your children in our camp."
Magnus looked the man in the eyes. "This is not yours or anyone else's camp. It is all of ours."
"Not anymore," the man said reaching up and striking Magnus across the face. Magnus was so stunned she fell to the ground.
"Are you crazy?" One of the men from the other side of the camp

rushed over. "Daniel will kill you for that."
"Not if he comes back, and she's already dead. He'll not know who did it. He's not going to kill us all. We'll tell him it was an accident. She is a witch just like her children. Who knows? She may have plans to kill us when we sleep tonight."
The man reached for Magnus, and one of the men yelled out, "No one is going to hurt Magnus."
"Yah," a man spoke up. "She has been nothing but kind to me."
"Me, too," another yelled out.
"I thought we all agreed," the man asked, a bit shaken.
"We agreed we didn't want them in camp but not to kill her," one of the men told him.
The man stepped back, and one man helped her up and helped her to a chair.
"We didn't mean for you to get hurt," he told her.
"I know," Magnus smiled sadly at him.
"We're just afraid for our lives, "another told her.
"I understand why everyone is afraid, and as soon as Daniel gets here, we will take our children out of the camp."
"Then you do understand?" one of the men asked Magnus.
"Of course we understand. Henasee and Ahaira are already moving out supplies out of camp."
Some of the people looked around and saw what Magnus was saying was true.
Magnus noticed everyone else had wandered back to their own spots, and there were no groups of men whispering in corners. She reached for the spoon and stirred the tea again.
"Why are you still wound up?" one of the men asked Jared. "We should burn her at the stake and her killer kids right behind her. No one is going to be safe with those witches on the island. Drink tea, right!" He spat on the ground. "No tea is going to stop the way those two kids like to kill. You didn't see the lady on the bed." He got closer for emphasis. "They almost drained all the blood out of the lady."
"I'd watch talking about her with the wrong person. Daniel will shoot you dead on the spot if he finds out you're talking about killing his wife."
"Well, maybe I'll just have to kill him, too," the man said, pulling

out a long knife out of its holder and rubbing his thumb across it.
"You're crazy," the man said and walked off.
"I'll show them crazy," the man laughed, looking over at Magnus.

"You don't want to go in there," Bernard told Daniel. "When we get the girls to shore, I'll bring some men back and bury them."
Daniel dropped his hand on Francine's door and followed Bernard down to the girls' room. Daniel's eyes filled with tears as he sees how much blood was on the floor. Reaching for the door, he stopped and looked at Bernard. "I won't have her hurt you. If I say get out, you get out."
Bernard started to argue.
"Promise you'll take care of Magnus and the new baby."
"Let's just get them and get out of here," Bernard told Daniel.
"Promise," Daniel said again.
"Ok," Bernard lifted his hand. "I promise. Now let's see what we're facing."
Daniel opened the door and was surprised to find everything in the room torn to shreds. "I don't see them," he said, looking in their beds and in the closet quickly. Stepping out of the room, they heard footsteps.
"That way," Daniel said, starting to run. "Girls, it's Daddy." Daniel could still hear the footsteps running away. "Girls, don't run from Daddy."
Bernard matched Daniel step for step. Reaching the deck, Daniel saw Beautiful for the first time. Her hair was haphazard, and her dress was dirty but besides that she looked fine. With her beauty intact, Daniel approached her. "Come, darling, we're going to shore to see Mommy." Beautiful reached her hand out to Daniel, and Daniel took it.
"Where is your sister?" Daniel asked Beautiful. Beautiful acted as if he'd never asked the question. "Beautiful, where is Precious?" Daniel asked again.
"Precious," Beautiful pointed to the staircase.
"I can get her," Bernard told him.
"We'll wait right here for you," Daniel said, watching for any changes for Beautiful to lose her beauty.
"I'll find her and be right back," Bernard said, heading down the

stairs again.

Finding Precious wasn't hard at all. Bernard could hear Precious humming from one of the rooms. Climbing over Ned, Bernard followed the sounds and found Precious sitting in her room with her doll.

"How did you get back in here?" Bernard asked her. "Your father and I were just in here looking for you."

Precious looked up at Bernard and smiled. Bernard noticed Precious's beauty was gone, but he was not afraid of her. Precious had never hurt anyone before. Reaching down to help her up, he held out his hand. Precious lifted a straight razor up and sliced deeply into his hand. Stunned, Bernard fell back against the wall. Bernard watched as she came closer to him with the razor. Just as she raised it to swipe at him again, the door flew open. Daniel slapped the razor from Precious's hand. Daniel watched Precious and wrapped Bernard's hand in a towel.

"How did you know?" Bernard asked him.

"Beautiful told me."

"She told you?" Bernard asked, looking at Precious.

"I asked her who hurt grandma and grandpa."

"What did she say?" Bernard asked.

"Me and sister," Daniel told him.

"Me and sister," Precious repeated behind them.

"Come in, Beautiful," Daniel yelled from the room.

Beautiful walked into the room and right up to Daniel. "Go to shore?" she asked Daniel.

"In a little bit, darling," Daniel said, more confident than he felt. "We are waiting for your sister's beauty to return."

Beautiful sat down, and Daniel watched as she handed Precious her doll and started to play with her. Within minutes, Precious was laughing, and her beauty started to return.

"If she's happy, her beauty returns," Daniel told Bernard. "Maybe that's what sets it off. When they're angry, their beauty goes away."

"Let's not test it out right now," Bernard whispered in pain.

"I agree," Daniel told him. "Let's have an adventure," he told his girls.

"Adventure," they both repeated.

"Uncle Bernard and I are going to take you on a boat ride to the island."

"A shore," Beautiful clapped and Precious repeated.

"A shore." Daniel clapped, too. "Let's go, girls," Daniel said, taking their hands.

"Don't forget your baby dolls," Bernard said, with as much enthusiasm as he could with his hand throbbing.

Carter watched as Daniel led the girls on deck. Bernard followed behind, his hand wrapped in a towel soaked in blood.

"What happened to him?" Carter asked Daniel.

"Nothing," Daniel said with a forced smile. "We are going on an adventure."

"Adventure," both girls laughed.

"A very fun adventure," Daniel told Carter.

"Ok," Carter got the gist of the statement." I will get our magic boat ready for my two beautiful passengers." Daniel watched as both girls laughed and clapped their hands.

"They like to be called Beautiful," he wrote down in his head. "A good thing to remember," he noted.

"Yes," Daniel said to Carter, "my very, very beautiful daughters would like to ride ashore on your magic boat."

"Magic?" Beautiful asked.

"Oh, yes," Carter exaggerated. "It sails across on top of the water, and if you're very, very good, you can put your hand in the water, and it will wash them all clean."

Daniel looked over at Carter, who shrugged his shoulders. "K, let's get going, ladies." Carter carried Beautiful down the rope, and Daniel carried Precious. Reaching up as far as he could, Daniel helped Bernard before he fell.

"There we go," Carter continued the game. "Who is going to help steer the magic boat?"

"Steer," Beautiful yelled.

"Steer," Precious repeated. Daniel started to panic. Making one of them angry in the boat could be disastrous. "Wait a minute, Daniel yelled over the waves. "I think there's enough room for both of my beautiful girls to steer the boat."

Both girls giggled and clapped their hands. "Let's put you here." He placed Beautiful by Carter. "And Precious can go here. Halfway to shore, we'll trade places." Both girls laughed and played with Carter and Daniel all the way to shore.

"Look where we are!" Daniel laughed, picking up Precious and carrying her to shore. "I bet we can find some magic here on the island." Carter continued talking and laughing all the way to the campfire.

"Where is everyone?" Daniel said, looking around for Magnus and Ahaira.

Daniel could see everyone else was keeping their distance. Which with the game of fun going on with the girls, he was glad they were. "You look for some magic with your girls, Daniel, and I'll be right back."

"Ok," Daniel smiled and took the girls to look for treasure behind a tree. "What's this?" Daniel smiled at a coconut.

"Mine," Beautiful said.

"Mine," Precious repeated.

"I see Daddy will need to find another treasure so both his beautiful girls can have one." When they both giggled and clapped, Daniel relaxed a little. Keeping up the happy game was starting to give him a headache. Where is Magnus? He sneaked a peek around the camp again. Carter shook his head at his men and hurried back to Daniel.

"This is going to be hard," Carter told him. "What are we doing, beautiful ladies?" Carter asked when Beautiful started to frown, looking at Daniel's face.

"We are looking for buried treasure," Daniel told Carter.

"You are looking in the wrong place, ladies. The treasure you want is down the shore." Daniel watched as Beautiful and Precious ran laughing down the shore.

"Where is she?" he turned and asked Carter.

"They think Jared has her."

"Jared?" Daniel screamed, bring Beautiful's attention.

"You better watch yourself, or we're going to have a very mean little lady on our hands."

" Not one, both," Daniel told him. "Precious is the one who cut Bernard."

"Bernard?" They both looked around and saw him sitting at a fire with one of the men caring for him. "Why would Jared take Magnus?"

"He thinks she and the girls are witches, and he wants them gone."
Daniel stopped walking. "What do you mean gone?"
"He talked about burning them at the stake."
"What?" Daniel yelled.
"Stop it," Carter warned him. "Those girls try to turn on these men and they'll shoot them, Daniel."
Daniel looked over at Precious and Beautiful laughing and picking up shells together. "They are just little girls, Carter."
"Little girls who need to find Ahaira," Carter reminded him.
"Yes, let's go," Daniel agreed. "We find her, and then I can look for Magnus. How are my beautiful daughters doing?" Daniel asked, approaching them.
"Eat!" Beautiful turned and asked him almost in tears.
"No, sweetie, don't cry. Daddy is getting you food right now." Daniel noticed Precious was starting to tear up, too. "What are we going to do?" he asked Carter.
"We're going to get them some food," Carter said, with a bright smile on his face. Carter ran like a clown skipping and jumping all the way to the other side of the camp. "What do you have ready to eat?" he laughed, running through everyone's camping areas.
Bernard looked up and yelled, "Get the children some food now!" Everyone in hearing distance ran and got something to bring to Carter.
"Here's some corn," one man told him.
"I've made corn biscuits," another one tells him. "Here's . . ."
Carter stopped listening and hurried away with two armfuls of food for the girls.
"Look what I've got for the best-looking girls on the island," Carter yelled, running up the beach.
Beautiful saw the food first and laughed and clapped. Seconds later, Precious was laughing, too. "Let's see what we have here," Carter put on a show, handing the girls piece after piece of food. Daniel took a few minutes to figure out what he was going to do next.

"There you are." Henasee ran down the beach toward them.
"Where's Magnus?" she asked, looking around.
"Look how beautiful our two lovely girls are," Carter motioned at Beautiful and Precious. Henasee stopped and looked at Beautiful

and Precious. Then she noticed the strained looks on the two men's faces.

"Ahaira and I have a wonderful surprise for you two."

Beautiful looked up with a smile. "Surprise?"

"Surprise?" Precious repeated.

"Yes, we are going to camp in a real live cave."

"Cave?" Beautiful asked.

"Cave?" Precious repeated.

"Yes," Henasee continued, "it's a house made of rocks."

"Rocks." They both clapped.

"After you're done eating, Carter and I will show it to you."

Both girls clapped and laughed.

"Thank you," Daniel mouthed to her and looked over at Carter. "We can do this." He smiled at the girls. "The most beautiful girls on the island get to sleep in a real live cave," he told them. Beautiful and Precious both laughed and clapped.

Daniel hurried back to the camp and headed right to Mack, one of the head men on the ship.

"Why do you think Jared has her?"

"He was sprouting off about her being a witch and . . ." Mack paused.

"What?" Daniel asked, getting in Mack's space.

"He hit her."

"He hit her!" Daniel screamed, and men backed away.

"He slapped her, and she fell. We told him he was wrong to do it."

"Yes," another man told Daniel, "we made him stop before he."

"Burned her at the stake!" Daniel screamed again.

"We were scared!" one of the men said, pointing at Henasee, Carter, and the girls up the beach.

"Magnus has showed you more kindness then you've show each other."

"Yes, she has," another man stepped forward, "and we told he so. We didn't know Jared planned on taking her. We all went back to our business, and she was just gone. It wasn't until you came ashore we realized Jared was gone, too."

"Damn it!" Daniel yelled into the crowd. "Magnus would have given anyone of you the clothes off her back if you needed it."

Most everyone in the crowd couldn't look Daniel in the eyes.

"I'll go with you to find her, Daniel," Mack told him.

"Me, too," another man said.

"You're right," another man from in back yelled. "I'm going."

Daniel shook his head, and he and four of his men headed down the beach. Picking up their footprints wasn't hard. No one had been on the island in quite some time. "He's taken her this way," one man yelled. Daniel raced ahead of his men.

"Over here," he yelled and pointed to where Magnus must have sat down. "She's tired, and it looks like he's dragging her," Daniel said to no one in particular. "I am going to drag him all over this island when I'm done with him." Daniel saw the fire before he saw Magnus or Jared.

"He's got her tied up over there," one of the men told him.

It took every bit of Daniel's strength not to march into Jared's camp and choke him with his bare hands. He knew Jared would have a gun or knife, but he was sure looking at Magnus tied to the tree with brush all around it. He was sure looking at her tired and scared. Even a bullet wouldn't stop the hatred he felt for this man until he shook the very life out of him.

"We need to get him away from her," Mack whispered. "If he lights that brush, it will go up in seconds."

"I thought of that," Daniel told him. "That's why I'm still standing here."

"I've got a plan," Mack told him.

"I'm listening," Daniel answered.

"I go in and pretend I've come to help him. When I distract him, you get her out of there."

"He's liable to kill you, Mack."

"I shouldn't have got caught up in everybody's fears, Daniel. Magnus has been a good friend to me. I owe her."

"Thanks, Mack. Just get her out of there. The first chance I have," Daniel promised.

Daniel watched as Mack walked nonchalantly into the camp.

"I come to help," Mack announced.

"How did you find me?" Jared asked.

"I smelt the witch," Mack laughed.

Daniel could tell Jared was starting to trust Mack and got ready to make his move.

"I say we light up the sky with this witch, and then find those to little witches and do the same to them."

Mack tried not to choke on his words. "Sounds good to me, Jared," Mack told him, "these kind of people have no rights living among us good folk."

Jared liked the sound of that and offered Mack a drink of his whiskey bottle.

"Don't mind if I do," Mack took the bottle from Jared and took the opportunity to turn him away from Magnus.

The pain in Magnus's arms was so severe she was light headed. Jared tied her tight, saying he had heard witches can turn into liquid and slide away. Magnus watched as Mack and Jared continued to talk and drink. Putting her head down, she released tears for her children, Daniel, and herself. Whispering into the night air, she said, "God, if this is how I am to go, please take care of my babies and Daniel." Magnus opened her eyes, startled by a hand on her back.

"Be very quiet, Magnus," Daniel whispered. "If Jared lights the brush before I can untie you . . ." Daniel didn't have it in his heart to finish the sentence.

"The girls?" she whispered.

"Safe," he answered. "Now hold still until I tell you to run."

"I twisted my ankle. I can't run."

"Ok, then. I'll carry you."

"Daniel," she cried quietly. "If you can't get me untied, step back."

"I'm not leaving you," he said.

"You must, Daniel. You must for our children."

Daniel worked with the ropes, but they wouldn't budge.

"He's coming, Daniel," Magnus whispered. "Get back."

Daniel moved back into the woods out of eye sight.

"I think now would be a good time to burn her."

"No," Mack said quickly.

"Why?" Jared looked at Mack. "You aren't out here to play games with me, are you, Mack?" Jared took out his knife. "You know I don't like no tricks played on me."

"I'm not playing no games with you, Jared. I just wanted to watch her squirm some more."

Jared laughed. "I see you are a mean one deep inside Mack. I want to watch her scream until dawn. Witch be gone." Mack flicked his fingers at Magnus. Magnus glared at Mack and then turned to glare at Jared.

"You won't be alive this time tomorrow night so have your fun," she spit at the two men.

"Daniel will kill you both for this."

"Daniel isn't going to do nothing to anybody," Jared laughed. "I'm going to kill him after I take care of you. He'll never know what hit him," Jared laughed.

Magnus turned away. The thought of anyone hurting Daniel was too much for her to think about.

"So," Jared laughed, "the witch does have feelings."

"She's playing with yah." Mack smacked Jared on the back. "She don't care about nothing but her spells and potions."

"I bet she wishes she had a potion or a spell now," Jared laughed.

Magnus looked up to the sky. "Please God, please. Let me show my children a good life a loving and kind life."

Blue smoke started to come from the fire Jared had made. Thick heavy smoke started to make him cough. Mack hurried to help Daniel untie Magnus as Jared continued to breath in the dark blue smoke. Magnus watched as the smoke twirled around only Jared and went down his throat. Coughing as if trying to get a tickle out of one of his lungs, Jared fell to his death.

Ahaira walked into the camp and looked at Jared. "I thought I heard him say he needed a potion or a spell." Magnus half laughed and half cried at Ahaira's expression on her face. She had just taken a man's life, and she was waiting for her thank you.

"Thank you, Ahaira."

"No one deserves to be burnt on the stake," she said as a matter of fact. "A true witch would not have died anyway and came back for revenge. Stupid people!" Ahaira spat toward Jared's dead body.

"Thank you," Daniel said to Ahaira as he got the last knot off of Magnus's ankles.

"The girls?" Magnus asked Ahaira, falling into Daniel's arms.

"They are sleeping like babies."

"Did the plant work?" Daniel asked Ahaira.

"We will know in time," Ahaira finished and walked out of the camp.

"Let's go find our girls," Daniel said, picking up Magnus and carrying her out of the camp.

Mack stepped in front of them. "I hope you know, ma'am, I didn't mean any of those things. I was just playing along with Jared until we could get you free."

Magnus put her hand out to him. "You're a good friend, Mack, thank you."

Mack smiled at Magnus and Daniel and stepped aside so they could head to the cave.

Magnus snuggled into Daniel. "I know about my parents," she said in his ear.

"I'm sorry, darling."

"They are in heaven together. I will miss them," she sighed. "They would never have survived without the other."

"That's how I feel about you, Magnus."

"Me, too, Daniel," she said holding on tighter.

"Are you all right?" Henasee reached them on the shore.

"I will be," Magnus smiled.

"The girls? How are they doing?"

"Ahaira says we'll know by the end of the week. She says they will sleep for some time." Magnus hugged Daniel. "What if when they wake up they are just our little girls?"

Two days, later Beautiful and Precious woke up with happy smiles on their faces. Magnus held out her arms to Precious, and Precious rushed into them.

"Mama," she smiled.

Magnus looked over and smiled shyly at Beautiful. She knew not to push her. "How's my Beautiful today?" Magnus's smile got bigger. Beautiful looked around the cave and ran straight for Magnus.

Daniel laughed. "She knows who she wants a hug from, darling."

Magnus held her two beautiful daughters until they squirmed to be let go.

"Daniel," Magnus said with tears running down her face, "their birth marks are gone."

Months went by on Noteese, and the girls' beauty had not gone away once. Beautiful and Precious were growing by leaps and bounds. Even the men were starting to be comfortable with the girls coming and going from the camp.

"They are breathtaking," Magnus said, watching Beautiful and Precious run up and down the beach chasing each other.

"We'll be going home soon," Daniel smiled.

Magnus rubbed her stomach. "And we'll be parents again."

"Yes, and Carter and I have dozens of Cart Carra plants already aboard the ship. Just in case." Daniel placed his hand over Magnus's stomach.

"In case, Junior comes out with an attitude," Magnus sighed.

Chapter 27
Spells are Made to be Broken

"We're going home," Carter told Henasee, holding her hand. "I'm not so sure how I feel about going home."
"I know what you mean," she answered. "Here, it's get up play, make food, eat and play."
"It hasn't been all play."
"There was that witch, spell, and potion thing," Carter laughed.
"Oh, yah," Henasee laughed back. "That!"
"I love you, Henasee," Carter said swinging her around to face him. "I was wondering how you felt about me? Or if you think you might one day feel something for me?"
Henasee broke free and ran down the beach. "If you catch me, you can have me," she laughed.
Carter started on a mad dash after her. Henasee jumped into the water and swam out to see where the two colors of water meet. Carter was only an arm's length behind her.
"See we did what we said we would do, Carter." Carter looked perplexed. "We said we would swim out here together." Carter smiled at her.
"I'm not sure who I love and who I want to be with, I'm young. But," she said taking off her top and tossing it in the water, "I'm glad I'm here with you right now."
Carter laughed and grabbed her into his arms.
"Me, too," he laughed taking her under the water.
Magnus walked down the beach to get her daughters. "Come on, girls it's time to get on the ship." Beautiful smiled over at Precious as she squeezed the life out of a lizard. "Go night, night," she laughed. Precious lets go of the dead minnow in her hand. "Go night, night," she laughed and ran with Beautiful to give her mother a big hug.

For more wonderful books, join me at: www.vickysiegrist.com

Ebony Arose: Ebony goes from rags to riches and from riches to heart brake.

Mother's Children Soldiers and War: Dedicated to Our Soldiers of The Red, White and Blue (God be with you)

Lost Beauty: Magnus didn't know her beauty was the price for her dreams coming true.

(Coming soon) Lost Beauty 2: Beautiful and Precious

Dearable Finds a Husband: Dearable finds out too late she has married the wrong brother.

Such a Little Girl: Dedicated to Such a Little Girl

Lost But Not Defeated: Clara never knew a friendship with a young Indian girl named Shanell could cause so much heartache.

Love Comes Home: Olivia and Oliver are meant to be together but everything is against them, even Olivia's own heart.

(Children's Books)

Our Magical Mad Place: Stephanie and her Grandma May have adventures as ten-year old girls. See what fun they have when their anger shows up in, Our Magical Mad Place.

Our Magical House: Stephanie and her Grandma May have all their wishes and dreams come true. Jumping on a trampoline couch made of green gelatin is fun but not as fun as driving your own turtle robot.

Casey Brings in the Paper: Sarah is trying to train Casey to bring in the paper. Casey wags her tail as if to say "you're good at that Sarah, real good! maybe bringing in the paper can be your job."

(Miniature Books) Read, Learn and Laugh

Off to The Vet We Go: Animals need great care that is why we take our pets there.

Shelter's Get Animals Home: Shelter's get animals home. No pet should ever be left on its own.

Elephant Should be Pains Name: It's not just a boo, boo, it's an Elephant!

Achoo Can Turn Red, Green and Blue: Achoo can change you too!